"Hush, Stella. It's all right now."

"Cade . . . I don't want to die. I—I thought I could accept it . . . whatever is going to happen to me . . . but not now . . ."

Her dark eyes glistened with tears as she gazed up at him. Her full lips parted. "Stop it, Stella," he whispered, and then, somehow, he was kissing her. . . . They were soft, gentle, desperately controlled little kisses that moved swiftly over her face, lingering on her warm, damp, salty lashes.

"It's all right," he murmured. "You don't have to be afraid. . . ." His arms pulled her close. She was shivering with cold. Cade held her with forced gentleness, tasting the tears that trickled down her cheeks. Inside, he was battling all his natural impulses. He wanted to sweep her up in his arms, carry her back to the cabin and warm her lovely, trembling body with his own—to kiss every intimate curve and hollow of her until she moaned with ecstasy. And then, when neither of them could resist any longer—

He forced his mind to break the dangerous train of thought. It could not happen, he told himself. He could not allow himself to imagine it. She had killed his brother, and he had a duty to perform. Nothing must keep him from what he had to do.

Dear Reader:

Harlequin offers you historical romances with a difference: novels with all the passion and excitement of a five-hundred-page historical in three hundred pages, stories that focus on people—a hero and heroine you really care about, who take you back and make you part of their time.

This summer we'll be publishing books by some of your favorite authors. We have a new book by Bronwyn Williams entitled *Dandelion*. It continues the story of Kinnahauk and Bridget and their grandson, Cabel. Brooke Hastings makes her historical debut with *So Sweet a Sin*, a gripping story of passion and treachery in the years leading up to the American Revolution. *Seize the Fire* is an exciting new Western by Patricia Potter. Caryn Cameron's latest, *Silver Swords*, is an adventurous tale of piracy set in Florida in the early 1800s. You won't want to miss these or any of the other exciting selections coming soon from Harlequin Historicals.

We appreciate your comments and suggestions. Our goal is to publish the kinds of books you want to read. So please keep your letters coming. You can write to us at the address below.

Karen Solem
Editorial Director
Harlequin Historicals
P.O. Box 7372
Grand Central Station
New York, New York 10017

Wind River

Elizabeth Lane

Harlequin Books

TORONTO • NEW YORK • LONDON
AMSTERDAM • PARIS • SYDNEY • HAMBURG
STOCKHOLM • ATHENS • TOKYO • MILAN

Harlequin Historical first edition August 1989

ISBN 0-373-28628-7

ELIZABETH LANE

has traveled extensively in Latin America, Europe and China and enjoys bringing these exotic locales to life on the printed page, but she also finds her home state of Utah and other areas of the American West fascinating sources for historical romance. Elizabeth loves such diverse activities as hiking and playing the piano. The current pet population in her home stands at one dog, three cats and two lizards.

Prologue

There were two of them—drunken miners, down from South Pass for a good time in Green River. One of them, a hulk of a man, used a bowie knife to slash his way into Stella Brannon's tent, knocking over a jug of sodium hyposulfite as he entered.

The crash woke Stella. She sat up just as the big man lunged for her. There was no time for her to grab the loaded Griswold & Gunnison she kept under her pillow. He pinned her to her cot and pressed a knife against her throat.

"Don't be skeered now, girlie. Jist be nice t' me an' my friend here, and we won't hurt ye none."

Stella recognized him now. He had been one of the crowd who'd gathered that afternoon to watch her photograph the work on the new railroad. There'd been nothing unusual in that. Stella was used to drawing onlookers. Photography, in 1868, was still a novelty, especially on the frontier. Here in Wyoming Territory, hers was likely one of the first cameras the settlers and miners had ever seen.

Even without the camera, Stella herself was enough to draw the eye of any man. She was tall for a woman, with a wealth of light auburn curls and a figure that tapered from a swelling bosom to a slender waist. Her features were more striking than beautiful. Her father, redheaded and Irish by descent, had once been involved in the Far Eastern trade. On his last voyage to the Indies, he had returned to Boston with a willowy Ceylonese bride, a flower of a girl, who had died soon after giving birth to a daughter. Stella had inherited her mother's large black eyes and pale golden skin—and something of her father's red hair, though the color was muted, like the tone of freshly cut cedar. The combination was strangely stunning, enough to stir any man's pulse. The fact that she traveled alone struck some men as an open invitation, which was why she kept the loaded pistol under her pillow at night.

But little good it did her now. Stella could feel the gun's hard contours beneath her head, but with the blade of the bowie knife cold against her throat, she dared not reach for it. She lay frozen as the miner leered down at her. He was a bull of a man, well over two hundred pounds. The thin streak of moonlight that shone through the rip in the tent illuminated a jowly face with a greasy smudge of black beard. A stubby black cheroot was jammed into one corner of his mouth. Without taking his eyes off Stella, he spat the cheroot onto the floor.

"Leave me alone," she whispered. "I've got money, a little. You can have it—"

The big man laughed. Stella shuddered at the evil grin on his face. The gun was there, she reminded herself. If she could catch him off guard she might have a chance to reach it.

"Purty gal like you ain't got no business sleepin' alone!" he grunted. "Me, now, I took one look at ye today, an' I says to myself, Gillis, old boy, she's gonna need some company tonight!"

Gillis. Stella burned the name into her memory as he licked his lips. The breath had begun to rasp in and out of his throat. If only she could reach the pistol....

Gillis's companion stood behind him, watching. He appeared to be tall and slender, though Stella, in her fear, was scarcely aware of him. He made no sound and did not move.

The big man shifted his weight and began to fumble with his trousers. Stella knew what was coming next. She would only have an instant to get the gun and use it. Like a cat, she tensed, gathering her strength.

His left hand tugged awkwardly at the stubborn trouser buttons. Yes, he would need two hands for the job. There was a chance... just a chance. Stella waited, holding her breath as he panted, swore and finally took the knife away from her throat. "Don't move, girl, or we'll slice up that purty neck good," he said. Then he reached back over his shoulder to hand the knife to his companion. "Hold this on 'er till I git through. Then you can have—"

With one lightning twist of her body, Stella reached under the pillow. Her hand closed around the gun and cocked it. But she was not fast enough. In an instant Gillis had grabbed her wrist.

"You hellcat!" he gasped. "I'll show ye." He began to wrench the gun from her hand.

Stella was a strong woman, and she fought with desperate fury, but she was no match for the burly miner. She felt the pistol slipping from her hand. Only the trigger—yes! The trigger was still hers. Her finger was locked around it, but she was losing her grip on the handle. She felt her fingers weakening, pulling away. She had to shoot now.... Now!

As the gun was ripped loose from her hand, Stella pulled the trigger. The shot went wild, but the sound of it startled Gillis. He dropped the gun and glanced around in sudden panic for his companion.

The second man had vanished.

Gillis hesitated, the air rushing in and out of his lungs. Then he leaped through the opening in the tent and disappeared into the night.

Stella lay on the cot, her heart drumming wildly, her eyes staring into the darkness above her. She was all right, she reassured herself. The men were gone. She was safe.

Still she lay trembling, the episode washing over her again and again, like the black waves of a nightmare. She should have known something like this would happen one day, she berated herself. True, she had spent many nights alone since her father died, leaving her his craft as a legacy. She had always felt safe, with the hefty Griswold & Gunnison under her pillow. But she would never feel safe again.

At last she forced herself to get up and light the lantern that hung near her cot. The brutes had broken some glass. She needed to see how much damage they had done.

The flame flared up in the chimney of the lantern, illuminating the brown darkness of the old army tent. Much of the area was cluttered with equipment—vats and trays for mixing chemicals, tripods, the extra camera and spare lenses, tins, jugs, towels and stacks of glass plates. Stella took a deep breath. The air smelled of chemicals and gunpowder, blended with the smoke from Gillis's cheroot.

Raising the lantern, she looked down at the floor. What she saw sent her reeling back toward the cot.

The second man, Gillis's companion, lay dead on the floor of the tent, a red stain on his chambray shirt.

Choking back dread and panic, Stella bent over him with the lantern. His face was young, the skin smooth and fair. A thatch of wavy hair, as pale as corn silk, swept back from a high, broad forehead. The finely molded chin bore no trace of whiskers. Only a downy, yellow fringe, carefully tended, adorned his upper lip. He could not have been more than seventeen or eighteen years old.

Stella had killed a boy.

Chapter One

Green River, Wyoming Territory, was a new town in the year 1868. Like others of its kind, it had sprouted overnight along the life-giving silver stream of the new Union Pacific Railroad. It was a makeshift place, thrown together out of logs, mud and clapboard, with nothing painted, nothing finished. Mud-stained canvas tents were scattered alongside the permanent buildings—if anything in such a state could be called permanent. Its outer bounds were marked by sheds and corrals, a few herds of white-faced Hereford cattle and massive piles of railroad ties.

Still, what this primitive town lacked in elegance it made up for in a sort of rawboned, youthful vigor. There were no old people here. Few women, either, for that matter, except for the busy handful that worked the bars and brothels along the main street. A passing journalist had summed it all up: Green River was a young man's town.

The jail was so new that its boards still smelled of pine sap. Its iron-barred cells, freighted in on the Union Pacific, had been assembled only weeks before. Cade Garrison stood next to the sheriff's desk and waited while the lanky Hoosier who served as the law in Green River fumbled through his chain of keys.

"She's in the back corner cell," the sheriff said. "I gave her a couple of blankets to hang up. Reckon a lady's entitled to a mite of privacy, even in here."

"Lady?" Cade had his doubts about the woman who'd admitted to shooting his younger brother, Jared, a week ago. Rumor had it she'd lured the boy to her tent, tried to rob him and then shot him in the chest when things got out of hand. "I'd hardly call a woman like that a lady," Cade said, his voice flat with bitterness.

"Oh, she's a lady, all right." The sheriff scratched his large beak of a nose. "You'll see that much when you meet her."

"Is she still sticking to her original story, about there being another man who attacked her?"

"She swears it's the truth. Big, black-haired fellow named Gillis, she says. Lit out after the shot was fired."

"Any truth to it, you think?" Cade sat down on the corner of the desk, stretching out his long legs. He was a lean, rangy man, tawny haired and sun burnished from years spent out-of-doors. At thirty-three, he was fifteen years older than his brother Jared had been.

The sheriff scratched his ear. "Don't rightly know for sure. A man fittin' that description was in town earlier that afternoon. Plenty of folks seen him. And they seen him later, headin' out of town with a wagonload of supplies, about sundown. I sent out a deputy to look for him, but he was gone without a trace. She could be lyin'...but then again, she mightn't be. Up to a jury to decide that, I reckon. Trouble is, the circuit judge won't be here for another fifteen days."

"In the meantime, you're just keeping her locked up?"

"Ain't got much choice. 'Sides, it's as much for her own good as anything. People liked your brother, Mr. Garrison. Nice lad he was—oh, full of the devil, I'll grant you. But in a fun-loving sort of way. He'd come down from South Pass about three weeks ago, lookin' for work on the railroad. He had a little money that he'd made in the mines, but he spent most of it on drinks and girls."

The sheriff paused to fish a cigarette paper and a small drawstring tobacco pouch out of his shirt pocket. While he rolled the cigarette, Cade waited in silence. He had visited

Jared's grave earlier that afternoon. Over that dismal mound of earth, he had made a solemn promise: to see that justice was done in the matter of Jared's death. But what was justice? he asked himself. Did it matter in the long run whether the woman was innocent or guilty? Jared was gone, and there was no bringing him back. Getting even didn't change anything—Cade knew that from experience.

The sheriff lit the cigarette and inhaled deeply. "Anyway," he said, blowing out a cloud of smoke, "everybody liked young Jared, and these miners stick together. The killin's got some folks pretty stirred up." He put the cigarette down and gazed intently at Cade. "There's been talk of not waitin' for the circuit judge."

Cade suddenly felt cold. "You mean a lynching?"

"It's happened afore. Never with a woman, mind you, but that don't mean it couldn't. Like I say, some folks are pretty stirred up. Jail's the safest place for the lady, least-wise for the next fifteen days."

"I see," Cade replied noncommittally, gazing down at his boots. Inside he was fighting back a churning sense of uneasiness, and it bothered him that he didn't understand why. The woman had shot Jared, whether by accident, as she claimed, or on purpose. Damn it, let them hang her! Why should he care?

"What about the tent?" he asked, changing the subject. "From what I understand, she claims the two men slashed their way in with a knife."

"Oh, the side of the tent is cut open, all right," said the sheriff. "But she could have done that herself to make it look like they'd forced their way in. The knife was found in the tent, next to your brother's body." He looked Cade up and down as he puffed the cigarette. His eyes seemed to be taking inventory of Cade's long, muscular frame, the broad shoulders, the sun-browned hands, callused from hard work. His eyes took in, too, the faded flannel shirt, the doeskin vest and the heavy Colt .45 that hung so naturally from Cade's hip it seemed almost like part of his body. "You a miner like your brother was, Mr. Garrison?"

"No. I've got a ranch in the Wind River Valley," Cade answered, remembering. The ranch was the reason he'd invited Jared out from Saint Louis that spring. He'd needed help running it and figured it would be a good chance for the boy. But life had been too slow there for Jared. Lured by the prospect of easy money, Jared had soon left for the goldfields at South Pass. A boomtown had sprung up there, where the Oregon Trail crossed the Great Divide.

"Wind River, you say?" The sheriff's eyes narrowed. "But that's Indian country! No white man could survive up there!"

"I'm an adopted Shoshone," Cade said calmly. "Chief Washakie did the honors when I married his granddaughter."

"Oh?" The sheriff's eyebrows shot upward. The expression on his homely face blended curiosity and contempt. Cade could all but see the questions flocking together like blackbirds in his mind.

"Let's see the woman and be done with it," he said, standing up and deliberately closing the subject. "What did you say her name was?"

"Brannon. Stella Brannon. Been widowed since the war, she says. Pretty thing, if I say so myself. Damned shame, all of this." Jingling the keys, the sheriff walked back toward the cells. As Cade followed, he could see the one in the corner, where a ragged, patchwork quilt had been tucked above the crosspiece of the bars, covering the door from inside the cell.

"Mrs. Brannon?" The sheriff's keys jangled as he turned them in the lock.

"Yes?" The voice that answered reminded Cade of rich, dark velvet.

"The boy's brother is here," the sheriff said. "Says he wants to talk to you."

There was a long moment of silence. "All right," she said, her voice low but firm. "Let him come in."

The sheriff swung the door open. Cautiously, his senses tingling, Cade raised a corner of the quilt and walked into the cell.

Stella Brannon sat on the edge of her bunk, poised like a wild creature, ready for flight or combat. Her head was held high, its angle defiant. Her slender hands clenched and unclenched nervously in her lap. She had been through a bad time, Cade reminded himself, and she probably expected more of the same from him.

His eyes took swift stock of her. He had expected some painted jade of a woman, someone clearly capable of luring an eighteen-year-old youth into her tent and trying to rob him. Now, looking at her, he found it difficult to reconcile what she had allegedly done with what he saw before him.

She appeared to be twenty-five or twenty-six, certainly no older, but then again, not a young girl. And she was beautiful, in a strange, wild way. Like a red fox, Cade decided. A wary vixen with chestnut hair, golden skin and eyes that were intensely dark, almost Oriental. They gazed at him now, blending fear and curiosity, sympathy and defiance.

"Mr. Garrison." She spoke his name in a low, throaty voice as she stood, hesitated, then glided toward him. She was tall, her bone structure long and fine. Her simple dark green dress, though wrinkled, was expensively made. Cade couldn't help noticing the style. He had left the East when the huge, hooped skirts were still in fashion—but clearly that had changed. Stella Brannon's dress had a long, narrow skirt that gathered to a small bustle in the back. The neck was high, the sleeves long—certainly not what a woman would wear for seduction.

Her hair was twisted atop her head and secured with a large ebony pin, but a wealth of curly tendrils had escaped their bonds to fall around her face. They glowed like a Renaissance Madonna's as she passed through a shaft of sunlight that slanted through the window of the cell.

She had killed his brother, Cade reminded himself. Whatever truth lay behind the matter, it was her hand that had pulled the trigger and fired the bullet that ended Jared's young life. Nothing could change that. He steeled himself as she stopped an arm's length from him and spoke again.

"Mr. Garrison, have you ever taken a human life?" she asked in a low, tense voice.

Cade remembered Antietam and Gettysburg. He remembered the Sioux raiding party that had killed Rain Flower. "Yes," he answered, his voice cold and emotionless.

"Then you must know—" She broke off, as if dissatisfied with the hollowness of her own words. Slowly she shook her head. "It was an accident. I swear it to you."

Cade thought of Jared's grave, the earth already dusty and blowing away on the autumn wind. They'd buried the boy the morning after the shooting. Cade, who'd not gotten word of it for nearly a week, had had no chance to see his brother's body. "Does it matter?" he asked bitterly. "Would proving your innocence bring Jared back?"

"Believe me," she said in the same low voice, "I would give anything I possess to bring him back for you."

"You should have thought of that before you pulled the trigger." Cade let each word sink in like a lead ball. He knew he was being cruel, but his own pain was so deep that he could not help himself.

Sparks flashed in the depths of the woman's strange black eyes. "Mr. Garrison, your brother came into my tent in the middle of the night! The man who was with him attacked me. We were struggling over the pistol when I fired the shot. It went wild—"

"The sheriff told me your story," Cade interrupted gruffly. "And if it's true, there's something else I'd like to know...." He took a deep breath. "What kind of decent woman would be spending the night in a tent in a place like Green River if she didn't want company? The hotel isn't much, I'll grant you, but it wasn't far off. You'd have been safe there, and this whole bloody mess wouldn't have happened."

Again the anger flared in her eyes. "Mr. Garrison, I am not what you imply I am," she said, clipping off each word with restrained fury. "And I did not invite your brother and his filthy friend to my tent. They forced their way in—"

"You still haven't told me why you weren't in the hotel."

She took a deep, painful breath, and Cade realized she was fighting for self-control. He had pushed her hard.

"My equipment," she said in a more subdued voice. "I take photographs for a living, and I'm good at what I do. But moving hundreds of pounds' worth of glass plates, camera parts, chemicals, trays, stands and paper isn't easy. What's more, I can't work just anywhere. I have to have a darkroom, where I can develop the plates without exposing them to light."

"I see." Cade remembered hearing about Mathew Brady during the war. Brady had hauled his photographic apparatus around in a large, enclosed van, which had doubled as living quarters on the field.

"I had a contract to do some photographic work for the Union Pacific," she said. "For the past few weeks I'd been working from a railroad car." She lowered her eyes and gazed down at her hands. "Originally, I'd planned to go back to Boston on the train again. But the more I saw of the West, the more I realized I wanted to spend more time here. I wanted to get away from the railroad, to photograph the mountains and prairies, the settlers, the Indians—especially the Indians!"

"A woman alone? You're out of your mind!" Cade snapped, using his disdain to mask a grudging flicker of admiration. The woman was a fool, he reminded himself. Her foolhardiness, if not her guile, had ended his brother's life.

She continued as if he had not spoken. "I had my things unloaded here in Green River. I was hoping to find a van for sale, but there were none to be had, so I found a wagon maker and hired him to convert an old buckboard for me. In the meantime, I set up my work in a tent."

"And you couldn't even leave it at night?" The irony in Cade's voice was unmistakable. It snapped something in her. She stiffened.

"Mr. Garrison, do you have any idea how irreplaceable some of those things are? Even the chemicals—I'd be lucky to find them any closer than Saint Louis. The plates, the camera itself, would be even harder to replace. As for the pictures I've already taken, they're priceless. To leave them alone in a place like this when an accident or even a bit of mischief could ruin everything I've done—"

"Mrs. Brannon, a bit of mischief and an accident, as you say, ended my brother's life!" Cade interrupted coldly. "I don't know about you, but I'd say that was worth a good deal more than a tentful of bottles and plates and bloody picture-taking equipment!"

She stood frozen in midsentence as he spoke, her eyes wide with pain and shock. He had cut her deeply, Cade realized. But, curse it, his own anguish was almost greater than he could bear. Jared—wild, young Jared—had been Cade's responsibility. He had invited the boy to come West in the first place. And when Jared wanted to leave the ranch for the mines, Cade had not forced him to stay. If he had, Jared would be alive. Bored, rebellious and chafing at the brotherly bit, but alive.

Stella Brannon's look told him she had heard enough. Deliberately she turned away and raised the quilt that covered the door of her cell. "Sheriff," she said in a commanding voice, "Mr. Garrison is ready to leave now. You may open the door."

She had sounded more like a queen than a prisoner, Cade reflected as he stared down into his half-emptied whiskey glass. And her eyes still haunted him. He had glanced back at her once as the cell door swung shut behind him, to see her standing where he had left her, a proud, lonely figure, those eyes gazing at him seeing . . . God only knew what!

Was she guilty? Cade asked himself for the hundredth time without finding a satisfactory answer. The sheriff was right in one respect: she did appear to be a lady. But looks could be deceptive. If she hadn't lured Jared into her tent, it wasn't because she wasn't pretty enough, that was certain. She was a stunner, with her light chestnut curls, her soft, sensuous mouth and a figure that even the modesty of her high-necked dark green dress could not hide.

Cade had known other redheaded women. They'd been fragile creatures for the most part, with porcelain skins that freckled at the lowering of a parasol, and delicate constitutions to match. Stella Brannon, he sensed, was different. Even in the wretched surroundings of the cell, she radiated an aura of quiet strength. He thought of her hands—large hands for a woman, slim, golden and capable looking. Those hands had killed Jared, Cade reminded himself.

Cade raised the glass and downed the rest of the whiskey in a single swallow. It burned its way down his throat like a long trickle of flame. He seldom drank. Liquor, aside from the taste, had little effect on him. He had only come into the saloon tonight to pass time while he decided what to do next.

Fifteen days was a long time, but he would have to stay around town till Stella Brannon's trial was finished. He owed that much to Jared's memory. Afterward—whatever the outcome—he would head back to the Wind River country. He would throw himself into the work at the ranch and try to forget about Jared. There was nothing else he could do.

As for the Brannon woman... Cade stared down into the empty glass, her image forming and disappearing in his mind. He had made a promise on Jared's grave to see that the boy's killer was brought to justice. Beyond that, her fate was up to the judge and jury. Innocent or guilty, what real difference did it make? Hang her or let her go—nothing would bring Jared back. And all the vengeance in the world could not remove one drop of grief. Cade had learned that long ago.

Feeling his way carefully around the hurt, he let himself remember Rain Flower, her doelike grace, her laughing brown eyes. He remembered the two sons she had given him, fine boys, swift and sturdy, as curious as two bobcat cubs.

On a day rich with autumn, he'd ridden home from a solitary hunt on the Bighorn, his two packhorses laden with salted meat and buffalo hides. He remembered still the clarity of that day, the lightness of his heart as he rode. The leaves of the aspens were like thin gold coins, the sky crossed with a long, trailing V of migrating geese. He looked forward to winter, to long nights in the warm cabin with the sweet sinuousness of Rain Flower's eager body, to the sight of his little sons tumbling naked among the furs that covered their bed. Perhaps by the time the snow was gone from the crags of the Wind River Mountains, there would be a third baby. A girl would be nice this time, he thought as he forded the last small creek and dug his moccasined heels into the flanks of his buckskin pony, anxious for the sight of home.

Only the blackened walls of the cabin, still smoldering, remained to greet him. The sheds and corrals had also burned or been pulled down, the horses driven off.

As for Rain Flower and the two boys... Cade shuddered at the memory. He had found his wife's body against one wall of the cabin, her clothes stripped away, her skull smashed by a war club. The younger boy, still a baby, had burned to death in the reed chest where his mother had hidden him. Cade's older son had been almost three—old enough to run. Cade had searched for half an hour before finding him fifty yards from the house, his small body neatly spitted by a Sioux lance.

After that, he had lost his reason for a time, Cade reflected, as he remembered trailing the Sioux raiding party with blood-maddened vengeance. It was not until the last of them—save one, who escaped—had died that Cade Garrison had come to himself again. He had crawled into a cave and slept for two nights and a day. When he awakened, the blood lust was gone from him. Only his grief remained.

And all the hate, the calculated revenge and the killing had not brought Rain Flower or his sons back to him.

So what did it all mean? Cade turned the empty glass in his hands. He felt numb inside. Mercifully numb, he told himself. Since Rain Flower's death, he had not allowed himself to feel anything too intensely. Even Jared's death, hurtful though it was, only pained him to a certain depth. Beyond that depth, the passageways were sealed. Never again, Cade had long since resolved, would he allow love to possess him so totally that the loss of it would drive him mad with pain.

The idea of vengeance no longer appealed to him. He knew the futility of it too well. But now he was dealing with a question of justice. Jared had been wrongfully killed. That called for some action in return.

Cade was startled out of his reverie by a touch on his shoulder. He turned and looked into the red-rimmed eyes of a man he had seen a few times at South Pass. A miner, Cade remembered, balding, with an oatmeal-colored beard and huge callused hands. "Buy you a drink, friend?" he asked, taking a seat on the stool next to Cade's.

Cade nodded his thanks, though he hadn't really planned on having another whiskey. The miner meant well, he told himself. Maybe he had known Jared.

"You're the brother o' the boy that was shot, ain't you?" the miner asked as the bartender poured another two fingers' worth in Cade's glass.

"That's right."

"Right sorry t' hear about the lad. Nice boy he was, though he liked the women a mite too much for his own good." The miner drained his glass and held it out to the bartender for more. "D'you see the gal what done it? Red-haired witch if I ever saw one. Eyes like a gypsy's an' a body to make the devil hisself look twice. An' her sa-shayin' around that picture-takin' machine smart as you please. Somethin' not quite decent about a woman what travels by herself, doin' a man's work."

Cade nodded politely and took a small sip from his glass. "What do you know about a man named Gillis?" he asked.

"Gillis? The one she claims was in her tent?" The miner hawked and spat a stream into the brass spittoon at the end of the bar. "He was lookin' at her that afternoon while she was takin' pictures. Eyes poppin' right outta his head, they were—though he weren't the only one, mind you. But I'll tell you one thing. If she says Gillis was in her tent, she's lyin'. Seen him myself, headed outta town with a buckboard, just afore sundown. Lots o' people seen him."

"And Jared?"

The miner shrugged. "Nobody can remember. He could have been around, I guess, but nobody seen him at the picture takin'." He leaned a little closer, the whiskey smell heavy on his breath. "Lissen now." The words sent out a small shower of spit. "Your brother had friends in this town and up at South Pass. We bin talkin' for the past hour about it."

The man glanced back over his shoulder to where a rough-looking group of miners and railroad men, maybe a dozen of them, clustered around two tables. All of them had their eyes on the pair at the bar, and Cade realized that his companion had been sent by them as a sort of spokesman. The idea made him uneasy.

"If there's something you want from me, you'd best come out and say it," Cade declared in a quiet voice.

"Want somethin'? Hell, no. Like I say, we're all miners, like your brother was. All we want is t' see justice done and done right!" He edged closer, and Cade suddenly knew what was coming next.

"That redheaded woman," the miner said. "Now you an' me, we know she done it. But her bein' a looker like she is, ain't no jury in the country that wouldn't turn her loose. An' I know the judge, too. He's got an eye for the ladies. That wouldn't help none, either. So we figger there's only one thing t' do—"

"You're talking about a lynching?" Cade was surprised at the tightness in his own throat.

"Like I say, we figger that's the best way to even out what she done to your brother.... Ain't never hung a woman afore." The miner licked his lips. "But I reckon there's a first time for everything."

Cade studied the man. He noticed the way the miner's big, blunt hands cradled his whiskey glass. He looked into the red-rimmed eyes and saw a hunger there. The man had wanted Stella Brannon, Cade realized. And the others at the table had wanted her, too.

"Ain't jist the men here, neither." The miner took a gulp of whiskey and washed it around in his mouth before he swallowed it. "There's others we can git. Ten, maybe twenty in all. An' you, naturally." He put down the glass and fixed Cade with a direct stare. "Reckon I don't really need to ask, but we can count you in, can't we?"

Cade stared down at a drop of whiskey that had spilled on the bar, reflecting the light of the railroad lantern that hung above it. He could feel something hard inside him, turning and tumbling like a rock in a creek bed. He needed more time to sort out his feelings, he realized. But maybe time had run out.

He drained his glass. "Yes," he said slowly. "You can count me in."

Chapter Two

Stella sat on her bunk in the darkness, fighting the urge to pace the floor of her cell. She'd tried that before. It only made her more agitated. Be calm, she told herself. Bide your time. The judge will be here in fifteen days. Surely he'll be a reasonable man. He'll see the truth of things.

She closed her eyes, took a deep breath and tried to relax. But she could not quell the worry that gnawed at her insides like a parasite. Something was wrong, and the awareness of it would not let her rest.

She thought of the man she had met that afternoon. Cade Garrison, the brother of the boy she had shot. For some unexplained reason, her heart had lifted when he walked into her cell. Here, she had thought as she looked into his calm blue eyes, was a man who would understand. A man who would believe her. But she had been mistaken. He was no different from the others: bitter, cynical and all too quick to believe the worst. Now she had to face the truth. Here, in this raw-built town at the end of the track, she had no friends, least of all the brother of the boy who had invaded her tent and died because of it. She was alone.

From the other side of the blanket, she could hear the snoring of a drunk who'd been locked into the next cell. Disturbing the peace, that was his crime. He would be on the street the next day. But her charge was murder. And what could she expect from a jury in this place? Cold fear crept through her as she stared at the walls of her prison.

The odds were high, Stella realized, that she would never leave Green River alive.

She stood up and walked to the window. It was a small window, open, but securely barred. She could see out of it only if she stood on tiptoe, something she often did. That little square was her one link with the outside world. Through it, she could see the stars and hear the sigh of the autumn wind. Sometimes she tried to imagine what lay beyond her view: the rolling, yellow plain, dotted with sage, rabbitbrush and wide-eyed pronghorn antelope; and beyond it, the towering peaks of the Wind River Mountains. Stella sighed. She had so desperately wanted to photograph that country before the winter snows came.

But even if the jury found her innocent, she would lose nearly three weeks—time she had planned to spend on the open road, using her camera to capture scenes from the lives of the settlers and miners, the Indians and the glorious untamed Wyoming wilderness. Now those precious days would be gone. By the time she got out of jail—if she ever did—the danger of early winter storms would make travel too great a risk for a woman alone.

Alone. The word echoed dismally in Stella's mind. She had been alone a long time now: four years since her father had died of his war injuries; six years since black-haired John Brannon had fallen at Shiloh in the same war, leaving Stella with nothing to remember him by except the thin gold band he had placed on her finger. They'd had five months together as man and wife before he marched off with the Union army, and it had been a long time now since Stella had been able to focus his face clearly in her mind or remember the sound of his voice.

Even the ring was gone. Stella had sold it a year after John's death, to buy the expensive plates and chemicals her father needed for his photographic work—the work she had carried on after his death. The work that had brought her to Wyoming.

Once again she agonized over her things: the camera equipment, the plates and chemicals and the hundreds of photographs she had taken during the past weeks. She had begged the sheriff to gather them up and lock them away someplace where they'd be safe. Don't worry, he'd assured her in his maddeningly easygoing manner. They'd be safe enough in the tent where she'd left them. There wasn't anybody in Green River who knew how to take pictures anyway, so who would bother them? He had dismissed the matter and would hear no more of it.

Stella's long fingers curled around the bars and tugged at them in frustration. What would happen to her work? Would it remain behind when she was gone? Or had it already been destroyed?

Some of it, at least, Stella knew to be good. She had spent two weeks in Saint Louis, mostly on the docks, piecing together a pictorial essay on river life—the steamboats and barges, the passengers, the dockhands, even the rats that scurried along the wharves. In Omaha, she had photographed the wild arrival of a cattle drive at the railhead, nearly getting herself trampled in the process. On the plains, she had taken pictures of buffalo at close range, while a railroad man stood guard with an old Sharps rifle. Then, sick with revulsion, she had recorded the slaughter of the huge beasts as a group of eastern businessmen on the train gleefully mowed the herd down with their shiny new Henrys. Stella would have been the first to admit that not all her photographs were "pretty." But they were honest. And they were history. The thought of their being lost or ruined—

"Sheriff!" She spun away from the cell window and lifted the quilt that covered the bars. The sheriff looked up from his desk. "Sheriff, I would like some paper and something to write with, please." Demands, Stella had learned, usually got a quicker response with this slow-moving man than did polite requests. In a moment she had what she wanted. The sheriff had passed a writing tablet, a pen and an inkwell through the bars. Thanking him, Stella lowered the quilt again. Then, lighting a candle, she dipped the pen into the ink and tried to forge her racing thoughts into a semblance of concentration.

"Dear Mr. Garrison," she wrote, then paused, suddenly doubtful. Of all people, why was she asking Cade Garrison for help? He was the last man on earth who would want to help her. She was wasting her time.

But she had nothing to lose by trying, and she could think of no one else to ask. Whether she lived through this experience or not, she wanted some hope, at least, that her photographs would survive.

But why ask Cade Garrison to take care of them? Stella wasn't sure what had given her the idea. Maybe it was his speech. For all his callused hands and weathered clothes, he spoke like a gentleman, a man of some learning. And she had caught a flicker of interest in his response when she mentioned her work. Cade Garrison had every reason to hate her. But if she could make him understand what those pictures meant, and if there was a chance he would save them, she had to try.

She continued the letter. "I know you'll think it strange, my asking you for help, but I've nowhere else to turn."

Again she paused, trying to imagine his reaction to such a letter. His image flooded her mind—the long lean strength of his body, the sun-streaked hair sweeping back from a face that was as proud and dark as an Indian's. If she'd had the chance to photograph him, she would have dressed him in buckskins, Stella decided, like the mountain men who'd opened the West forty or fifty years before. There was a wildness about Cade Garrison that made him look out of place in the drab little town of Green River, like an eagle that had drifted down from its home on some rugged peak. He seemed to belong to the sky, to the mountains, to the wind.

But he would not help her. The more she thought about him, the more certain she became of it. The realization hit her as soon as she recalled his eyes. They were cold eyes, and blue as deep ice in wintertime. Stella had seen grief in those eyes, and contempt. Any interest he might have in her photographs would be outweighed by the force of those emotions. She had killed his brother. She could expect no help from Cade Garrison.

Wearily she tore the sheet from the writing tablet and crumpled it in one hand. Her spirit seemed to crumple with it. For four years she had been alone—proud of her independence, leaning on no one. She had crowded her days with work, enough work to ensure that she would collapse into exhausted slumber at night. She'd had no time for loneliness. And no time for love. Oh, decent, kind men had pursued her; she had fled from them all. Why? Stella asked herself now. She could have married again. She could have been sheltered and protected, if not happy.

Had she loved John Brannon so much? They had married young—too young to really know their own minds. And those few months they'd had together had been tense and awkward, their lovemaking clumsy at best. Perhaps if they'd had more time together, things would have smoothed themselves out. As it was, by the time John had marched off to war, Stella was on the verge of admitting she had made a serious mistake. She had wanted a man. She had married a boy. And Shiloh had robbed him of his chance to grow up.

Maybe that was the trouble, Stella told herself. She had made one bad choice, and she was afraid of making another. That was why, when she met an attractive man, the first thing she did was look for some flaw in him—and she invariably found it.

A sudden longing flooded her—for life, for laughter, for all the things she would miss if her days were to end here, in this wretched little town. She thought of the sunrises she would never see, the new lands she would never visit, the photographs she would never take…and perhaps, out there somewhere, the fulfillment of love she would never know.

Stella stared out through her tiny square of window. She could see a star—only one—twinkling like a drop of ice against the black sky. Another day had ended, a day filled with frustration, fear and dying hopes. And tomorrow would be the same. She turned away from the window. The floorboards of her cell creaked lightly as she walked back and forth, like a caged leopardess.

Things were happening much too fast to suit Cade. He had joined the lynching party, he told himself, in the hope there might be time to talk some sense into the leaders, or at least to send a warning to the sheriff. But he had hoped in vain. The vigilantes had surrounded him from the moment of his consent, and they were in no mood to listen to reason.

There were twenty-two men now, besides himself, and the blood lust was on them like a fever. Once, Cade had come upon a pack of dogs running amok in a herd of sheep. Some of the dogs he had recognized from neighboring ranches. They were docile farm pets—guardians of cows and chickens, companions of small boys on their adventures. But the instincts of the pack had taken over. The dogs were racing among the herd, attacking with a viciousness that left thirty sheep dead before the pack could be driven off.

Now, as he looked at the men around him, Cade experienced the same sickening dread. These were ordinary men—miners, railroaders and townsmen. But the pack instinct had caught them up, and they were like wolves on the trail of fresh game. Many of them had smeared their faces with lampblack before leaving the saloon. Their features were lurid in the flickering torchlight. Muttering, laughing and cursing, they surged down the street toward the jail.

Cade moved with them, a battle raging in his own mind. What was he doing here? Why was he going with these men? He had rationalized that he wanted to try to save the woman, but he had done nothing, and in a few minutes it would be too late. Maybe he didn't really care whether they hanged her or not. She had killed Jared, hadn't she? He, of all people, should be happy to see her punished.

The big miner, his oatmeal-colored beard smeared black, nudged Cade. "Some of us, we bin thinkin'," he said with a sly grin. "Her bein' the kind of woman she is, it'd be a powerful waste not t' take out a little trade afore the hangin'. Know what I mean?" He jabbed Cade with his elbow and winked lewdly. "Fact is, since it was you that lost your brother, might even be fair t' give you first go at her, eh?"

Cade looked at the man. He saw the hunger in those eyes and in the loose-drooping lower lip that glistened with moisture. Behind him, the others pressed close, warm, sweating, reeking with lust and liquor. Cade felt the excitement. It ran through them all like a hot current. He could hear it in their damp, heavy breathing and in the urgent murmur of their voices.

The madness of the pack. Cade's own pulse was racing. He thought of Stella Brannon's soft lips, her warm, curving body, the wild, russet cascade of her hair. A man would have to be crazy not to want her. But not like this. Great heaven, not like this!

Cade brought himself up short. He was a man, like the others. A male animal, with an animal's instincts. But he was a human being, as well, born with the ability to reason, to make rules of human decency and abide by them. This drunken mob had passed the point of decency. They no longer knew or cared what they were doing. And if Cade didn't try to stop what was about to happen, he would be no better than the worst of them.

He thought of his promise to Jared—to see that Stella Brannon was brought to justice. Was this justice? he asked himself. When it was done and she was hanged, would he feel that he had kept his vow?

Cade looked at the faces of the men around him. Suddenly his uncertainty changed to iron resolve. He had to do something, and if he did not do it at once, all hope would be lost.

Nothing he could say, he realized, would dissuade the mob now. They were caught up in the instincts of the pack, wild with woman hunger. Words would accomplish nothing. Either the men would not hear or they would turn on him.

He had his gun, but the others were armed, too. He could never hope to hold them all at bay while he got Stella Brannon to safety. But he had to do something fast. In minutes they would be at the jail; then they would be inside, and it would be too late. Once they caught sight of Stella, there would be no stopping them.

The pitch-pine torches crackled and hissed as the miner nudged Cade again. "Well, Garrison, what do you say?" he asked.

Cade thought fast. Once, along the Bighorn, a grizzly bear had caught him in the open without his rifle. No man can outrun a charging grizzly for any distance. Cade, in desperation, had ripped off his buckskin coat and flung it on the ground. The bear, catching Cade's scent on the coat, had paused long enough to tear the garment to shreds. By the time he'd finished, Cade had reached the timber and shinned up a tall tree where the grizzly could not follow.

The miner was waiting. His blackened face glistened with drops of sweat, reflecting the torchlight. Cade took a deep breath. "That's fine," he said. "But I'm thinking of something else."

The muttering vigilantes fell into silence, waiting for him to go on. "I'm thinking," said Cade, "that the woman isn't enough. I'm thinking of the *place* my brother was murdered. Her lair."

The muttering had begun again. Some of the men were taken with the idea. Others resented any delay in getting to Stella.

"To the tent!" Cade shouted, raising his fist in the air. "Burn it! Destroy everything in it! Let's go!" Seizing a torch and praying that the others would follow him, Cade charged back up the street, toward the far end of town where a string of tents, Stella's among them, had been pitched alongside the new track. The men hesitated for an instant, then surged after him.

Green River was a small town. The tents were only minutes away, and there wasn't a man who didn't know where
Jared Garrison had died.

Cade stuck his torch in the ground. Its light flickered
through the slash in the tent's side. Cade caught a glimpse
of glass jars and jugs, of boxes, bundles and stacked-up
equipment. Damned shame, he thought. He had an idea,
at least, what the things in the tent meant to Stella Brannon. But he knew of no other way to save her life.

"Smash it all!" he shouted. "Everything! Then burn this
hellish place!"

In a frenzy of destruction, the men swarmed over the
tent. Cade heard the crash of shattering glass, smelled the
pungent odor of the chemicals. Then, in the next moment,
he had faded into the darkness and was running back up
along the track toward the main part of town. Only once
did he pause to catch his breath and look back over his
shoulder.

Stella's tent was already in flames.

Stella had tried to sleep, then given the idea up as impossible. There was something in the air tonight. Something ominous. She shivered in her cell, more from
uneasiness than from the chill of the September night. She
had seen nothing unusual. She had heard nothing. Yet, her
senses were screaming. What was it? What was out there in
the darkness?

The sheriff had gone home for the night. He had left his
deputy, a homely young man, slow of wit but brave
hearted, to guard the jail's two prisoners. The deputy had
settled back, put his boots on the desk and fallen asleep.
Stella could hear his deep breathing, interspersed with occasional snores. It was clear he did not share Stella's apprehension.

She turned back to the window once more. It was foolish, this edginess, she told herself. It would only cost her a
night's rest, and slumber was her only respite from the

worry and tedium of her situation. She would lie down again. Maybe this time sleep would come.

As she lay back on her bunk, the image of Cade Garrison flashed into her mind, throwing her even deeper into turmoil. Every instinct told her to call him back, to plead for his help, to trust him. And reason argued just as passionately that he was her enemy. She had shot his brother. He was angry and bitter, and he was the last man on earth who would be sympathetic to her plight.

Again she saw his face—the proud, jutting features, the sweeping mane of sun-streaked hair. And the eyes. Stella had glimpsed a wolf one early morning on the plains. Its eyes were a startling blue, intense in their paleness. Cade Garrison had eyes like that.

She closed her eyes, and Cade Garrison's image vanished. The greasy, bearded face of the man named Gillis pressed in on her. She could feel his brutal hands. She could feel the cold steel of the pistol in her grip, the trigger against her finger. She could hear the explosion of the shot as she fired....

Stella sat bolt upright. No, she told herself. It was not a gunshot she had heard. It was the abrupt slamming of the front door, followed by Cade Garrison's shouting, rough with urgency.

"Where's the sheriff?"

"Gone...gone home." The deputy sounded as if he had just been awakened. Stella pushed the quilt aside and saw Cade shaking the young man's shoulders.

"Listen to me. There's a mob of drunken men coming up the street. They'll be here any minute, and they want the Brannon woman. We've got to get her out of here."

The deputy blinked himself awake. "Look, mister," he said. "Ain't no safer place in Green River than right where she is. Ain't nobody gonna get her out of that cell! Not while I'm here!"

"Listen, you fool!" Cade leaned over the desk, his height and his broad, muscular shoulders all but overpowering the young man, who was still half-slouched in his chair. "There are more than twenty of them! And they're armed! If you think you can stop them—''

The deputy stood up. He was almost as tall as Cade, but he was skinny, all knobs and knuckles. His bony chin jutted determinedly. Stella could see the ring of keys lying on the desk. ''Look,'' he said. ''I got no authority to open these cells. If you want to go and git the sheriff—''

''Damn it, there's no time!'' Cade rasped. ''They'll be here any minute, and you won't stop them. If they can't use the keys, they'll shoot the lock. They'll drag her out, and they'll kill her.''

He turned for the first time and faced Stella, who stood gripping the bars of her cell. His blazing eyes met hers across the room.

''Mr. Garrison, is it true?'' she asked, her throat tight with fear. ''They really mean to kill me?''

''So help me, they'll be here any minute! Tell this young fool to get you out of here!''

''I have one question to ask you.'' Stella spoke above the pounding of her heart. He was gazing at her, a desperate, silent fury etched into every line of his face. There were smudges of lampblack on his clothes. His eyes were bloodshot.

He moved closer, so that he and Stella were separated by no more than an arm's length. ''Ask it and be quick!'' he demanded in a rough whisper.

''You say there are twenty men coming to hang me. There's something I don't understand.''

''What's that?''

''You. I shot your brother. You've more reason to want to see me hang than any of them. Yet you're here. Why?''

He glared at her, seething with exasperation. ''Of all the—''

''How do I know this isn't some kind of ruse to get me out of this cell so you can turn me over to them?''

Cade exploded in a burst of impatience. ''Damn it, you *don't* know! Not any more than I know what in hell's name I'm doing here! But I know one thing. If we don't get you away from this place, you won't survive the next half hour!" He spun back to the deputy. "Either you unlock the cell or I take the keys away from you and do it myself!"

The deputy had picked up the keys. In a curiously child-like gesture, he put them behind his back and began to edge around the desk. "Look, mister," he said. "I told you before. I ain't got no authority to open them cells, an' unless I want to lose my job—"

A cracking blow from Cade's fist cut the deputy off in midsentence. He staggered backward, dazed by the impact of the punch on his jaw, then sagged to the floor, unconscious.

For an instant Cade stood looking down at the young man. Regret and pity flickered like brief shadows across his face. Then he bent down and scooped up the keys where they'd fallen on the floor. In two long strides, he had reached the door of Stella's cell and was turning the key in the lock. "Come on," he said as the door swung open. "Let's get out of here."

Stella hesitated. The cell, at least, had been safe. What would happen if she put her life into the hands of this strange man who had every reason to hate her? She looked at Cade where he stood, impatient, ears to the wind. Could she trust him? Again, instinct and reason battled in her mind.

"Come on!" he growled. "That, or I leave you here and they can bloody well hang you!" He turned his back on her and headed for the door.

Stella made her decision. "I'm coming!" she said, snatching up her skirt and following him.

The jail's only exit was through the front door. Cade opened the door and peered cautiously around it. Above his head, Stella could see the dark sky and the stars.

"They're coming up the street," he said tensely. "Less than a block away. We've got to make a run for it now. Come on, and pray they don't see us." Stella felt the pressure of his strong fingers on her arm as he slipped out the doorway, pulling her behind him.

They flattened themselves against the outside wall. Stella, her head pressing hard to the left, could see the torches now, coming up the empty street and moving closer, like a swarm of fireflies. From a nearby saloon came the sound of a piano, clinking out "Camptown Races." A bottle crashed against the side of a shop as the mob approached. A man laughed drunkenly.

"Come on!" Cade whispered, sliding along the front wall of the jail and pulling her after him. The jail was not large, but the distance from doorway to corner seemed very long. Stella had heard of a vigilante mob in Lincoln that had tied an accused killer behind a horse and dragged him nearly a mile to the tree where he was to be hanged. "T'weren't much left of him by then," someone from the old town had told her. "Then when they got the noose on him, they tied it wrong, so's it choked the poor bugger 'stead of breakin' his neck like it ought to. 'Tweren't more'n a week went afore they caught the feller what really done it. They'd gone an' hung the wrong man, y'see."

Stella flattened herself against the wall as Cade slipped around the corner. She moved as he moved, like his shadow, her heart pounding. She made the turn, then stopped, suddenly held fast.

"Come on!" Cade tugged at her arm. "We've got to run for it!" He glanced back at her. "What's the matter?"

"I-I'm caught!" Stella yanked at her skirt. It was firmly hooked on a nail that stuck out from the corner of the building. The mob was breaking into a run.

Cade cursed under his breath. The blade of his knife flashed in the darkness. The moonlight glinted on his pale hair as he bent low and slashed at the hem of Stella's skirt. She could hear the vigilantes coming closer, their pounding footsteps muffled by the dusty street. "Hurry!" she whispered to Cade.

She fell against him as her skirt came free. His arms steadied her for an instant. Then the two of them were running along the side of the jail, around to the back. Through the thin clapboard walls, Stella could hear the men storming inside, cursing as they found her gone.

"My horse—" Cade said. "It's in the stable, behind the hotel. We'll have to circle back."

He moved as he spoke, pulling Stella with him. She stumbled over a rock in the dark. The momentary pain made her gasp.

The vigilantes were spreading out now. She could hear them behind her, bursting out of the jail. One of them cursed as he found the torn piece of her skirt.

Stella could see the stable ahead of them. It was little more than a shed, a place thrown together with scrap lumber, where visitors could shelter their horses. The stable was dark, and no one seemed to be around.

Cade and Stella crossed a patch of moonlight and darted inside. There, at last, Cade let go of her arm. She fell back against the wall, breathing hard.

The horses were moving around in their stalls—huge, snorting shapes. Cade seemed to know which one was his. In the darkness he found the blanket and saddle and put them on the horse's back.

Stella clung to the edge of the wide doorway, watching and listening. "They're coming closer," she whispered. "Hurry!"

Cade did not reply, but the nicker of the horse and the familiar clink of the bit against its teeth told her he was putting on the bridle. Stella could see torches now, coming around the back of the jail, moving fast. It made sense that they would check the stable. Yes, they were coming. They were running now, like hounds on a hot trail. She could smell the smoke from the pitch-pine torches. Their blackened faces gleamed like coals in the light of the leaping flames. "Hurry," she whispered. "For the love of heaven—"

"I'm ready," Cade said. "Come on."

The horse loomed big and warm in the darkness of the stable. Cade mounted, then reached down and caught Stella's waist with his arm. "Hold on tight," he said, swinging her up behind him.

The mob was closing in. "Garrison!" one of the men

bawled. "If you be in there, give us the girl! Hand her over or, by hell, we'll hang you, too!"

"Come out, Garrison!" another voice shouted. "Come out now, or we set fire to the place!"

Cade held the stamping horse in check for an instant. "Hang on tight," he said between his teeth. "And keep low!"

Stella's arms tightened around his waist. His body was as taut as a bowstring. "Now!" he said, and he dug his heels into the horse's flanks.

The leaders of the mob had reached the stable entrance. The horse exploded out of the opening, right on top of them. Stella glimpsed upturned faces in the torchlight. She felt the impact as the horse reared, striking out with its hooves, hitting flesh and bone. She heard shrieks of pain.

"We'll git you for this, Garrison!" a voice bawled. "We'll git you, and the girl, too!"

A hand grabbed at Stella's skirt, almost pulling her down. She clung hard to Cade as the horse surged forward and broke free. The lynch mob howled behind them as they thundered out of the stable yard.

Someone had started shooting. "Down!" Cade rasped. "Keep low!" He reached back with his left arm and pulled Stella to one side. Then he angled the horse's path, keeping his own body exposed to the fire, protecting hers.

Bullets whined around them—wild, drunken fire that rained like hot hail. Stella felt Cade flinch. Then, suddenly, they were clear of the place. The shouts of the vigilantes faded behind them as they plunged into the darkness. Stella felt the wind. It tore the pins from her hair, setting it loose to stream out behind her.

She pressed tight against Cade's back. Her hand moved up his arm and came away sticky with blood. "You've been hit!" she exclaimed.

Cade did not answer. She felt the tension in his body. She could almost feel the conflict in his mind as they rode together into the wild, black night.

Chapter Three

In a few minutes they had left the town behind them. Stella gripped Cade tightly as the horse thundered through the sage, up hills and across gullies in the darkness. She was seated sideways on the horse's rump, and every jolt threatened to throw her to the ground.

"I can't hang on this way!" The wind seemed to carry her voice backward, away from Cade's ear, but he heard her. His head jerked to one side. Stella saw a high, brushy knoll in the direction he had indicated. It stood out, a black silhouette against the stars.

"We'll stop up there," he said.

Stella huddled against his shoulder. This was a nightmare, she told herself. Any minute now she would wake up and find herself back in the jail in Green River. Or better yet, she would wake up on the train or at home in Boston, safe in the discovery that the shooting of Jared Garrison had been a nightmare in itself.

The horse was climbing now, zigzagging its way up the slope. Stella felt herself sliding down its sweaty rump. She clasped Cade hard. His hand reached back to steady her, but he did not speak. What was he thinking? she wondered. Why had he saved her? What did he plan to do with her?

The moon was higher now. A week past fullness, it hung like a waning lantern above the distant hills, casting the rocky outcrops and clumps of rabbitbrush into stark, black tracery.

The horse's hooves sent small cascades of loose gravel tumbling down the slope. Cade reined to a halt as they reached the top. Stella let go and slid to the ground. For the first time, she got a good look at the horse. It was a massive roan stallion, its coat blood-red in the moonlight.

The breeze was chillier here and rich with the smell of sage. Stella shivered. Her hair was whipping in the wind. She turned to let it blow back from her face.

Behind them and below, she could see the town. It lay dark in the moonlight, lifeless except for the flicker of torches up and down its main street. Cade had dismounted. She heard him laugh behind her, a bitter sound. "Look at them," he said. "Running in circles, like a pack of hounds who've lost the scent!"

Stella shivered again. "Do you think they'll follow us?"

"Not tonight. But we'd be smart to be well away from here by morning. That's when they'll come after us."

She ran a hand through her wind-tangled hair. She'd brought nothing with her, she realized. Not a comb, not a blanket, not a change of clothing or even a warm shawl. She had no food and no money. Nothing. An irrational anger began to grow in her, a rage at her own helplessness. She was completely at the mercy of this cold, bitter stranger.

"What do you plan to do with me?" She gazed down at Green River, where the torches were beginning to scatter and go out, one by one.

"You ask that as if you thought I *had* plans." Cade laughed, but again there was no humor in the sound. "When I rode into town, the last thing I expected to do was leave with a woman." He was silent for a moment, his boot scuffing at a rock. "I can't very well take you back to Green River," he said slowly. "And I can't take you to South Pass City, either. That's the first place the vigilantes—and the law—would look for you. I'll have to find someplace to hide you." He took a deep breath. "It wouldn't be for long.

Only till the circuit judge gets here. Then I plan to turn you over to him . . . for trial."

The last word struck Stella like a blow. She spun around to face him. His eyes were like pale flints in the moonlight.

"You killed my brother," he said. "I promised on Jared's grave that I'd see justice done. It would be a blot on his memory if I did anything less."

She turned away from his brutal gaze and walked to the edge of the hill. "Then why did you bother to save me? Why didn't you just let those . . . *animals* have me?" She turned back to him, her temper suddenly flaring. "Why didn't you just join them?"

He gazed back at her. She could see the blood soaking into his sleeve, and she remembered his wound. It would need tending—but no. She had asked him a question. She wanted an answer, first.

For a long moment he did not speak. The wind was cool and damp, promising a storm.

"I've seen what vigilantes can do," he said. "Not only to the person accused, but to themselves. Some bloodthirsty beast gets into them. They do things—things they'd never do in their right minds. I didn't want to see that happen because of Jared. And I didn't want to be a part of what they'd have done to you."

"And yet you would turn me over for trial."

"That's different. I'm in favor of justice. I demand it, in fact, when my brother's death is involved."

"Even if I'm innocent?" Stella met his cold blue eyes. "Look at me! How can you believe your brother's death could have been anything but a horrible accident?"

Cade's throat moved as if he were forming some bitter retort, but he pressed his lips together, biting it back. "Not having been there when it happened," he said, "I'm not in a position to say whether you're innocent or guilty. I'll have to leave that to the jury."

Stella stared at him, this grim paradox of a man, who had risked his life to save her and yet would not hesitate to turn her over for judgment when the time came. She could not read the expression in his eyes or fathom what was going on in his mind. Yet, she sensed that some struggle was raging inside him—a struggle she could not understand.

What could she say to him? Stella's mind groped for a reply that would push aside his cold, angry determination. She searched and came up empty.

Cade cleared his throat. "We'd best get moving," he said. "If they trail us at dawn, we'll want to have a good start on them."

"Your wound—"

"It's nothing. The bullet grazed my arm, that's all. It only stings."

"There's no sense in letting it bleed." Stella was already bending down, tearing at the eyelet ruffle on her petticoat. "Take off your shirt. This won't take long."

"All right, but hurry." Cade unbuttoned his shirt and pulled it off his left side, wincing as fragments of blood-soaked flannel tore loose from his flesh. His bare shoulder was smooth and hard muscled, his chest broad, with a frost of pale gold hair.

Stella had ripped loose more than a yard of the ruffle. "You don't have any whiskey, do you?" she asked. "It would help keep the wound from festering."

"No. There's water, but don't take time to wash it now. That can wait till morning. Just wrap it, and we'll get moving again."

The wound was a dark, sticky slash on Cade's arm, but his skin was cool to the touch. He smelled of pine smoke and leather, a good aroma, warm and clean.

Stella began the wrapping—tight enough to stop the bleeding, but not so tight that it might cut off the circulation. She could hear the sound of his breathing, deep and low, close to her ear. Her mind was as busy as her fingers—grasping, probing at the situation.

And then she remembered. "My things!" she exclaimed, suddenly frantic. "My camera, my plates..."

She felt him stiffen under her hand, but he did not reply.

"We can't just leave them down there," she insisted. "We've got to save them. It's worth my life to save them!"

"That's impossible," he said in a quiet voice.

"You don't understand!" she cried. "That's my life's work down there! It's more than that. It's my *life!* I can't just go off and leave everything to the mercy of whoever comes along."

"Don't be a fool," he growled. "Be still and listen!"

"I can't leave without my pictures and equipment!" Stella's hands quivered as they continued to wrap Cade's wound. She could see his blood soaking into the lace. "I can't go without them, and I won't. You can ride off and leave me here!"

"Don't be a child! Listen to me!" His voice was like a lash. "It's too late to save your things!"

"What?" Stella froze, the end of the lace dangling from her hand.

"The vigilantes went through your tent before they came to the jail. They smashed everything. Then they set fire to the place. There's nothing left worth saving."

She stared at him in icy disbelief, unable to speak.

"And as long as you're listening, I might as well tell you the rest of it," he said. "It was my doing. I led them there."

Stella heard his words. Rage and bewilderment churned up inside her as they penetrated.

"Why?" The question exploded out of her.

"They were coming after you. I did it to buy time—enough time for me to get you out of that jail."

Stella resumed her wrapping of the makeshift bandage. She moved mechanically. She felt numb, as if something in her had died. She thought of her father's cameras, of the chemicals and equipment she'd find no replacement for in a thousand miles—even if she had the money to buy them. She thought of the photographs, hundreds of them. The people, the moments, the skill and timing that would never come together again. The sense of loss was overpowering. She looked at Cade Garrison. We're even, she thought. I killed part of him. Now he's killed part of me.

"Damn you!" The words burst out of her. "You should have left well enough alone! You should have let them hang me and saved my pictures, instead! Damn you!"

Cade stood silent while she split the end of the lace bandage and knotted it around his arm. Her hands were trembling. He had known, of course, that she would not take well to the news about her things. But he had not realized how deeply the loss would strike her. A pang of regret shot through him—but no, he told himself quickly. There had been no other way. If he had not chosen to sacrifice her photographs and equipment, she would be in the hands of the vigilantes by now, more than likely raped and dead.

Instead, she was here beside him, furious but alive. Cade could see her out of the corner of his eye. Her head was bent over the knotting of the bandage, her hair blowing around her face, hiding her expression. In the moonlit darkness, her hands gleamed like ivory. They were almost Oriental in their movements, making even the tying of a knot a study in grace.

One of those hands had fired the gun that killed Jared, Cade reminded himself again. And the pain of Jared's death was still strong. He let the pain surround him, let it flow into his veins like blood. He thought of Jared's face, his reckless ways and careless laughter. Stella Brannon had stilled that laughter forever.

She stood so near to him that he could almost feel the warmth radiating from her skin. He could hear her breathing and see the rise and fall of her breasts beneath the fabric of the dark green gown. Even he could not deny that she was a beautiful woman. That beauty had lured Jared to his death, Cade reminded himself as he fought back the warm tide of desire that rose from deep inside his body. He had saved her from the vigilantes. But he had no claim on her, save one: she had killed his brother.

"Let's go," he said gruffly, pulling his shirt over the bandage. The sleeve was stiff where his blood had dried in the wind. She watched him like a cat as he buttoned the shirt and tucked it into his trousers.

"One question first," she said in a voice that was drained of emotion. "You say you plan to turn me over for trial. Does that mean that I'm your prisoner, or am I free to leave you?"

Cade shrugged as he turned toward the horse. "Does it matter right now? Where could you go? There's no place that's safe for you."

"Will I be safe with you?" He had mounted, and she stood on the ground, looking up at him.

"Safer than you'd have been if you'd stayed in jail. Come on." He reached down to pull her onto the horse. She hesitated, deliberating. Then, setting her jaw, she allowed him to swing her up behind the saddle. She sat astride this time, her gown bunching around her legs.

"Where are you taking me?" Her voice was flat, as if she no longer cared.

"North. Till I find a place where you can stay." Cade had given the matter some brief thought. South Pass City was only two days' ride, but it wouldn't be safe for either of them. Stella was a fugitive, and he had aided in her escape. The vigilantes, or the law, could be after them both.

The roan responded to a nudge of his heels. As the animal broke into a trot, Cade felt Stella's arms slide tensely around his waist. He steeled himself against her warmth.

"I've got some friends," he said. "A buffalo hunter and his wife. They've got a cabin on the Little Sandy, not far from the Wind River Valley. They'd take you in for a week or two. Probably be glad for the company."

"And you?"

"I'd leave you there while I went on up the valley to my ranch. The place needs tending." And that was true. It was lucky he'd been down to a handful of horses and cattle when he'd gotten the news about Jared. If there were Sioux around, he'd be fortunate to have any stock left when he returned. "I'd likely stay just long enough to check on things," he said. "Then I'd be back to take you to the judge."

"What makes you so sure I'd still be there when you came?"

"You'd be a fool to run off. There aren't any other cabins or towns within a half day's ride. With winter storms due anytime and the Sioux still in the area, you wouldn't have a chance on your own."

"The Sioux?" He felt her stiffen behind him.

"Let me explain." The horse was picking its way down the steep slope now. Cade let the animal have its head while he talked. "The Wind River Valley is as close to paradise as any place in Wyoming. The mountains shelter it from storms. It's got plenty of good water, rich soil and the thickest, greenest grass to be found. It makes a fine wintering place for stock, for game . . . and for Indians."

"But the Sioux? I thought their range was farther east, in the Dakotas and the Bighorn country."

"It is. But in the summer, bands of them move down into the Wind River to hunt and raid. They can be dangerous." Cade swallowed a lump of bitterness. No one knew better than he what the Sioux could do.

"When winter comes, the Sioux leave the valley," he continued. "That's when the Shoshone return from their summer range in the South."

"I was told the Shoshone were friendly to whites." Stella's arms tightened as the horse slipped on a loose rock, lurched and regained its footing.

"They are," he answered her question. "The trouble is, this time of year, you could just as easily run into Sioux, instead. And that long red hair of yours would make quite a trophy for some hotheaded young brave. So wherever I leave you, I'd strongly recommend that you stay put."

"I see." She fell into silence as the trail leveled off, but Cade was acutely aware of her nearness. His body tingled where her arms encircled him and where the taut points of her breasts touched his back. He had not been this close to a woman since Rain Flower's death. The slow, raw hunger that was seeping up in him now was a thing he had tried to forget. He fought it, as he knew he must.

By tomorrow night, he calculated, they would arrive at the cabin where his friend Knute Aarnson lived. The Aarnsons liked company. They would take Stella in for a few days, he was sure. Until then, he would keep his distance from her. He would use his grief, his outrage over the senselessness of Jared's death, to maintain that distance.

A wolf howled from somewhere off in the hills. Cade felt Stella shiver behind him. "Don't worry," he said. "Wolves are afraid of humans. Chances are you'll never see one up close."

"It's not that," she said. "I'm not afraid. But it's such a lonely sound. It reminds me of every sad thing I've ever known."

And what sad things had she known? Cade wondered. Those dark, haunting eyes of hers seemed to hold a thousand secrets, and for a moment he wanted to learn them all. But he brought himself up short. Knowing her would only make things harder. The less he found out about her life, the better.

"Tell me about your brother," she said.

"You want to hear about the man you shot?" The irony in Cade's voice was genuine.

"Yes, if it doesn't pain you too much. I-I've wondered a lot about him, you know. There in that cell, I had time to wonder about all sorts of things."

For a time, Cade did not answer her. He concentrated instead on guiding the horse. They had come off the hill now, and the rolling plain stretched before them, mottled black and gold with the shadows of clouds. "Jared was only eighteen," he said at last. "And he was like a lot of boys that age—restless and full of life. Wild, some would call him. But not in the bad sense of the word. It's just that he couldn't seem to wait for things to come in their own time. He wanted everything life had to offer and he wanted it all at once. He'd have been a good man once he got that out of his system." Cade paused, letting the bitterness well up in him once more. "Unfortunately, he never got that chance."

"I'm sorry," Stella said. "I'm truly sorry. But I can't help wondering what your brother was doing with a man like Gillis, in my tent, in the middle of the night."

Cade waited for her to continue. Now she would plead her case again, insist that Jared, with Gillis, had forced his way into her tent and that the shooting had been an accident. But she said no more. Silence hung between the two of them, dark and heavy.

Cade spurred the roan to a gallop. Here on the open flat was the best place to put distance between themselves and whoever might follow. Later they could stop and rest.

Clouds were rolling over the horizon, blotting out the stars. The night wind strengthened, carrying with it the smell of rain. Cade's heart sank as his ears caught the distant rumble of thunder. Neither of them was prepared to spend the night in a storm. His coat, his oilskin poncho and a change of clothing had all been left behind in the hotel. And Stella had only the clothes on her back. If the wind turned cold on them and the rainstorm turned into an early blizzard, they could be in serious trouble.

He scanned the horizon. Somewhere up ahead, if he remembered right, lay an outcropping of rock, honeycombed with small caves. It was their one chance of shelter. Praying that his bearings were correct, he made for it.

Stella clung to his back in silence. Cade could feel the tiredness in her arms and sense the apprehension in her tense body. "Hold on," he said. "I'm heading for a place where we can get out of the weather."

He felt her nod, and that was all. Ten minutes later, the storm struck, pelting rain, ice-cold. It fell in blinding sheets, soaking them both to the skin in minutes. Cade could see no more than a stone's throw in front of them. In desperation, he gave the horse its head. Animal instincts were sharper than those of a human. If there was shelter to be found, the horse had the best chance of finding it.

Behind him, he could feel Stella, huddled tight against him, shivering with cold. Silently he cursed the missing oilskin. If he had not left it in the hotel room, it could have kept both of them dry.

The horse, at least, seemed to know where it was going. It plodded steadily forward, head lowered against the storm. Wind howled around them, whipping the sage into dancing nightmare shapes.

A bold of lightning split the sky, so close that the crack of thunder was as sharp as a rifle shot. In the flash of blue light, Cade saw the outline of the rocks. They were just below the horizon, a blocky mass, perhaps half a mile off. With a shout, he spurred the horse toward them.

The rain had turned to sleet by the time they reached the rugged outcrop of dark red sandstone. Cade, who had sheltered here before, dismounted and led the horse under an overhang, away from the wind. Then he turned and put his hands around Stella's waist to lift her from the horse. Her clothes were soaked; her teeth were chattering. She seemed numb, slow to respond. "Put your hands on my shoulders," he said. She did as she was told, and he swung her down off the horse's slippery rump.

For a moment she stood in the circle of his arms. Cade could feel her shivering beneath her gown. He could feel the smooth curve of her waist beneath his hands. The thin, wet fabric clung to her breasts, revealing every detail of soft fullness and tautly erect nipples. In spite of himself, his body responded to her nearness. He felt a deep stirring, a sudden flame leaping low in his vitals.

Her eyes were huge and dark in her pale face, her hair wet and glistening, like a mermaid's. In his mind, Cade fought her. He battled the rising waves of desire that surged up in him again and again. He steeled himself against the urge to bring her closer, to taste those soft, rich lips, to strip away her wet clothes and warm her flesh with his own.

Summoning all his will, he forced himself to release her and turn away. "We have to get you warm," he said gruffly. He moved back to the horse, bent low and busied himself with the cinch. His bedroll and other gear had been left behind in Green River. But at least when he'd saddled the horse, Cade had thrown the saddle blanket on first. Now that blanket was all they had. It smelled like the horse, but it was thick wool, dry on the underside and warm from the horse's own body. He slipped it off the roan's back and wrapped it around Stella's shivering shoulders. She snuggled into it with a weary little sigh, her hands pulling it tighter.

Cade picked up the saddle. "The biggest cave is back inside. Come on." He led the way through the maze of boulders and sandstone ledges, honeycombed with odd, cavelike recesses. His own clothes were dripping. Each gust of wind that struck through the openings in the rocks chilled him to the bone. The pain in his wounded arm was a dull, throbbing ache. Wrapped in the blanket and as silent as a shadow, Stella followed him.

The largest of the caves was about fifteen feet deep and tall enough to stand in. Cade had camped here once or twice before, and other travelers used it, too, from time to time. The air in the back of the cave still smelled of burning sage and charred meat. A black circle on the sand, near the entrance, marked the spot where a fire had been. Cade's eyes strained into the darkness. There against one wall of the cave—yes! He exclaimed elatedly. Whoever had been here, they'd not used up all the wood they'd gathered. The small pile of dry sagebrush was just enough for a fire.

In a few minutes he had a small blaze flickering on the floor of the cave. Stella moved close and held her hands above the flames. The warmth seemed to bring her slowly back to life. She savored it for a long moment before she spoke.

"What now?" Her voice was like the tone of a cello. It stirred something in Cade—a memory of another life, so far removed from the present that he had all but buried it. The flare of dark red satin, the fleeting taste of vintage Burgundy, the fading notes of a Schubert sonata... He looked down at his hands, and the memory vanished.

"We rest here till first light," he said. "If we get an early start, we should reach the cabin of my friends, the Aarnsons, by nightfall." He studied her where she crouched beside the fire, her skirt a soggy mass. She had put aside the blanket as the fire warmed the cave, but she was still shivering. "You'll never get warm unless you get out of that dress," he said.

Her eyes widened. The hesitation in them filled Cade with sudden perplexity. The kind of woman Stella Brannon was reputed to be shouldn't have any compunctions about taking her clothes off in front of a man. Yet her modesty seemed genuine . . . and was oddly touching.

"Don't be silly," he growled. "Take it off and spread it on that rock to dry! If you're worrying about me, you can stop! I won't come within ten paces of you! I'll even turn my back, if you insist!"

Slowly she rose and walked toward him. Her black eyes flashed a strange, quiet defiance. "That won't be necessary, Mr. Garrison," she said coldly. "I know that your only interest is in keeping me healthy for my trial. I won't disappoint you by catching pneumonia."

Still looking at him, she began to undo the buttons at the neck of her dress. Her eyes held his in a challenging gaze that defied him to look down. Cade was aware of the movements of her fingers as they freed each button. But he saw only her eyes—intense eyes, full of mystery, the irises almost as black as the pupils. They held his as a magnet holds steel. He was acutely aware that she had opened her dress to the waist, but he could not look down at her body. If his eyes so much as wavered, she would know it.

The dress slid from her shoulders. Cade was aware of the sound and motion of it. Only when it fell in a wet circle around her feet did she break off looking at him. She bent swiftly, picked up the dress from the sand, shook it and walked away from him with it. Cade caught a glimpse of white corset and petticoat before she wrapped herself in the saddle blanket once more. Her bare arms gleamed like brass in the firelight as she spread the dress on a boulder to dry.

Slowly Cade let out his breath. For all the chill of his wet clothes, he was perspiring. What was she, this woman—

bold as a whore one moment, prim as a nun the next? And what the devil did she think she was trying to do to him?

"We'd better get some sleep," he said, breaking the awkward silence between them. "Keep the blanket. I'll be fine. I've slept worse off than this." And he had, Cade reflected briefly. Much worse. Once, in a Dakota blizzard, he had saved his own life by shooting a buffalo, gutting it and crawling inside the still-warm carcass. Before that, in the war, he had slept on the battlefield, with Confederate artillery whining overhead and the moans of wounded men filling his ears. There had been other nights, after Rain Flower's death... But this was not the time to remember them. Not now.

Stella had curled like a cat on one corner of the blanket, pulling the rest of it over her. Not really a comfortable-looking way to sleep, Cade observed, but she was exhausted. Already her eyes were closed, her lashes black against her cheeks. The blanket rose and fell with her breathing. In the flickering golden light of the fire, her face was as soft as a child's.

Cade moved the empty saddle closer to the fire and leaned back against it. His clothes were beginning to dry. He was warmer now, almost comfortable. But he could not settle down to sleep. His eyes wandered around the cave, coming to rest again and again on the sleeping form of Stella Brannon.

What was she? he asked himself. Sometimes when he looked at her, he saw what he wanted to see: an adventuress, strong willed and unprincipled; a woman who would lure a young man into her tent, then shoot him when things got out of hand.

Yet other times, like now, it was her vulnerability he saw. He remembered how she had endured the storm tonight—shivering, weary, but without a word of complaint. He remembered the gentle hands that had bound his wounded arm.

Well, one thing he did know. He had to keep his distance. Stella was a beautiful woman. She stirred feelings in him that he had tried hard to bury. Even now, as he looked at her, Cade felt a subtle tremor of desire. His eyes traced the long curve of her hips and legs beneath the blanket. His gaze lingered on her face, on her closed eyelids and the delicate, shadowed hollow of her throat.

For a moment his mind broke free of its iron restraints. He pictured her standing before him, the way she had when she'd taken off her rain-soaked dress. He visualized her fingers, undoing each button, the damp fabric sliding off her satiny shoulders, down her arms . . .

But this time he seized her by the waist and jerked her hard against the length of his body. As he pressed her close, he could feel the parting of her thighs through the thin petticoat. He heard her gasp as he bent his head and buried his face in the warm, fragrant cleft between her breasts. . . .

No! Cade forced himself to stop. To even think of possessing her was as dangerous as fondling a rattlesnake. He would be a fool if he let himself weaken.

With effort, he forced the thought of her from his mind. Instead, he thought about Jared. He pictured his young brother, lying dead on the floor of her tent. He pictured the smoking pistol in her hand. Yes, it was working. The coldness was creeping back into his veins. He was safe now. The danger was past. He could do what he had to do.

Resolutely he turned his back on Stella Brannon. He put his head on the saddle and closed his eyes. He was bone weary, but sleep would still not come. His churning mind and the dull pain in his arm made rest impossible. Cade lay staring at the ceiling of the cave as the fire flickered and slowly died. Outside, the storm spent itself. The drumming rain faded until, at last, the only sound he could hear was Stella's soft, even breathing.

Chapter Four

Stella opened her eyes to a leaden dawn. The ground was cold through the rough blanket, the air heavy with moisture from last night's rain. Where the fire had warmed the darkness, there was only a heap of black ashes.

Gingerly she stretched her cramped legs and sat up. Exhaustion had allowed her to sleep soundly, escaping the nightmare for a few blessed hours. But it was morning now—time to face the reality of what had happened. Time to put her losses aside and go on.

That, she knew, was what her father would have told her to do. Six years ago, when she'd gotten the letter about John's death, he had put his arms around her. "Grieve for him, lass," he'd murmured. "Then take what you have and get on with life. Looking back and feeling sorry is nothing but a waste."

Stella had taken his counsel. With all her love and energy, she had flung herself into learning his profession. Photography had become her life, and now that life, too, was gone, destroyed by lust and vengeance.

"Take what you have and go on," her father had said. But this time she had nothing. Worse, she was a fugitive from the law. How would she find the strength to start over again?

She rubbed her eyes and looked around. The empty saddle lay on the floor of the cave, on the other side of the dead fire. Cade Garrison, however, was gone, as was Stella's dress.

Perplexed, she wrapped herself in the horse blanket. Her feet, still in their tight-fitting, high-button shoes, tingled as she walked out of the cave.

The morning air, stinging cold, smelled of damp earth and sage. The rocks, pale mauve in the half-light, glistened with raindrops. Stella could not see Cade, but she could hear the faint nicker of his horse. She followed the sound through the maze of boulders.

Cade was leaning on an outcrop of rock, staring at the sky. "The storm's passed us, I think," he said without turning around. "It'll be warm enough once the sun comes up."

"Where's my dress?" Stella fought back a wave of sudden, senseless rage. Seeing him had brought reality crashing in on her like an avalanche. Her equipment and supplies, her priceless photographs—gone, everything. And it was Cade Garrison's doing. She knew that her anger was irrational—after all, he had saved her life—but on this chilly, wretched morning, she could not help feeling as she did.

"There." He nodded toward a clump of sage. "It was still wet when I got up. I thought it might dry faster out here in the air." He turned slowly and looked at her for the first time. Yes, he did have eyes like a wolf's, so pale they were almost silver. Stella pulled the blanket tighter around her body.

"We've got to get moving," he said. "You'll find your dress a bit damp, I'm afraid. But it should dry fast once the sun comes up."

The dress was spread on the top of the sage, damp, as Cade had said, and cold. Stella picked it up with one hand, holding the edges of the blanket together with the other. "I won't be long," she said, striding back among the boulders, toward the cave.

Ducking under the overhanging entrance, she dropped the blanket next to the saddle and slipped the dress over her head. The fine wool gabardine was clammy against her skin. She shivered as she tugged it into place, thrusting reluctant arms into icy sleeves, hooking the buttons at the waist, then moving upward, her fingers stiff with cold.

It helped to keep moving. Stella walked around the cave as she worked the damp loops over the dainty, round buttons. What a shame there was no more dry wood, she thought, gazing at the blackened remains of the fire. That small blaze had warmed her bleak world last night. It had given her courage. Silently she thanked the unknown traveler who had left those few sticks of sage unburned and out of the weather.

As she finished the last button and turned to leave, something caught her eye—something black and no bigger than her thumb, oddly out of place in the red sandstone hollow of the cave. She walked back to where it was lying behind a rock, as if it had been tossed there.

Recognition struck her like a blow as she saw what it was. Her head felt light. Her throat constricted as she cried out, "Cade!"

He was there in an instant, pistol drawn and alarm written across his face. "What?"

"Gillis." She was trembling. "He smoked black cheroots, just like this one. I remember. Oh, dear heaven!"

Cade stared at the black stub where it lay on the red sand. Then he crouched beside her, picked it up and studied it. "This doesn't prove a thing, you know," he said. "It may or may not be Gillis's. And even if he was here, there's no law against that. Half a dozen witnesses saw him leaving town hours before Jared was killed. He could have camped here on his way back to South Pass."

"You don't understand!" Stella clenched her fist in frustration. "I didn't remember till now. Gillis was smoking one of those when he broke into my tent. He tossed it on the floor. When I saw that I'd killed your brother, it threw me into such a panic that I forgot about the cheroot—till now! That cheroot was evidence! If I'd remembered it in time, it could have proved that Gillis was there! It could have saved me! Don't you see?''

Cade opened his fingers and let the black stub drop to the sand. Stella could only guess what he was thinking—if he believed her at all. It was too late now. The evidence was gone, burned in the blaze that had destroyed the tent. Gone. Like Jared.

He stood up and wiped his hand on his trouser leg. Stella saw his throat move as he swallowed. For a moment she thought he was going to speak. Instead, he shook his head and turned away. ''Let's ride,'' he said.

They headed north, toward the distant mountains. Cade pushed the roan as hard as he dared. Now, while the land was flat and the day fresh, was the time to cover ground. It would be slower going once they began to climb.

Stella clung to his back, shivering in her damp dress, but keeping her complaints to herself. He liked that in her, Cade admitted grudgingly. She didn't whine about things that couldn't be helped—a rare quality in a woman.

He remembered how she'd cried out his name when she found the cheroot in the cave. She'd given him a start. For a second he'd thought she'd stumbled across a rattlesnake. Then he'd seen her face—the dismay, the frustration. All of it over a stub of tobacco that could have been tossed there by anyone.

Was there anything to her story that Gillis had dropped his cheroot in her tent? Or was she just trying to confuse him? Her distress had seemed real, but was it? If she was lying, Cade reminded himself, it wouldn't be the first time a beautiful woman had tried to deceive him. He'd be a fool to let himself believe her without proof.

The sky glowed like an opal as the sun pushed over the hills. The day ahead would be clear and warm, thank heaven. Steady riding would get them to the Aarnson cabin on the Little Sandy by nightfall. His friends would take Stella in. Then he would be safe from this torment of her arms reaching around him, her firm, lovely breasts pressing into his back, her slim thighs curving behind his where she straddled the horse. He would be free of her for a time. Then, perhaps, he would be able to think straight.

Cade fixed his eyes on the horizon and pressed the roan to a lope. He would look ahead, he promised himself—ahead to the Wind River and home.

Stella's spirits rose with the sun. The dawn had begun with a mud-gray sky that matched her mood. Little by little, however, the clouds had paled to platinum streaked with amethyst. The first rays of sunlight had brushed the desert, and suddenly it was beautiful.

She had seen country like this from the windows of the train. It had moved past her then, like a yellow-gray blur, monotonous in its vast sweep. Now, from the back of the roan, she saw how each clump of sage caught the light, how pools of shadow moved and dissolved like quicksilver on the land. Startled jackrabbits shot out from under the very hooves of the roan, to go bounding across the flat and out of sight. An eagle circled and cried overhead, its coppery wings black against the sunrise.

Cade's back was a broad shield from the wind. Stella clung to the smooth leather of his vest, bobbing with the horse's motion and letting the sunlight warm her. Slowly she felt her strength and spirit returning. Those first bleak moments of dawn seemed far away now. True, her situation was grim. But she was far from beaten. She would fight, she resolved, and she would survive to take pictures again. Somehow, God help her, she would come through all this.

Cade was silent. Stella could feel the cold-steel resistance in his body. She weighed like a stone on his back, she knew. He would be anxious to leave her with his friends and depart for the Wind River Valley. And what then? Would Cade's friends help her? Would it be worth the risk to run away before he returned? She had no answers to those questions. She could only hope she would know what to do when the time came.

At the top of a small rise, Cade pulled the roan to a halt. There were rocks here, broad and flat, with hollows where the rain had collected. "We'll water the horse and fill the canteen," he announced. "It may be our only chance for a while."

Stella slid off the horse. Her legs were already stiff. They'd be worse, she knew, before the day was over, but she would not give Cade the satisfaction of hearing her complain. She was hungry, too. Ravenous.

"There'll be no breakfast, I'm afraid," he said, reading her mind. "Cooking a grouse or a rabbit takes more time than we've got, and since we're not exactly loaded down with provisions—"

"It's all right," said Stella. "I can last if you can."

"My friend Knute Aarnson is a good buffalo hunter. If you can hold out till tonight, there'll likely be meat and biscuits." He knelt down and submerged the flat, tin canteen in one of the pools to let it fill. The roan lowered its head and lipped at the water.

Stella found another rain pool and drank from her cupped hands. Then she splashed her face, rinsed her mouth, and ran her fingers through her tangled curls. Cade watched her, squatting on his haunches, his eyes narrowed.

"Your stallion..." she said, groping for something to ease the awkward silence. "He's an extraordinary animal. To cover so much ground with two people on his back—"

"Yes," said Cade, warming a little for the first time. "I breed his sons and daughters on my ranch. I've been offered a fortune for him, but I wouldn't take it. The worth of some things is beyond buying and selling."

"How did you come by him?"

"He was given to me—by my father."

"You brought the horse all the way from the East?"

"No." Cade hesitated a moment, then continued. "I meant my Shoshone father, Chief Washakie."

Stella stared at him. His wary eyes gazed back at her, measuring her reaction. Was she shocked? Was she repelled?

"I don't understand," she said at last. "You can't be a Shoshone—not with blue eyes and blond hair."

"I was adopted by the tribe three years ago. They... winter near my ranch." His jaw tightened, as if he were biting back something else, something he was not ready to tell her.

"And the Sioux?" she asked, remembering what he had said earlier.

"Washakie's enemies. And mine." He stood up in one liquid motion, twisted the lid onto the canteen and reached for the roan's bridle. "Let's get moving."

He swung himself into the saddle and caught her up behind him. Stella held on tight, feeling the ripple of the roan's steely muscles as it broke into a trot.

They came over a hill and startled a small herd of pronghorn antelope. The delicate creatures stared at them with wide, velvety eyes, then wheeled and fled, white rumps flashing as they bounded over the sage.

Cade laughed, an unexpectedly pleasant sound. "It's a good thing for them we weren't hunting," he said. "What you just saw is typical of pronghorns. They always want to stop and take a look at you before they run away. Often as not, that kind of curiosity gets them shot."

"They're beautiful," Stella said. "I could never shoot one."

"You could if you were hungry enough. They're not bad eating."

"Don't talk about eating. You'll only remind me of how hungry I am." Stella brushed her hair out of her eyes. "Why don't you tell me how you came to be an adopted Shoshone?"

She had said the wrong thing. He stiffened slightly, and Stella sensed the quiet closing of a door inside him.

"I've heard of Washakie," she persisted. "I was hoping to photograph him before...before my profession went up in smoke." She closed her eyes and willed herself to be calm. Even the mention of her loss brought a fresh stab of anger and regret, but whining about it would not bring back even one of the precious images she had captured. Not any more than it would bring back Jared Garrison.

"Tell me something," she said. "Is it true that Indians don't like to be photographed? Someone told me once that they think the black box is a trap to steal their souls."

"Oh, it's true of some," Cade answered. "But not Washakie. He's seen enough of the white man's gadgetry to know that there's no magic in it. I expect he'd have been very gracious about posing. And he'd have made you a good subject. He's a very majestic old man."

"Would you tell me about him?"

Again Cade hesitated, then nodded. "I'll tell you a story about him—something that happened just last year."

"I'd like to hear it," Stella said.

"You'd have to know Washakie to fully appreciate it. In his younger days he was a terror in battle. The Crow, the Blackfoot, the Sioux—they all feared him. But he's getting old now—closing in on seventy, I'd say." Cade paused to guide the roan up a rocky bank, then went on with his story.

"The tribe has always had its share of young hotheads—braves who've resented the way Washakie keeps them in line. A bunch of them were talking one night, saying how the old chief ought to step aside and let a younger man—one of them—lead the Shoshone. Washakie overheard them. The next morning, he was gone."

"Gone where?" Stella shook her tangled curls, savoring the warmth of the sun.

"Nobody saw him for almost two moons. Then one night he reappeared. Walked into the firelight like a big, white-haired ghost and flung down seven fresh Sioux scalps. 'Let the one who would take my place count as many,' he said."

In spite of herself, Stella gave a horrified gasp. "That's awful!" she murmured.

"This isn't Boston or Saint Louis." The edge had returned to Cade's voice. "Washakie, in his own way, is the most civilized man I've ever known."

"Then maybe you've been away from civilization too long," Stella said, pricked by his reaction.

"I came west after the war," Cade said. "And I saw more murder, cruelty and deceit between *civilized* Yanks and Rebs than the whole Indian nation ever dreamed of!"

Stella weighed the bitterness in his words, groping in vain for a satisfactory answer. She wanted to believe that he was wrong, but she was haunted by the irony of what he had said. Was it Indians, after all, who had killed her husband? Was it Indians who'd banded into a drunken mob and set out to hang an accused woman in Green River? Was it Indians who had caused the death of Jared Garrison?

Cade accepted her silence without question. For a time they rode without speaking. Then, toward midmorning they came up over a low rise. Shading her eyes with her hand to look ahead, her breath caught in sudden amazement.

Mountains. Stella had seen mountains in the East, but she had never seen mountains like these. High above the far horizon they loomed, thrusting great, craggy peaks into the sky. Blue in the distance, cold, rugged and wildly beautiful, they defied ordinary words. Stella ached for her camera.

Cade spoke at last. "You're seeing the Wind River Range. My ranch is just beyond, in the Wind River Valley."

By the time they reached the foothills, the sun was descending in the western sky. Cade felt a prickle of anxiety as the trail cut into a patch of aspen. Out on the plain, he had felt safe. There the country was open. A traveler could see for miles in all directions and have ample time to get away if danger appeared. The hills, however, were different.

Cade knew this country as well as any white man alive. Most of the time he passed through it with little to fear. He had a swift horse, a good Spencer rifle and, since Rain Flower's death, a fearsome reputation among the enemies of the Shoshone.

This time, however, the Spencer had been left behind in Green River, along with the spare shells for his Colt .45. The roan was carrying double, and Cade's companion was a woman—a young and pretty woman whose long chestnut hair would inflame any brave who saw her. For protection, he had nothing but the Colt, loaded with six bullets.

"Is something wrong?" She had sensed his uneasiness.

"Nothing out of the ordinary. But it wouldn't be a bad idea to keep your voice down."

"How much farther is it to your friends' cabin?" she asked softly.

"Two hours, or so. With no delays, we should make it before dusk."

"This is Indian country, isn't it?" There was whispered excitement in her voice and, Cade hoped, a little healthy fear. He knew she was an adventurous woman. He could only hope she had the good sense to be cautious, as well. Otherwise, she might not live long.

"Most of Wyoming is Indian country. A good place to be quiet."

"That makes sense," she conceded after weighing his words for a moment. Then she said no more. Cade had to admit he liked that in her. He had known a number of beautiful women. Most of them had acted as if the earth, the sun and the planets all revolved around their charms.

This woman was different. Her attention, he had noticed, was usually directed outward, away from herself. Not once had he heard her complain because her dress was damp and wrinkled, or because she had no comb for her hair. Instead she had taken in everything—the desert, the mountains, the birds and animals she saw—with the eagerness of a child.

Since Rain Flower's death, Washakie had pressed Cade to take his choice of the young Shoshone maidens. "Your heart will never heal while you are alone," the old chief had said. Still, Cade had put off making a decision. He had loved Rain Flower. She had given him the warmth of her body, the music of her laughter and two fine sons. She had made him happy—and yet his life with her had not been complete. Something was missing. But until now he had not realized what it was.

Rain Flower had lived her life in the mountains and plai.s of the West. For all her beauty and goodness, she had never read a book, never seen one of Shakespeare's plays or heard a Mozart sonata. She knew nothing about history, science, philosophy or religion. She did not know the name of the president, or why the Civil War had been fought.

Cade suddenly realized that he had missed those things; he had missed the sharing of common ground, the give-and-take of ideas that could bring two people almost as close as lovemaking.

Last night the hunger for Stella's body had almost driven him wild. Today he was experiencing a different kind of hunger. Stella was an intelligent woman, articulate and cultured. Everything she was spoke to him of a world he had left behind—a world that he found himself longing to remember. He felt a desperate need to talk with her, to open his mind to hers and let her words flow into him like gentle rain.

The pressure of Stella's hand on his arm shattered Cade's reflections. Danger. The sudden awareness of it was so strong that it made the hair bristle on the back of his neck.

The roan was following a narrow trail that wound to the top of a wooded ridge. Cade halted the horse and rose in the stirrups, every sense alerted.

The September sky was like blue glass, the wind so still that even the aspen leaves hung limp. Only the scolding of a whiskey jack disturbed the afternoon silence.

But there was something in the air. Even Stella had felt it and warned him with her touch. Now Cade strained his eyes and ears, alert for the faintest rustle of a leaf or stirring of a twig.

It was his sense of smell that finally triggered the alarm in his mind. Smoke. It hung lightly in the air, like a memory, its bitter pungency blending with the smell of the damp earth. A camp fire, Cade concluded, or the remains of one, at least, for the smell was not fresh. Someone had camped in the area the night before. Who it was, or whether they were still nearby, was anyone's guess, but he couldn't proceed safely till he found out.

He slipped silently from the saddle. "Stay here with the horse," he whispered to Stella. "If anything goes wrong, don't wait for me. Ride for your life!"

Her black eyes opened wide, the pupils large even in the sunlight. "I couldn't just ride off and leave you!" she insisted in a low voice.

"Head north," he said, as if she hadn't spoken. "The second river you come to will be the Little Sandy. Follow it upstream far enough and you'll come to the Aarnsons'. Understand?"

"Yes, but—"

"Don't hesitate. If anything happens, I'll have a better chance on my own."

Her lips parted, ready to protest again. Then, seeing the sense in his words, she slowly, reluctantly nodded.

Cade handed her the reins as she moved into the saddle. Then he snaked through the underbrush to the top of the ridge. Inching forward on his belly, he peered over the top.

The hollow below was clumped with birch-white aspen trees, their leaves yellow gold in the autumn sunlight. Cade searched the area for movement. Everything seemed quiet, but he had to be sure.

Moving with stealthy grace, he edged his way down the slope. Now he could see the small clearing where a fire had been. The ashes were cold and black, quenched by last night's storm. There was no sign of life around the place, but Cade still felt uneasy. Something was not right.

From somewhere up the slope, he heard the harsh call of a crow. The sound froze him where he stood. The pounding of his heart seemed to fill his whole body as he listened.

The call came again as one of the big black birds glided over the top of the ridge. Cade relaxed a little. It had been a real crow, after all, not a human signal. Maybe he was feeling apprehensive for nothing.

Keeping to the trees, he made his way to the bottom of the hollow, where the camp fire had been. He would take a moment to check the area, Cade resolved. Then he would get back to Stella and be gone.

Years of hunting with the Shoshone had taught him how to approach a strange place. He moved like a shadow, his lean body blending with the trees, his leather boots treading so softly that not a twig was disturbed. For all his outward calm, his nerves twanged like bowstrings. Death was here. He could feel it.

The drone of flies surrounded him as he stepped into the open. Cade knew then, with a sickening certainty, what he would find. It was only a matter of following the sound.

The dead man lay sprawled facedown at the far edge of the clearing. He was a miner, from the looks of him, dressed in a faded wool shirt, mud-spattered trousers and heavy work boots. His skull showed through, bare and bloody, where a fist-sized section of his scalp had been hacked away.

Steeling himself, Cade seized one of the man's stiff arms and turned the body over. For a fleeting moment he had thought the poor devil might be Gillis—but, no. The man was dun haired and middle-aged. A stranger. Gold panning on the Big Sandy, more than likely, before his luck ran out.

There was no time to bury him. Cade turned the man over again, the way he'd found him. Then he looked around.

Footprints in the soft earth told the story: the miner's hobnailed boots; the shod prints of a horse that had likely been stolen; and the moccasin tracks. Cade could distinguish half a dozen different sets. Sioux didn't usually come this far south, but it was their work, all right. Washakie would kill any Shoshone brave who took a white scalp.

Cade was still bent over the tracks when a movement on the hillside caught his eye. Instinctively, he ducked into the brush. When he looked back up the slope, his heart stopped.

Six mounted Sioux, leading a seventh horse, were moving in a slow line along the top of the ridge. They were headed directly toward the place where he had left Stella.

Chapter Five

Something was bothering the roan. Its ears twitched back and forth. Then it began to strain at the bridle, stamping its hooves and swinging its great head. Stella, who had dismounted to stretch her screaming leg muscles, looped the reins around her hands. The rough leather edges bit into her fingers as the stallion danced and jerked.

"Easy, big fellow," she muttered. What could be disturbing the creature? She was familiar enough with horses. This one seemed more agitated than fearful. Its tossing and straining were almost eager, as if it had scented one of its own kind.

Yes.... The realization shook her. Echoing her own thoughts, she heard the still-distant whinny of another horse. She flung her arms around the roan's muzzle and pressed close to stifle its answer. The roan fought her, its massive strength almost dragging her off her feet.

Where there were horses, there would be men. Indians, perhaps, or vigilantes. Whoever it was, the odds of their being friendly were slim, Stella realized. And Cade was out there somewhere—separated from her, perhaps by the intruders themselves.

He had told her to wait. He had also told her to take the roan and get away if anything went wrong. Stella clasped the snorting stallion's muzzle and tried to listen for any sound, any clue that would tell her who was coming. She'd be a fool to panic needlessly, she told herself.

Again she heard the nicker of a horse. The sound came from somewhere up the ridge, closer than before. If she moved up the slope a few yards, she might be able to get a look at whoever was coming before they saw her. Otherwise, if she stayed where she was, they would soon be right on top of her.

The roan was getting even harder to control. She could not risk lashing the reins to one of the slender aspens while she crept up to the ridge. She would have to take the horse with her.

She clasped the satiny, steel-muscled neck. The roan's musky sweat stung the raw places on her hands as she urged the stallion forward.

Toward the ridge, the trees thinned out. Scarcely daring to breathe, Stella crouched behind a boulder and stared up at the skyline. One hand clasped the reins of the fidgeting horse. The other shaded her eyes.

There—coming along the top of the ridge. Stella felt a thrill of terror as she saw them. Six Indians, riding single file, leading a seventh horse. They sat like bronze statues on their ponies, dark and haughtily erect. The leader had a rifle slung across his knees. The others carried bows, with arrows bristling from buckskin quivers. They were no more than a hundred yards away, she estimated, and headed straight for her.

Were they friendly or hostile? Stella realized to her dismay that she did not know the difference between one tribe and another. If they were Shoshone, she had nothing to fear. Otherwise—

The roan went into a sudden frenzy. It tried to rear, jerking the bridle so hard that Stella's arm was almost wrenched from its socket. She grabbed for the reins with her other hand and was yanked over onto her back. As she hung on frantically, the stallion flung back its head and shrieked out its primeval challenge at the oncoming ponies.

The Indians stopped. They had heard the roan, and now they saw it—a magnificent steed, fit for a chief. Still gripping the reins, Stella lay low in the brush and watched them kick their ponies to a trot. Now, before the Indians saw her, was the time to turn the roan loose. The big stallion was a prize. She could only hope they would go after it, giving her time to hide or escape.

The roan was jerking wildly on the bridle as it tried to rear. Stella relaxed her hold, expecting the horse to break loose; but somehow, in the struggle, one of the reins had become tangled around her wrist. The stallion's constant pulling kept it stretched tight. She could not let go.

The Indians were coming closer. Stella struggled desperately to free her hand. If the roan bolted, she could be dragged to death. If the Indians spotted her ... She did not even want to think of what might happen then.

Cade's image flashed through her mind. Where was he? Did he know what was happening? Maybe—the thought made her blood run cold—maybe the Indians had already dealt with him.

They were closing in now, fanning out as if to cut off the stallion's escape. They must have seen her. If she could only manage to gain her feet ... If she could somehow get into the saddle ...

She froze at the sound of a gunshot from the foot of the slope. The Indians were stopping, turning, though none of them had been hit. A pistol, even a Colt .45, was useless at that range.

The Indian leader wheeled his pony one way, then the other. He seemed to be hesitating, torn between the prize of the stallion and the lone enemy down in the hollow.

The whang of a second gunshot settled his mind. He twisted back to face the others, raised the rifle in the air with both hands and threw back his head. The hills echoed with his war scream. In the next instant, all six of them were charging down the slope, their ponies' hooves clattering on the loose rocks.

Hauling down on the reins with all her weight, Stella struggled to her feet, then urged the roan to the top of the ridge. She could see the Indians. By now they were nearly halfway to the bottom of the slope, where Cade waited for them, alone and on foot, with four bullets left in his pistol.

Catching the stallion off guard, she flung herself across the saddle and struggled to a sitting position. The roan snorted and danced in protest, but did not try to throw her.

Cade, she realized, could have saved himself by remaining hidden. Instead, he had drawn the Indians away from her by firing two of his precious bullets. In doing so, he had exposed himself to almost certain death. There would be no more than four shots left in his Colt. There were six Indians.

He had ordered her to ride for her life if anything went wrong. That would be the sensible thing. But she owed him his brother's life, as well as her own. She had to do something to even the debt, no matter what it cost her.

A third shot rang out. This time the Indians were within pistol range. One of them flinched, then slumped and slid from his pony. Five Indians, and no more than three bullets were left.

They had paused briefly on the hillside to assess Cade's position and nock their arrows. Stella took a deep breath and dug her heels hard into the roan's flanks. The stallion shot off the ridge and headed down the slope at a breakneck gallop. She clung to its neck, keeping low as it leaped and skidded, sending cascades of loose gravel down the steep hillside.

She had chosen a course parallel to the way the Indians had gone. At the sound of sliding rocks and breaking brush, the five braves spun around. Their surprise bought her a few precious seconds. She was almost even with them before they started shooting.

Flattening herself like a tick against the roan's neck, Stella swung around them. An arrow whined past her ear. Another lodged with a solid chunk in the fork of the saddle, pinning her skirt to the leather.

Out of the corner of her eye, she could see the Indian leader fumbling with the rifle. He did not seem to know how to use it, thank heaven. Some of the others, as well, seemed reluctant to shoot at the stallion. Shrieking, they gave chase, instead.

Stella caught a glimmer of movement in the woods below as another pistol shot rang out. The leader's rifle went flying as he clutched his bleeding shoulder. No more than two bullets were left in the Colt. But Stella knew where Cade was now, and she was bearing down on him fast.

The Indians thundered behind her. Their ponies were no match for the big stallion's power, but on the treacherous slope they were more agile. Little by little, they were gaining, closing in around her.

Cade's fifth shot dropped an Indian who was reaching for the roan's bridle. Behind her, Stella could feel hands clutching at her skirt. Frantic, she jabbed her heels into the stallion's sides. The roan leaped forward with a suddenness that jerked the Indian from his pony. Stella heard him scream as he fell.

Cade was in the open now, crouched to spring. As Stella swept past him, he leaped up behind her, onto the back of the saddle. She could feel the sudden shock of his weight, feel the hard press of him as he leaned forward, his arms reaching around either side of her to seize the reins. "Hang on tight," he muttered.

The roan, responding to his master's touch, surged ahead like a cannon shot. Stella wrapped her arms around the massive neck and hung on. She could feel the throbbing chest muscles and the pulse of the stallion's great, pounding heart. The russet mane lashed her face. Somewhere behind them, the shouts of the remaining Indians were growing fainter.

They galloped out of the hollow at an angle and skirted the sage-dusted foothills, moving toward the blinding blaze of the late afternoon sun. Anyone coming after them, Stella realized, would have to ride into the sun, as well, and would have a hard time seeing their quarry. But this was an unnecessary precaution. The Indians appeared to have been left behind.

That did not stop Cade, however. He pressed the roan ruthlessly, as if he were being pursued by some demon. Stella could feel him behind her, his muscles as hard as iron, his breath rough and warm against her ear.

She kept low in the saddle, giving herself up to the flow of the stallion's motion. Her head swam with the musky perfume of sage, sweat and rich, damp earth. The wind sang in her ears and swept through her. She was alive— more alive, she suddenly realized, than she had been in years! She had raced with death—hers and Cade's—and she had won!

Yet, she sensed, Cade did not share her exhilaration. He was a grim shadow behind her, driven by some wildness, some deep, black force she did not understand.

He cut back into the hills and made for a low, brushy knoll. Only when they had gained the top did he rein in the heaving stallion and slip to the ground.

Stella gazed back the way they had come. From the knoll, she could see the desert, stretching south till it blurred and blended with the deepening sky. To the north, the Wind River Mountains rose like the towers of some mythical kingdom, their granite crags purple in the evening light. The wind was cool and sweet.

Cade scanned the horizon, his mouth tight. Stella dismounted and let the stallion's reins drop to the ground. Then she smoothed her torn skirt and walked over to where he stood. She had had enough of this cold wall of silence he had built around himself. If that wall could be broken, now, she resolved, was the time to break it.

"Cade..."

He turned to face her, his eyes blazing with a strange, pale fury. "You little fool!" he exploded. "You could have been killed! Of all the crazy, reckless things to do—"

And then there were no more words, because his arms were crushing her tight against his chest; his mouth was hard and hungry on hers. His lips devoured her, moving with tender savagery from her mouth to her face, her closed eyelids, her throat.

Stella whimpered as he kissed her, cruelly almost, with the pent-up frenzy of a man who had been too long without physical love. She was too hungry herself, from years of being alone, to fight what was happening now. Little quivers of ecstasy shot through her as she met the urgent stab of his tongue with her own, and she realized that if Cade had a mind to, he could take her, right here in the open, on the cold, damp earth. He could take her, and she would have no more will to resist him than she would to stop breathing.

Then a sudden chill seemed to pass through him. Abruptly he thrust her away and stood gazing down at her, his chest heaving. Stella could almost see the conflict raging behind those icy eyes. He was reminding himself of who she was and what she had done. The barrier was swinging into place again.

When he spoke, his voice was razor edged with bitterness. "Forgive me. I forgot why you and I are here. This . . . mustn't happen again."

"It will happen only if you choose to let it." Stella forced herself to speak calmly, hiding hurt that was like the jab of cold steel inside her. "And now, if we want to reach your friends' cabin tonight, shouldn't we get moving? The light won't last an hour."

Cade took up the reins of the horse and swung into the saddle. In a moment, Stella was up behind him and they were cantering through the sage into the evening wind.

She clung to the saddle, still shaken by what had happened. She could feel his need for her almost as strongly as she felt her own, but she could not break through the guard he had built around his emotions.

As for her own feelings . . . But what did it matter? Her explosive encounter with Cade had stirred responses she had not even known she possessed. But she was facing a wall. Even if Cade could forget that she had killed his brother, there were other conflicts raging inside the man— strange forces, she sensed, that would not allow him to love. If she could not turn away from him, she thought, he would break her heart.

Cade pressed the horse to a rolling gallop, forcing Stella to wrap her arms tightly around his waist. She felt his muscles contract as he steeled himself against her touch. Briefly she closed her eyes, trying to pretend that nothing had happened between them. But pretending did no good. Cade's kisses still bruised her lips; his nearness tortured her memory.

They had been riding by moonlight for nearly an hour, following the river, when Cade spotted Knute Aarnson's cabin. A wave of relief swept over him. He had begun to fear that somehow, in the dark, they had missed the place. His resolve, he knew, was not equal to spending another night alone with a woman who stirred a throbbing desire in him every time he looked at her.

Stella's wild ride down the slope, in defiance of all odds, had moved him beyond words. His emotions, so deep that he could not deal with the reality of them, had burst out in anger and fallen apart in a jumble of lust, tenderness and need. In short, he had made a complete fool of himself.

For most of the past two hours, Stella had clung to him in reproachful silence, her warm body a torment behind him. Half a dozen different times, Cade had been on the verge of breaking that silence to explain, to pour out his need, to come to some kind of reconciliation with what had happened between them. But each time, the forces of pride, mistrust and caution had stopped him. He had lowered the barriers between them once—with calamitous results. Best leave well enough alone.

But suddenly, now that they were safe, the journey had taken on a strange bittersweetness. He found himself wanting to prolong these last moments with her, to draw something from them that would leave a warm remembrance.

He had slowed the roan to a walk. All the old conflicts battled inside him. With great effort he forced them aside.

"Stella?"

She did not answer, but he felt her stir behind him. Her hair smelled of rain and sweet, young meadow grass.

"I'm a strange man, Stella. Sometimes I behave in ways that aren't easy to explain."

Again that questioning silence.

"Maybe it's because I've been away from your so-called civilization for so long. Maybe it's because I've seen so much death that it's done things to me—" Lord, what was he saying? He wasn't making a great deal of sense, even to himself.

"If you're trying to apologize, there's no need for it." Her low-pitched voice sent a thrill through him. "We're alive. We can be grateful to each other for that and forget about the rest."

"Stella, I vowed justice."

"Justice has many faces, Cade."

He took a deep, sharp breath. "If I said I didn't care about you, I'd be a liar. But I can't let that change my mind."

"I never expected you would." There was bitterness in her voice. "You're not that kind of man."

"Sometimes I wish I was! It would simplify things!" Cade nudged the roan to a brisk trot. He had not done well, he admitted ruefully. The old fears had swirled up in his mind again, and now this talk was becoming dangerous. Any more of it would bring him to the point of betraying himself.

The cabin was close now. In the moonlight he could see the outline of its sod roof and log fences. The lantern in the window beckoned like the light of a sanctuary.

Approaching an isolated frontier cabin in silence was never a good idea. "Knute!" he shouted. "It's Cade!"

The lantern flickered and moved. Yes, it was all right. He had reached a point of safety. He would see Stella settled in the cabin with the Aarnsons. Then he would spend the night in the shed and be gone in the morning, gone before the sun rose—gone before she could awaken and call him back.

The front door of the cabin swung open as they cantered into the yard. The man who stepped out, holding a lantern and a rifle, was as big as a bear, with a great bush of a beard and thinning, light brown hair.

"Cade!" he boomed. "You some kind of crazy man? These hills are crawling with Sioux! You're lucky—" His jaw dropped as he saw Stella.

"Well, I'll be...!" A grin spread across his kind, homely face. "Got yourself a bride, have you?" The grin widened as he looked Stella up and down.

"No, not this time." Cade lowered Stella gently from the back of the horse before swinging out of the saddle himself. Then he introduced Stella to his friend. "The lady's tired and hungry, if you can spare a plate and a bed for her," he said. "Come on with me while I put away the horse, and I'll explain why she's here."

"She's welcome for as long as she needs a place." Knute turned to Stella. When he spoke, his deep, bullfrog's voice was hushed. "You go on inside," he said. "My wife's there. Her name's Karin. She's from the Old Country, but she speaks pretty good English. She'll be right glad to see another white woman. Maybe you can cheer her up a bit. She's been poorly since she lost the baby."

Cade had begun leading the roan toward the shed. He stopped and turned. "Karin lost her baby? When?"

"About ten days ago. Almost lost her, too. Just us two, alone here. Not much I could do. It ... was a boy, Cade."

"Damn it, I'm sorry, Knute. Really sorry."

"We named him after you. Karin, she wanted to give him a name, even when he ... didn't live. We hoped you wouldn't mind."

"Mind? It's an honor, Knute." Cade turned away and led the roan into the darkness behind the cabin. Knute, after ushering Stella toward the open doorway, followed him.

Outside the cabin, Stella paused a moment to stretch her aching legs and smooth her rumpled skirt. She was bone weary and ravenous, but Karin Aarnson's plight had touched her. It would take a strong woman to endure life in an isolated cabin and to survive the loss of a child under these wretched conditions. Frontier wives like Karin must be forged from a special steel, she told herself as she knocked gently on the open door, then stepped inside the cabin.

It was a small place, dimly lighted by one tallow candle that sputtered from the mantel. Stella could make out the stone hearth, where a blackened iron pot nested on orange coals. A pair of snowshoes hung on the far wall, above what appeared to be a crude bed. Next to the bed was a hand-carved cradle—poignantly empty. In one corner, strips of drying meat dangled from wire hooks above a clutter of dirty pots and utensils.

"Karin?" Stella's whisper was loud in the odd silence of the tiny cabin.

A rocking chair moved in the shadows beside the fireplace. The candlelight flickered on a huddled form.

"Ja?" The reply was so faint that Stella scarcely heard it, but she moved toward the voice, picking her way between a stack of kindling and a heap of wooden bullet boxes.

"Karin?"

The woman in the chair was wrapped in a rough, woolen blanket, its folds half concealing her face. When she did not get up, Stella knelt down on the hearth in front of the rocker.

"Hello, Karin. I'm Stella. Knute told me to come in."

Karin Aarnson leaned forward, the blanket falling back behind her. The pale face revealed by the yellow glow of the candle was as delicate as a child's, the eyes large and filled with pain. Flaxen hair hung in loose tangles around her thin shoulders.

"Hello. I—I am happy to meet you," she whispered, her English hesitant but somehow charming. "I— Please. This place. It looks so bad. I have been—how do you say it?—I have not been very well."

"Don't worry, I understand. Your husband told us about the baby." Stella reached out and clasped the frail hands. They were as rough as a field laborer's, nothing but bones and calluses. "Knute said I might be able to stay here a few days. If that's all right with you, maybe I can give you some help."

"Help?" Embarrassed, Karin glanced around the cluttered, dingy cabin. "But you are a guest. Knute helps me some, but with me so sick he cannot hunt—"

"Then maybe I can at least be worth my keep." Stella squeezed the work-worn hands, already feeling protective towards this fragile child-woman. "It must have been awful for you here, having your baby and losing it, with no woman to help you," she said softly.

"*Ja*, it was awful." Karin's voice quivered slightly. "Poor Knute. My poor husband. He so wanted a son." As she gazed at Stella, she began to tremble. One tiny, choking sob worked its way up out of her throat, followed by another.

Stella felt something break loose inside herself. "You poor girl," she murmured as Karin began to cry in earnest. "You poor, poor thing!"

Karin's frail body shook with sobs. Stella gathered her close and held her as she wept, releasing a storm of pent-up grief, fear, loneliness and despair.

"There," Stella whispered. "Go ahead and cry. You'll feel better for it." She rocked Karin gently, smoothing the tangled hair with her fingers.

That was how Knute found them a few minutes later when he and Cade came back into the cabin with the lantern. *"Det er godt,"* he muttered awkwardly, gazing down at his wife. "It's healthy for a woman to cry over things, I heard once. Gets it out of her system. Sometimes . . . I wish I could do the same thing."

The return of the men halted Karin's emotional outburst. While she dried her eyes on the hem of her white flannel nightgown, Knute filled two tin plates with buffalo stew from the big, black pot on the fire. "Eat hearty," he said, slapping them down on the split-log table. "It's not fancy, but there's plenty."

The stew, which smelled like heaven, was thick with meat and dumplings and seasoned with wild onion. To wash it down, Knute filled tin mugs with steaming barley coffee. It was plain fare, but hot and good. Stella fought the temptation to wolf down her portion. Cade, she noticed, ate sparingly and said little. What was he thinking? she wondered. And what had he told Knute Aarnson out there in the shed?

Knute sat at the table and did most of the talking while Karin stayed huddled in her rocker, only picking at the bowl of stew he had brought her. From time to time, her reddened eyes darted shyly to her husband.

"My wife is from Oslo," Knute explained, leaning back in his chair. "Her family lived just down the street from my big brother, Hans. Good people, Hans told me. Had money for books and fine clothes and schooling, even a carriage. They lost it, though, the house and all, when the father's business failed."

Knute's eyes lingered gently on his wife as he took a generous gulp of barley coffee. "The family was on the street. My brother took Karin in as a servant, but she was a proud girl. Said she wanted to go someplace where nobody knew about her father's disgrace."

"So they sent her to you?" Stella glanced at Karin, who managed a shy, sad smile.

Knute flushed. "They showed her my picture, and she liked it. It was taken in my younger days, you see, before I started losing my hair. My brother stood in for me at the wedding. Made things not so hard that way, to have us married before she left Norway. I met her train at Omaha. I-I'd been needing a good woman for a long time." His gaze moved to where his wife sat. In his eyes, Stella glimpsed both tenderness and anguish. It was clear that he loved her. But was he aware of what he'd done, bringing a gently reared girl like Karin to a life like this?

"Then you haven't been married long?" Stella asked.

"Two years this past summer." Knute put down his mug and leaned toward her, his plain, round face furrowed with concern. "Cade says you need a place to stay for a while. To tell the truth, that's an answer to my prayers. Karin needs another woman here. I've tried to take care of her since the baby—I just can't. I don't know how."

"Then I'll be grateful to be of some use," Stella said. "And I may as well start being of use now." Over Karin's feeble protests, she stood up and began to clear away the empty plates and mugs. It was good to be needed. It made everything less awkward.

Cade stood, too, and stretched his legs. During the meal, Stella had felt his eyes on her. They were less cold than before, she sensed, maybe because the two of them were no longer alone. He felt safer here, less mindful of the need to keep the barriers high.

"It's getting late," he said to Knute. "I'll do fine with a blanket in the shed. That way, Stella can bunk in here."

"Suit yourself, friend." Knute tossed him a ragged patchwork quilt.

Cade caught it deftly, then turned and walked back toward the fireplace, where Karin still sat, huddled in the rocker. He bent low for a moment, so that his face was almost level with hers. "Thank you for your hospitality, Karin," he said gravely. "I'm sorry, very sorry about your baby."

The red blotches around Karin's eyes had faded by now. Seeing her in the glow of the lantern, Stella realized for the first time that Knute's wife was pretty. She gazed at Cade and managed a wan smile that showed small, slightly crooked teeth. "Thank you, Cade," she murmured in her thickly accented English. "As always, you are welcome here."

"Good night, Knute...ladies...." Cade paused at the door, the quilt over his arm. For a long, vibrant moment, his eyes caught Stella's and held them. Their intensity almost made her weak, and suddenly she knew what he was planning. He had seen her to safety. He would rest a few hours, and then, while he still had the strength, he would leave. She would awaken in the morning to find him gone.

A sudden sense of loss swept over her. She had met this man twenty-four hours ago, and her life had changed forever. Now, the reality of his leaving loomed like a bleak winter storm. Riding behind him on the red stallion, her arms around his waist, she had felt herself one with the earth, the wind and the soaring eagles. She had felt the vital forces of her own life and his, flowing together.

As he opened the door, her lips parted, ready to call out his name, to beg him to stay. But she could not speak, and the moment was lost. He tore his gaze from hers, turned and was gone, closing the door behind him.

Steeling herself against the loss, Stella washed the dirty dishes while Knute piled a front corner of the cabin with buffalo hides and covered them with a flannel sheet for her to sleep on. The hides were hairy and strange smelling, but Stella was exhausted. The prospect of sleeping anywhere that was safe and warm was good enough for tonight.

Darkness afforded the only privacy in the tiny, crowded cabin. After Knute had helped his wife into bed and blown out the lantern, Stella slipped out of her dress, petticoat and corset and into the lace-trimmed muslin nightgown that Karin had lent her. As she spread the tattered blanket she'd been given over the flannel sheet, she could hear Knute in the far corner of the cabin, unbuckling his belt and dropping his heavy boots on the floor. The bed frame creaked as he climbed in next to Karin. Then all was quiet.

Huddled under the blanket, Stella closed her eyes. She was dizzy with weariness, but sleep would not come. Her mind kept seeing Cade, standing in the doorway, his eyes drinking her in, as if he were seeing her for the last time. She remembered the feel of his arms around her, his warm, ravenous lips on hers....

Knute Aarnson had begun to snore, a soft, snuffling sound that filled the tiny space of the cabin. Stella covered her ears with the blanket and tried to shut out the noise.

Cade was just outside, she reminded herself, sleeping in the shed. She could go to him, awaken him gently and, if nothing else, they could talk. That way, at least, his going would not leave so many things unsaid between them.

But no, reason and caution argued. Cade's passion to see justice done in the matter of his brother's death overruled any feelings he might have for her. He had told her as much. Going to him now would only make things more difficult.

Go to sleep! she scolded herself, turning over and smoothing the lumpy wrinkles out of the blanket. There's no use churning over something that can never be! You'll only cause yourself grief!

She closed her eyes, took a deep breath and let it out slowly in an effort to relax her aching muscles and quivering nerves. Knute's snoring had become slower, more rumbling as he drifted into deep sleep. Stella lay still, trying not to let the sound bother her and trying not to think about Cade.

But it did no good. Cade was too near, and there were too many unspoken questions in her mind. She could not let him ride away in the dawn with those questions unanswered.

With her heart pounding like a tom-tom, she stood up, wrapped herself in the quilt and stole out of the cabin.

Chapter Six

Cade moaned softly as he slept. In his dream, Stella was there, leaning over him, her fragrant, chestnut hair enfolding them both like a curtain of rippled silk.

His arms reached up and drew her down to him. Her bare breasts were rose-tipped ivory, full and round in the moonlight. He buried his face in their deep, warm cleft, losing himself in their softness as the fire filled him. He wanted her more than he wanted food and air and freedom, more than he had ever wanted anything in his life.

"Stella...." He whispered in his dream. "Stella...."

"Cade." The low whisper jarred him awake. Instinctively, he groped for his pistol, but as his fingers touched the cold steel, he realized who it was. The dream clashed head-on with reality and shattered as he sat up.

"Is everything all right?" he asked, still dazed.

Stella knelt beside him, the quilt pulled around her body, the moonlight making a soft halo of her hair. "I couldn't sleep," she said. "You're leaving in the morning, aren't you?"

"I've got things to do." It was almost frightening, how easily she read him. "I'll be back in a few days," he said.

"And then?" She settled onto the ground beside him, tucking the quilt around her bare feet. "Surely you're not taking me back to Green River. They'll hang us both!"

"I didn't plan this, Stella. Not any of it."

"Including what happened this afternoon?"

Cade swallowed hard. "Years ago, in Saint Louis, I knew a gypsy woman," he said. "She threw knives just the way you throw questions."

"Is that where you learned to dodge so well?" She spoke softly, but Cade felt the barb in her voice.

"I've always been an impulsive man, Stella. There've been times in the past when I've given in to those impulses and paid a heavy price for it. This afternoon—" he paused to draw a deep, painful breath "—this afternoon can't happen again. You're a beautiful, exciting woman, and you saved my life. But that doesn't change the fact that my brother died in your tent."

"Then what are you going to do with me?"

"Damn it, I don't know yet!" The words spat out like bullets from a Gatling gun. "I told you, I didn't plan this!"

She accepted his retort in silence, pulling the quilt tighter around her shoulders. Cade was immediately sorry. He hadn't meant to hurt her, but this woman had a fearful ability to arouse strong feelings in him.

He half expected her to cry or to get up and go back into the cabin. That's what most women Cade knew would have done. Instead, she remained where she was, huddled in the blanket, gazing through the open door at the starry sky. The night was diamond clear, chilly with the promise of coming winter. The cry of a wolf echoed far off in the darkness.

It seemed like a long time before she spoke again. "When we were riding in, you started to tell me something—something about having seen a great deal of death. Why didn't you finish?"

"Maybe I thought better of it." His answer was only half-true. He had also lost his nerve. It wasn't easy, the thing he'd contemplated telling her.

"The war?"

"Partly."

She took a deep breath, as if she were about to plunge off a precipice. "Cade, my whole future is in your hands right now. It would help me understand my own position if I knew more about the kind of person I'm dealing with."

"I was married," he said slowly. "To an Indian girl. Chief Washakie's granddaughter. She gave me two little sons."

No answer from her. Wasn't that what he'd anticipated? Could he have expected any response except shocked silence?

She was still looking at the sky. "What happened to them?" she asked in a hushed voice.

"I came back from a hunting trip and found them all dead. A raiding party of Sioux had done it."

"Cade—" She turned and laid a hand on his sleeve. He braced himself against her warmth. Now that he had told her this much, he was determined to finish, even though she would not like what she was about to hear.

"The tracks were still fresh enough to follow," he said. "Over the next few weeks I trailed those Sioux up into the Bighorn country. One by one, like some animal gone mad, I killed them. I could even tell you how—"

"No!" Her hand had frozen on his arm. Her voice was a taut whisper. "No, that's enough, Cade."

"Later on, after I'd had time to look back on it, I was sick with disgust at what I'd done. It was senseless, all of it, I realized. The blood of the whole Sioux nation couldn't bring back my wife and sons."

Stella was silent beside him. What was she feeling? Cade wondered. She would be shocked, certainly, and repelled. He couldn't blame her for that. Anyone would be.

"Do you understand at all?" he asked her. "Do you see why I couldn't let them hang you back there in Green River?"

"And why you're saving me for the law?" Her voice had a bitter twist to it. "You want to get your justice legally this time, with no blood on your hands. I can understand that much, but it doesn't help. It doesn't change anything for me."

"One way or another, this has to be resolved." He gazed at her, his emotions in turmoil. Part of him wanted to take her in his arms, stroke her hair and rock her like a child. Another part wanted to crush her lips with his, as he had that evening. Still another part of him wanted to push her away, to shield himself from the revulsion she must surely be feeling after what he had told her.

"Maybe you'd better go back inside," he said. "You don't want Knute and Karin to get the wrong impression."

A long, tearing sigh escaped her. "Cade—"

"There's nothing more to say, Stella." He restrained himself as he watched her rise. He was being cruel, he knew. But to hold her, to reassure her with promises he could not keep—that would be infinitely worse.

She left him without another word. He watched her pale form fade into darkness, aching to call her back. Maybe he ought to stay tomorrow, he thought. Knute could use his help for a day. And that would give him a chance to make things right—

No. He broke off the thought before it had a chance to form. There was no way things could be right between Stella and himself. Not under the circumstances.

Leave while he still had the resolve—that was the only thing to do. Sleep for a few precious hours, then be off before dawn. Maybe once he was away from here, without Stella's presence to cloud his mind, he'd be able to think clearly. Maybe then he'd be able to make the right decisions and hold firm to them.

With a sigh of frustration, Cade turned over and pulled the ragged quilt around his body. He was weary enough to drop, but his thoughts were churning wildly, shifting one way, then another. He closed his eyes, determined to sleep. But the image of Stella's face stayed with him, as pale as a moon in the darkness of his mind.

Stella lay on her bed of buffalo skins, wide-awake. For hours she had stared into the darkness, trying to sort out the implications of what Cade had told her.

She'd heard of mountain men and trappers pairing up with Indian girls. Squaw men, that's what people called them—an awful, dirty-sounding term. Somehow it didn't seem to fit Cade Garrison at all. And yet it did. She'd only be deceiving herself if she denied it. Cade had loved a woman—a Shoshone. She had given him two sons. And he had gone mad with grief when they died.

She shuddered as she tried to imagine the rage it must have taken to track down and kill each member of the Sioux raiding party. Cade was a violent man, capable of fearsome lusts. And yet he had risked his own life to save her after she shot his brother.

It didn't make sense, and neither did Stella's own feelings. She was shocked and repelled by what he'd told her. Yet she could not help feeling pain for him. Cade Garrison, she sensed, was a man who carried deep emotional wounds. Some of those wounds were still raw, and they would be a long time healing.

Stella turned over and tried once more to settle herself on the lumpy hides. How could she have walked away from him like that, without even trying to understand? Maybe it wasn't too late. Maybe she could go out to him again, and this time they could talk more sympathetically.

She listened to make sure Knute and Karin were asleep. Then, wide-eyed in the early morning darkness, she slipped out of bed and tiptoed across the splintery floor.

Her hand was on the door latch when she heard it—the snort of a horse and the sound of hoofbeats in the darkness, passing alongside the cabin, then growing fainter. She did not have to open the door to know who it was and what had happened.

Stella's eyes closed with the sudden pain of loss. She was safe here and among friends, but somehow, she had never felt more alone.

Cade was gone.

South Pass City lay in a long pocket of the high, treeless plain, near the point where the Oregon Trail crossed the

Great Divide. It was bigger than Green River, and more of a town. But there was an element of isolation here, a loneliness foreign to settlements that mushroomed along the tracks of the Union Pacific. The winds were colder here, the blizzards deeper, and the homemade whiskey expensive and foul.

Here notorious outlaws walked the streets unafraid; and here, in one of the hillsides, was a crude dugout with a wooden door, where women and children took shelter during gunfights and Indian trouble.

Cade had not really planned to come to South Pass. His early departure from Knute's place, however, had bought him some time. With luck, word of the jailbreak would not reach here for another day or so, and he needed a new rifle to replace the Spencer he'd left behind in Green River. South Pass City was the only place where he knew he could buy one.

He had another reason to be here, as well, though he'd tried to push it aside. Stella's reaction to the cheroot stub in the cave still troubled him, as did the fact that nobody in Green River had seen Gillis since the shooting. If anything could be gained by nosing around and asking a few questions, he owed it to Jared—and to Stella, blast it—to do so.

The matter of the rifle was easily taken care of. The one-legged pirate who ran the General Store often took guns in trade from miners who couldn't pay their accounts. From the stash in the back, Cade selected another Spencer—newer than the one he'd lost—and four boxes of bullets. He also replaced the lost oilskin poncho. This time of year, the weather could turn nasty and strike with less warning than a rattlesnake. He didn't want to be caught unprepared again.

The street outside was an ankle-deep river of mud that squashed into ruts under the passing wagon wheels. Miners, loaded down with gear, grub or ore samples, trudged through the mire, as unheeding as cattle. Two mongrel dogs, mud from nose to tail, chased each other around a corner of the Claims Office. The day was cool here, with a brisk, menacing wind.

There was only one place to go if you wanted information. Cade stowed the bullets in his saddlebags, tied the rifle and the rolled-up oilskin to the saddle and led the roan up the street.

The saloon, a weathered, clapboard structure with an outside stairway leading down from the rooms on top, was the busiest place in South Pass. As he entered, Cade met a blast of warmth. Someone had put too much coal in the potbellied stove; the air swam with heat waves and tobacco smoke. The wooden floor was caked with muddy tracks.

At the bar, Cade ordered two fingers of brandy—expensive stuff, but at least it wasn't home brewed. After he'd paid the plump, swarthy woman behind the bar, he took the glass and sat down at an empty table.

The place wasn't half-full, but then it was not much past midday. The serious drinking and gambling wouldn't begin till after dark. The men who sat around the bar or huddled at the tables were just passing time, waiting.

"Buy me a drink, mister?"

Cade had seen the girl before. Martha Jane was her name, and she'd drifted in last spring from some mining town in Montana. At sixteen, she could drink like a man and curse like a mule skinner, and Cade had heard that her performance upstairs was nothing short of amazing.

"Sit down." Cade nodded toward an empty chair. A girl like Martha Jane might be able to provide him with some answers to his questions.

"Ain't allowed till you've paid."

"All right." Cade fished in his pocket. "Here. Order whatever you'd like."

Martha Jane went to the bar and came back with a glass of something that could have been either whiskey or tea. "There." She grinned, plopping down across from Cade. She had rusty hair—darker than Stella's and even more unruly—and her complexion was as speckled as a trout's.

Her broad shoulders and handsome, almost mannish features, contrasted garishly with the low-cut purple satin gown she wore.

"So how are things in South Pass?" Cade eased into the conversation.

"Not so good. I been thinkin' I might light out come spring. Hear it's mighty nice in the Dakotas."

"What's wrong? Is this place getting too civilized for you?"

"Hell, it's not that!" Martha Jane quaffed her drink and wiped her mouth with the back of her hand. Her face was flushed and damp from the heat in the room. "Look around. This town's got the death curse on it. The Oregon Trail won't amount t'nothin' but a cow path now that the railroad's through. An' there's already talk o' the gold mines peterin' out. Mark my words, mister, in a few years there won't be nothin' here but coyotes an' rattlesnakes. Me, I don't aim to stick around that long!"

Cade took a deep breath. "Martha Jane, I came here to ask about a man. I was hoping you might know something about him."

"Hell, I know lots of men!" She gave Cade a good-naturedly lewd wink. "What's his name?"

"Gillis. He's got a claim up here somewhere."

"Gillis? Big coyote with a black beard?"

"That's right. Sounds like you know him."

She grinned, showing handsome, horsey teeth. "Comes in here almost every night. But don't get the wrong idea. I ain't never been upstairs with him. He's sweet on one of the other girls." Martha Jane leaned forward, pressing her breasts against the edge of the table as she lowered her voice to a whisper. "That's why he comes here. Her name's Amy, and she's...well, sweet. Not like me. There she is, right over there."

Cade followed the direction of Martha Jane's gaze. The girl was painfully young beneath her rouge, with wide blue eyes that still showed traces of innocence. Her yellow hair hung in strings down her back. Her pink satin gown, which

looked as if it had been taken in to fit, was stained and
faded.

"Amy's skeered to death of Gillis," Martha Jane continued. "She always hides upstairs when he comes, but he
knows she's here. Ruby over there puts a high price on her
'cause she's so pretty. She says that if Gillis can come up
with enough money, he can have her. But Amy says she'll
run away afore that day comes."

Cade took a long, slow sip of the brandy. "You knew my
brother, didn't you?" he asked her. "Jared Garrison—tall,
blond, not much older than you."

"Jared?" Her breath caught, and Cade realized that
Martha Jane must have known Jared well in some respects. "So he was your brother. Funny, I've seen you in
here afore, but I never made the connection between him
and you." She lowered her voice. "I heard what happened. I'm right sorry about it. I liked your brother. I really
did."

"Did he know Gillis? Were they friends?"

Martha Jane shrugged. "They both came in here a lot.
Sometimes they played poker at the same table. But
friends? I wouldn't call it that. They knew each other, that's
all."

"Martha Jane Canary!" The plump woman behind the
bar shrilled like a harpy. "Less'n that fellow's takin' you
upstairs, his time's done! You got to pay attention to the
other customers!"

"Bitch!" Martha Jane muttered under her breath. Then
she gave Cade a sly look, "You want to? I could show you
a real good time, mister."

Cade shook his head. "I've got a lot of ground to cover
between now and sundown," he said, excusing himself as
gallantly as he could. "It looks like for now I'll have to
make do with my fancies."

"Martha Jane!" Ruby's voice rasped like a saw against
green lumber.

The girl stood up, moving with defiant slowness. "Got
to go," she whispered.

"One more thing," Cade said, suddenly remembering. "Gillis. Does he smoke?"

"All the time. Little black cheroots. Don't ask me where he gets 'em. Must have a whole trunkful stowed up at his claim." Her eyes darted to the woman at the bar. "I got to go. Really. Come back tonight. Maybe he'll be here."

"Thanks." Cade watched her swing off to another table. Then he took the time to finish his brandy, sipping it slowly, before he got up and left.

Pity he couldn't have stayed around to meet Gillis in person, Cade reflected as he rode away from South Pass. He would like to have asked the fellow some questions. But the risks were too great. Someone could arrive very soon with news of the jailbreak. When that happened, he wanted to be far away.

As he rode, he reflected on his conversation with Martha Jane. The black cheroots fit in with Stella's story; however, part of him was still skeptical. It wouldn't be the first time a beautiful woman had lied to him, Cade reminded himself. And if he had been as cautious seven years ago as he was now, he would be back in Saint Louis, living in wealth and comfort.

But it did no good to dwell on the past. He had found a new home, and the Wind River Valley was in his blood. Apart from the loneliness, he was content amid the wild beauty of its peaks, forests and meadows, with the Shoshone as his brothers. The thought of returning to it now, even for a short time, filled him with a sense of peace.

He would have to decide what to do about Stella. But there was time, he reassured himself. She would be safe with the Aarnsons for a few days. And he, too, would be safe—from the lure of her dark velvet voice, her soft lips and warm, curving body; and from the hunger that filled him whenever she was near.

Yes, it was for the best, he told himself as he turned the roan into the wind. He had to do the right thing, make the right decisions. With Stella beside him, it was all he could do to think, let alone reason. He needed solitude, needed the blessed quiet of the Wind River. There, perhaps, wisdom would speak as strongly as passion, and he would listen to its voice.

Late morning sunlight slanted through the freshly washed front window of the Aarnson cabin. Inside, the floor had been swept, the bed changed, the dishes washed and put away.

Stella stood behind the rocker, brushing the tangles from Karin Aarnson's fine blond hair. The back of the brush, she noticed, was silver, inlaid with tortoiseshell. It seemed out of place in this rough setting—as out of place as its fragile, young owner. What a shock Knute's way of life must have been to Karin. It was a wonder she'd survived it at all.

"Sit down and rest, Stella," Karin protested. "You are not a servant here. You do too much!"

"It feels good to be busy." Stella paused to smooth out a snarl with her fingers. "Helps keep my mind off... things."

"Yes." Karin's small hands formed a knot in her lap. "Knute told me what happened to you—all of it. Even the jail and the men who tried to hang you. What an awful thing. You must be a very strong person."

"And you," Stella said slowly, "must be a very kind person, to take in someone who has been accused of murder."

Karin turned, her hair pulling taut in Stella's hands. "You don't know..." She struggled with the words. "To be so alone in this place. No woman friends. You don't know how happy I am that you are here."

"Thank you," Stella murmured, touched. "That means a great deal to me." Gently she resumed her brushing. "Living here must be hard for you, Karin. Do you miss your life in Norway?"

"Norway! Oh..." Karin lapsed into a long silence that spoke eloquently of the memories that haunted her. Soft beds and carpeted floors, crystal chandeliers, music lessons and tea with little cakes. Parties, balls and sleigh rides. Parents, brothers, sisters, friends . . .

"Knute is very good to me," she said softly. "He tries— he works so hard to keep me fed and warm and safe, but . . ." She drew a deep breath, as if she were pulling in her feelings. "I would ask him to go back to Norway, but I know better. Here he has this land. In Norway he could only work for his brother. For himself, he would have . . . nothing."

"You love him, don't you?" Stella murmured, amazed. Knute was at least twice the age of this child, and certainly not the sort of man one would expect to turn a young girl's head.

The color rose in Karin's pale, thin face, and for that instant she was beautiful. "You know how I married his picture. When I got off the train in Omaha and saw him . . . he looked so different. And then when he brought me here, I saw this cabin and I wanted to turn around and go right back to Norway."

"But you stayed." Stella brushed a lock of Karin's hair around her finger to see if it would curl.

"He was so good. So gentle. At first I stayed because I didn't want to hurt him. Then—" Karin's next words were spoken in a whisper. "At first he did not touch me. Not for many, many weeks. He wanted to wait, he said, till I was ready." Karin gave a small, nervous laugh. "I was so young. So—how do you say it?—innocent. I did not even know what he meant. Only after I told him that I wanted to give him a son, that was the first I really understood—"

She turned in her chair so that she was looking up at Stella. Her eyes glistened with tears. "I failed him, Stella. A man like Knute needs many sons, and I am not strong enough to have them. I-I'm not even strong enough to do my share of the work in this place." Karin shook her head in despair. "My poor Knute. Sometimes I even think it might have been better if he'd married an Indian woman, like Cade did—"

Immediately Karin's hand flew to her mouth. Her pale green eyes widened in alarm. "Oh, forgive me, I—"

"It's all right," Stella said swiftly. "Cade told me about his wife and sons." She began to braid Karin's hair, her fingers moving with furious speed. She'd told herself that it didn't matter, this business about Cade's Indian wife and children. It was not even her concern. But she had to admit that it had gnawed on her. What else could have kept her awake last night when she was so tired?

"Did you know Cade's wife?" she asked Karin.

"No. He never brought her here. And she died soon after I came." Karin winced as Stella's fingers caught a hidden tangle. "I've seen other Indians, though. Some of them came here last winter to beg for food."

"Shoshone?"

"I don't know. But they were awful—so dirty and wicked looking. I—I was never so frightened in all my life. Knute had to make them go away. If Cade's woman was like them . . ."

A shiver went through Karin's thin body as she spoke. She let the thought hang on the air while Stella tied off her long single braid with string and added a pink ribbon. Knute's wife looked fresh and pretty.

Stella kept busy for the rest of the day, flinging herself into the cleaning and washing with a fury born of desperation. It didn't matter, she told herself again and again. Cade's past was his own business. It shouldn't concern her. But that night, just before she sank into exhausted slumber, she finally admitted that it did matter. There were things she had to know.

Knute might be able to help her, she thought. He and Cade were close friends, and men talked to each other. When she had the chance, Stella resolved, she would ask him.

That chance came the next afternoon.

They were in the cleared area behind the cabin. Knute, stripped to the waist, was scraping a buffalo hide that he'd stretched on a log frame. Stella was seated on a stump, peeling a panful of potatoes from the root cellar. Karin was in the cabin, making biscuits for supper.

Knute glanced up at her, squinting beneath his bushy eyebrows. "I'm beholden to you, Stella," he said. "You've made quite a difference in Karin. It's good to have her up and about, dressed and doing things—"

"Karin's trying, but she's still not very strong," Stella answered. "She's been through a hard time, Knute."

"*Ja*, I know." Knute had a habit of throwing Norwegian words into his conversation, something his more educated wife seldom did. "Karin's had a hard life here. And she's young, just a girl. If—" he sighed deeply "—if I had the money, I would take her and move to California, I think. Maybe there, things would be better." His eyes wandered to the tiny grave at the edge of the clearing, surrounded by a sad little wall of piled-up stones. "I'd planned to take her to South Pass City to have the baby. There's a doctor there, and women who could help. But when her pains started so early..." He bent over the hide again, plying the knife ferociously to hide his grief.

"Don't blame yourself. You couldn't help what happened," Stella said softly. "At least you were able to save Karin."

"*Ja*, thank God for that. If I'd lost her, too..." He swallowed hard. For a few minutes he worked in silence. Then he spoke again.

"Cade is very taken with you," he said, the simple words full of shadowed meaning.

Stella felt her heart jump, but she forced herself to speak calmly. "Is that what Cade told you?"

"*Nei*, not in words. But I know him." Knute paused to clean his knife blade on the rough bark of the frame, then attacked the hide once more. "I met him in Laramie right after he came west, and we wintered together part of the first year. I know almost all there is to know about Cade Garrison, and I never saw him so churned up over a woman before!"

"But you know why he brought me here—"

"*Ja.* And it's got him all tore up inside. That's why he didn't stay around here any longer than he did."

"Tell me about him, Knute," she said, grateful for the opening. "He seems so closed up, so angry, as if he had a wall of porcupine quills around his soul!"

Knute wiped the blade again. "I know. He's had a lot of hurt, that man."

"Tell me, Knute. Please." Stella spoke softly, trying not to betray the urgency she felt inside. She had to know about Cade. If there was any way to understand him, she had to try.

Knute began scraping the hair from the buffalo hide once more, but slowly this time, as if he just needed something to do with his hands while he talked.

"Cade's from Saint Louis. His family's still there, and they've got money. *Uff da!* A fortune! From the early days of the river shipping business."

Yes, it was beginning to make sense now, Stella thought. Even in his worn and faded range clothes, Cade had the air of a gentleman about him. "Then what's he doing out here?" she asked, puzzled. "He could be living well."

"Woman trouble." Knute did not look up from his scraping. "And not an ordinary woman, this one. She was married. To the lieutenant governor of Missouri."

The afternoon was silent except for the rasp of the knife on the damp buffalo hide. Knute was quiet, too—so quiet that at last Stella could stand no more of it.

"What happened?" she demanded, her emotions suddenly churning. How much did she really want to know about Cade Garrison? How much could she stand to hear?

Knute shrugged his big, sunburned shoulders. "The old story. The rich, powerful husband. The beautiful, bored wife. And, naturally, the foolish, hot-blooded young man."

"Cade?"

"Cade. Hot-blooded and the best shot in the state. She picked a good one, that Lavinia!"

"Oh!" Stella had cut herself on the knife. She put her finger to her mouth to stop the bleeding.

Knute raised a bushy eyebrow. "You can listen or you can peel potatoes, *ja*? Not both."

Stella put the pan on the ground. Her finger still stung where she had cut it. "All right. Go on, Knute."

"It was a long time ago, you understand. Just before the war. Cade was different then—young and not so careful as now. And she was a bad woman. She used him."

"How?" Stella felt uneasy. The sun was too bright, the Indian summer afternoon too warm.

"Her husband. She was careless on purpose, and he found out. He challenged Cade to a duel."

Knute stopped scraping the hide. His eyes met Stella's. "Cade didn't want to hurt the man, you understand. The lieutenant governor, he shot first and missed. Cade shot into the air. He thought that was the end of it. But when he turned to walk away, the fool grabbed another gun from his second. He shot Cade in the shoulder."

Stella was dimly aware that she had stopped breathing.

"Cade killed him," Knute said. "He had to."

"And Lavinia?"

"She waited long enough to get her husband's money. Then she ran off to Paris—with the riverboat gambler she had loved the whole time."

Stella felt the breath leave her. Yes, she thought, that explained a great deal. Cade's anger, his mistrust . . .

"The lieutenant governor had dangerous friends," Knute was saying. "Cade had killed the man in self-defense, but he could not stay in Saint Louis."

"So he came west?"

"Not then. He joined the army. The war was just starting. Before it finished, Cade got wounded in the side. After that was when he came west. That was when I met him."

"And he told you all this?" Stella gazed down at her hands, still shaken by what she had learned.

"*Ja*. Like I say, I know him pretty well."

"And his wife? His Shoshone woman?"

"So, he has told you." Knute furrowed his heavy brows.

"Only that she gave him two sons. And that they were all killed by the Sioux."

"Cade's war wound had never healed right," Knute said. "He was hunting in the Wind River when it went bad again. He would have died, but the Shoshones found him. They took care of him."

Stella nodded her understanding. She could imagine the rest. The wounded stranger, the tender, young Indian girl. Nature taking its course. Suddenly she did not want to hear any more. Each new revelation about Cade's past stung her like a lash, and she had had enough whipping for one day.

She picked up the pan of potatoes. "I think I'll finish these in the cabin," she murmured. "Karin might be needing some help."

Knute gave her a knowing glance, then returned to his scraping. Stella had left him and walked slowly back around the cabin, lost in thought. She had just rounded the corner when her eye caught a slight flicker of movement in the trees.

She raised her head, instantly alert, eyes and ears straining. She saw nothing, heard nothing. Yet, her senses prickled with the vague sensation that she was being watched.

That was silly, she told herself. It was only a bird or a leaf catching the light. There was nothing to worry about.

Resolutely, she walked to the edge of the clearing and peered into the dim shadows of the forest. There was nothing there. Nothing but pine trees, dark and thick, their needles carpeting the earth.

She shrugged off her apprehension, went back into the cabin and busied herself with helping Karin. It was foolish to worry, she told herself. Her imagination had simply gotten the best of her.

But in spite of everything, the feeling remained with her, lingering in her uneasy mind for the rest of that day.

Chapter Seven

Karin sank into the rocker, exhausted after a morning of making loganberry preserves, pouring them into clay jars and sealing them with wax. Her drawn face was beaded with sweat, her small hands stained crimson with berry juice.

Stella gave her a concerned glance. "Now you've overdone it," she scolded good naturedly. "I told you you'd be sorry if you didn't rest."

"Yes, I know." Karin dabbed at her face with the frayed hem of her apron. "But Knute loves loganberry jam in the winter. The berries would have spoiled if I'd let them go even one more day."

"I could have done it by myself, if you'd only let me," Stella said. Karin's determination to be up and doing her share was a real worry to her. Knute's young wife was still so weak that she trembled when she walked.

"I'll have to do things by myself when you leave," Karin said. "I may as well—how do you say?—get used to it."

"You'll make yourself really ill if you're not careful."

Karin shook her head stubbornly. "No. I will not be ill. I can't be. If I am ill, Knute will not leave me to go hunting. We'll have no meat and no hides—and no money! Oh, Stella, I wish you could stay! It's so lonely here when Knute is gone! I hear noises in the forest. They frighten me so—"

"Hush," Stella said softly. "I'll stay as long as I can. But when Cade comes back—"

"No!" Karin protested. "I can't believe he would take you away from here and let you go back to jail. Not Cade!"

"I killed his brother, Karin." Stella spoke softly. "A thing like that isn't easy to forgive."

"But Cade is such a kind person." Karin argued. "Last winter, when Knute hurt his leg and could not hunt, Cade brought us meat. Every week he came, even in the snow. While he was here, he would chop enough firewood to last us till he came again. And me . . . always he treats me like a lady. He makes me feel like I was back in Oslo." Karin's long braid switched as she shook her head. "No, Cade is like a brother to Knute and a very big brother to me. Perhaps if we both asked him to let you stay—"

"It wouldn't do any good, Karin. Cade may be a good man, but he's stubborn. He made a promise on his brother's grave, and he means to keep it."

"Yes." Something flickered behind Karin's eyes. "Jared meant very much to him."

"You knew Jared?"

Karin nodded slowly. "Not well. But yes, he came here with Cade a few times. He—" She broke off and lowered her eyes.

"What is it?" Stella asked.

"Nothing. He . . . tried to kiss me once, that's all. Knute and Cade had gone off hunting that morning. Jared had told them he didn't feel well enough to go along. He—" the color rose hot in Karin's cheeks "—he came up behind me. He told me I was the prettiest girl he'd ever seen. And he asked me if I'd ever wondered what it would be like to make love to a man my own age. Then he tried..." Karin's hands twisted the hem of her apron as she struggled with the words. "Forgive me. It's just that I never told anybody—"

"What did you do?" Stella asked gently.

"I—I told him to let me go. I told him that I was a married woman, and if he didn't leave me alone, I would tell Knute and Cade when they got back."

"And he did? He left you alone?"

Karin nodded, her lips pressed tightly together. "He laughed. He said he was only teasing. But I knew better. I did not stop being afraid till Knute came home."

"And you never said a word to Knute?"

"It would have only caused trouble between Cade and Knute. Cade always stood up for his brother." Karin tried to rise, then collapsed into the chair again with a nervous little laugh. "You are right. I did too much today. If you will help me to the bed, I think I must rest awhile."

Stella settled Karin on the bed with a quilt tucked around her. Then she began to sweep the kitchen, her mind in turmoil. Karin's revelation had brought back memories of Jared Garrison standing silent in her tent while Gillis attacked her. What if Gillis had been successful? she wondered. Would Jared have raped her, too? The idea sent a cold shiver through her body.

Cade had admitted that Jared was wild. And Karin's story certainly bore that out. It stood to reason— But, no! Jared was Cade's brother. Something in her refused to believe that a brother of Cade Garrison's could be capable of such an awful act.

And maybe that was part of the trouble, Stella told herself as she swept the dirt from the splintery floor. Maybe Cade refused to believe it, too. If she was innocent, that meant Jared, his own brother, was guilty.

The dilemma loomed large and black, overshadowing even her worry about Karin. Cade would be returning soon to turn her over for trial. In less than two weeks, she could be on her way to prison—or the gallows.

And muddled into it all, somehow, was the realization that Cade had stirred her. In their brief time together, he had touched depths in her that no man had ever touched. And she had touched him, as well, she knew.

But did it mean anything? That question haunted her, too. Cade seemed as drawn to her as she was to him, but that had not weakened his resolve to turn her over to the law. Why was he so unmoving? Was it because he did not care for her, or was he so duty-bound that he refused to listen to his heart?

Cade was a man with a turbulent past, Stella reminded herself as she finished sweeping and put the broom in the corner. That past, she sensed, was the key to who and what he was. Somehow, for whatever reason, she needed to understand him.

She passed the fireplace and paused to stir the beans that simmered over the coals in the big iron pot. Raising the wooden spoon to her mouth, she blew on the hot liquid and tasted it. Not enough onions, she decided. She would have to go down to the root cellar and get more.

Out of the corner of her eye, she could see Karin, asleep on the bed. The quilt rose and fell with the shallow rhythm of her breathing. That, and the buzzing of a horsefly on the windowsill, were the only sounds in the warm, cluttered cabin.

Stella opened the door and stood on the threshold, letting the autumn breeze cool her sweat-dampened face. How small the world seemed here—just the cabin and the clearing around it, surrounded on three sides by a towering wall of dark green pines. It was unsafe to go beyond the edge of it, Knute had told her. The trees were so thick and so alike that one could become lost in minutes. And there were wolves, bears and mountain lions in the forest, as well, to say nothing of Indians.

Only on the side that faced the Little Sandy did the trees open up a little. A span of two hundred yards separated the river and the cabin, most of it thick with willows and scattered clumps of pine. The river, Knute insisted, was the most dangerous place of all. He would not allow either Stella or Karin to walk the winding path through the willows unless he was along with a rifle, and he carried most of the water himself, in two big, wooden buckets suspended from a yoke that rode his powerful shoulders.

A good man, Knute Aarnson. Stella saw him now, coming up the path, bent under the weight of the buckets. Impulsively she slipped out the door and ran to meet him.

Maybe they could talk, she thought. He might have some
answers to her questions about Cade.

She hurried down the path, savoring the feel of the wind
in her hair. How much longer would she be able to run free
like this? she wondered. How much longer, before iron-
barred doors clanged shut behind her again, this time forever?

"Knute!" she called out to him, then stopped short as
she saw the alarm on his rugged face. "What's the matter?"

"Nothing, I hope." His eyes appraised Stella, as if he
were speculating how well she might stand up to a crisis. "I
saw some fresh hoofprints in the mud at the edge of the
creek," he said. "No shoes. That means Indian ponies."

Stella gave an involuntary gasp.

"Please—" Knute shook his head "—you mustn't let
Karin know. She's terrified of Indians."

"Would they attack us?"

"I hope not, but you never can tell." Knute shifted the
weight of the yoke on his shoulders. "Can you shoot a rifle?"

"If I have to." Stella felt her pulse quicken. "You think
they're Sioux, then?"

"No way to tell from the tracks. I haven't had much Indian trouble before. I always figured that was because of
Cade."

"Because of Cade?"

"*Ja.* He's bad medicine to the Sioux. Since he wiped out
the raiding party that killed his wife and children, they
mostly leave him alone. Whatever the reason—fear, superstition, respect—they don't seem to bother him much."

"Or his friends—is that right?"

Knute had begun to walk again, plodding under the
weight of the heavy water buckets. "I don't know for sure.
But either Cade's medicine has rubbed off on me, or I've
been plain lucky."

"Then let's hope your luck holds out." Stella walked
alongside him, swinging her arms in an effort to appear

untroubled. The breeze, however, had suddenly become chilly; the clear, autumn sunlight harsh and glaring. The croak of a raven from the top of a pine had an ominous tone to it, like the voice of doom. She found herself shivering.

"Knute, what was she like—Cade's Indian wife?" she asked. "Did you know her?"

"I met her just one time," Knute said. "She always stayed in the Wind River, you see. He never took her with him when he went out."

"And . . . what did you think of her?"

"She was the most beautiful Indian girl I ever saw. Sweet and very shy." Knute shifted the yoke again and glanced at Stella, his eyes questioning. "I think Cade chose her because she was exactly the opposite of Lavinia."

"But he loved her?"

Knute nodded slowly. "*Ja*. He loved her. When she died, a part of him died, too."

"I see." Stella walked a few paces in silence, her eyes on the path.

"It troubles you?" Knute asked.

"What?"

"That he took a woman of another race."

"No—no! My own father took a woman of another race. She became my mother."

"Ah!" Knute's gaze took in Stella's dark eyes and golden skin; he nodded his understanding. "But something troubles you, *ja?* Is it that he loved someone else so much?"

Stella's silence answered his question.

"Ask yourself this," Knute said gently. "If he had not loved her, would Cade be the man he is? Would you care for him so much?"

"Knute—" He had probed too deeply, touching a tender spot.

"*Jeg beklager,*" he said. "Forgive me. It's not my business how you feel."

"But Karin is your business." She decided to change the subject. "I'm worried about her, Knute. She's just not regaining her strength. And she won't rest. She keeps working till she drops."

Knute did not reply for a long moment. Stella could hear him breathing hard as he walked, straining under the weight of the buckets. When he finally spoke, it was so softly that she had to bend close to hear.

"After Karin lost the baby, I wrote a letter to my brother, Hans," he said. "I asked him to send me Karin's passage back to Norway."

"Karin doesn't know?"

He shook his head.

"Knute—" Stella touched his arm "—Karin loves you. It would break her heart if you sent her away."

"It might be the only way to save her," Knute said. "I brought her to this wild place because I needed a wife. But I was a fool. Karin isn't strong enough for such a hard existence. She will die if she has to stay here much longer."

"But isn't there some other answer?" Stella protested. "You could move into one of the towns, or pick up and go someplace like California. Things would be easier there. You could even go back to Norway with her."

Knute's sigh racked his whole body. "Stella, I don't have a penny. In the past, I've made money hunting buffalo. But this summer, with the baby so close, I couldn't leave Karin alone. I've hardly been hunting in months. Sometimes I think that maybe, with her safe in Norway, I could earn enough money for a new start somewhere else...."

"And then you'd send for her?" Stella asked hopefully.

"*Nei*, it could take years," Knute answered in a pain-dulled voice. "Karin's young. She could find a new life. How could I ask her to wait that long...for me?"

"Have you talked this over with Karin?" Stella asked softly.

Knute's silence answered her question.

"You should, Knute. Karin's your wife. You can't just send her away without her having some say in the matter."

"I wanted to wait till Hans sent her passage—and he will. My brother is a good man."

"But is that fair to Karin? To just do it, like that? A woman has a right to know her husband's plans."

Knute plodded along in silence for a few steps. Then he sighed. "I hate to say it, but you're right. Karin should know."

Stella touched the great, solid shoulder, aching for him. "When do you plan to tell her?"

The water sloshed in the buckets as he shrugged. "Soon. As soon as I can find a good time."

They were nearing the cabin now. Knute was silent, his shoulders bent, his heavy brows knotted above the bridge of his nose. How would Karin react to his news? Stella wondered. Karin seemed to love her big, gentle husband. But the thought of going back to the safety and comfort of Norway, back to her family and her old life, might be a blessed relief for her. Her existence in this wild, lonely place had been bleak beyond words. No woman could be blamed for wanting to leave it.

Stella was so preoccupied that she'd almost forgotten about the Indians. Not until Knute spoke did the sense of danger suddenly seize her again.

"Stay inside till we're sure they've gone," he said softly. "Remember, no word to Karin. Indians make her so afraid—"

"But shouldn't she know?"

"*Nei*, not unless she has to. Believe me, you have never seen her when there are Indians around. She goes wild with fear."

Knute set one bucket down in the yard, then carried the other inside to the kitchen. Karin was still asleep, curled beneath the ragged quilt, the end of her pale gold braid falling across her cheek. She looked as soft and innocent as a child.

Stella busied herself in the kitchen, using some of the water Knute had carried in to wash the dishes. Her movements were mechanical, like a puppet's; her nerves as taut as bowstrings. Every sound—the creak of a floorboard, the distant call of a magpie, the wind in the pines—set off alarms inside her.

You're being silly, she told herself. Knute said those Indians weren't likely to attack. They're probably miles away from here by now!

Still the fear lingered, dark and heavy inside her. She had heard stories about Indians and what they did to their victims. The memory of her one encounter with them only served to make those stories more real.

But enough of this! Stella picked up another dish, took a deep breath and began to hum softly to herself.

The minutes crawled by. Knute prowled the cabin, checking the windows and the door. Karin, awake now, was sitting up on the bed, watching him with wide, puzzled eyes.

Stella finished the dishes and turned toward the fireplace to stir the pot again. It was only then she remembered that the beans she was cooking needed more onions.

The door to the root cellar was outside, along the north wall of the cabin. The onions, she reminded herself, were not really worth the risk of going outside. Yet, for some reason, she felt a compelling need to go. It was as if, perhaps, by risking her safety for something as trivial as a few onions, she could lessen her own fear.

"I have to get something from the root cellar," she told Knute. "I'll only be a minute."

Knute looked worried, then shrugged. "All right," he said.

The small trapdoor that led down to the cellar was just a few strides away, around the corner of the cabin. Stella crouched beside it for a moment, her senses straining for any sign of trouble.

The wind had died. The pines stood silent vigil around the cabin, their cool shadows blending into impenetrable green darkness. There was no movement, no sound anywhere except for the call of a blackbird from the river. The stillness of the woods was strangely frightening. Stella could feel her heart fluttering against her ribs like a wild bird in a cage.

Shrugging off her uneasiness, she raised the small door and slipped down the crude steps that had been carved out of a single, heavy log. The darkness and the rich aroma of damp soil closed around her as she reached the bottom. She took a deep breath. It was strange how safe she felt down here, surrounded by solid earth. Strange, how much she wanted to stay.

But she had forgotten that the root cellar was right under the part of the cabin where Knute and Karin's bed stood. She could hear them talking now, both of them in Norwegian, and the sound came down clearly through the thin cracks in the floor. She could understand only a few words of the language, but she realized, from the tone of what was being said and the repeated mention of the name Hans, that Knute was telling Karin of his plan to send her back to Norway.

Stella used the light from the open trapdoor to find the onions she needed. By now she could hear the sound of Karin weeping, pleading with her husband to change his mind. It was clear that in spite of the hardships and in spite of her frail health, she could not bear the idea of leaving him.

Suddenly Stella realized what little privacy the two of them had had since she came. The darkness of night and the fact that they spoke a language she did not understand were clearly not enough. Knute and Karin needed some time alone—even if it was only a few minutes—to express their feelings openly.

She would wait, she resolved, until they'd had some time to talk. When things quieted down again, then she would go back up to the cabin.

She sat down on a heap of pumpkins, newly harvested from the Aarnsons' vegetable patch. By now her eyes were well accustomed to the darkness. She could see bins of potatoes, carrots and onions along one rough, earth wall. Another wall was lined with crude shelves, these mostly bare except for a few dusty jars of preserves and four big jugs of Knute's whiskey.

Karin and Knute had lowered their voices. Maybe they were resolving some of their difficulties, Stella told herself. Maybe, by some miracle, they would make everything right between them, and she would return to find them in each other's arms.

And maybe, Stella continued in her fantasy, another miracle would happen. Cade would come back again, convinced this time that she was telling the truth about Jared's death. Together they would find a way to clear her of all the charges, and then...then—

A scream shattered Stella's reverie—a scream of sheer, stark, animal terror. The voice was Karin's.

Stella leaped to her feet and started for the steps. Her head had almost cleared the ground when she saw the arrow just outside the trapdoor, still quivering where its point had struck the earth. Above her, she heard the bark of Knute's rifle and the sound of Karin screaming again.

Half climbing, half falling, she scrambled down the chiseled steps and flung herself against the back wall of the cellar. For a moment she lay there, sweating and sick with fear. This is the end, she thought. The end of everything.

Then, slowly, her courage returned. She could not just lie here, she told herself. She had to do something.

Knute's rifle rang out again, and Stella heard an Indian shriek. How many of them were out there? she wondered. And what could she do to help Knute?

She climbed on top of the pumpkins so that her head was directly under the floor. "Knute!" she shouted through one of the cracks. "What can I do?"

"Stay where you are!" Knute bellowed. "No way you can get up here!"

"How many are there?"

"Can't tell! They're back in the trees! Maybe a dozen!" Stella could hear the sound of bullets sliding into his rifle. He fired again, cursing as the shot whanged off a tree.

"Knute, if you could get me a gun—"

"How, damn it?"

"You could chop a hole in the floor and drop it down to me. Then I could hold them off from this side."

There was a long pause. "You can shoot, *ja*?"

"Yes, I can shoot!" Just ask the good citizens of Green River! Stella thought bitterly.

"Just a minute, then." He fired another shot into the trees. Then Stella could hear him moving around the cabin, rummaging beneath the bed. In the next instant he was chopping away at the floor with a hatchet. The wood was beginning to splinter. Stella could see a thin beam of light through the opening.

"Hurry!" she whispered, then gasped as an arrow, trailing flame, whistled through the trapdoor and struck the ground at her feet. She doused the fire with dirt, coughing as the acrid fumes scorched her throat. This arrow had done no harm, but there would be others. Dread tightened like a noose around her heart.

Knute was no longer chopping at the floor, and Karin had begun to scream again—hysterically this time, over and over. Stella could hear Knute's voice as he tried to calm her. She could hear Karin thrashing around like a wild animal in her terror; and faintly, over the sound of Karin's screams, she could hear the crackle of flames.

Helpless, Stella listened to the struggle above her head. From the sound of their footsteps—Knute's heavy, Karin's light and quick—she could almost visualize what was happening. The roof was ablaze above their heads, and Karin, in her mindless fear, was trying to run outside.

"Knute!" Stella shouted. "The floor! Chop a bigger hole, and I'll help you get her down here!" But she was shouting at nothing. The conflict overhead only grew wilder.

Suddenly Knute's footsteps faltered. He staggered backward, and Stella realized he had been hit. Crazed with fright, Karin spun away from him and ran screaming for the door. Her footsteps paused as she slid the bolt back. Then she plunged out into the yard.

Stella could still hear her screaming. Karin was running away from the cabin now, toward the woods, toward the Indians. They would take her alive, and then—Stella pressed her hands to her face, shuddering violently as she thought of what the Indians would do to a pretty girl like Karin.

From overhead, Stella could hear the scrape of Knute's body as he dragged himself across the floor toward the window. She could hear the crackle of the blazing roof and Karin's screams, growing even more frantic now as the Indians closed in on her.

A single shot rang out from the cabin. The screams stopped abruptly as Knute's body slid to the floor. Then there was no sound but the hissing, popping flames, burning into the sap-rich pine rafters.

In the darkness of the cellar, Stella huddled beside the pumpkins, choking back wild sobs. The love it must have taken for Knute to drag himself up and pull that trigger! Now they were gone, both of them. Knute and Karin Aarnson had died together.

And she was alone. No, not alone, she reminded herself as she heard the creak of a floorboard overhead. The Indians were close by, and if they found her she would not be as lucky as Knute and Karin had been. Her death would be much slower than theirs.

She could hear the Indians ransacking the burning cabin, crowing over each new prize they found and shouting to the ones who had stayed outside. Any minute now they would discover the cellar. She had to do what she could. Hurriedly she rearranged the heap of pumpkins, stacking them near the wall in a long row. That done, she lay down behind them, flattened herself against the wall, and pulled some of the pumpkins over on top of her body. It was not a very good hiding place, but it was all she had. There was, perhaps, one chance in ten—no, one in a hundred—that the Indians would not see her.

They had left the cabin now, driven out by the fire. Stella could hear whoops of elation as they discovered Knute's big piebald horse, still tied in the shed. She could hear the animal's nervous whinny as they led it outside. Soon, she thought. Soon they would be coming down.

Through a crack between the pumpkins she could see the open trapdoor and a square of bright blue sky. She kept her eyes on it, waiting, watching, her mouth dry and her heart drumming.

At last she heard a shout, and an instant later the square of sky was blotted out. Stella held her breath as the first Indian came cautiously down the steps, his knife flashing in the thin column of light. His chest was bare, his face streaked with yellow war paint. A lone eagle feather was thrust into the back of his long, braided hair. He blinked, trying to adjust his eyes to the sudden darkness of the cellar.

A second Indian swiftly followed him, this one younger and more slender than the first. The two of them stood there at the foot of the carved log, glancing around and muttering in their strange tongue.

Smoke from the burning cabin was beginning to seep through the floor, creating a dim haze in the dark cellar. The air swam with its pungent, bitter odor. The first Indian coughed, cursing in his own language. He nudged the second Indian's arm, urging him, perhaps, to leave this place.

Frozen to the floor, Stella felt the stinging smoke enter her lungs. She fought the desire to gasp and cough. That smoke was her ally, she told herself. If she could keep silent long enough, it would drive the two braves away.

As she lay there, struggling against her own reflexes, a third Indian came down through the trapdoor, his bulk blotting out the sky. At first, Stella could not see him well, silhouetted as he was against the light. He looked to be taller than the other two and more powerfully built. His long hair flowed loose around his broad, bare shoulders.

He spoke gruffly to the two younger braves, his angry voice spitting out each syllable. He appeared to have sent them down into the cellar to find something, and they had disappointed him. Now they shrank away from his rage as he kicked over the bins of potatoes and onions, then turned and began to range around the cellar like a prowling bear.

Stella stifled a gasp as he moved into the light. His proud features were cruelly handsome, with a thin scar running the length of his face, just missing his left eye. Where it entered his hair, the scar had created a streak of white that stood out starkly against his wild black locks.

A chill ran through her as she looked at him, and suddenly she knew what he had wanted to find. The Indians had been watching the cabin. They knew there were three people living there. And afterward, with Knute and Karin dead, they had not found her. One look at the big Indian's face told Stella he was not ready to give up.

The smoke was thicker now, floating in ghostly layers through the dark cellar. One of the younger braves was coughing, his hand clasping his throat. Stella shrank against the cold dirt wall, willing herself not to breathe as the big Indian glared into the darkness.

He was going to find her. If he so much as nudged one of the pumpkins, he would know she was there. It would only be a matter of time till he did just that.

What would they do with her then? Stella could only pray that the end would be swift. She was not afraid of death, but the thought that Cade would return to find her gone— or worse, to find her body—filled her with deep regret. She would never really know him, never feel his anger, his passion, his love. Whatever they might have shared would be lost.

The floor of the cabin was beginning to smolder, the red glow showing through the cracks. The powerful Indian glanced up at it, then moved closer to Stella's hiding place. His moccasined foot brushed one of the pumpkins.

Any second now, he would find her.

Chapter Eight

The sky was rose and amber above the Wind River peaks, the grass still silver with frost. Cade paused on a ridge, his eyes tracing the path of the Little Sandy in the valley below. Soon, he thought. Soon.

He nudged the roan and they started down the slope, leading the spare horse he had brought for Stella. As he rode, he mulled over the decision he had made—a decision that tempered justice with mercy.

After too many sleepless nights, Cade had finally faced the truth. He could not bear to take Stella back to the explosive situation in Green River. Still, he could not simply let her go. If he did, he would be leaving her a fugitive from the law—legal prey for every ruthless bounty hunter in the country. And she would not have an easy time hiding. Her spectacular beauty would be noticed and remembered anywhere she went.

A solution had to be found, and it had come to Cade after days of soul-searching. The U.S. marshal in Laramie, Sam Catlin, was a friend of his, and a fair man if there ever was one. Cade would take Stella there and enlist Sam's help. At the very worst, Cade told himself, Sam would see that Stella got a fair trial.

It had not been an easy choice, but once made it had brought him a measure of relief. He could only hope that Stella would not fight it. Her willingness to go with him would make everything less difficult.

The roan's hooves spooked a grouse, who shot skyward in a rocket burst of sound and feathers. Cade watched the bird's short, blurred flight. His hand stroked the neck of the startled horse, soothing it.

Inside himself, he felt a profound loneliness. It had come on him the night he'd ridden away from Stella. When he saw her again, he realized, it would only be replaced by the ache of desire. There was no way around it—he wanted her badly.

He thought about the long ride to Laramie. It would be filled with temptation, he knew. Once again, they would be traveling alone, and there'd be at least two nights, probably three or four, they would have to spend on the trail. It would take all his strength to resist her, but he had made up his mind to do just that. If he weakened, he would be lost.

Cade's heels nudged the roan's flanks, urging the big red stallion to a trot. Now that Stella was so near, he felt a growing sense of anticipation, an uncontrollable need to be with her. Half-angry at himself, he pulled in on the reins, as if trying to rein in his own emotions. There were things he had to accomplish, he told himself, and he had to be strong. If he could not get his feelings under control before he saw her, there would be no hope for him later on.

A vague chill of uneasiness settled over Cade as he rode into the valley. The feeling seemed oddly out of place in the calm of the morning—a morning whose cobalt sky promised a beautiful day. The sun had risen above the Wind River crags, flooding the land with light. The aspen leaves danced on the trees, glittering like thin gold coins. On such a day, two years ago, he had ridden home from a hunt in the Bighorn country, his body eager for Rain Flower's love. Strange, how vividly that day came back to him now, as if he were living it over again. The clarity of the day, the anticipation...

It hit him suddenly, like cold lightning. Half-wild with dread, he kicked the roan to a gallop, jerking hard on the lead of the second horse to make it follow. Nothing had told him, but he knew what he would find when he reached the Aarnson place. Lord help him, he knew.

He covered the last mile in minutes, splashing across the Little Sandy, thundering through the willows, hoping with all his soul that he might be wrong. But when he reined up at the edge of the clearing, he saw that his ghastly premonition had been right. Nothing was left of the Aarnson cabin but charred ruins.

Numb with shock, Cade dropped the reins and dismounted. A magpie, perched on the blackened chimney, scolded him raucously as he approached. There was no other sign of life around the place.

He stepped over what had been the threshold. The ashes were cold, not even smoldering. At least two or three days had passed since the cabin had burned, he guessed. The floor was littered with charred timbers and blackened remnants of what had once been a home—here a teakettle, there a tin plate, a spoon and the iron rings from a wooden bucket. In the far corner, he could see the burned remains of Knute and Karin's bed.

Choking back his feelings, he forced himself to look for bodies. He would not believe they were all dead, he told himself. Not until he found them.

He searched the square area of the cabin, avoiding the section of the floor that had covered the cellar. The boards there had burned so thin, it would be easy to break through and fall. But he could see there was nothing there—or anywhere else, for that matter. There were no bodies in the cabin.

Half relieved and half puzzled, he stepped outside again and began to circle the clearing. He found one Sioux arrow stuck in the ground, then another. And there were footprints, too many and too jumbled to give him any clear idea of what had happened. He could see moccasin tracks, some of them covering the older prints of Knute's hobnailed boots. The line of flat-heeled slipper prints would have to be Karin's. And Stella's—yes. He crouched low, his fingers tracing a spot where one of her delicately pointed high-button shoes had pressed. He swallowed hard, churning inside. If only...

No, he told himself firmly. He would not think about what might have been. And he would not give in to his grief until he'd learned all he could about what had happened here. Bracing himself against what he might find, he widened his circle and kept on walking.

At the edge of the clearing, in a straight line from the cabin's front door, the grass was smeared with dried blood. Cade felt his heart lurch, but he tore his gaze away from the red-brown stains and kept moving. It wouldn't do any good, staring at the blood and wondering whose it was, he told himself. Nothing would do any good now. Knute and Karin were gone. And so was Stella.

In spite of his efforts, Cade felt his eyes blur. As he stopped to blink them clear, he caught sight of something stuck to the trunk of a dead pine. The hair on the back of his neck rose as he realized what it was.

A feather, a large one from the tail of a hawk, had been fixed to the bark. Its broad tip had been dipped in blood.

Cade felt hot and bitter rage rise up in him. That feather answered all his questions. Not only did he know that Knute and Karin and Stella were all dead; he knew they had died because of him.

Red Hawk had returned.

He left the feather where it was and moved on around the clearing. Here and there the grass was trampled, but he saw nothing more until he came to the spot where Knute and Karin had buried their baby.

Graves! There were two fresh graves, flanking either side of the tiny mound where the baby lay, each marked by a simple cross of bound twigs. Cade's mind reeled. Could a passing stranger have done this—found the baby's grave and buried the parents on either side of it? The possibility seemed farfetched. Yet, the only other explanation was even more incredible.

With his heart pounding, Cade bent low and examined the soft earth. Yes! His spirits leaped. They were everywhere—those narrow, pointed shoe prints, as delicate as a doe's, all around the graves!

Cade's iron control broke. "Stella!" His cry echoed through the forest.

There was an instant of silence. Then the black timbers covering the cellar shifted and tumbled aside. He saw the glint of the sun on her coppery hair, and then in a moment she was running to him across the clearing.

"Stella!" He reached her in midstride and caught her in his arms. Yes, she was real and solid. She was warm. She was alive. "Stella...Stella..." Whispering her name over and over, he covered her face with kisses—her eyes, her cheeks, her sweet, soft mouth.

She was sobbing. He felt her body quiver against him and tasted the wet salt of her tears. Cade let her cry, pressing his lips against her tangled hair as he cradled her close. Lord, what she must have been through! What it must have taken for her to dig those graves and drag the bodies into them!

"Cade—" She looked up at him, struggling to choke back the sobs. Her dark eyes were bloodshot, her face streaked with soot and tears. To Cade, she had never looked more beautiful. For a few short moments, the battle that raged inside him lost all meaning.

"Hush," he whispered, stroking her hair. "You don't have to talk about it. Not till you're ready."

"It was Knute's whiskey that saved me," she whispered, still fighting for control. "I was in the cellar, hiding. After the others were dead...they...the Indians came down, three of them. They were looking for me...but the cabin was burning. The air was full of smoke. They came so close..." She broke into sobs again.

"Hush...." Cade kissed her closed eyelids. Her lashes were wet with tears.

"Just when I was sure they would find me, one of them saw the whiskey—four jugs of it," she said. "They...they took it all. The smoke was awful by then, and they went away."

"And you buried Karin and Knute?" Cade asked gently.

"Yes . . . the next day. They'd been—" She broke into a fresh torrent of sobs.

"There. . . . You don't need to tell me." Cade held her close. He knew what the Sioux did to the bodies of their victims. And knowing Red Hawk, he'd have spared no pains.

"You saw the Indians?" he asked softly.

"Not all of them. Just the three. One of them—" Her breath caught. "One of them was big, with a scar—"

"And a white streak in his hair?"

"Yes! You—"

"Red Hawk. He's an old enemy of mine." Cade's voice was flat with bitterness.

She looked up at him, her eyes still fearful. "Your wife and sons . . . ?"

"Red Hawk led the war party that killed them. He. . . was the only one who got away from me. Now it appears he's come back to even the score."

"Knute said the Sioux always left you alone. He said you were bad medicine."

Cade shook his head. "It's true they haven't bothered me much. But I'd say that's mostly because of Red Hawk. I disgraced him, you see, by killing his braves. Revenge is the only thing that can mend his reputation."

"So he wants you saved till he gets his chance?"

"That's right." He released her and let his eyes travel from the charred ruins of the cabin to the two fresh graves. "This," he said, his throat tight with bitterness, "is just Red Hawk's way of letting me know he hasn't forgotten."

She shivered beside him. "Cade, what are we going to do?"

Cade steeled himself once more. "I've got a plan," he said. "Hear me out, Stella. Please."

The morning sun was higher now. Its rays slanted through the charred timbers, making odd geometric patterns on the floor of the cellar. Stella glanced around the place that had been her only shelter for the past three days.

No, she told herself, it was best not to think about what had happened here—the terror, the desolation she had felt. It was best not to remember the ordeal of burying Karin and Knute, then, waiting alone, clinging to her hope that Cade would come. She had been through a nightmare—and she had more to face. There was no sense in looking back when so many problems lay ahead.

Resolutely, she forced the memory of the past four days from her mind. Then, with swift-moving fingers, she began to unfasten her dress.

Cade had brought her an old flannel shirt, a pair of breeches with a belt, a broad-brimmed Stetson and some beaded Indian moccasins. Not only would they be more comfortable than a skirt to ride in, they would make her less apt to be noticed. From a distance, at least, she would look like a boy.

With a twist of her shoulders, she let the tattered, dark green dress fall to the ground. Her lips still stung from the urgent pressure of Cade's mouth. Her body still felt the crush of his arms. They had needed each other for those first few unrestrained moments. But Stella was no fool. Nothing had changed, she told herself as she buttoned the baggy plaid shirt. Cade's resolve was as strong as ever.

The trousers were so large that she had to roll up the bottoms and cinch in the waist with a belt. A fine picture she would make riding into Laramie! she thought. The lady from the East, come to town for her rendezvous with justice! She smiled bitterly at the image and went on dressing.

She had accepted Cade's plan with little hesitation. It made sense—at least more sense than any other course. She would never be safe in Green River, and she could not run from the law forever. Turning herself in to Cade's friend Marshal Catlin seemed the best chance of proving her innocence.

It was not a sure chance, she knew. A cloud passed over her spirits as she pictured herself walking to the gallows or spending years of her life in prison. There was a risk, a dangerous risk.

But there were risks in everything, she reminded herself. She had just survived an Indian attack and a three-day ordeal of hiding. Somehow, she would find the strength to survive the next few weeks, as well.

She came out of the cellar, blinking in the sunlight. Cade, she saw, was at the edge of the forest, staring down at the graves.

Stella walked over and stood quietly beside him. He would not touch her now, she knew. He was too full of grief, too full of anger. And he had regained his determination to go ahead with what had to be done.

They stood for a last time beside the graves of their friends, both of them knowing better than to speak. Finally he turned toward her. His pale wolf's eyes burned into hers, as if something in him were saying goodbye to her. Then, abruptly, he turned away again and strode toward the horses.

"It's getting late," he said, his voice harsh. "Let's ride."

The mare Cade had brought for Stella was the best of his herd—a deer-footed Appaloosa that Washakie had traded from the Nez Percé tribe. The two of them made a striking pair, Cade thought, giving them a sidelong glance. The mare was perfectly proportioned and deep mahogany in color, with tiny white spots scattered over her broad rump, like stars in the sky. As for Stella, she rode with a grace that even her baggy men's clothes could not hide. Her long hair was twisted up and tucked under the Stetson, and she held her head high, like a duchess. With that figure, Cade realized uneasily, no one would ever mistake her for a boy.

They had been riding most of the day, keeping to the back trails, where they would not be spotted. At midday, they had forded the Sweetwater, Stella guiding the mare without fear into the eddying current. Lunch had been venison jerky, eaten in the saddle. She had accepted the dried, salted meat without complaint, chewing on it hungrily. For the three days she had spent hiding in the cellar of the burned-out cabin, she explained, she had lived on carrots and raw potatoes. She had been afraid even to go to the river for water.

"I heard the horses when you came," she had continued in her rich, cello voice. "And I thought...I hoped—But I was so frightened. It could have been the Indians coming back, or someone like Gillis. Then, when I heard you call me..."

She had stopped speaking and looked away from him. Cade had felt himself churning inside. He ached to tell her how he had felt when he saw her tracks around the graves, when he had realized she was alive. But no—he brought himself up short. That would only make things more difficult when they reached Laramie.

Laramie. The place was beginning to loom large and black in Cade's mind, and with every mile they covered, his spirits grew darker. Sam Catlin would help if he was able, but Sam couldn't work miracles. If Gillis couldn't be found or had a good alibi for the time of Jared's death, the evidence against Stella would be overwhelming.

And what then? Cade asked himself. Could he accept a guilty verdict as justice? Could he stand by and let Stella hang or go to prison? Those questions had kept him in turmoil all afternoon.

Their trail, most of it through open country, had skirted the south end of the Wind River Range. Soon they would be coming up on South Pass City.

Too bad it wasn't safe to go into town, Cade reflected. Stella, he knew, was exhausted. She needed a good meal and a night in a decent bed. By now, however, word of the jailbreak would have spread like a blazing brush fire through the mining settlements. Neither he nor Stella could afford the risk of being seen. They would have to pass through the next valley to the north and sleep on the trail.

He swung around in the saddle and glanced at the sky. Broad, linty clouds were piling in from the west, moving fast. He didn't like the looks of them. Even this time of year, they could be the forerunners of an early blizzard—the kind that froze young buffalo calves in their tracks and buried wagons in snow up to the axles. Weather was never a thing to be taken lightly on the unsheltered Wyoming plains, not even in October. All Cade's instincts told him to start looking for a place to hole up.

"Cade, look!" Stella's worried exclamation startled him out of his thoughts.

"Where?" He reined in the horse, all his senses tingling.

"Up there, on that ridge. No, wait. It's gone now."

"What did you see?" Cade shaded his eyes, then reached for the field glass in his saddlebag.

"It looked like a man on horseback. But the sun was in my eyes. I'm not sure...." She gazed toward the ridge, squinting against the glare of the afternoon sunlight. "It could have been an antelope."

"Not likely, this close to a town." Cade swept the horizon with the glass, seeing nothing. "We'd best get moving. Keep your eyes open."

He spurred the roan to a canter. The sooner they got away from this place, the better he'd feel, Cade told himself.

He'd planned to skirt the north edge of the mining country, then follow the Sweetwater down to the point where it joined the North Platte. From there it would be a simple matter to cut south, across the open plain, to Laramie. That was the easiest route and, unfortunately, the most predictable. If they were seen, it wouldn't be hard for a posse to move ahead of them and set up a trap. And then there was the weather. A fall blizzard could be as deadly as any man-made ambush. Silently, Cade cursed his dilemma.

"What are you thinking?" Stella had moved in close to him.

Cade dismissed the temptation to comfort her with a lie. If there was danger, she needed to know it. "We seem to be stuck between bad alternatives," he said.

"You think we've been seen, then?" Her voice was calm.

"We can't be sure, but we've got to assume that we have."

"We could head for the mountains."

Cade glanced north. Clouds were slipping in over the Wind River peaks. In a big storm, the mountains were safer than the plains. They gave a measure of shelter from the icy killer winds that howled unchecked across open country.

"We could," he said, weighing things. "But it would cost us time. There's also the chance of running into Indians."

She shuddered. "And if we just keep riding?"

He made a quick visual sweep of the surrounding country, not liking what he saw. They were heading east through a long, narrow valley, with sage-covered hills on either side of them. If they had been spotted, it would be a perfect setting for a trap.

"Cade?" An anxious note had crept into her voice.

He took one more long, critical look at the sky. There were more clouds now, milling like wild horses in a catching pen. And a breeze had sprung up, carrying the unmistakable smell of cold and moisture.

Cade had lived too long in the West to ignore the danger signals. If a storm was coming, heading for the mountains was the best of two bad choices. At least in the mountains there would be shelter. A cave or even a heavy stand of pines would do if the storm was a small one. A truly big storm, however, could drive them all the way to the Wind River Valley.

His eyes made a last survey of the area where they were riding. The shortest way out was straight up the steep, brushy slope that flanked their trail. "Come on," he said, indicating the route with a jerk of his head.

The ground was treacherous, covered with loose gravel and patches of shale. Cade hung back and let Stella get ahead of him. The small-footed mare was as nimble as a goat, but the roan's size and power worked against him. The big stallion's hooves slipped and plunged as it struggled for a foothold. Stella glanced back over her shoulder, then hesitated.

"Keep going!" Cade shouted. "I'll catch up!"

Moments later, when the roan lurched its way over the top, Cade found her waiting for him just below the ridge.

"Let's go!" he said gruffly, both pleased and annoyed that she had not gone ahead without him. "Now's our best chance to gain some distance!"

Stella nodded and turned her horse without a word. Cade let her get a lead while he gave the red stallion a few seconds' rest. His eyes followed her zigzag path down the slope. She was leaning forward in the saddle to encourage the mare, her hands confident and sure. The Stetson had blown back in the wind, leaving her hair to stream free, like a banner. Even now, in this time of danger, he was struck by her beauty.

The landscape darkened as a bank of clouds scudded across the sun. The breeze had become a stinging wind that tore at Cade's hat and whipped clumps of sage and rabbit-brush into a waving frenzy.

There was no time to be lost. Cade spurred the roan and followed Stella down the hill.

The late afternoon sky was black with clouds. Steady and cold, the wind blew through the pines, howling its song of darkness and danger.

Stella and Cade had fled north, through the foothills, into the very shadows of the Wind River peaks. Even here, the wind was a staggering force. At times, Stella felt as if it would pluck her right out of the saddle.

The mare was tiring. She had run well, but her stamina was no match for the roan's. Her sides were heaving, and her hooves were beginning to falter. Soon she would be too spent to go on.

Stella, too, was fighting exhaustion. Her head ached; her lungs burned. Under the sheepskin coat Cade had lent her, she shivered with cold.

They were climbing the wall of a canyon now, on a dizzying trail that wound through rocky outcrops and clumps of pine. All afternoon she had followed Cade's lead without question. He knew where to go in these mountains, she told herself. She had to trust his instincts. It was her only chance of survival.

Cade, a stone's throw ahead of her, looked back over his shoulder. Even in the dim light, Stella could see the concern on his face.

"Can you keep up?" he called out over the wind. "It's getting dark. I don't want to lose you."

She shook her head, too weary to speak.

He turned the roan and came back to her. "It's not much farther to the top, and then we'll be on level ground. Can you walk?"

She willed her cold-numbed lips to move. "I can try."

"It would warm you up a little and rest the mare."

Stella nodded wearily and tried to pull her right foot out of the stirrup. She had been in the saddle so long, however, that her leg refused to move.

"Here." Cade slipped off his horse and came around to free her foot. "Just relax and let yourself fall," he said, holding up his hands. Stella reached out to him. As she slid out of the saddle, he caught her and gently lowered her to the ground.

For a long moment she stood there in the circle of his arms, her feet tingling, her knees unsteady. Even now, she could feel the battle raging inside him as he balanced her, fighting her nearness.

She looked up at him and saw that his own face was lined with fatigue. How much longer could they go on, she wondered, before they both dropped in their tracks? When would they find shelter?

"Cade—"

"Hush." His voice was a rasp of weariness. "Listen to me, Stella. You're tired, I know, but we've got to keep moving. This storm is a big one. If we stop here, we could get snowed in till we freeze or starve. Besides, we've come this way for a reason. I know this canyon. There are some big rocks at the top of the trail. When we get up there, it won't be too hard to start a slide.''

"Why?" She was too tired to reason it for herself.

"We may have been seen back there in the valley, and since there's undoubtedly a price on your head, we can't dismiss the chance that somebody might trail us. If they do, the trail will end right here. Can you make it to the top?''

Stella gazed past his shoulder. The rocks stood out like nightmare shapes on the horizon, solid black against the churning clouds. They looked frighteningly steep and very far away. "I can make it," she whispered.

Awkwardly, he pulled her close and held her for the space of a few heartbeats. His coat was rough against her face, his breath hard and heavy in her ear.

"That's a good girl," he murmured, releasing her. "Now try walking."

Stella took one unsteady step, then another, the wind whipping her hair. She was stiff and sore, but the feeling was coming back into her feet. "I'll be all right," she said.

"Come on, then. Lean on your horse if you need to."

She took the mare's bridle and followed Cade upward through the darkness. Around them, the wind blew in whistling gusts that threatened to pluck them off the trail. Stella clung to the solid weight of the mare, fixing her eyes on the pale rectangle of Cade's buckskin jacket ahead of her. Icy flecks of sleet had begun to fall, swirling madly on the wind.

Suddenly Cade stopped, and Stella realized they had reached level ground. They were standing on the rim of the canyon, surrounded by pine trees and big, rugged boulders. The wind was even stronger here. Stella slumped lower to keep from being blown off balance.

Cade looked over his shoulder. "Are you all right?"

Stella was too cold and tired to speak. She simply nodded.

He handed her the stallion's reins. "Take the horses back away from the edge and keep them there," he said.

His words came to Stella through a mist of exhaustion. Numbly, she did as she was told. The horses snorted and shook their heads as she led them into the shelter of the trees. Their frosted breath blew away on the wind.

Cade had found the trunk of a fallen pine and braced it under a massive boulder that rested on the lip of the canyon. Stella watched him through clouds of blowing sleet as he flung his weight onto the makeshift lever, pushing down with all his strength.

The earth groaned as the boulder shuddered. Cade rested for the space of a few breaths, then threw himself onto the lever again. This time the massive rock began to move. It creaked forward ever so slightly, loosening in its bed. Then, as Stella watched, its weight caught the edge of the precipice, and it went crashing over.

Cade had flung himself backward. He scrambled to his feet as the rock bounced and tumbled down the wall of the canyon, tearing out trees and loosening cascades of dirt and rock. For a few seconds the roar seemed to fill the whole world. Then everything was still.

Through the whirling mist of sleet and darkness, she could see Cade walking toward her, his arms open. She wanted to run to him, but her legs would not obey her mind. No sound came from her throat when she tried to cry out.

He was moving faster now, running toward her. Everything was all right now, Stella told herself. The cold had become warm, the song of the wind as sweet as a summer's breeze.

"Stella...." His voice came to her from a distance. She was floating, drifting away from him.

"Stella!" For an instant she saw his face clearly. Then his features blurred before her eyes, and she plummeted into blackness.

Chapter Nine

Stella drifted on a churning sea. Its currents spun and eddied, carrying her in and out of fitful dreams. Sometimes she heard voices—John's ... her father's. At other times, it was her own voice she heard, crying out in the blackness.

The waves washed over her, blotting out her sight, cutting off her breath. Sucking whirlpools tried to pull her down. In her desperation, she moaned and struggled. She reached out...

And suddenly there were hands, strong and warm, reaching through the dark mist to clasp hers. She clung to those hands. She felt their strength as they drew her up out of the current. Then she sensed that she was moving slowly toward a face with pale blue eyes....

"Cade," she whispered.

"I'm here, Stella."

"Don't leave me, Cade."

"I won't leave you. Lord help me."

She opened her eyes. He was bending over her, his face worried.

"Cade—"

"Shh," he whispered. "Lie still. You've been through a bad time."

Stella's eyelids dropped, then fluttered open again. She was lying in a bed, she realized, in a warm room. Behind Cade's head she caught a glimpse of a lantern hanging from a log rafter. Sunlight streamed in through an unseen window.

"Where am I?" she murmured.

"In the Wind River Valley. This is my home, Stella."

"What?" She struggled to sit up, but she was so weak that she fell back on the pillow again.

"Don't try to move," he said. "You were burning up with fever by the time we got here. I—almost lost you."

"How long have I been here?" Stella lifted her head, trying to see her surroundings.

"Three days."

"Three days!" She sank back into the pillow, unbelieving.

"You've been delirious."

"And you took care of me?" Stella stirred in the bed and realized she was wearing nothing but a long flannel nightshirt, buttoned down the front. There was no sign of her own clothes. In spite of herself, she felt her cheeks flush.

"There was no one else." He stood up and walked away from the bed, avoiding her gaze. "You've had nothing to eat. We'd best get some broth down you."

She followed him with her eyes as he walked to the massive stone fireplace on the far wall. An iron pot hung from a rack above the fire. Cade bent over it and ladled some steaming broth into a wooden bowl. Slowly he walked back to the bed, blowing on the hot liquid to cool it.

"Take as much as you can," he said, sitting lightly on the edge of the bed. "It will make you feel stronger, I promise." He sat the bowl on a stool while he slipped an extra pillow under her head. Stella tried to help, but she was so weak she could barely raise her arms.

The broth was brown and thick, its aroma so delicious that it almost made her dizzy. When he blew on a spoonful and held it to her mouth, she took it hungrily. As she swallowed it, however, she realized there was something strange about this broth.

"What's the matter?" he asked.

"It's—it's got a bitter taste to it. Not bad, really. Just . . . odd."

He nodded. "I put a bit of yarrow and willow bark in it. The Shoshone give it to their warriors after they've been wounded in battle. It strengthens the blood, they say."

"Superstition?" Stella ran her tongue gingerly across her upper lip, tasting another drop.

"I thought so at first," Cade answered. "But it works. A lot of their medicine does work. I've seen it." He dipped another spoonful out of the bowl and held it toward her. Stella hesitated, stared at the spoon and then opened her mouth.

A smile tugged at his lips. "That's it. You're a real warrior."

She swallowed the second spoonful, grimaced, then nodded for more. The strong, brown liquid burned its way down her throat, its warmth stealing into her limbs.

"The mare!" she exclaimed, suddenly remembering. "Did she make it all right?"

"She's fine," Cade said with a nod. "She's out in the corral right now, eating her fill of oats."

"And the storm?"

"It was a big one. Blocked all the mountain passes. We almost didn't get here."

"What about Laramie?" she asked slowly.

"We'd never make it out of here through the snow-drifts. Laramie will have to wait."

Wait. The word sank like a stone in a quiet pond. Strange, Stella thought, the conflicts that stirred and shifted inside her. She had dreaded the very idea of reaching Laramie and turning herself in. Now, however, she suddenly realized she would not be at peace until the matter of her innocence was resolved.

She finished the last spoonful of broth and sank back into the pillows. The bitter tang of yarrow and willow bark trickled through her body. Yes, Stella admitted, she did feel stronger.

Cade had wandered back toward the fireplace. This cabin was much larger than the one where Knute and Karin Aarnson had lived. There were braided rugs on the floors and two leather-cushioned rocking chairs in front of the fireplace. A cupboard with glass doors divided off the kitchen area, and part of one wall was lined with bookshelves. There were, perhaps, a hundred books, their tooled leather covers worn soft from handling.

"Mine, from Saint Louis," he said, following her gaze to the books. "I . . . had Jared bring them for me when he came out last spring."

The name stung Stella like a whiplash. "Cade, I—"

"Don't." He cut her off, his voice quiet. "Nothing can undo what's happened or bring my brother back. But I can't go around pretending he was never part of my life. Jared brought me a whole trunkful of my books, and I was more grateful than if he'd brought me a trunkful of gold!"

He walked back and forth before the fireplace as he spoke, agitated, like a great cat in a cage. Stella watched him from the bed, her mind groping for a way to comfort him. But there was nothing she could say.

"I'm sorry," he said, stopping abruptly and speaking too fast. "You've been lying sick in that bed for three days, and I haven't even asked you if there's anything you need." He moved to the foot of the bed and glanced up toward the ceiling. "You'll be wanting some privacy. I've rigged some hooks along this rafter where a quilt can be hung. It will be almost like a bedroom for you. I always planned to add another room someday, but for now—" He broke off and gazed at her, one eyebrow lifted. "What's the matter? You look puzzled."

"I am, a little," Stella admitted, glancing around the cabin. "There's no other bed. Where do you sleep?"

The look that flitted across Cade's face told her he was not amused. "Don't worry, it's all been quite proper. There's a loft. See the trapdoor, just above the bookshelves? I've been sleeping up there."

"Oh, I didn't mean—" Stella could have bitten her tongue. "How do you get up there?"

"There's a ladder. I put it up at night. You'll see." He turned his eyes away. "You could be here awhile before a thaw clears the passes," he said. "So we might as well set up a living arrangement you can be comfortable with. Before I hang the quilt up for you, is there anything else you need?"

Stella hesitated. He sounded as if he were anxious to dismiss her, she thought. Hang the quilt; put up one more barrier. He was doing his best to maintain a safe distance between them, and for a moment she thought it might be just as well to let him go ahead.

But no, she decided. She had only just opened her eyes. There were things she wanted to know, things she wanted to see, first. "There is something I'd like," she said. "I want to look outside. I want to see where we are."

"Do you think you can walk to the door?"

"I can try." Stella sat up slowly and pulled aside the covers. Her long, bare legs were as pale as birches against the sheets.

"Here—you'll be cold." Cade took the quilt he had been about to hang and held it out for her, like a robe. As Stella's feet slipped to the floor, he wrapped her in it. "Careful, you're still shaky," he said, moving behind her with his steadying arms.

"I'll be all right." Stella stood close to him. She could feel the warmth of his body through the quilt. His breath stirred her hair.

"Can you take a step?"

"I'll try." Her legs were liquid. She willed one bare foot to move, shifted her weight onto it and stumbled.

He caught her skillfully. "Here," he said, sweeping her up in his arms, as if she were no heavier than a child. "Tomorrow's soon enough for you to be walking. This is the only way we're going to get you anywhere today."

He strode across the cabin with her, toward the door. There he paused for a moment. "Close your eyes," he said, sliding back the bolt. "Don't open them until I tell you."

Stella shut her eyes tightly. She heard the door creak as it swung open, and she gasped as she felt the shock of fresh, cold air. The sunlight flashed like fire through her eyelids.

Snow crunched under Cade's boots as he walked. Stella counted his paces: ten . . . fifteen. She felt the world spinning as he moved. Nothing seemed steady or safe except his arms, holding her.

At last he stopped. "There," he said. "Open your eyes."

Stella blinked, dazzled at first by the brightness of the sun on the snow. Then, little by little, her eyes adjusted to the light.

"Oh!" she gasped. "Oh, Cade!"

The mountains filled her eyes—towering granite crags, so high that they seemed to hold up the sky. Their rugged hollows glittered with snow. Their skirts, velvety with pine, swept down to enclose the valley floor.

From where Cade stood, holding her, the land sloped downward to a narrow lake, as dark as a sapphire against the snow. In the distance, the white landscape was dotted with small, moving forms.

"Deer," Cade said. "Sometimes we get elk and buffalo, too. You can see them quite well with the field glass."

"The Wind River Valley." Stella shivered and nestled into the enfolding warmth of the blanket. "Where's the river?"

"It's a half day's ride from here," Cade said. "This is only a small arm of the valley. But all the land you can see from here is part of my ranch."

"It's beautiful." She shivered again as a stray breeze brushed her hair.

"You're getting cold," he said, his arms tightening around her. "We'd best get you back inside."

"Only a minute more." Stella filled her eyes with the mountains, the trees and the snow. She filled her lungs with the sunlit air. For a moment she gave in to a sense of total bliss. The beauty of this place was intoxicating.

"We'd better go back inside before you catch a chill out here," Cade said. "There'll be plenty of time to see this when you're stronger."

"Oh, very well." Stella sighed and relaxed against his chest, feeling the deep rise and fall of his breathing as he carried her back to the cabin. He was right, she told herself. There would be time—time to rest, time to gather her strength for Laramie. In the meantime she was safe. And she was in a beautiful place—perhaps the last place where she would ever be free.

The weather had turned colder. The sunlit days were crystal sharp; the nights left rich traceries of frost on the windowpanes. In the mornings, when Cade went out to see to the horses, the ice on their trough was as thick as his thumb.

Stella was rallying. Every day he noticed changes in her. At first she had been content to keep still, lying back against the pillows in the big, brass bed, reading his books and accepting the broth and the hot gruel that he fed her. To Cade, those days had taken on a bittersweet innocence. She had been as pliant and as trusting as a child, and he had cared for her with all the tenderness in his heart. In the presence of her helplessness, the fires of his lust had burned low, giving them both a time of rest.

But no longer. Her strength was returning, and with it the vitality that inflamed him every time he looked at her. Once more, the days were torture for him; the nights a hell of wanting her.

Yesterday she had noticed the big copper tub hanging on the back of the cabin. This afternoon she had insisted on a bath. Cade had hauled the tub into the cabin and helped her as she piled the cooking pots with snow and hung them over the fire to melt. It had taken the better part of an hour before the tub was full of warm water.

While she bathed, he had taken the rifle, saddled the roan and ridden into the foothills with the idea of hunting. This would be a good day to bring down a buck, he told himself. Fresh meat would keep well now that the weather had turned.

He had left Stella the loaded Colt, with orders to fire it as a signal if she needed him. "I won't be far," he promised. "I'll hear it."

He had planned a leisurely hunt, but once in the saddle he found himself riding hard, as if the very hounds of hell were chasing him. The snow flew under the roan's pounding hooves as they hurtled fallen logs and clumps of brush. Once they startled a doe, which went bounding off through the bare aspens on its steel-spring legs. Cade reined in and watched it till it vanished over a hill. His hand did not even move to draw the rifle from its scabbard.

This was no way to hunt, he admonished himself. Tearing breakneck through the hills like a fool, spooking all the game for miles. What was the matter with him? What was he running away from?

Stella. Even her name sang in his blood. He thought of her now, curled warm and glistening in the tub, the water rippling around the contours of her slim legs and soft, golden breasts. He pictured her hands, smoothing the soap into every silken curve and hollow of her body. And even at this distance, he felt the compelling surge of his own response.

Cade cursed under his breath. The real hell of it was that no part of the picture was left to his imagination. The night they'd fled from the storm, he had carried her, shivering and delirious, into the cabin. The blizzard had soaked her to the skin, and she was hot with fever. He had laid her across the foot of the bed and stripped away her icy clothes. Then he had lifted her burning body in his arms and placed it under the quilts.

She had been out of her head, only half-conscious, and by the next morning her fever had risen so high that he feared for her life. Frantic with worry, he had bathed her in wet cloths to cool her fiery skin and forced spoonfuls of willow-bark tea down her throat. For more than twenty-four hours he had not left her side.

At last her fever had broken, and she had soaked the sheets with sweat. Only then had he dared to relax his vigil. He had put dry sheets under her, slipped her into an old flannel nightshirt and gone to sleep, exhausted, in one of the rockers.

While Stella was ill, his concern had outweighed everything else. He had cared for her, forcing his mind away from all thoughts of passion. But now that she was getting well, he found himself remembering. His mind recalled every sweet, intimate detail of her body: the long, smooth curve of her hips; the swelling mounds of her breasts, their tips like small, perfect rosebuds; the vibrant, russet bloom between her thighs.

Once he had seen the sketch of a goddess, taken from the wall of a Hindu temple in Ceylon. Stella's body possessed the same sinuous grace, the same incredible tapering from full, rounded bosom to tiny waist. Every time he looked at her now, the memory of that body lashed at him, driving him to a near frenzy of desire.

And there was no help for him. This place, the Wind River Valley, was Stella's only sanctuary from the world; and, ironically, he was her only protector. When the storms let up and the passes thawed, he would escort her to Laramie to face what had to be faced. How could he expect to do that if he gave in to temptation? How could he let himself love her, then turn her over to the law?

With a sigh of resignation, Cade headed the stallion for home. By now, Stella would be through bathing, and she'd need him to help haul the heavy tub outside and empty it. Earlier in the day, she had said something about wanting to see more of the valley. This afternoon, with the sun gleaming bright in the cold, cloudless sky, might be as good a time as any to do it.

She was sitting on the porch when he arrived, her skin fresh and pink from scrubbing, her hair curling damply around her face.

"You look like a mermaid fresh from the sea," he said. "But you'll catch your death, sitting out here like this."

"Nothing that feels this good could possibly be bad for me," she argued, wrinkling her nose. The impish gesture intrigued Cade, as if he'd just glimpsed a new facet of her nature. "I put a blanket over the tub," she said. "The water's still warm, if you want to use it."

"Thank you, but no," he said swiftly, though the idea did have some appeal. Since her coming, he'd washed himself from a basin in the privacy of the loft, and he still felt a trifle hesitant about bathing downstairs, with Stella around. He did not want to embarrass her, he told himself—but no, it was more than that. Under such intimate conditions, he was afraid that his own desire would betray him.

Still, the idea of a warm bath...

"Leave it, if it's not in the way," he said, compromising. "Maybe later I'll change my mind. If it's cooled too much, we can always heat a little more water."

"It's a lovely day," she said, gazing up at the peaks. "Look how the snow catches the sun."

"You said you wanted to see more of the valley? How do you feel about this afternoon?"

"Today? Now?" She had swung back around to face him, her dark eyes dancing with anticipation. The sudden flash of her beauty made him ache. "Oh, that would be wonderful! I can be ready as soon as my hair dries!"

Within the hour they were cantering through open country, ringed with pine and scattered with willow clumps along the streams. The sky was deep cobalt blue, the snow so dazzling that it made them squint.

"Look!" Stella pointed to a herd of elk in the distance. Cade handed her the field glass, and she gasped as she focused on a huge bull. "Cade! His antlers! They're as long as his body!"

"Those old boys grow them big," Cade said. "He'll lose that set in the next few weeks. Then, by summer, he'll have grown more."

"Can we get closer?"

"I wouldn't advise it. Their mating season is on, and a bull elk in rut can be dangerous, even to someone on horseback."

"You love this country, don't you?" She had lowered the glass and was looking at him now, her eyes warm and curious.

"It's the most peaceful spot I've ever known," he said, though the words struck him as strange. In this valley, he had lost Rain Flower and his sons. In this valley, he had taken his terrible revenge upon the Sioux. But even these memories could not change the way he felt about the place. It was a haven, a shelter from the ugliness of the outside world.

"But don't you ever miss your old life? The bustle of a big town like Saint Louis? Friends? Parties? The theater?"

"Sometimes," Cade admitted, swinging the roan in closer so they could talk more easily. "I try not to let myself spend too much time thinking about it."

"What do you miss most of all?" she persisted

"You won't laugh?"

The sunlight glistened on Stella's russet hair as she shook her head.

"It's music I miss the most," he said. "Before the war, my parents used to hold concerts in our home, and I never got tired of listening. Sometimes the silence here..." His voice trailed off, leaving the sentence unfinished. "I've even thought of ordering a fiddle or a guitar and trying to learn it, but it would be years before I could play well enough to suit myself. I haven't much patience with things that take time."

"I know what you mean," she said. "I play the piano a little. My teacher said I had a real talent—but I chose to concentrate on photography, instead. Still, the thought of never hearing music again . . . I—I don't think I could bear it!'' She spurred the mare and shot ahead of him, skirting the edge of the trees. Cade knew what she was thinking. If she hanged or went to prison for shooting Jared, there would be no more music, no photography, no life left for her at all.

"Cade!" She had reined in her horse at the edge of the trees. "Come see these tracks!"

When he reached her side, he saw that she was staring down at some enormous prints in the snow. "They look like they were made by some giant man, walking barefoot!" she said, her voice blending awe and fear.

"Grizzly bear," Cade said. "And a big one, judging from the size of those tracks."

She shivered. "Do you think it's close by?"

"The tracks look fairly fresh. But I wouldn't worry. With two of us here, both on horseback, it will probably stay well out of sight."

"But they do attack people? And horses?"

"A grizzly that's hungry or in a bad mood will attack anything. But I'll wager this one's just looking for a place to spend the winter." Cade kept the tone of his voice casual. He did not want to spoil the lightness of the afternoon by scaring her, which is what would happen if he told her about the time he'd seen a huge, wounded grizzly bring down a man on a galloping horse. The big bears were as mean, tough and irascible as any animal in the world, and Cade usually gave them a wide berth.

He glanced down at the tracks again. They were fresh—too fresh to suit him. "Come on!" he said, wheeling the roan. "I'll race you back to the lake!"

She laughed, kicking the mare into an explosive burst of speed. Down the hill and across the flat they galloped, Cade holding back the long-legged roan a bit so she could stay even. Her hair streamed behind her as she rode, like the flag at the head of a cavalry charge. Her face glowed in the icy air.

They were nearing the lake now, where the land inclined downward. Stella was riding full tilt, pressing to the limit, when the mare hit a patch of treacherous ground, a steep slope where the snow had melted slightly, then frozen again with a thin coating of ice.

As Cade watched in horror, the mare's hooves began to slip. The Appaloosa fought for balance. Then, in the next instant, she lost her footing and crashed, taking Stella with her.

Cade flung himself off the roan in time to see them tumble down the slope in a wild flurry of arms and legs, coming to a stop in a heavy drift at the bottom.

By the time he reached them, the mare had struggled to her feet, unhurt. Stella, however, lay with her eyes closed, her hair spreading like blood on the white snow.

"Stella!" He lifted her in his arms. For a moment her body hung limp. Then—blessed relief—her eyelids fluttered and lifted. She moaned softly. Her dark eyes gazed up at him.

"Are you all right?" he asked.

She shifted her limbs cautiously, then nodded. When she tried to speak, however, her words came out between sobs.

"I—I was so afraid," she gasped. "When the horse went down, I thought—I thought—"

"Hush, Stella. It's all right now."

"Cade, I don't want to die! I thought I could accept it— whatever is going to happen to me—but, not now...."

Her dark eyes glistened with tears as they gazed up at him. Her full lips parted.

"Stop it, Stella," he whispered, and then, somehow, he was kissing her—soft, gentle, desperately controlled little kisses that moved swiftly over her face, lingering on her warm mouth and her damp, salty lashes.

"It's all right," he murmured. "You don't have to be afraid." His arms pulled her close. She was shivering with cold. Cade held her with forced gentleness, tasting the tears that trickled down her cheeks. Inside, he was battling all his natural impulses. He wanted to sweep her up in his arms, carry her back to the cabin and warm her lovely, trembling body with his own, to kiss every intimate curve and hollow of her until she moaned with ecstasy. And then, when neither of them could resist any longer—

He forced his mind to break the dangerous train of thought. It could not happen, he told himself. He could not even allow himself to imagine it. She had killed his brother, and he had a duty to perform. Nothing must keep him from what he had to do.

"We need to get you back to the cabin," he said. "Do you think you can ride? It's not far now."

"I'll try."

He helped her mount the skittish mare, and they rode the last mile in awkward silence, both of them lost in thought. At the corral fence, she dismounted herself, before he had a chance to assist her. "I'll help you with the horses," she said.

"No, you're cold and you've had a nasty fall. Go on inside. I'll take care of it."

She did not argue. He stood watching her as she walked back to the cabin, graceful even in the faded, ill-fitting wool coat and trousers she wore. Conflicting emotions clashed like armies in his mind. He wanted her. And he had a feeling she felt the same way about him. But he was not ready to face the consequences of giving in to desire. The price was too high.

Cade cursed under his breath. The truth, he admitted, went much deeper than his promise to Jared. Love without hurt was something he had never known. Lavinia's treachery had burned him; Rain Flower's death had left him emotionally frozen—until now. Until Stella.

But how could he let go of his feelings again when the risks were so great? he asked himself. How could he expect her to love him, when so much difficulty lay ahead? Even if the charges against her were dropped, she would not want to stay in Wyoming. She would return to her life in the East, where he could not safely go, and he would lose her.

Yes, restraint made sense, Cade thought. By holding back, he would be protecting both himself and Stella from the hurt that was sure to come. And yet, the pain of his aloneness was so intense, his need for her so deep, that sometimes it was all he could do to keep from crying out with it.

The cabin door closed behind Stella, leaving him alone. Cade unsaddled the horses and then turned his attention to getting some firewood. If he didn't chop some more now, he calculated, there was a chance they'd run out by morning.

The wind had freshened. It rippled through the pines and blew shimmering clouds of snow across the pasture. Cade turned up his collar, hefted the ax and went to work.

Stella lay alone in Cade's brass bed, gazing at a thin ray of moonlight that slanted through the window. It was well past midnight, she knew. But she could not sleep. Her mind was too busy, going over and over the things that had happened.

Cade had puttered around the yard for a time, chopping wood and feeding the horses. Then he'd hiked back down toward the lake with the shotgun and returned with two freshly killed snow geese, which he'd cleaned, plucked and hung in the cold. By then it was evening, and the round, golden moon had risen above the distant hills.

In his absence, she had prepared a supper of vegetable stew and hot biscuits. He'd been hungry and appreciative, but that was all. There had been no move to take her in his arms again. Once more, Stella realized, the barriers were in place.

After supper, he had added more hot water to the tub and gotten ready to take a bath. Without being asked, Stella had snatched up a copy of Homer's *Iliad* and retreated behind the quilt.

Strange, she'd mused, these proprieties they followed. After what they had been through together, it would have seemed more natural to have stayed, helped him out of his clothes and offered to wash his back. It was not as if she had never seen a man's body. She was, after all, a widow.

But Cade's cool reserve had made her hesitant. She had not wanted to embarrass him or be sent back behind the quilt like a misbehaving child. So she had curled up on the bed with the book, its pages a blur before her eyes, its words a meaningless jumble.

She remembered the look on his face when he'd taken her in his arms, the excruciatingly restrained passion in his kisses. Cade wanted her, she knew. But physical desire and love could be worlds apart. To believe that Cade could love the woman who'd killed his brother—no, that was asking too much.

And what about her own situation? Stella had slammed the book shut in a turmoil of indecision. Weeks from now, she could be dangling from the end of a rope or facing years in prison. As things stood, they had no future, she and Cade. They had only the present—and soon, even that would be gone.

Taking a deep breath, she had put the book down on the bed, stood up and pulled the quilt aside. Cade, in water to his waist, had looked at her with startled eyes but said nothing as she walked around behind him and soaped her hands.

"Stella—" He spoke as she touched him.

"Hush," she whispered, beginning to massage the lather into his broad, bare shoulders. "It's been much too long since I washed a man's back."

She let her hands move slowly, circling the muscled ridges of his shoulder blades and gliding down the long groove of his spine. He responded to her touch the way a wild animal responds to stroking—liking the feel of it, but tense, resisting full surrender to the pleasure.

"I had a wonderful time today," she said. "I'm sorry I spoiled it by falling."

"You didn't spoil it," he said. "I'm just thankful you weren't hurt." He took a deep breath. "Stella, I want you to promise me something."

"What?" She had picked up the soap again and was working up more lather on her hands.

"The valley is beautiful, but it can be very dangerous. There are wild animals... Indians... the chance of accidents like the one you had today. Promise me you won't go out riding alone. I... don't think I could stand it if anything happened to you."

"I promise," she said, though the thought passed through her mind that his concern was ironic. In the near future he'd be turning her over to the law for possible hanging. Would he be able to stand it then?

Her thumbs rubbed small knots of tightness from the back of his neck. His skin was warm to the touch and fragrant with the rich, clean aroma of the soap. Never mind the future, she told herself. It was out of reach, out of control. Now—that was all that mattered. The crackling warmth of the fire, the drops of water glistening on Cade's sun-bronzed skin. Now was all she had. "Put your head back," she said, her voice as soothing as her hands. "I'll rinse the soap out of your hair."

She had retreated behind the quilt again while he got out of the tub and dried himself. Not until she felt the sudden chill of cold air and heard the splash of pouring water did she venture out again.

Cade had emptied the tub and was just closing the door. He stood lean and golden in the firelight, a white towel wrapped around his hips. Stella's mouth opened softly as she gazed at him. She had never realized a man's body could be so beautiful.

He bolted the door, then walked toward her. "No," he whispered. "Don't move."

Slowly, he lifted his hands and cupped her face. His eyes blazed passionately into hers, but his touch was as restrained as if he'd been holding a child.

"Thank you, Stella," he said softly. Then he bent his head; his lips brushed hers in the briefest, tenderest of kisses.

"Cade—" She strained toward him, but he shook his head.

"You're the loveliest thing I've ever seen," he said, his voice rough with tightly reined emotion. "But if I followed my natural inclinations right now, we could both end up sorry. I'm going up to the loft now, while I'm still able."

"Cade, I—"

"Not another word. We'll talk tomorrow, in the cold, sensible daylight." He'd kissed her again, even more gently than the first time. Then, before she could react, he had turned away and was putting the ladder up to the loft.

Now, hours later, Stella lay wide-eyed and restless in the moonlight. She could feel the beating of her own heart, the pulse of life in her veins and the throb of desire deep in her body.

Tomorrow they would talk, he had said. Tomorrow they would be sensible. But how many tomorrows did she have left? How many nights like tonight?

The only man who had ever made love to her was John. Their times together had been frustrating at best—clumsy and full of misunderstandings. Stella had never known the full giving of herself to a man. She ached to know it now, tonight. With Cade.

What did it matter whether he loved her or not? she asked herself bitterly. What did anything matter, when, in a few weeks she could be dead or locked away for life?

The howl of a wolf, echoed by another, floated down from the hills. The loneliness in the sound made Stella shiver. Perhaps Cade had heard it, too. Perhaps he was awake, as she was, tormented and feverish with need.

The wolf howled again, its call wild and haunting in the night. Stella sat up and brushed the quilt aside. In the moonlight, she could see the rails of the ladder that led up to the loft. She could see each rung, each step.

Almost without willing it, she felt herself moving, gliding across the floor till she reached the foot of the ladder. Then, with her heart in her throat, she began to climb.

Chapter Ten

Cade lay awake on his bed of buffalo robes, listening to the faraway call of the wolves. The sound filled him with loneliness and a sense of deep need.

He remembered how Stella had touched him, the slow, sensuous way her hands had caressed his shoulders and glided along his back. He had fought her, resisting the pleasure she had given so sweetly. Why, he asked himself, when he needed her so? What were his principles worth tonight, in this cold, lonely darkness?

He pictured her now, asleep in the bed below him, her hair spilling soft and red across the pillow. He imagined pressing his face to that hair, dizzying himself with its fragrance, then finding the bare curve of her neck with his lips—

"Cade...." Her whisper broke the silence. He heard the creak of the ladder as she reached the top.

"Cade." She spoke his name again, her voice like dark red velvet.

His throat was so tight that he could not answer. This was a dream, he told himself. But, no—she was moving toward him in the darkness. He could hear the light pressure of her weight on the floorboards, the delicate rush of her breathing.

"Here I am," he said, finding his voice.

She was beside him then, kneeling, still in her night-shirt. "Hold me, Cade," she whispered. "I've been alone so long."

Without a word, he lifted the edge of the buffalo robe and drew her down beside him. She quivered like a bird as his arms closed around her. Her heart drummed wildly beneath the swelling curves of her breasts. It would be best to send her away, Cade told himself. That would be the sensible thing, the wise thing. But he could no more let her go than he could stop the blood from pulsing through his veins.

"Stella...." With a growing sense of wonder, he nuzzled her hair, her eyes, her warm, eager lips. Her arms crept around him. Her trembling hands explored the lines of his bare back, their touch sending ripples of pleasure through his whole body. She had come to him. She wanted him. And he wanted her—so urgently that, in the heat of his desire, his resistance was melting away like spring snow.

Even now, he felt the compelling surge of his own arousal. He was painfully ready for her. Still, he hesitated, half-afraid of hurting her, half-afraid to believe this was really happening.

"Are you sure?" he murmured against the fragrant hollow of her neck. "I don't want you to be sorry."

He felt the shake of her head. "I won't be sorry," she whispered, her breath moist in his ear. "Whatever happens, whatever lies ahead for us...I want to look back and remember this."

A feeling of pure joy shook Cade to the depths of his soul. He felt his frozen emotions breaking through their cold, hard walls. The sudden sense of freedom was so sweet that it almost brought tears to his eyes.

"Stella—" He swept her closer and felt her body mold eagerly to his through the thin nightshirt. She whimpered as his lips claimed hers and his tongue began its gentle, darting invasion of her mouth. Her hips pressed against him, swaying back and forth like a dancer's. Yes, she felt him; she knew.

He slipped the nightshirt from her body. She lay trembling in his arms, her skin like warm satin against his own, her hands moving with delicate urgency over his chest and shoulders and down the curve of his back.

Then he began to kiss her with an exquisite slowness that prolonged the delicious, tingling sense of anticipation. His mouth caressed her face, her throat, her breasts, moving lower until she began to moan softly, to whimper and plead.

"Cade... now... oh, please, now!"

Yes, now. Cade felt his life bursting inside him as he took her. Stella, he thought. My angel. My salvation. Stella.

There were no barriers now. No holding back. His need filled her as his passion swept them both toward mounting crescendos of ecstasy.

"Cade..." she whispered wildly, "love me, Cade...." She quivered in his arms as they exploded together in a burst of rapture that carried them beyond the threshold of every pleasure either had ever known.

Stella closed her eyes and nestled her face against Cade's chest, savoring the roughness of his hair and the warm, clean aroma of his skin. She felt an overwhelming tenderness toward him, this man who had taken her on a journey that was as new as life and as old as time. It was as if she had never known, till now, what it meant to be a woman, what it meant to give herself to a man. She shivered with contentment and pressed closer to him.

His arms tightened around her. She felt his lips nibbling softly at her hair. Neither of them spoke. Words would only break the spell and bring reality crashing in upon them once more.

For this brief time, they had heaven within their grasp. Stella clung to that heaven with all her strength. There would be consequences later, perhaps even regrets. But she could not undo what had been done. And she would not. She had given herself to Cade. She had known his passion.

Whatever happened later on, nothing could ever take this memory away from her.

Stella stirred sleepily beneath the buffalo robes and opened her eyes. Sunlight was streaming into the loft through a crack beneath the eaves. Incredibly, it was morning.

"Cade?" Her hand reached out for him, but he was gone. The hollow where he had lain beside her was cool and empty, almost as if he had never been there at all.

She closed her eyes, savoring the warmth of the bed and the sweet aroma of Cade's body on her skin. Little by little, she relived each precious detail of last night's love-making. Her hands brushed the places where Cade had caressed her.

Why had he gone this morning without waking her? Maybe it was only that he had chores to do and wanted to let her rest. Maybe when he had finished he would come back to her, his body cold from the dawn air, needing her warmth, needing her love again. Maybe...

She indulged in the fantasy, keeping the truth at bay for a few moments longer. Reality, she knew, was as harsh and glaring as the morning sunlight. She and Cade had come together out of a deep, compelling need. But their love-making had not resolved any of the problems between them. If anything, it had only made things more complicated. Stella sighed and sat up. She knew that Cade had not wanted to be here when she awakened. And she knew why.

She groped for the discarded flannel nightshirt. Pulling it around her, she crept across the loft to the top of the ladder. "Cade?" she called out tentatively, thinking he might be downstairs.

There was no answer.

Slowly she began to climb down the ladder. How would Cade react when he saw her? she wondered. Would the barriers be firmly in place again, or would he be as tender as he'd been last night? And what would she say to him?

ARE THESE
THE KEYS TO YOUR NEW
CADILLAC COUPE DE VILLE?

INSTRUCTIONS:
With a coin, scratch off the silver on your lucky keys to reveal your secret registration numbers. If they match, return this entry form—you instantly and automatically qualify to win a brand new Cadillac Coupe de Ville!

YOUR UNIQUE SWEEPSTAKES ENTRY NO.

№ 1H821163

☐ **YES,** please enter me in the Sweepstakes and tell me if I've won the $1,000,000.00 Grand Prize, or any other prize. Also send me my four *free* Harlequin Historicals plus a *free* mystery gift as explained on the opposite page!   246 CIH YBB2

NAME	(PLEASE PRINT)	
ADDRESS		APT.
CITY	STATE	ZIP

☐ No, don't send me my free books or the free mystery gift, but do enter me in the Sweepstakes.

NO POSTAGE
NECESSARY
IF MAILED
IN THE
UNITED STATES

BUSINESS REPLY MAIL
FIRST CLASS MAIL   PERMIT NO. 717   BUFFALO, NY

POSTAGE WILL BE PAID BY ADDRESSEE

HARLEQUIN
READER SERVICE®
MILLION DOLLAR SWEEPSTAKES
901 Fuhrmann Blvd.
P.O. Box 1867
Buffalo NY 14240-9952

DETACH ALONG DOTTED LINE

Their first meeting, she knew, would be awkward, full of strain and uncertainty for them both.

Stella had almost reached the bottom of the stairs when she heard the whinny of a horse outside—a strange horse, not Cade's roan or the Appaloosa mare. Her hands froze on the rails in sudden, paralyzing panic. She had felt so safe here in this valley. Now that sense of safety was shattered. Someone was outside—someone who had not been here the night before.

Her eyes darted around the cabin. Cade's rifle was gone from its place beside the door. But he did not seem to have left in a hurry. He had taken the time to build a fire. He had even hung a pot of porridge over the flames to cook before going outside.

The window curtains were drawn, shutting off her view, but Stella caught the sound of men's voices coming from the direction of the corral. She strained her ears, trying to catch a word, a clue as to who might be outside. That was when she realized they were speaking in a language she had never heard before.

She was still clinging to the ladder in wild uncertainty when she heard the sound of boots on the porch, stomping off the snow. In the next moment Cade swung the door open and stepped into the cabin.

His face was ruddy with cold, his tawny hair tousled by the morning breeze. His eyes flashed uneasily as he looked at her, then glanced away.

"Cade—"

His eyes met hers again, their expression closed this time. "No, it's all right," he said.

Stella did not know if he was speaking about last night or referring to their morning visitors. Only one thing was evident; Cade was once again trying to put up a wall between them.

"Who's out there?" she asked in a whispered voice.

"Washakie. His people have arrived in the valley, and he's come to pay his respects. Get dressed, and I'll invite him in."

"Just Washakie? He came alone?" Stella hesitated, still grasping the ladder.

"Yes. Why?"

"Nothing. It's just that I heard voices outside before you came in. Indians, speaking their own language."

"That's right, Stella, you did." Bitter amusement flickered across Cade's windburned face. "You heard two Shoshone talking—Washakie and me."

"Oh." Stella's hand went to her throat as the realization struck her. She had thought she knew Cade Garrison. But there were facets of this complex, turbulent man that she had never seen. Even though they had made love last night, he was still, in many ways, a stranger.

"Hurry," he said. "We don't want to keep our guest waiting."

Stella darted behind the quilt and began to rummage through the trunkful of clothing Cade had provided for her. What a shame she had no dress to wear, she thought. It didn't really seem fitting to meet the great chief of the Shoshone wearing an old shirt and baggy men's trousers. But that was all she had; it would have to do.

She pulled on clean clothes, splashed water on her face, and ran a brush through her tangled hair. "I'm ready," she said. "Go ahead and show the chief in."

Cade walked to the door, then paused before stepping outside. His eyes met Stella's in a swift, penetrating glance. "Remember, you are meeting my father," he said, then was gone.

His words sank in slowly as Stella waited for him to return with Washakie. She had known that Cade was an adopted Shoshone, but she was just beginning to learn how much that adoption meant to him. He spoke their language and called their chief his father. His own lost children, she reminded herself, had been half-Shoshone.

An unexpected current of fear surged through her as the door latch moved. The last Indians she'd encountered had very nearly murdered her. Cade had assured her that the Shoshone chief was friendly. Still, after what she had been through, Stella told herself, she could not be blamed for feeling as she did.

Her heart caught in her throat as the door swung open. The man who stood beside Cade—yes, she thought giddily, they actually *looked* like father and son. The resemblance between them was almost uncanny.

Washakie was tall, as tall as Cade, and though his long hair was silver white, his body was lean and powerful. Even in his faded wool shirt, well-worn leather leggings and patched blanket, he was a regal figure—every inch a chief. Stella ached for her camera. The portraits she could have taken of such a man!

"Won't you come in?" she said swiftly, remembering her manners.

A faint smile flickered across Washakie's handsome, hawklike features as he stepped across the threshold. His presence seemed to overflow the cabin, as if a great bull elk had walked in through the doorway.

"He understands quite a bit of English." Cade had come in behind him and closed the door. "But he feels that speaking the white man's tongue is beneath his dignity. He prefers to use an interpreter." He turned to Washakie and spoke a few words in Shoshone. The sound of them was like nothing Stella had ever heard before—full of oddly musical, birdlike tones that defied conventional English vowels and consonants.

The old chief replied with a voluble cascade of speech, smiling, nodding, pausing now and then to glance at Stella. His dark eyes were as sharp as a raven's and bright with curiosity.

"What is he saying?" Stella turned to Cade.

Cade hesitated. His chest rose and fell as he took a deep breath, then dutifully translated. "He says his heart is happy because his son has come home with a wife. He says that I have been alone much too long, and that he welcomes you as a daughter.

"Oh. . . ." Stella felt a rush of emotion. She stared down at her hands, unable to look at either man. "Cade, shouldn't you explain . . . ?"

"I already have. But my explanation doesn't make much sense to him." Cade took another deep breath. "By Shoshone custom, you see, a woman who sleeps a night in a man's lodge is looked upon as his wife. The kind of legalities we attach to marriage have no place in their traditions."

Stella flushed. "You mean that in his eyes—"

"Yes. From the standpoint of Shoshone law, you are my wife, Stella." Cade spoke evenly, his eyes betraying nothing. But Stella knew he was thinking about last night. Yes, she realized, hot color rising in her face. In the fullest implication of the words, she had indeed slept in his lodge.

She lowered her eyes, sobered and confused. What forces had last night's impulsive act set in motion? she wondered. What did Cade expect of her now? Did he, also, think of her as his wife?

"And what about later?" she asked, wanting to test his feelings. "What will happen when I leave here?"

Cade's eyes flickered, then hardened. "That, too, Washakie will accept," he said in a low voice. "It is not unknown for a Shoshone woman to leave her husband."

Stella felt a jab of cold pain, like a sliver of ice inside her. Quickly she smiled to hide it. "Please invite the chief to sit down," she said, moving toward the fireplace. "And would you ask him if he'd like some breakfast?"

"I'm certain he would," said Cade. "Surprisingly enough, he's quite fond of porridge."

Washakie sat majestically in the big rocker before the fireplace. Stella dished him up a bowl of steaming porridge topped with brown sugar, which he cradled on one big, brown hand, a pewter spoon held awkwardly in the other. He ate slowly, blowing on each bite, stopping now and again to nod his approval or to say something to Cade, who sat in the opposite chair.

Stella hovered awkwardly in the background. Before coming west, she had read several books about Indians. Indian women, she knew, were expected to tend to their duties when their men were discussing important matters. They were not permitted to join in male conversation or to express their opinions in front of guests.

Was that what Cade expected of her? Stella asked herself. Was it her proper place to play the submissive Shoshone bride while the men talked? The very idea made her bristle.

Squaring her shoulders, she picked up a stool from the kitchen, carried it to the fireplace and put it next to Cade's chair. "May I join you?" she asked, sitting down.

She glanced from one to the other. Washakie raised one grizzled eyebrow in surprise, but did not appear to be offended. Cade simply nodded.

"I was just telling the chief about your photography work," he said. "He has questions that I can't answer."

Washakie's eyes, set deep in their wrinkled folds, danced like a child's as he spoke. The questions came in bursts of Shoshone, punctuated with jabs of his spoon.

Cade translated for Stella. "He says the black box has taken his picture a number of times. At first he believed it was some sort of magic. Now he knows the black box is just a machine. Still, he would like very much to know how it works."

Stella was surprised and pleased by the old man's interest. "Tell him that someday soon I hope to get another camera," she said. "When I do, I'll be happy to show him everything."

Washakie shook his head emphatically, and Stella realized he had not waited for Cade's translation. There was a note of impatience in his abrupt reply.

A hint of a smile, like a flicker of sunlight in a shadowy forest, passed across Cade's face. "My father says he has waited for a long time to learn about the black box. It would be a kindness if you did not make him wait any longer. He realizes you have nothing to show him, but you could explain—"

"Oh, Cade." Stella thought of the chemical processes, the complicated steps involved in producing a finished photograph. "I don't know if I can!"

"Try," Cade said gently. "Keep it as simple as you can. Maybe between the two of us, we'll be able to put it in terms he can understand."

Stella took a deep breath and began. She explained how the glass plates had to be coated with light-sensitive chemicals in a darkroom, how each plate was covered with a black shield to protect it till it could be placed in the camera, and how the shield had to be carefully removed—all of this while the chemicals were still wet.

Every few sentences she stopped to let Cade translate, watching him as he struggled to explain terms for which there were no equivalent words in Shoshone. Washakie listened attentively, shaking his great, silvery head when he did not understand some point, crinkling the corners of his eyes and nodding when, at last, he did.

As Stella explained how the picture had to be focused and how, when everything was ready, the lens cap was removed for a few critical seconds to expose the plate, she felt something strange happening. Strong feelings had begun to well up inside her like water from a long-dead spring— feelings of rage, frustration and profound sadness, as if she were mourning a part of herself. She struggled against them, trying to hold them back, but they were too powerful to be suppressed. By the time she had finished describing how the plate was developed, she was fighting back tears.

"Stella..." Cade had noticed. His blue eyes narrowed with concern. "Are you all right?" he asked.

"I'm sorry!" She pressed her hands to her face in an effort to contain the overwhelming rush of emotion. "It's just that I-I've tried so hard not to think about what I lost. I didn't realize till now how much being able to take pictures meant to me!" She was choking back sobs now, feeling helpless and foolish. Even Washakie was staring at her. What must he think? she wondered.

The old chief said something to Cade—a question, perhaps. Cade's reply was quick—a few words of explanation. Then Washakie turned and spoke to Stella, his voice soothing. She could not understand the words, but the gentleness in their tone was like the touch of a hand on her shoulder.

She remembered Cade's story—how, only last year, this white-haired patriarch had galloped off in the night and returned with the bleeding scalps of seven enemies. She tried to imagine the savagery involved in such an act, to reconcile it with the image of the kindly old man who sat before her.

And Cade— The realization struck her now as she remembered what he had told her. He, too, had destroyed his enemies. He had hunted down the Sioux who had murdered his wife and sons and killed them one by one. Cade, in his own way, was as much a savage as the man he called his father. And yet he had cared for her while she lay ill. He had made love to her with exquisite tenderness.

Who was Cade Garrison? The contradictions in him puzzled and disturbed her. How could she be so drawn to the man, and yet so repelled by what he had done?

Cade's voice broke into her thoughts as he translated Washakie's words. "My father says that he grieves with you for the loss of your black box. But only the box is gone. The knowledge of how to make pictures is still in your mind and in your hands. One day you will get another picture machine, and it will be as if you had lost nothing at all."

Cade's eyes were tender now as he spoke, and yet they avoided hers. He was remembering, perhaps, that the loss that pained her now had been, in part at least, his doing.

When Stella answered, she was in control again. "Tell him, please, that I am grateful for his kindness and for his wisdom. And tell him that when I get another camera, I would like very much to take his picture."

Washakie beamed as he heard Cade's translation. Then, as if he had finished with the matter, he rose from his chair and murmured something to Cade.

"He brought a gift for you today," Cade said. "He would like you to come outside and see it now."

"Oh—"

"He says he is sorry that it's not another black box, but he hopes that when you see it, the tears will leave your eyes."

"Tell the chief he is very kind," Stella said. But Washakie was already at the door. He stood there, beckoning imperiously, a hint of a smile on his broad, handsome face.

Stella threw on a coat and followed him outside, blinking as the dazzling sunlight filled her eyes. The icy morning air clouded her breath. The pines stood blue-black against the glittering snow.

Washakie's horse, a towering piebald, was tied to the corral fence. It danced and snorted, its massive hooves pounding the snow to mud where it stood.

Cade had turned the roan out into the pasture to let it run. Stella could see it racing along the far fence, head thrown back, tail streaming like a comet. The Appaloosa mare stood at the far corner of the pasture, nickering anxiously. Something was clearly agitating all the horses. But what was it?

Cade was just behind her. She heard his voice, close to her ear. "Look," he said.

At first she did not see the filly. Its coat blended so perfectly with the snow that only its swift-moving shadow was clearly visible. Not until it paused in front of a stand of pines did Stella really get a good look at it. Then she gasped in wonder. Never had she seen such a horse. It was like a picture from a child's fantasy book—as delicate as a fawn and as white as ermine.

Washakie gave a low whistle. The filly pricked up its ears, snorted and cantered toward him, where he stood at the fence with Stella and Cade. Its elegant head stretched over the rails. Its delicately tapered nose nuzzled Washakie's sleeve. The old chief spoke; Cade translated for Stella.

"He says this filly was raised at his fireside, like a pet. She is very tame, but she is still too young to be broken. In the spring, when the snow is gone, then she will be ready for you to ride. Her name is Snow-in-Summer."

"She's really for me?" Stella ran a finger down the filly's satiny cheek, torn between wonder and hesitation. She had never seen a more beautiful animal, but under the circumstances, how could she accept such a generous present?

Cade seemed to read her thoughts. "Take her," he said softly. "To accept Washakie's gift is to accept his friendship. He will be hurt if you refuse."

Stella pressed her face against the filly's neck, breathing in the warm, musky aroma of its damp coat. She was deeply touched by Washakie's kindness. Yet, at the same time, she felt herself being pulled into the circle of the chief's power. The gift, she knew, was a tie to bind her to Cade, to this place and to him. Emotions warred and tumbled inside her. One part of her ached to belong—to accept Washakie's gift, to let herself be accepted as his daughter and, by extension, as Cade's woman. Another part of her argued that she merited none of this. She was a fugitive from the law, wanted for the murder of Cade's brother. Everything she had found in this valley—the beauty, the warmth, the sense of belonging—could be snatched away from her, leaving nothing behind except bitterness.

"Cade?"

"Yes?" He stood behind her. She could not see his face.

"Does he know about your brother? Does he know how I came to be here?"

There was a long pause. "He knows," Cade answered quietly.

She took a deep breath. "Then tell the chief—your father—that I would be honored to accept his gift."

Washakie smiled and nodded his vigorous approval. Then he spoke more words in Shoshone—words that Cade did not translate.

"What did he say?" Stella glanced sharply at Cade.

"Please understand that he means well." Cade's eyes flickered, as if trying to avoid her gaze. "He said that the filly can be mated to my red stallion to produce many fine sons and daughters . . . and it is his hope that you and I will also give him many grandchildren."

After Washakie's departure, Cade spent the rest of the day working on the corral fence. The winter ahead would be long, the wolves and other predators hungry. He wanted to do what he could to keep the horses safe. Stella seemed so taken with the beautiful white filly. Losing it, he reflected, could be awfully hard on her.

He welcomed the work. It was good to have something physical to do, something to keep him outside, removed from the torment of Stella's nearness.

Last night . . . the memory haunted him. For that brief time, everything had seemed so simple. He had wanted her; she had wanted him. There had been nothing to stop their passionate coming together. Only now, in the harsh light of day, could he see the morass they had stumbled into.

Nothing could alter the fact that Stella was wanted for murder. That he cared for her and that they had made love, could not erase reality. It only made that reality more painful.

And there were other realities, as well. Cade labored furiously on the fence, splitting timbers with the heavy maul and pounding them into place along the rails. Sweat ran down his body beneath the heavy wool shirt as he tried to work the frustration out of his system, all in vain. His desire for Stella was like a raging fever. None of the old mental tricks, like thinking of how she'd caused Jared's death, worked anymore. He wanted her so much that he was almost afraid to be alone with her.

And now it was evening—a time when all realities would have to be faced. The sky was crimson above the Wind River peaks, its color staining the snow a glimmering, translucent red. The pines were masses of black in the dusk. Beyond the corral, the windows of the cabin glowed with light and warmth. The tantalizing aroma of Stella's cooking drifted on the evening breeze.

Stella had spent most of the day fussing over the filly— leading it around, brushing its coat and feeding it tidbits from the kitchen. What the fence had been for him, Cade suspected, the filly had been for her. It was a refuge, an excuse to avoid a confrontation that was bound to be painful. He had no trouble understanding that.

But it was no good, he told himself as he straightened his weary back. These games of evasion they were both playing could not continue; they had to talk. They had to try to make some sense out of what had happened and decide what to do next. He simply did not trust himself to leave things to chance. If he did, their passion for each other would destroy them both.

Cade made sure the horses were secure in their stalls. Then he closed the corral gate, fastened the latch and walked slowly back toward the cabin.

Chapter Eleven

Beans and bacon. The tantalizing aroma swirled all around Cade as he opened the door and stepped into the warmth of the cabin. Stella was bent over the pot, stirring with a wooden spoon. Her face was pink from the heat of the fire, her curls tumbling damply onto her face. She looked so pretty, Cade thought.

"Sit down. It's ready." She nodded toward the table with its two place settings, then bent to check the biscuits that were browning in the Dutch oven.

"It smells good." Cade poured water into the basin and soaped his hands. He had been prepared to push right into his serious talk and get it out of the way. But he could tell that Stella had worked hard on supper, and he was wolfishly hungry. No sense spoiling a good meal with unpleasantness. The talk could wait.

"This is my father's recipe," Stella said. "He claimed he got it from a one-eyed ship's cook he met in Singapore. But knowing my father…" She shrugged and laughed, but there was a note of uneasiness in the gesture. She knew as well as he did, Cade realized, that some sort of reckoning was at hand. Like him, she was braced for it.

"Singapore? Your father must have been an interesting person," he said, making conversation.

"First mate on a clipper. He'd been all over the world. But after I was born, he stayed home to raise me. He was a ship's chandler in Boston for a while—till he discovered photography. He went a little mad over it, I'm afraid."

"He was good, I take it?" Cade sat down at the table.

"A master." She ladled up the beans. "He worked with Mathew Brady during the war. Took a lot of pictures that eventually wound up with Brady's name on them, including some of Lincoln."

"What happened to him?" Cade got up and helped her with her chair, their bodies brushing self-consciously for an instant. Then he sat down again.

"Gettysburg," she was saying. "He was taking pictures close to the front and caught a burst of shrapnel. He lived—" Her breath caught sharply, and Cade sensed the lingering pain of the memory. "He lived for more than a year. But he was an invalid, totally bedridden the whole time. That was when he started teaching me about photography. I was his legs, his hands. He taught me everything he knew. That was his legacy to me."

Cade nodded sympathetically. He was just beginning to realize what the loss of Stella's cameras and plates had meant to her. No wonder she had cursed him when she found out he had encouraged the mob to destroy them. "I never told you I was sorry—about your things, I mean," he said.

"You saved my life."

"If there'd been some other way—"

"Evidently, there wasn't." She had lowered her eyes and started eating, taking small spoonfuls and blowing delicately on each one. "And what about your family? Knute told me you were from Saint Louis."

"That's right," Cade said, realizing that if Knute had told her that much, he had probably told her about Lavinia, as well. "My parents are dead. My brother runs the family shipping business."

"He's the oldest?"

"No. I am." Cade took a bite of flaky biscuit. "Out of three brothers and two sisters. Jared was the baby of the family. Spoiled for it, if the truth be told. That's why they sent him west, to me. I suppose they thought it would make a man of him.''

She glanced up at him, her dark eyes profoundly sad, and for a moment Cade expected an outburst of apologies. Instead, she simply shook her graceful head.

''Do you go back often?'' she asked softly.

''To Saint Louis? No, I've never been back. But I keep in touch with the family. Sometimes when I go into South Pass, I find a letter waiting.''

''And now even that...'' Her voice trailed off, then rallied. ''Since you rescued me, you can't safely go anywhere. You're as much a fugitive as I am!''

Cade ate his beans in silence. Yes, she was right, he reflected. In rescuing Stella, he had made himself a pariah. He could not even go into South Pass City to pick up mail from his family or to send letters to them. He would not even be able to sell horses, livestock and supplies from his ranch. In a few months, he could be out of money.

''Would they come here after us, do you think?'' she asked. ''The vigilantes, I mean—or a posse.''

Cade thought a moment, then shook his head. ''It's not likely. Right now the snow's pretty deep in the passes. And even if it weren't, most of them are afraid of the Indians. I think we're safe here for the time being.''

''But it's no good for you this way. You've got to turn me over to the law, and soon.'' Her words came so abruptly that they startled him. He put his spoon down and stared at her.

''It isn't fair to you,'' she said. ''It's bad enough that I shot your brother. I don't need to be responsible for ruining your reputation and making you a wanted man, as well!''

''Stella, nobody forced me to get you out of that jail,'' he protested. ''I did it of my own free will and, damn it, I have no regrets!'' Surprisingly, even to Cade, the words rang true. He *didn't* have any regrets, he realized. Given the same circumstances—even knowing what the consequences would be—he would not hesitate to rescue Stella again.

"Not even any regrets about last night?" she asked, her voice too even, too calm.

The question had caught him off guard. *He* was the one who'd planned to bring up last night. He'd had it all thought out.

"Stella—"

"No, let me be the one to say it." Her spoon was poised in midair, her eyes unwavering. "We needed each other last night. And it was good—for both of us, I'd daresay. But it doesn't change anything, Cade. It won't undo anything that's happened."

"You're sorry, then?" Cade found himself asking.

She lowered her eyes for a moment, then looked up at him again, her expression subtly different. "No," she said, her voice so low that he had to strain to hear it. "It was like nothing that's ever happened to me before. It was a time I'll keep and remember as long as I live. I'm anything but sorry."

"Then—"

"It's not that simple. You may be a Shoshone, but I am not. The fact that I've slept one night in your lodge doesn't make me your woman, Cade. It only makes things more complicated."

"Stella, if you're asking for an apology—"

She shook her head. "I was the one who came to you."

"What you're saying, I take it, is that I'm not to expect you again tonight."

The color deepened in her face. How damnably beautiful she looked.

"Not tonight. Not any night. I—I owe you a great deal, Cade. More than I can ever repay. But as soon as it's possible to leave, I want you to take me to Laramie. I want to get it over with."

She had spoken her peace. Now she sat looking at him, her eyes large and dark in the lantern light, her delicate chin resolutely set.

"Stella, if it will make things any easier, I feel the same way you do," Cade said gently. "We've both been alone for a long time. We're both awfully vulnerable. If we just let things take their natural course—" he shook his head "—we'll start lying to ourselves and each other. We'll start believing that everything's all right, even though we both know better."

"And we'll put off going to Laramie, for one reason, then another," she said. "Oh, Cade—"

"It's all right. I understand. I think we both do."

"Then—"

"Let's eat our supper before it gets cold."

The rest of the meal was divided between silence and polite, impersonal conversation. Cade could feel the strain in her and in himself. Each of them, he sensed, had more to say—much more. But, by common consent, they had closed a door between them.

After supper he excused himself and went outside to bring in some firewood for the next morning. The night air was icy, his breath a cloud of mist in the dark. He took his time with the wood, pausing every few steps to look up at the sky. In the east, the moon was rising, full and golden above the distant hills. How sweet it would be, he thought, just to lie with Stella in his arms and watch that moon through the window. They wouldn't even have to make love, if he could just have her there, warm, soft and fragrant beside him, the whole night. Dear God, it had been so long—

But no, he reminded himself. They had just resolved that issue, he and Stella. Strange, how it had come about. He had planned to broach the subject himself, but she had been well ahead of him at every turn, thrusting boldly where he had been hesitant. There had been nothing left for him except to agree with her.

Cade hefted the small stack of logs and walked slowly back toward the cabin. Something else, he realized, was troubling him tonight. For the first time, as he listened to Stella, he had become aware that she was as anxious as he was to resolve her part in Jared's death. And that was strange—considering that she could end up dead or in prison for it.

He muttered a curse under his breath. His experience with women told him to be skeptical. Yet all his instincts urged him to trust her.

Cade paused, balancing the wood on one arm while he unlatched the door. Only one thing, he decided, was certain.

Stella Brannon was quite a woman.

Stella lay alone in bed, the pillow still damp where she had vented her tears. She had done it, she congratulated herself bitterly. She had made the noble choice and salvaged her pride in the process. Cade had been neatly disarmed, the fateful words snatched from his mouth before he could be the first to speak them.

But it had been a hollow victory. She felt that hollowness now as she lay there, wanting him even more tonight than she had wanted him the night before—wanting again the feel of his arms pulling her close, the silky roughness of his naked body locked to hers. Wanting the sweet sense of belonging to him, wholly and without question.

It had been easier last night. She had simply given in to her desire and gone to him. Now that was out of the question; she had seen to it herself. Rightness had won out over need—a cold, lonely triumph.

Stop it, she scolded herself. You're a grown woman, Stella Brannon, not a foolish young girl! You made the only intelligent choice! Now stop mooning and accept it!

She turned over, fluffed her pillow and closed her eyes. In spite of everything, she was weary. As she drifted into fitful sleep, her dreams tormented her. She saw Gillis's leering eyes and smelled the whiskey on his breath as he pressed the knife to her throat. She saw the face of Jared Garrison, so hauntingly like Cade's, as he lay, death pale, on the floor of her tent. She heard the fear-crazed screams of Karin Aarnson and the single gunshot that silenced them forever.

Stella moaned in her sleep, choking on her own fear as Red Hawk's grim features swam into focus. They grew larger and larger, until they filled her nightmare. Then, slowly they began to fade until nothing was left but a dim, red mist. She could see something in the mist, something tall and angular. In her dream, she moved closer until she was standing at the foot of it, looking up. She gasped out loud as she realized it was a gallows, with a hangman's noose dangling from its crossbeam.

She tried to run away, but her legs would not move. She was being pulled upward, as if by some huge, invisible hand, closer and closer to the noose. Her screams were silent, torn from her throat without sound. She struggled wildly, exhausting herself as the gallows began to fade. Even the mist was darkening now, growing blacker and blacker. She was sinking into it. Her struggles lessened, grew fainter, until at last, mercifully, the nightmare ended and she slept in peace.

Stella did not awaken the next morning until she heard Cade stirring in the kitchen. She stretched, yawned and stayed where she was, behind the hanging quilt. She knew his routine by now. Usually he built up the fire, started a pot of coffee and maybe some oatmeal porridge and then went out to see to the horses. That was her cue to get up, and she generally managed to be washed, combed and dressed by the time he came back inside to eat breakfast.

She waited till he had gone outside. Then she slipped out of bed and into her clothes. The night's sleep had helped. She felt rested this morning, strong enough to deal with her newfound resolve. She would keep busy, she promised herself. She would be industrious and cheerful, and she would keep herself at a comfortable distance from Cade. That way, maybe she'd be able to get through the day with her emotions under control.

Still barefoot, she pattered over to the fireplace to check the porridge and the coffee. Then she went to the washstand, where she splashed cold water on her face, rinsed her mouth and ran a brush through her hair. The face in the washstand mirror was glowing with health. The climate in the Wind River must agree with her, she mused.

Cade had not come back inside. Strange, she thought. Feeding and watering the horses usually took him no more than ten or fifteen minutes. What was keeping him out there?

She pulled on her thick wool stockings and tied her moccasins over them. Then, slipping into one of Cade's jackets that hung by the door, she stepped outside.

The sky was clear, the day already promising to warm. Maybe the sun would begin to melt the snow in the passes and on the plain, she thought. If so, her time of reckoning in Laramie could be close—days away. Stella shivered, anticipation and dread clashing in her mind.

Cade's tracks, the freshest ones, led around the corner of the cabin toward the shed. She was following them, her eyes so intent on the snow that at first she did not notice the cluster of figures standing near the corral. When she looked up and saw them, she gave a little gasp.

Four Indian women, swathed from head to foot in bright-colored trade blankets, stood staring at her.

"Oh!" Stella swallowed her fear. There was nothing to worry about, she assured herself. These women had to be Shoshone, and they would not have come here except out of friendship or curiosity.

"Hello," she said politely, thinking she would have to get Cade to teach her a few simple phrases in their language.

One of them, a stout-framed squaw of about fifty, answered in a short burst of Shoshone. Then, as if at a signal, all four of them descended upon Stella.

"No! Wait!" Stella protested as they surrounded her like a flock of chattering birds. Curious hands tugged at her clothes and pinched her skin. Her red hair seemed especially fascinating to them. They pulled and jerked at it, tangling their fingers in its curls as they jabbered and commented to one another.

"Please..." Stella had wanted to be friendly, but she was not used to this. She felt as if she were being picked apart. A small kernel of panic began to grow within her. When were these women going to stop? And where was Cade?

When one young squaw tried to thrust her finger into Stella's mouth to look at her teeth, Stella knew she had reached her limit. Half angry, half fearful, she pulled away. "Cade!" she called out. "Cade, help me!"

He came around the corner of the shed, an ax slung over his shoulder. When he caught sight of her, he laughed, the sound ringing loud in the stillness of the valley.

"It's not funny!" Stella protested. "They're hurting me!"

"All right." He spoke a few words in Shoshone, and the women began to move off. "Forgive them," he said. "They mean well. It's just that they've never seen a white woman up close before. They're very curious, that's all."

Stella brushed her tangled hair out of her face. "I want to make friends with them," she said. "But to have all four of them pinching and pulling at me like that—"

Cade added a few words of explanation in Shoshone. The women murmured contritely. From a safe distance now, Stella studied them, seeing them for the first time as individuals.

The oldest one, clearly the leader, had the look of a Roman matriarch. Her strong, proud features would have done justice to an ancient coin, and her bright blanket was flung around her body with the authority of a toga. Beneath an unruly thatch of iron-gray hair, her eyes were sharp, penetrating and shrewd.

The two who stood on either side of her were still girls and appeared to be sisters. They were pretty and plump, both of them, their black hair greased and pulled tightly back from round, good-natured faces. By turns, they kept stealing glances at Stella, then looking back at each other and giggling.

Cade stepped to the side of the older woman. "Stella," he said, speaking in a respectful tone, "I would like you to meet She-Bear, the eldest daughter of Chief Washakie." He hesitated. His pale eyes, seeking Stella's, were full of unspoken questions as he added, "I have the honor of being her son-in-law."

Stella's lips parted in surprise, but she quickly regained her poise. "Tell She-Bear that I, too, am honored to meet her," she said, hiding a rush of bewildering emotion. What was it to her that Cade's Shoshone wife had been this woman's daughter? Should it matter that this whole part of his life was strange and foreign to her?

"These are her nieces," Cade nodded toward the two plump girls, who responded by looking at their feet and tittering. "Shy Fawn and Little River."

"I'm pleased to meet you," Stella said with a friendly smile that sent the two girls into paroxysms of giggles.

The fourth woman had been standing behind the others, her blanket covering her hair and part of her face. Now Cade spoke to her and she stepped forward, the blanket falling back to frame her small, elegant head.

Stella saw that she was young—twenty, perhaps—and stunningly beautiful. Her face was a perfect oval, her eyes as large and soft as a doe's, her skin like polished mahogany against the bright red blanket. Her hair was parted down the middle and swept back in two glossy wings before being caught into a single braid down her back. When she moved, Stella realized that the young woman was with child, and her time was very close.

Cade spoke again. "Stella, this is She-Bear's daughter, Moon Bird." His eyes caught Stella's sudden, questioning look. "Yes," he said, meeting her gaze. "Moon Bird is my wife's younger sister."

Stella murmured a greeting, only half-aware of the words. Seeing Moon Bird was like catching a glimpse of the woman Cade had loved. She was filled with conflicting emotions—sympathy, admiration, jealousy—all at the same instant.

"Moon Bird's husband was a young war chief, killed by the Sioux last spring," Cade said. "Widows have a difficult time, especially in the winter, with no man to do the hunting, so Washakie has taken her into his household. In the spring, after her widowhood has lasted a full year, then she'll be ready to marry again."

"She's lovely," Stella said, realizing that the sorrow in Moon Bird's eyes only added to her beauty. "I wouldn't expect her to have any trouble finding a new husband."

"Oh, no. Half the braves in the tribe will want her. Some of them have already spoken to Washakie."

"I can see why," Stella said, but she had noticed the direction of Moon Bird's gaze and the way her dark eyes softened when Cade spoke. Many braves might want her, but if Moon Bird could have her way in the matter, it was clear she would choose the white warrior who had married her sister.

Stella forced back her own emotions. "Is it wise for her to be up and about in her condition?" she asked Cade.

Cade did not answer her question, and she realized his attention had shifted back to She-Bear. The older woman was speaking to him in Shoshone.

He turned to Stella. "It would please her if you invited them into the cabin," he said. "And it might be nice to give them something—a little flour or sugar, or the biscuits left over from last night would be fine."

Stella looked at the Indian women and tried to mask her nervousness with a smile. "Would you ask them to come with me, please?" she said to Cade.

"Why don't you ask them yourself?" Cade said. "This is what you say...." He spoke a short phrase in Shoshone, slowly, so that Stella could hear every syllable. "Try it," he said.

Stella tried laboriously to imitate the strange sounds. Her efforts sent all four of the women into gales of laughter. But the ice was broken. They followed Stella into the cabin, and the rest of the visit went well.

After they had gone, the four of them trudging off in a line across the melting pasture and into the trees, Stella sank onto the edge of the porch. Cade, she noticed, was smiling at her.

"You didn't do too badly," he said, easing himself onto one of the lower steps.

"Oh...." Stella groaned and shook her head. "Do you think I gave them enough flour and biscuits? They kept looking at me!"

"You were a very gracious hostess, under the circumstances," Cade said. "They seemed quite pleased."

Stella gazed at the sets of narrow moccasin tracks, already dark where the pressed snow was soaking into the ground. "I wish I'd had my camera," she said. "And I wish I could have really talked to them. Could you at least teach me their names in Shoshone?"

"I could." Cade stretched his arms, clasping his hands around one knee. "But most Shoshone names are long and hard to say. This, for example, is She-Bear's name in Shoshone...." He uttered a string of syllables so complex that Stella threw up her hands in surrender.

"But Washakie's name is Shoshone, and it's easy," she protested. "The names can't all be that bad."

"But most of them are a bit hard to pronounce," Cade said. "Washakie got his name as a youth, when he killed his first buffalo. He took the skin that covered its skull, dried it and made it into a rattle that he carried with him. That's how he came to be called Washakie, the rattler. What his name was before that—" Cade shrugged "—no one remembers."

"Has he always been so friendly to whites?" Stella asked.

"Always," Cade answered. "In fact, about nine years ago, his refusal to go to war almost cost him the leadership of the tribe. But believe me, it's not out of any great love for his white brothers. Washakie's first concern is for the Shoshone. From the beginning, he was smart enough to realize that their best chance of survival was an alliance with the whites. And he's made sure that alliance wasn't just one-sided. In return for his help and friendship, he's insisted on decent treatment for his people."

"Has it worked?"

"Not always, I'm afraid. There've been plenty of broken promises. But yesterday he told me that the government had offered him this land, the whole Wind River Valley, as a reservation for his tribe. He's very pleased about it."

"And what about the Sioux?" Stella asked, remembering what Cade had told her earlier. "Will they still come here to hunt?"

"Washakie is hoping the army will help him chase the Sioux out for good. But until that happens, he's going to have to deal with them himself," Cade answered. "And that brings me to something else."

Stella looked at him expectantly.

"In other years, Washakie's band has set up their camp in this arm of the valley, down there by the lake," he said. "They like that spot because it's sheltered from the wind and because it's close to water. I've welcomed them because their company makes the winters here less lonesome."

"Will they be camping here this winter?" Stella asked. "I think I'd like that."

"They will if you say it's all right." Cade shifted his position on the step so that he was looking directly up at her. "Washakie, you see, is a sensitive person. He was afraid that you, as a white woman, might be nervous about having his people around. He didn't want to make trouble between you and me because of it."

Stella gazed out at the pasture, where Snow-in-Summer was frisking in the morning sunlight. "Is that why he gave me the filly?" she asked.

"No. He did it because he's a generous man, and he wanted you to be pleased," Cade said. "I know him. That's the way he is."

"But it shouldn't be up to me," Stella protested. "This is your land and theirs, not mine. Besides, I might not even be here much longer. Look at the snow. It's melting. Soon you'll be able to take me to Laramie.''

Cade stared at the sky, his pale eyes narrow. "Maybe," he said, his voice sounding detached and faraway. "But Washakie wants your consent before he moves the camp. May I tell him he has it?''

"Of course.''

Cade stood up and cleared his throat. When he turned back to face Stella, something in his expression had changed.

"You're not telling me everything," she said, reacting to her own instincts. "There's something else. What is it?''

Cade sighed. "I didn't want to alarm you. I know what you must have gone through when Knute and Karin died—''

"The Sioux...." Stella felt her throat tighten.

"Washakie tells me he's seen signs that they're in the Wind River Valley. Tracks. Campsites with the coals still warm. Arrows...''

"Is it Red Hawk?''

Cade shook his head. "That's hard to say. From the signs, it looks like a small hunting or raiding party, but no-body's actually seen them." His hand brushed Stella's shoulder. She felt her whole body respond to his touch. "Don't worry," he said. "Even if it is Red Hawk, we'll be safe here, with Washakie's band close by.''

"And what about when we leave here? What then?''

He seemed to avoid her eyes. "Washakie would send along an escort as far as the Sweetwater. We'd be all right after that.''

Stella gazed out across the pasture, the October sun warm on her face. The sky was like polished turquoise, with only a few wispy clouds drifting above the Wind River peaks. Behind her, she could hear the sound of melting snow, dripping off the eaves of the cabin. Soon, she thought, this peaceful interlude would be over. She would be making the grim journey to Laramie, to face what had to be faced.

"One question," she said to Cade.

"Ask it." His voice was calm, his manner relaxed, as if he, too, had fallen under the gentle spell of the morning.

"Do you have a Shoshone name?"

"I do. Washakie gave it to me when I was adopted by the tribe. Would you like to hear it?"

Stella nodded, then laughed when he gave her the Shoshone version of his name. "No, I'll never be able to say it. What does it mean?"

"It means Yellow Wolf."

"Yellow Wolf." Stella turned the name over in her mind. "Yes, I like it," she said. "It suits you."

Later, after Cade had saddled the roan and gone off to speak with Washakie, Stella remembered Moon Bird. She had meant to ask Cade more about his beautiful sister-in-law, to learn, perhaps, what was behind the way she had looked at him.

But, no. She forced the very idea out of her mind. Cade's relationship with Moon Bird, if any, was none of her business. If she questioned him, he would only think she was jealous—an emotion to which she had no right. Cade, she knew, planned to spend the rest of his life here, among the Shoshone. It made all the sense in the world that his choice for a second wife would be the sister of the woman he had loved.

As for herself... Stella gazed out across the pasture, her eyes tracing the trail the roan had left in the melting snow. If the law ruled that she had to pay for killing Jared Garrison, there was no point in her making any plans at all. But if the jury found her innocent and set her free, there would be no limits to what she could do. She could return to the East, invest in more photographic equipment and go anywhere in the world. She would put Cade firmly behind her—grateful for what she had learned, but knowing it was for the best. The Wind River Valley was Cade's home, and the Shoshone were his people. If she were to stay, she would be as out of place as poor little Karin Aarnson had been.

Not that she had a choice, she reminded herself. For all that had passed between them, Cade had given no sign that he would ask her to stay. It was one thing for him to feel physical desire for her, quite another for him to build a life with the woman who had killed his brother.

Restless, she got up from the porch step and walked out to the pasture fence. Snow-in-Summer, hoping for a tidbit from the kitchen, nickered and trotted over to her. The velvety pink muzzle poked eagerly at Stella's pockets.

"Nothing for you this time, sweetheart," Stella murmured, stroking the silky white face. "Oh, what a beauty you are. And what a shame I won't be around this spring to ride you!" Overcome by sudden emotion, she pressed her face into the warmth of the filly's neck.

Chapter Twelve

By midmorning, Washakie's band had begun to move into the valley. Stella viewed the spectacle from the safe distance of the porch at first, using Cade's field glass to get a closer look.

"As long as you want to see what's going on, you may as well do it from up close," Cade said. "Give me a minute to saddle the horses, and I'll take you over there."

Intrigued but hesitant, she lowered the glass. "You're sure they won't mind?"

"They'll be too busy to pay much attention to us. Come on. It's a sight you won't soon forget."

Before she could protest, he was off to saddle the red stallion and the Appaloosa mare. He came riding back around the cabin on the roan a few minutes later, his face concerned.

"Your mare is limping," he said. "She must have twisted something when she slipped and went down with you the other day. It's probably nothing, but we'd better give her a rest. Do you mind riding double?"

"Why not? I've had plenty of practice!" Stella laughed. "Let's go."

He leaned down toward her and held out his arm. Stella let him swing her up behind him in the saddle, much as he had the night they'd ridden away from Green River with the lynch mob howling behind them. It felt natural, somehow, to sit behind Cade on the roan once more, her hair flying in the breeze, her arms wrapped lightly around his waist.

They skirted the pasture and galloped down around the small, frozen lake. "Remind me to get you a horse you can ride while the mare's mending," Cade said. "There'd have been plenty for you to choose from, but I sold most of my herd last spring. The only reason I had the Appaloosa is because I'd kept her for breeding."

"Do you always do that? Sell off your horses?"

"Usually. Spring's the best time to do it, because that's when the miners and settlers are most apt to need them. The horses that aren't sold, I turn over to Washakie, to run with his herd till fall. Otherwise, the Sioux would steal them."

"I saw the braves herding horses. There were hundreds of them! Are any of those horses yours?"

"Oh, just forty or fifty head. They'll have my brand on them. You can have your pick from the ones that are broken." He laughed. "Owning that many horses makes me a rich man by Shoshone standards, if not by the rest of the world's. Only Washakie has more."

Yes, a rich man, and a fine catch for a pretty, young Shoshone widow, Stella mused. Then she was immediately annoyed at her own reaction. She had crossed that emotional bridge once already, she reminded herself as they rode into the bustling camp. She'd be a fool to go back over it again.

The burgeoning village was a maze of activity. Cade wheeled the roan hard to avoid a bundle of lodgepoles swinging from the side of a trotting Indian pony. Stella had to grab his waist to keep from sliding down the stallion's slippery rump. Children and dogs raced almost under the roan's hooves. Some of the women were unloading rolled-up buffalo hides and leather parfleches from the pack-horses. Others were lashing the long lodgepoles together to make the frames for the teepees.

Stella caught a glimpse of She-Bear directing several younger women as they erected a huge pole framework near the middle of the camp.

"That will be Washakie's lodge," Cade said. "Those are his wives and his unmarried daughters. She-Bear, as a widow, doesn't have any real status, but at times like this, she runs them all."

The women, Stella noticed, were doing most of the work. "Where's Washakie?" she asked. "Where are the other braves?"

"Hunting, most likely," Cade said. "The camp will need meat once the lodges are up."

"But that's not fair!" Stella protested. "Look, those poles are heavy! The men should be doing that!"

Cade chuckled sardonically. "I'm afraid you're arguing with centuries of tradition, Stella. The women move the camp, the men hunt. It's always been that way."

But Stella had scarcely heard them. She had just spotted Moon Bird, struggling to raise a heavy lodgepole. Her body was perilously round beneath her shapeless cotton dress.

"No!" Stella was off the horse like a shot, her hands grasping the rough pole, taking the burden of its weight.

"You mustn't try to do this!" she scolded Moon Bird. "It's bad for you! You could hurt yourself or your baby!"

Moon Bird seemed to understand, but she was not ready to give in. She tightened her own grip on the pole, her jaw set, her lovely eyes defiant. By now She-Bear had also caught sight of what was going on. She bore down on the two younger women, her words like the sharp chatter of an angry blue jay.

In desperation, Stella turned to Cade. "Make them understand! Moon Bird shouldn't be doing this kind of work!"

Cade had dismounted by now. He spoke quietly to She-Bear, who clearly did not welcome the interference. Her reply, again, was swift and sharp.

Cade translated for Stella. "She says that all the women are needed to help. Moon Bird is healthy, and she cannot be excused from her share of the work." His eyes and voice softened. "I know you mean well, Stella, but you can't expect to step right in and change their traditions."

Stella glanced at Moon Bird, who was still clinging to the pole. For all her tenacity, she looked weary. Her pretty face was drawn and, though the day was not warm, her forehead was beaded with sweat.

"Look at her. She's not having an easy time," Stella said to Cade. "Tell She-Bear that if she must have someone to help, I'll take Moon Bird's place."

"Stella—"

"Would you at least ask her, Cade? Please."

The look he gave her blended amusement, exasperation and, perhaps, a grudging approval. He turned and spoke to She-Bear, who lifted her eyebrows in surprise, looked Stella up and down and finally grunted her acceptance.

Cade ushered Moon Bird to a seat on a stack of firewood. She sank down wearily, following him with her eyes as he walked back to his horse. Then, at a command from She-Bear, the work commenced again.

Stella's muscles strained as she helped raise the towering lodgepoles, bracing them while they were anchored into place. She-Bear was no gentle taskmaster. Her sharp tongue lashed at everyone, including the red-haired stranger who had taken over her daughter's work. Much of her prodding, in fact, seemed to be directed right at Stella.

Under her jacket and warm flannel shirt, Stella felt the sweat running down her body. She lunged to catch a swaying pole, slipped against the muddy earth and would have fallen if Cade had not stepped in and caught her. She felt his arms bracing her body, steadying her until she regained her footing. Then, suddenly she realized he was working at her side, ignoring the giggles of the younger women as he helped balance the poles and anchor them to the ground. "Thank you," Stella whispered.

When it was finally finished, Washakie's lodge was a splendid structure—strong, light and surprisingly roomy. Stella straightened, massaged her aching back and glanced around the camp. By now most of the other tepees were finished, as well. Cooking fires crackled in the open, fed by kindling the young children had gathered. In a few chaotic hours, the camp had taken on the well-ordered bustle of a village. A small miracle, Stella thought, wishing once again that she'd been able to save her camera. The photographs she could have taken today!

"Well done!" Cade's voice behind her was like a swift hug, warm and hearty.

"You, too." Stella turned her head and smiled up at him, feeling a new sense of kinship with this man, with the place he called his home and the people he called his brothers. Today she had crossed barriers that she'd once thought were impassable.

Then, out of the corner of her eye, she caught a glimpse of Moon Bird, standing beside She-Bear. Both women were looking at her, the mother with ill-disguised disapproval, the daughter with hot-eyed resentment. The sight of them sobered Stella. Some things never changed, she reminded herself. She was still very much an intruder here in the Wind River Valley. In the eyes of She-Bear and her daughter, she would remain an intruder until she left.

Well, that day was not far off, Stella resolved. As soon as she got a chance to talk with Cade alone, she would ask him to take her to Laramie. The snow from the early fall blizzard was melting. Soon the passes would be clear again. The plains would be safe until the next big winter storm. Now, while they had the chance, would be the time to go.

Cade was walking back toward his horse. As she turned to follow him, Stella felt a cool breeze lifting the damp tendrils of hair from the back of her neck. She glanced up at the sky and saw that a blanket of clouds, as thick as newly clipped wool, had drifted in above the peaks.

The roan snorted and shook its russet hide as Cade swung himself into the saddle. Stella, her muscles aching, clasped his hand and let him pull her up behind. She-Bear and Moon Bird watched with sullen eyes as she wrapped her arms around his lean, hard body and held on.

The ride back to the cabin was unhurried. Cade gave the stallion its head, letting it pick its own way among the bristling clumps of yellow grass. Stella leaned lightly against the back of his buckskin jacket. The work on the tepee had been tiring and, she realized, she had not fully recovered from being ill. It felt good just to rest against Cade's strong back while the roan took its time in getting home.

"You overdid it back there," he scolded her gently. "You'll be due for a nap when we get back to the cabin."

"I only wanted to help," she said. "But they didn't even thank me."

He was silent for a few moments. "They're proud people, Stella. Within their lifetime, they've seen most of their hunting ground go to the whites. They've seen most of the buffalo killed. Now, instead of the great hunts of old times, they're forced to live on handouts from their white brothers. They don't like charity—not any more than you or I would."

"You're saying that I shouldn't have offered to help."

Cade shook his head. "Your helping was kind and generous. I'm just warning you not to expect a big show of gratitude."

"I see," Stella murmured, knowing well he had not fully explained the reasons behind She-Bear and Moon Bird's animosity. Perhaps he hadn't even noticed. Men tended to overlook things like that—things that almost any female would spot at once.

"Don't be discouraged," he said. "They're good women. They'll be friendlier once they get to know you."

Gathering her courage, Stella pounced on the opening. "They may not get much chance to know me. The snow is melting, Cade. By tomorrow, most of it will be gone. There'll be no more reason to put off taking me to Laramie."

Cade did not reply at once, but she felt the muscles tighten beneath his jacket, and she wondered if she had made him angry. The wind that ruffled her hair suddenly seemed colder.

At last he spoke. "Look at the sky, Stella."

She lifted her head and gazed past his shoulder, toward the jagged line that separated the rocky peaks from the sky.

Clouds were scudding in from the west—cold, gray banks of clouds that churned and tumbled like the sea. Stella had seen such clouds before, and she knew this time what they would bring. Speechless, she stared at them, emotions warring inside her. Laramie, again, would have to wait. And her life here, in the Wind River Valley, would continue a little longer.

As they reached the cabin, Stella felt the first tiny, cold flake on her cheek. While Cade secured the horses in their stalls, she hurried to gather firewood and carry it inside. By the time they had finished, the wind had picked up, tossing the thin flakes around like handfuls of down.

By nightfall, the air was a swirling, stinging mass of white. The snow had covered the shallow grass in the corral, and drifts were already forming along the pasture fence.

Cade lifted the ax and brought it down hard. The block of firewood he was chopping split cleanly in two, the sound echoing like a gunshot in the wintery silence. His breath came in cloudy puffs as he bent to gather up the chips that were scattered over the crusty snow.

A week had passed since the storm. The snow was no deeper than with most fall blizzards, but the cold spell that had set in was unusually bitter. It froze the trough solid every morning and left icicles as long and thick as Cade's arm hanging from the eaves of the cabin.

Then there was the wind. It eased up during the day, but at night it howled around the cabin like a lonesome timber wolf. It rattled the windows, whistled through the rags Stella stuffed under the door and made the flames dance crazily in the fireplace.

That wind—yes, Cade thought—that was what made the nights so bad. Lying there alone in the loft, listening to that eerie, mournful sound, while Stella lay in the bed below, her woman's body warm and out of reach. There were times, during those long, windy nights, when Cade felt as if he would die from wanting her. But he could not go to her, he knew. And she did not come to him.

The days were easier. There were things to do then: hunting, chopping wood, caring for the horses and visits to the Shoshone camp. Stella had picked out a spunky black mustang from the herd, and she often rode alongside Cade when he went to visit Washakie. She had discovered the children of the band, and while Cade talked with the chief, she would gather them around her, teaching them simple finger games and passing out small treats from the kitchen. Cade marveled at the way she seemed to communicate with them—neither she nor they speaking a word of one another's language.

Even the women in the camp were warming to her, though She-Bear and Moon Bird were as distant as ever. Cade was not blind to the reason why. Washakie himself had mentioned She-Bear's intention to keep Cade as her son-in-law, and it was plain that She-Bear viewed Stella as an obstacle to her plan.

Which was a shame, Cade reflected, since he had already made up his mind that he did not want to take another bride from among the Shoshone. He had loved Rain Flower well, but these past few weeks with Stella had made him acutely aware of what had been missing from his life. He needed a companion who could share his love for books, music, art and poetry, someone he could talk with about the world he had left behind. Someone who, one day, might travel with him to see that world once more. He did not want to die, he realized, without hearing Beethoven again, without seeing *Hamlet* and *Lear*, or viewing some of the world's great paintings. He needed someone who understood that. Someone like Stella.

But, no. He brought the ax down on a log with an abrupt whack, as if cutting off the very thought. The obstacles between Stella and himself were too great to overcome. And until the matter of her guilt in Jared's death was resolved, she was a woman without a future. That was a harsh way of putting it, but it was the way things stood, and there was little he could do to change them.

The evening wind tugged at Cade's Stetson as he gathered up the cut logs. From the cabin, he could smell the antelope haunch that Stella was roasting over the fire. There would be fresh biscuits to go with it, he knew, as well as potatoes and carrots from the root cellar. He had been working outside most of the day, and he was ravenously hungry. He hurried with the wood.

It was beginning to snow again—not the thick wet snow of a heavy blizzard; it was too cold for that. The flakes that were falling now were dry and scanty, no more than swirling ice flecks on the wind.

Something caught Cade's eye as he glanced up from retrieving a stray piece of kindling. A figure on horseback was moving through the twilight, coming toward the cabin from the direction of the lake.

Cade thought it was one of the Shoshone at first. Then he heard the echoing "hallooo," a sound an Indian would never make, and he realized his visitor was a white man.

His first thought was for Stella. If the approaching stranger was a lawman or a bounty hunter, she could be in great danger. He ought to get into the cabin, he thought. He could hide her in the loft before the intruder got much closer.

He had started for the porch when he heard the voice again. "Cade! Cade Garrison! Is that you, you son of a hound dog?"

"Sam?" Disbelief echoed in Cade's voice as the figure swam in and out of focus in the swirling snow. Cade's eyes made out a tall scarecrow of a rider in a broad-brimmed hat, hunched forward against the biting cold. He blinked, still not quite daring to believe his eyes or ears. There would be no need to take Stella to Laramie now. Incredibly, Laramie had come to them.

United States Marshal Samuel T. Catlin reined his horse alongside the corral fence and slid wearily out of the saddle. His thick eyebrows and bristling mustache were iced with frost from his breath. "Hell, but it's cold!" he grunted. "Thought I'd freeze my backside to the saddle before I got here."

Cade held the horse, a powerful, rangy bay, while Sam stomped the circulation back into his feet. He couldn't help wondering why the veteran lawman had braved the fearsome weather and the Indians to come here. There was always the chance that Sam's appearance had nothing to do with Stella, he told himself, but he wouldn't bet money on it; this visit had to be more than just a social call.

"How did you get through, Sam?" he asked, trying not to sound worried. "I thought the passes would all be blocked with snow."

"And they would be, except for this god-awful wind." Sam flexed his gloved hands and brushed some of the frost from his grizzled face. "Blowed some of 'em cleaner than the back of a newborn shote. But it's been tough goin' in this cold. Hope to hell you can spare a bed and a hot meal."

He took the reins from Cade and began to lead the big bay toward the shed. As they passed the cabin, he took a deep breath and smacked his lips appreciatively. "Sure smells good. Biscuits and all, I can tell." He gave Cade a shrewd, sidelong glance. "You never were much of a cook, you know, son. I always said that's what comes of growin' up rich." He plodded along in the snow for a few steps while Cade wondered what to say next.

Sam cleared his throat. "Heard about your little ruckus down in Green River," he said. "I figured I'd find you up here."

"She wants to give herself up, Sam," Cade said, almost relieved that the marshal knew. "We were coming to find you in Laramie. If it hadn't been for the snow—"

"I never talk business on an empty stomach." Sam unbuckled the cinch from under the bay's belly and hefted off the saddle. "Found through long experience that hunger muddles a man's judgment, and I haven't had a bite since dawn. Feed this nag here, and let's get some vittles down me. Then we'll talk."

Cade poured a bucket of oats while Sam slipped the bridle off the bay. The horse snorted as it lowered its big head. Its mouth munched and snuffled eagerly at the oats.

"So much for him," Sam said. "Now, let's us go on inside. I've heard quite a bit about this red-haired lady friend of yours, and I'll confess I'm downright anxious to meet her."

Stella was bent over the fire, basting the antelope roast, when she heard Cade come in. It was not until she turned around that she saw the lanky stranger standing at his side.

Startled, she gasped. Her hand went to her throat. The man was so covered with snow and frost that he looked like an unearthly winter ghost.

"It's all right, Stella," Cade said quickly. "This is Marshal Sam Catlin from Laramie. It seems he didn't wait for us to go and find him."

Something inside Stella sank like a stone. She had thought she was ready to face the law and resolve the matter of her guilt. Now she realized that she was not ready at all. She needed time, she told herself frantically—time to sort out the feelings that clashed and tumbled inside her, time to strengthen herself for the awful consequences that would come to pass if she could not prove her innocence.

Without being asked, Sam Catlin strode over to the fire. He was taller than Cade and as thin as a lodgepole, with close-clipped gray hair and a bristling mustache that overhung his long, prominent jaw. When he took off his snow-encrusted sheepskin coat, Stella saw the massive pistol that hung at his hip.

"Lordy, I forgot what warm feels like!" he said, rubbing his hands together. "But I've not forgot my manners. Right pleased to meet you, Missus Brannon. Seems you've caused quite a stir."

"I'd planned to turn myself in to you," Stella said. "Ask Cade."

"Already did. But business'll keep till I've filled up this hole in my gut. Those biscuits smell mighty good."

"I'll set another place at the table." Stella moved like a marionette, strings pulled taut. Beneath her icy calm surface, she was feeling more like a trapped animal. She battled the urge to run out the door, leap astride Cade's big roan and bolt for the hills. Freezing, starving, getting eaten by the wolves—anything would be better than becoming a prisoner again.

Cade carved the roast while Stella dished up the vegetables and biscuits. The meal was eaten in an atmosphere of tension—a tension to which Sam Catlin seemed oblivious. He ate heartily, praising the food and interspersing mouthfuls with comments about the weather, the railroad and the Indians. Stella and Cade sat on either side of him, responding in monosyllables, forcing themselves to eat.

Cade seemed especially restless. Stella, watching the play of the firelight on his features, sensed that he was struggling to hold words and emotions in check—a struggle that he did not seem to be winning.

At last, as the marshal was sopping the last of the gravy from his plate with the last biscuit, Cade spoke up.

"Blast it, Sam, you can't take her in now. Not in this weather. You barely made it here yourself. And that's not the worst of it. Washakie says he's seen fresh signs of Sioux in the area. I can't let you—"

"Relax son." Sam wiped his mouth with a napkin and leaned back in his chair. "I hadn't planned on taking her in. Leastwise not this trip. To tell you the truth, right now I've got bigger fish to fry."

Stella put her fork down and stared at him. "Then, what—"

"Just give me a minute, and I'll tell you." Sam's eyes, set deep beneath grizzled eyebrows, shifted from Stella to Cade and back again. "Listen good, now. Far as you two are concerned, I only stopped by because I was in the neighborhood. The real reason I'm up this way is that I've been trailin' a wanted man—a dirty galoot who killed a dance-hall girl in Laramie last week. I tracked him as far as the north pass, then lost the trail in this damned blowing snow.

But lessn' he's made it out some other way, he could still be here in the Wind River. Thought I'd better warn you to keep a sharp eye out.''

"Killed a girl, you say?" Cade asked.

"That's right. Amy Corrigan, that was her name. Pretty little yellow-haired thing—before he got to her. Seems she'd left South Pass just to get away from him. But he followed her to Laramie, used her and then carved her up pretty good with his knife. Lord, there are some sights a man would like to forget...."

Stella glanced toward Cade. His right hand was gripping the edge of the table so hard that the fingertips were white. Why was he reacting so strongly? she wondered. What did he know?

"The girl lived long enough to tell us who did it," Sam said. Then he paused for dramatic effect, as if he were about to lay a set of four aces on the table.

"It was a miner from South Pass," he said. "Big, black-bearded fellow named Newt Gillis."

Chapter Thirteen

Sam picked up his coffee cup and took a long, slow sip. "Let me make one thing clear now," he said. "I heard how you claimed Gillis was in your tent, Missus Brannon, and how you said you were fightin' him off when you shot young Jared. After seein' what Gillis did to the Corrigan girl, frankly, I'm inclined to believe you."

Stella closed her eyes, relief welling up in her so hard that it made her throat ache. "Thank you," she whispered. "Oh, dear God, thank you."

"Not so fast, now." Sam set his empty cup down with a sharp rap on the table. "I said *I* believed you. But the sad, hard truth is, lady, that in the eyes of the law, what I think personally doesn't amount to a hill o' beans! Circumstantial evidence, that's what they call it. Gillis could murder half the women in the territory, and that still wouldn't prove he was in your tent when you say he was!"

Cade spoke up quietly. "Sam's right, Stella. Without evidence or a confession from Gillis, you're no better off than before."

Stella fought back sudden tears as she forced herself to face the truth. "I know," she murmured. "I know that much about the law."

"I'll be leaving at first light," Sam said. "By rights I ought to arrest you now and take you with me. But Cade's right about this weather. It's too cold. Too dangerous for a woman out there." He turned to Cade. "I want your word on it. You'll bring her to Laramie soon as the weather clears."

Cade hesitated, then glanced at Stella, who nodded. "You have it," he promised.

"After I leave here, I'll be cutting south and then west to Fort Bridger," Sam said. "Be there a few days just resting up. Then I'll head back to Green River and catch the train for Laramie. Since you two will be travelling by horse, I should be waiting when you get there."

"Why Bridger?" Cade asked, puzzled. "It's a good three or four days out of your way."

"I know." Sam yawned wearily. "But they're holding a prisoner for me there. Some devil who's wanted in three states. It's my job to get him back as far as Cheyenne. Besides, from what I heard, Gillis has a friend or two around the fort. There's always the chance he'll show up there. He may have thrown me off his trail this time, but he can't survive alone in the mountains all winter. Not unless he's half grizzly bear and can hibernate." Sam yawned again and stretched his long, sinewy arms. "Well folks, I'm all tuckered out. Got anyplace a body can rest?"

"I'll rig another bed in the loft for you," Cade offered. "I'm afraid it's ladies only downstairs."

"Long as I don't have to sleep standin' up," Sam said. Then he turned to Stella. "I'm much obliged for the tasty supper. Now, don't you lose any sleep, hear? I always like to help out a lady, and I'll do everything I can to see that this mess is straightened out."

"Thank you," Stella murmured. "That's all I ask."

After the men had gone to bed, she lay staring at the moon through the window, too agitated to close her eyes. Hope was a cruel emotion, she reflected. It kept a body constantly on edge, fraying the nerves, muddling the mind. If Gillis was captured, if he confessed to having attacked her in her tent, Sam Catlin would see to it that she went free. If not—

From the loft above her, she could hear the faint rumble of Sam's snoring. She turned over, punched her lumpy feather pillow into shape and tried once more to go to sleep. So many *ifs*! If Gillis could be found... If he could be taken alive... If he could be made to talk before he went to the gallows... If the judge believed Stella's story—no, if *Cade* believed it—somehow, that mattered most of all.

Restless and wide-eyed, she lay there, weighing the pieces of her life, one against another. It was nearly dawn before she drifted off at last, into a deep, uneasy slumber.

Sam had ridden off before daylight, in spite of Cade's urging that he stay for breakfast. "No, that would only take time," he'd said, slapping the saddle onto the big bay and jerking the cinch tight. "I've got a lot of ground to cover before sundown, and the weather's threatening to turn nasty again. I'd best get moving!"

While Sam bridled the horse, Cade had cut some thick slices of the antelope roast and wrapped them up along with some of Stella's bread. "Take this, at least," he'd insisted, pressing the small bundle on Sam. "You'll be hungry later on."

"That's right kind." Accepting the offering, Sam had swung his lanky frame into the saddle. "And I'll pay you back with some friendly advice, son." He looked sternly down at Cade, where he stood in the snow. "I can see you're taken with that girl, and I can't say as I blame you. She's as pretty as a red fox—makes me wish I was a few years younger, myself." His eyes narrowed. "But go slow. Don't let yourself get tangled up to where you'll get hurt. I'll do what I can to clear things. But if that can't be done, I'll have to take her in. It's the law, and it's my job, Cade. And there'll be hell to pay if you try to stop me."

"I know, and I understand." Cade gazed up at him. "Godspeed, Sam. Good luck."

Sam nodded, wheeled the horse and was off in a flurry of snow. Cade stood watching him till he vanished into the trees. Then he turned back toward the shed, Sam's words still ringing in his ears.

It was good advice, he told himself. It was true that Gillis's crime had helped Stella's case, but he couldn't let that change things. He would have to continue as he had before, keeping his feelings under tight rein. Otherwise, he realized to his dismay, when the time came, he would never be able to let her go.

He gazed at the sky, already growing pale above the distant hills. As long as he was up so early, he resolved, it would be a good morning for a short hunt. With luck, he could bring down a deer or some late migrating birds and be home before Stella was awake. There would be no danger in leaving her—not with the Shoshone camp so close by. No man, red or white, would be foolhardy enough to violate the circle of Washakie's protection.

Swiftly, before he could change his mind, he saddled the roan. Now all he needed was his rifle from inside the cabin. He would get it quietly, without waking Stella, and be off.

His boots were caked with snow. He kicked them lightly against the edge of the porch before he opened the door to the cabin, closing it softly behind him as he went inside. The Spencer was propped in a corner, next to the fireplace. Cade slipped a few bullets into his pocket and picked up the rifle, leaving the Colt behind for Stella, as he usually did.

The fire was getting low. He reached for a log and placed it on the coals. That would be enough to keep the cabin comfortable till she woke up, he told himself as he paused to warm his hands. Then she could build up the fire and start breakfast herself.

The quilt that concealed Stella's bed hung at the far end of the cabin. Behind it, there was no sound or movement, but he felt himself irresistibly drawn toward it. Maybe he ought to make sure she was all right before he left, Cade rationalized, moving softly in that direction. It would only take a few seconds. Then he'd go.

Reaching the quilt, he pushed it gently aside. Stella lay there in the bed, sleeping like a child, her tousled hair spread in soft disorder over the pillow. One arm was flung lightly above her head; the other lay bent across her breasts. The expression on her face was so peaceful, so innocent, that it tugged at Cade's heart.

This woman had killed his brother, he reminded himself. Even if the shooting had been accidental, there was no question that her hand had pulled the trigger.

In the past, that reminder had worked. It had almost always brought him up short when his attitude toward Stella Brannon showed signs of softening. Now, seeing her there, so tender and vulnerable, he found that the words had an empty ring to them. Was it because of the news Sam had brought? Or was it something else?

Since last night, he had been keeping Sam's story about Gillis at a distance, almost as if he were afraid to examine it too closely. Why? Cade asked himself now. It was clear that Gillis was capable of doing exactly what Stella claimed he had done. The only thing lacking was the proof that he had actually been in her tent when Jared was killed. With the law on Gillis's trail, there was at least a fair chance of getting that proof.

He ought to be glad for Stella, he thought. He ought to be relieved that she was one step closer to establishing her innocence. What in heaven's name was wrong with him? Was he such a ghoul that he *wanted* to see her judged guilty?

Jared. The realization hit Cade like a punch in the stomach. If his younger brother was not the innocent victim of a conniving woman, what was he? What could he have been doing in Stella's tent, if she had not lured him there? Why had Jared been with a man who'd turned out to be a rapist and a murderer, and how could he have just stood there and watched while Gillis attacked a woman? The questions loomed before Cade like a great, black pit. If Stella's version of how Jared had died turned out to be true, those questions would haunt him to the end of his days.

Stella stirred and moaned softly in her sleep. Cade lowered the quilt and retreated a few steps. It wouldn't do to have her awaken and see him looking at her that way. Besides, he reminded himself, he had been about to go hunting.

He checked the fireplace to make sure the new log was burning. Then he slipped outside, latching the door behind him. Even if he didn't see any game, he told himself, the ride would do him good. It would give him a chance to do some much needed thinking.

The roan, saddled and ready, was tied to the corral fence. At first Cade did not see the bundled figure standing beside it. When he did, he was so startled that he raised his rifle. Then he realized it was a woman—an Indian woman.

"Yellow Wolf, husband of my sister." The whispered voice, speaking in Shoshone, was Moon Bird's. "Forgive me. I must talk with you."

She stood gazing up at him, her body painfully swollen with her dead husband's child. Even now, her face was hauntingly beautiful, very like Rain Flower's had been, and yet not the same. Not the same at all.

"Iron Bow has asked Washakie for me," she said. "He has offered a fine riding horse and a new rifle...." She laughed bitterly. "There was a time when I would have been worth seven times that much, but now—"

"Iron Bow is a kind man and a skillful hunter," Cade said swiftly, also remembering that Iron Bow was no longer young and that he already had one wife. "You and your child would never go hungry."

"And you think that is all that matters to me?" She turned on him suddenly, hissing like an angry cat. "You fool! Can't you see that it's you I want? If you talk to Washakie today, before he gives Iron Bow an answer—"

Cade shook his head gently. "If you do not wish to marry Iron Bow, just tell Washakie how you feel. He would never force you—"

"But *you* will not speak to him!" Her face was stricken.

Cade sighed. A lie, he realized, would be even more heartless than the truth. "You are a beautiful woman, sister of my wife. Many fine men will want you, I know. But as for myself, I have decided not to take another bride from among the Shoshone. I am sorry—''

"It's the red-haired one you want, then!" Moon Bird interrupted waspishly. "But she does not plan to stay! Washakie told me so!"

"There are other reasons," Cade said quietly.

"But I would be your second wife, Yellow Wolf, if that was what you wanted." Moon Bird's tone and expression had changed. "You could have your white woman, too. For me, it would be better than being second wife to Iron Bow." Her fingers plucked at Cade's sleeve. "Remember when you were married to my sister, how I used to come to your house and make a game of learning your language? Even then I wanted you. Even then, I dared to hope you would take me, too, when I was older."

"That was a long time ago," Cade said gently.

"Not so long that I don't ache for you every time I think of it." She moved closer to him. "I still remember the white man's words you taught me, and I still want to be yours. You could speak to my grandfather—''

"No," Cade said, forcing himself to speak plainly. "I loved your sister, but things are not the same. *I* am not the same—''

"It's the white one who has changed you!" Moon Bird exclaimed. "Since she came to this valley, you are no longer one of us! You are no longer Shoshone!

"You'll be sorry!" She turned on her heel and spun away. "I'm going back to Washakie and tell him that I want to marry Iron Bow. When it is too late for you, Yellow Wolf, then you will see what a fool you have been!"

Cade watched her stalk away through the snow, waddling slightly in her advanced state of pregnancy. He knew that she wanted him to run after her or call her back. But no, he decided, it was better to leave well enough alone. He was embarrassed for Moon Bird, but the girl would be all right. She was as strong willed as she was beautiful. Today she would lick her wounds; tomorrow she would set her sights on someone else.

Shaking his head, he put a boot in the stirrup and swung himself into the saddle. Yes, he reflected as he nudged the roan to a trot, this would be an excellent time to go hunting.

Stella turned away from the window, upset with herself for having watched the entire scene. Whatever passed between Cade and Moon Bird was none of her business, she told herself for perhaps the tenth time. Still, there was no mistaking the intense emotions involved in what she had seen. A lovers' quarrel of some sort, she surmised with a sigh. A bit of jealousy, perhaps, on Moon Bird's part.

Whatever the cause of it, the confrontation had ended badly. Cade had galloped off with his rifle, probably to hunt, and Moon Bird was storming her way back to the Shoshone village.

Stella pattered over to the washstand and began to brush her hair with hard, rough strokes. She really hadn't meant to watch, she told herself. The sound of the door closing had awakened her, and she had glanced outside, expecting to see Cade with Sam Catlin. Instead, she had seen Moon Bird and, to her chagrin, she had not been able to tear her eyes away.

Cade's relationship with Moon Bird was his own business, she reminded herself as she pulled the flannel nightshirt over her head and flung it on the chair. She had enough problems of her own without getting involved in matters that didn't concern her. She would just have to put the scene out of her mind.

She dressed swiftly and snatched a quick bite of crusty bread for breakfast. Then she took three carrots and went outside to check on the horses.

The filly and the mustang were frisking around the pasture, snorting and nipping playfully at each other. As soon as they saw Stella with the carrots, they trotted toward the fence, their breath misting on the frigid morning air. The Appaloosa mare came more sedately from the shed, her limp noticeably better today. Already, their winter coats were growing so thick and shaggy that they caught the burrs. Stella had spent an hour yesterday just combing them out.

She fed them the carrots, scratching their ears and murmuring nonsensical little love phrases. They responded by nuzzling at her pockets and mouthing her hair. Stella laughed, enjoying the feeling, using it to warm the chill that seeing Cade and Moon Bird had left inside her.

As she turned to go back inside the cabin, her eyes caught sight of Moon Bird's fresh moccasin tracks in the snow. She could see the line of prints across the pasture where Moon Bird had trekked all the way from her village—too far, Stella reflected, for a woman in her condition. Here Moon Bird's tracks met Cade's—yes, this was where they had stood and talked. Then Cade had mounted and ridden off, and Moon Bird had ...

Stella blinked. There were no moccasin tracks leading back toward the Shoshone camp. Instead, the small footprints went for about twenty yards in that direction, then turned back and followed the trail that Cade's roan had taken.

Puzzled and worried, Stella tried to piece together what had happened. It looked as if Moon Bird had started back toward her village in a huff, expecting Cade to call her back or go after her. When, instead, he had just ridden off, she had been upset enough to turn around and try to follow him.

Stella's eyes traced the roan's trail till it disappeared in the trees. From the way the snow had been thrown up, she could tell that Cade had been riding at a good, swift trot. That speed would have put him far ahead of Moon Bird. In all likelihood, he would not even have known she was trailing him.

Stella sighed. The girl was an impulsive fool. With the birth of her child so near, she was taking a terrible risk. But then, in her senseless anger, that could be exactly what Moon Bird intended. Cade would be forced to blame himself for any mishap that befell her, and his guilt would be his punishment.

Exasperated, Stella turned away from the tracks. Let Moon Bird play her silly game, she told herself. It was not her problem! She had more important things to worry about!

Turning swiftly, she started back toward the cabin. She had almost reached the porch when another realization struck her hard—so hard that it stopped her in her tracks.

Moon Bird had not gone running off into the forest alone. She carried another life with her—a small, helpless life, which could already be in grave danger.

Stella glanced up at the sky. The dawn was overcast. Dark clouds, heavy with moisture, were scudding in above the Wind River peaks. The breeze was damp and slightly warm.

By now she knew the signs. More snow, probably within the hour. There was no time to be lost. Swiftly she darted inside the cabin, where she snatched up the pistol Cade had left, along with a knife and, as an afterthought, a warm blanket from the bed, which she tied around her waist. Then she ran back outside to saddle the mustang.

Half an hour from the cabin, Cade had brought down a two-point buck. By the time he had dressed the carcass and tied it to the back of the saddle, the air was thick with feathery white flakes.

The short excursion had been good for him, he reflected as he circled back through the softly falling snow. It had given his mind the chance to clear a bit, to digest Sam's news and put Stella's situation in its proper perspective.

The truth, he decided, was the most important thing of all. And in getting to that truth, he could not let himself be blinded, either by his desire for Stella or his loyalty to Jared. He had to force himself to be clearheaded, to see things as they really were and to act accordingly. If Stella was innocent and his brother had been involved in a vile act, he would have to accept that and let her return to the world she had left behind. If her innocence could not be proven—

Suddenly Cade found himself unable to finish the thought.

Impatient, he spurred the roan hard. The big stallion shot forward, and they raced for home, plunging over logs and leaping small gullies in the blinding, whirling snow.

Cade felt as if he were on fire, burning with a rage he was at a loss to explain. He only knew, somehow, that he had to get back to the cabin, back to Stella. He had to feel her in his arms, feel her lips, soft beneath his crushing kisses, feel her body, arching to meet his—that was truth, raw and simple. He needed her.

By the time he cleared the foothills, the landscape was covered with a fresh layer of white. Through the falling snow, Cade could see the cabin. Everything looked quiet— perhaps too quiet, he mused uneasily. There was not even any smoke coming out of the chimney. Stella must not have put any more wood on the fire. Why not? he wondered. Could she still be asleep at this hour? Could she be ill?

The white filly stood under the sheltering eaves of the shed, the spotted mare in the open, a few yards away. There was no sign of Stella's black mustang. When Cade dismounted and led the roan inside, he saw that her saddle was gone, as well.

Maybe she'd ridden to the Indian Village, he speculated as he unloaded the dead deer and hung it from a hook on one of the crossbeams. She must have gotten lonesome by herself and gone to visit Washakie and the children. Surely that was all, he reassured himself. She would be back soon, laughing, running through the snow...

The roan, still saddled, turned and looked expectantly at its master. Cade sighed. No, he would not be able to rest until he knew Stella was safe. He led the stallion outside, mounted again and set off at a gallop for the Shoshone village.

As he entered the outskirts of the camp, he sensed that something was not right. The usual bustle and clamor—

barking dogs, chattering women, crying babies—had dimmed. An air of disquiet hung around the place.

An agitated figure came hurrying toward him. It was She-Bear, her hair disheveled, her handsome face distorted with worry. "You have news of my daughter!" she exclaimed.

Cade shook his head. "You're saying that Moon Bird is missing?"

"No one has seen her since before dawn! Her tracks led toward your house, Yellow Wolf.... See, the snow has already covered them—"

"Moon Bird came to my house very early this morning, as I was leaving to hunt. We talked for a few minutes. Then, as I rode away, I saw her walking back toward the village. That was the last—"

"She never came home! She is lost, and my grandchild with her!" She-Bear tore at her hair in a gesture of mourning and began to groan in a loud voice.

"Where's Washakie? I must speak with him."

She-Bear pointed, and Cade saw the chief standing outside his lodge. He dismounted and made his way among the morning camp fires.

"A long life, my father." Cade greeted the old man formally.

Washakie's face was shadowed with concern. "No word of my granddaughter?"

"Not since I saw her headed back toward your village this morning. And Stella is missing, too. Her horse is gone. Has she been here?"

Washakie shook his head slowly, and Cade felt something tighten around his heart.

The old chief scratched his chin thoughtfully. "Could it be that one has followed the other? With both of them gone—"

"We've got to find them!" Cade said. "The snow's already covered their tracks, but we'll have to try."

"I'll get a rifle and my horse," said Washakie.

* * *

The white flakes were falling harder now. They clumped on Stella's lashes, blurring her vision. The cold wind bit her face with icy teeth. She huddled in the saddle, urging the black mustang on with kicks from her half-frozen feet.

By now, Moon Bird's tracks were nothing but shallow depressions, their outlines softened by the fresh snowfall. Stella's eyes ached as she followed them, peering ahead through the thick-standing lodgepole pines that seemed the same everywhere she looked. This was hopeless, she told herself. The tracks were getting fainter, the forest thicker, the wind colder. Soon it would be impossible to go on looking. What would she do then?

With one gloved hand, she brushed her blowing hair away from her face. She had no choice except to go on, she realized. There were two lives at stake. As long as there was a chance Moon Bird might be out here, she could not give up the search.

The whiteness swirled around her as she pushed deeper into the silent forest. Her eyes were intent on the ground, on the faint, snow-filled hollows that told her where Moon Bird had walked. She had to keep those tracks in sight. She had to follow them, whatever it cost her....

A sudden snort from the mustang made Stella flinch, and she realized her mind had been drifting. The tracks were sharper now, and up ahead she could see something against the snow—something red, lying in a heap at the foot of a big boulder.

Stella's heart lurched into her throat as she slid out of the saddle and plunged toward it. Perhaps she was already too late—but no. As she came closer, she heard a moan and saw a writhing movement. It was Moon Bird, lying there in her red blanket, her body doubled up with pain.

Stella leaned over her and raised the blanket's edge. Moon Bird's eyes, gazing up at her, were like a wounded hawk's, cold with hatred. She was a proud woman, Stella reminded herself, and she would not welcome aid from someone she considered her rival. But this was no time for pride. It seemed that Moon Bird's child was about to enter the world. She needed help.

The snow was coming down in sheets. Glancing around, Stella spotted the trunk of a dead pine. The tree had long since fallen over, but its top had caught in some thick brush before reaching the ground. The way the branches lay, Stella observed, they could form the framework for a crude shelter.

Swiftly she crawled underneath the trunk, brushing the snow from the ground and breaking off the dry branches that were in the way. Then she turned to Moon Bird, where the girl lay twisting on the ground. Pointing to the tree trunk, she tugged at Moon Bird's blanket. "Come on," she urged, hoping Moon Bird would know what she wanted. "Try to get up."

Moon Bird's hostile eyes flashed their understanding. "Wait," she hissed in startlingly clear English. "Wait for the pain."

Stella's eyes widened in amazement. "You speak—"

"Not now!" Moon Bird's beautiful face contorted with agony. The contraction was long and wrenching. When it had passed, she turned over, struggled to her knees and crawled underneath the fallen tree. There she spread her own red blanket on the earth, where Stella had brushed away the snow. No sooner had she finished than another pain seized her. She clenched her jaws hard, but did not cry out.

Stella took the blanket she'd brought from the cabin and draped it over the fallen tree, creating a sort of makeshift tent. She was about join Moon Bird beneath it when she remembered her horse. In her concern for Moon Bird, she had not even taken time to drop the reins to the ground.

Quickly she glanced around. The black mustang, true to its half-wild nature, was gone. Its hoofprints, leading off through the trees, were already filling up with snow.

It had been Washakie's suggestion that they check the cabin again before heading into the woods. It made sense,

Cade agreed as they galloped back around the lake. Maybe Stella had returned in his absence. Maybe she and Moon Bird would both be there.

"Look!" Washakie pointed to something in the yard. Cade's heart leaped as he recognized the black mustang. Stella was back! he told himself. She was all right!

But as they got closer, he realized something was wrong. The mustang, still saddled and bridled, was loose in the yard. It trotted back and forth, whinnying anxiously.

Washakie grunted. "That horse has run away," he said, and suddenly Cade felt sick and cold inside. Stella was out there somewhere, in the forest. She could have been thrown. She could have run into Gillis or Red Hawk. She could be hurt, even dead.

"I'll check the house," he muttered. "We might as well be sure no one is there."

He spent precious moments dismounting, going up to the cabin and looking inside. It was empty—the fire out and Stella's bed unmade as she had left it. Heartsick, he gazed at the place where she had slept, remembering her warmth and tenderness. That was when he noticed that one of the blankets was missing from the bed.

He checked the covers to make sure. Yes, one blanket was gone, the brown one that usually lay on top. Why would she take it? Cade's mind worked furiously as he tried to make some sense of what he knew. Moon Bird had been angry, and she had not returned to her village. Stella had gone sometime afterward, taking the blanket and—yes, he took a moment to check—she had taken the pistol, as well.

As he stepped out onto the porch, Cade's mind reached the inevitable conclusion. Moon Bird, her rage exceeding her common sense, had followed him into the forest. Stella must have gone after her.

He returned to Washakie and told him what he had found. The old chief nodded. "I think you must be right," he said. "When we find your woman and my granddaughter, they will be together."

"*If* we find them. Their tracks are covered, and I've only a general idea of where I rode when I went hunting."

"We will find them, my son," Washakie said. "Listen, while you were inside your cabin, I learned something from this black horse."

Cade gazed at the old man, puzzled.

"Look at his tracks," said Washakie. "They are still too fresh to have been covered by snow. If we follow them swiftly, back to the place where he came from—"

"Of course!" Cade stared at the trail of hoofprints where they came out of the trees, wondering how long the horse had taken to get home and how far it had wandered. There was a heavy chance they would lose the trail in the snow, but they had to follow it. It was the only real lead they had.

"Let's go!" he said. "Pray to your gods that we aren't too late!"

Stella crawled into the shelter beside Moon Bird. The loss of the horse was not the end of the world, she tried to reassure herself. They would just have to wait till the baby was born and Moon Bird was steady enough to walk back, that was all. Maybe by then the snowstorm would be over.

Moon Bird was lying on her side, her dark eyes glittering with pain and mistrust. She'd moved over, however, to make room for Stella under the blanket.

"Where did you learn to speak English?" Stella asked as she eased down beside her.

"Some from Yellow Wolf, when he was with my sister," Moon Bird answered sullenly. "More later, from missionaries. They tried to baptize me, but I only wanted to learn—" Her words ended in a small gasp as another painful contraction racked her swollen body. Stella waited till the pain had passed before she asked her next question.

"But why haven't you spoken to me before?"

Sweat beaded Moon Bird's forehead. She pressed her lips in a tight line, refusing to answer. Only her eyes spoke. Their searing gaze told Stella all she needed to know.

A sudden gust of wind caught a corner of the brown blanket, threatening to snatch it away. Stella clutched at the edges in a frantic tug-of-war, tucking them under her own body to hold them in place. Outside, the snowflakes fell in wet clusters, so heavy that they landed on the blanket with splattering thuds.

Stella raised up on one elbow. "I'm not your enemy, Moon Bird," she said. "If I were, I wouldn't be here."

Moon Bird simply shook her head. Her eyes were still defiant as she clenched her teeth against the onset of another contraction. The force of it arched and twisted her body, but she did not cry out. She had too much pride to show pain before a rival. Instead, she endured, breathing deeply until at last her tortured muscles relaxed and she lay on her back, staring up at the blanket.

"Do you think it will be soon?" Stella asked softly.

Moon Bird nodded, then caught her breath as another pain seized her. This time, its intensity was so great that her lips parted in a low moan.

"Go ahead. You can even scream if you want to. It's all right." Stella tried to sound reassuring, but she had never helped with a birth before. She could only hope the baby would come easily and that she would know what to do.

Moon Bird moaned again, her body twisting violently. It was time, Stella realized as she raised the girl's skirt. "Push," she urged. "Push hard!"

Moon Bird's voice rose to a thin scream as her body contracted; Stella, crouching beneath the low cover of the blanket, helped ease the squirming little being out with her hands.

"A boy!" she exclaimed, her throat tight with emotion. "And listen to him! He's already caterwauling like a young cougar!"

While Moon Bird rested, Stella tried to clean the newborn as best she could. Then she wrapped him in the warmth of her own coat. As the small black eyes blinked up at her, so alive and alert, she fought back a rush of tears. Thank heaven she had found Moon Bird in time. Thank heaven the birth had been so easy, the child so healthy and strong.

Now, as Moon Bird took the child, she even managed a wan smile. She lay back on the blanket and gave him her breast, her lovely face as serene as a Madonna's. It was as if, in giving birth to her son, she had let go of all her bitterness.

While she waited for the afterbirth to come, Stella raised the edge of the blanket and looked outside. The whole world was white—so white it hurt her eyes. Dazzling snow lay over everything, in a layer as deep as her longest finger could reach. And the flakes were still falling in a blinding, blowing swarm that showed no signs of letting up.

Sobered, Stella lowered the blanket. She realized now that she had underestimated the danger to Moon Bird, the baby and herself. Reaching safety would not be a simple matter of bundling up the child and walking back to the cabin. The snow had already obliterated the trail they had left. Now they would have no way of finding their way home. They were stranded here, with no food, no dry wood for a fire and no matches.

Just then the gleam of Cade's pistol caught Stella's eye. It lay on one corner of the blanket, where she had dropped it when she used her coat to wrap the baby.

That was the answer! Surely Cade, and maybe Moon Bird's family, as well, would be looking for them by now. A signal shot could be heard for a long distance, even in the storm. Excitedly, her mind began to plan. She could fire the first shot now, the next one in an hour, then . . .

Stella picked up the heavy Colt .45. As she inspected the cylinder, her heart sank like a solid lead weight.

The gun was empty.

Chapter Fourteen

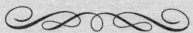

Cade cursed the snow. It filled the air with a solid whiteness so intense it was blinding. It whipped mournfully around the legs of the horses and formed treacherous drifts that covered logs, rocks and holes.

He and Washakie had long since lost the tracks of the black mustang. They were simply looking now, tired, discouraged and all but lost themselves. The storm beat upon them, driving them to exhaustion. But as long as Stella and Moon Bird were missing, they could not give up the search.

At Cade's suggestion, they had stopped at the last spot where they'd been able to see the mustang's tracks. Tying Washakie's red bandanna to a tree to mark the place, they had ridden in a series of circles, each one wider than the last. Sooner or later, he reasoned, if they made a careful pattern, their search would be rewarded.

But the snow had made things almost impossible. Only the old chief's uncanny sense of direction kept them from getting hopelessly lost. As it was, they returned at the end of each circle to the fluttering red bandanna, more and more discouraged.

It was Cade who finally voiced the fear that haunted them both. "Something must have happened to them," he said, brushing the snow from his face. "The Sioux—"

"No!" Washakie interrupted. "After so many years of life, I can feel when the Sioux are nearby. I can *smell* them! There have been no Sioux here!"

"Then...someone else, an animal..." Cade said, trying to grasp the fear by voicing it. "My friend the marshal told me about a bad man, an evil man, who had come to the valley—"

"We have found *nothing*, my son," Washakie reminded him. "No sign of anyone or anything. This—" he swept his arm in a cutting arc through the snow "—this is our enemy. This is what we must fight. We must make a bigger circle, then an even bigger one. And we must use more than our eyes. We must use our ears, our noses, our minds! Only then will we find them!"

Cade took a deep breath. Dread and despair were like tight steel bands around his body, but he knew Washakie was right. They had to keep circling. It was their only chance of finding anything at all.

His eyes peered through the stinging snow. "Let's go," he said, nudging the roan to a cautious walk. "If they're out here, if they're alive, we'll find them."

Stella lay on the edge of the thin blanket, the cold from the ground seeping into her body. Her limbs felt leaden, her eyelids heavy. She knew that she would freeze if she did not try to move, but in the tight confines of the shelter, she could do little more than flex her hands and feet.

Wrapped tightly in her coat, the baby lay between her and Moon Bird. It sucked at its fists, making contented little smacking noises. Stella listened, still awed by the newness, the miracle of that small life.

Moon Bird stirred and raised her head. "Thank you," she said softly. "You did not have to follow me. You did not have to help. I owe you...much. My baby's life...." The words trailed off as she struggled with feelings too deep to express in her simple English.

It was Stella's turn to be silent. She had taken one life. Now, perhaps, she had done something to weight the other side of the balance.

"He looks like his father," Moon Bird murmured, gazing down at her tiny son.

"Cade told me how your husband died," Stella said. "You must have loved him very much."

Moon Bird gave a bitter little laugh. "Love? What is that? It was Yellow Wolf I wanted. But his eyes were only for my sister. So I married another man. Then . . . she died. And it was too late for me."

"But now you're both free!" Something twisted inside Stella as she spoke. "It's not too late, after all!"

Moon Bird breathed deeply, in and out. Stella was conscious of the snow growing heavy on the frozen blanket that sheltered them.

"You say it is not too late?" Moon Bird's voice was bitter. "If you believe that, then you are blind! He looks at you the way he looked at my sister!"

"That can't be!" Stella protested her deepest hope—the hope she had not dared voice even to herself.

"You helped me. I can only pay you back with the truth. You are the one Yellow Wolf wants."

Stella closed her eyes, resisting the words, fighting their implications, yet wanting desperately to believe they were true. "What will you do, Moon Bird, if you don't marry Yellow Wolf?" she asked gently.

"Another man wants me." Moon Bird spoke proudly. "Iron Bow is a leader of our tribe. He has many horses and a big lodge. I—I will never go hungry."

"Then I wish you well." Stella suppressed the impulse to reach out and squeeze Moon Bird's hand. The girl had swallowed enough of her pride. She would not welcome the gesture, or even understand it.

Moon Bird drew her baby closer. "Do you think someone will find us?" she asked softly.

"They'll find us." Stella tried to sound cheerful, but her voice rang hollow in the tiny space of the shelter. With no food, no fire and the cold draining the strength from their bodies, they were in grave danger. If no one found them before dark, they would freeze.

She flexed her fingers, trying to keep them warm. She wanted to live. She wanted to see Cade again, to feel his arms holding her close once more. "Come to me...." she whispered, as if he could hear. "Come...."

Toward evening the wind died and the snowfall began to thin. The setting sun glowed like a burning coal above the horizon, turning the snow-covered landscape a ghostly, iridescent pink.

Cade's whole being dragged with the weight of despair. He and Washakie had been searching for hours. They had looked till their eyes burned from the whiteness of the snow. They had spent their voices trying to shout above the wind. All for nothing.

"It could be that they made their own way home," Washakie said, sighing wearily. "Even now, they could be warming themselves by the fire."

Cade glanced at him. The old chief had searched valiantly all day, but now he looked unspeakably tired, his eyes red and hollow, his white hair hanging damply around his care-lined face. Washakie had always been a vigorous man, but he was seventy years old, Cade reminded himself. He could become ill, or worse, if he stayed out much longer.

Torn, Cade stared out into the darkening woods. Once the clouds cleared, the night would be bitterly cold. If Stella and Moon Bird were out there, with no shelter and no fire, they could freeze to death.

Cade glanced at Washakie again. "Let's make one more circle," he said, forcing himself to sound optimistic. "Then we'll go home. You may be right. They may be waiting for us."

Washakie nodded his agreement. They nudged the horses and set out again, through the strange, rosy twilight. If they found nothing, Cade promised himself, he would recruit a group of young braves and come back with torches. He would not give up until Stella and Moon Bird were found.

They had completed, perhaps, half the circle when Washakie, who was in the lead, signaled a halt.

"What is it?" Cade reined in beside him.

"Shh! Listen!"

Cade paused. "I don't hear—"

Washakie placed his finger on his lips, a jabbing, emphatic gesture. Cade strained his ears and still heard nothing.

"Down there!" Washakie pointed to a spot where the snow appeared to have drifted over a fallen tree. Another instant and the old chief was out of the saddle, clawing furiously at the drift with his hands.

Only when Cade had sprung down to help him did he hear the faint cry coming from under the snow. It sounded like—yes, it was! It was a baby!

"Stella!" Without waiting for an answer, Cade plunged his hands into the drift. His fingers found the roughness of the thick, wool blanket. With Washakie's help, he shoved away the layers of heavy snow, then lifted the half-frozen blanket clear of the fallen tree.

Stella and Moon Bird lay huddled together on the ground, so numb with cold they could scarcely move or speak. Only the baby, swathed in Stella's coat and warmed between the two bodies, had enough life to protest. It was squalling lustily.

While Washakie took care of Moon Bird, Cade bent over Stella and lifted her in his arms. Her eyes were open, gazing up at him, but her flesh was cold. In this weather, with no coat, he realized, there was no way she would have survived the night.

He stripped off his sheepskin jacket, warm from his own body, and wrapped it around her; she moaned softly as he cradled her close. All questions aside, right now the only thing that mattered to him was that she was alive and safe.

Washakie, with the sudden strength of a man half his age, had already lifted his granddaughter and her child onto the saddle of his horse. With an easy, catlike spring, he swung himself up behind them. Moon Bird, who had been more warmly dressed than Stella, appeared to be in good condition. She was able to sit up and hold her whimpering son in her arms. Stella, however, had given up her coat for the baby. The cold had sapped so much of her strength that she was almost limp.

Cade looked down into Stella's cold-reddened face and realized that she had very nearly given her life for Moon Bird and the child. There was no way such a woman would have lured young Jared into her tent to rob him. Nor would she have deliberately pulled the trigger that ended the boy's life. A wave of guilt for the way he had treated her washed over him.

"Let's go," Washakie said, holding back his restless horse. Cade lifted Stella carefully into the saddle and steadied her while he mounted. Then he cradled her in his arms, letting the chief break trail as they rode home through the deepening purple twilight.

Once they'd cleared the trees, Washakie turned his horse toward the distant fires of the Shoshone camp, leaving Cade and Stella to ride the rest of the way alone.

By now it was dark. The constellation of Orion, the hunter, was above the western hills, the three stars in his belt like great, brilliant jewels against the velvety sky.

Wrapped in Cade's jacket, Stella had been content to let herself rest. She needed the support of Cade's arms around her, the solid feel of his chest against her back.

"You must be cold," she said, forming each word with numb lips. "I think I can spare your coat if you want it back."

"Keep it. We'll be home in a few minutes." His lips brushed her hair as he spoke. "How do your hands and feet feel? We'll want to check them for frostbite when we get inside."

"They feel all right," Stella said, wishing it was easier to speak. She wanted to tell him how frightened she had been, how she had been torn between staying under the blanket and going out to find help, and how, in the end, the weight of the drifting snow had made their tiny shelter a prison. But all that could wait. There was time now. She was safe. She was with Cade.

They rode into the yard, breaking trail through the deep drifts. Snow was piled high on the roof of the cabin. It lay in zigzag rows along the rails of the pasture fence. Stella peered anxiously through the darkness and was relieved to see her black mustang in the corral, silhouetted like a paper cutout against the white snow.

"You may owe your life to that fool horse," Cade said. "If Washakie and I hadn't followed the trail he left when he came home, we never would have found you."

"Then maybe I can forgive him for running away." Stella found that the words came easier this time.

"That's my girl. No use holding a grudge," Cade's chuckle was deep and mellow in the darkness. Something about him was subtly different tonight, Stella mused. He seemed less reserved, more open. Maybe he was just relieved at finding her safe. Or maybe . . .

He halted the roan next to the porch, slid to the ground and eased her out of the saddle—as gently, she thought, as if she'd been made of rare porcelain. Just as gently, he carried her inside the cold, dark cabin and lowered her into one of the rockers. Then he started back outside to put the roan away.

"I'll only be a few minutes," he promised. "Then, when I come back, we'll see what we can do about getting you warm."

She sat in the darkness and waited for him, flexing her hands and feet to increase the circulation. The tingling sensation was painful at first, but soon the numbness began to leave her fingers and toes. She was going to be all right.

Cade came in with an armload of dry kindling from the shed. He put it down by the fireplace, then paused to light the lamp that hung from a rafter. The flame flickered as it caught the wick, casting a yellow glow around the cabin.

"That's better." Cade bent down and began to stack the kindling in the fireplace. "We'll soon have—"

"Cade!" Stella reached out and clutched his shoulder. "Look at the kitchen! Someone's been in here!"

He spun around, instantly alert. One hand reached for his rifle. "Keep down and don't move," he said.

Like a stalking cat, he inspected the cabin. The kitchen had been ransacked. Cupboard doors were flung open, their contents hastily scattered. Flour, sugar and oats were spilled across the floor, crisscrossed by huge boot tracks.

"Gillis!" Stella gasped, her throat tight with horror. "Your friend Sam said he'd tracked him into this valley!"

"There's no way to be sure." Cade swung the rifle back toward the bed. The covers had been torn loose, the mattress pulled to one side. "Whoever it was, he was in a hurry. It looks like he was searching for food, money, bullets— anything he could get his hands on. But as far as I can tell, he's gone."

Their eyes met, then moved upward, toward the loft. "I'll check up there." Cade took the lantern and mounted the ladder, his rifle cocked and ready. Stella held her breath as the floor creaked overhead. An eternity seemed to pass before she heard him announce, "It's all right. There's nobody up here."

He came back down the ladder, the lantern flooding the cabin with light again. "I'll just check outside," he said.

"Be careful."

Again she waited while he looked, her heart pounding with a fear so strong it was almost irrational. She had felt so safe in this cabin. Now, what had happened here seemed almost like a violation of her own body.

She jumped, startled by a sudden sound, then realized it was only Cade stomping the snow off his boots on the porch. By the time he swung the door open, she had almost regained her composure.

"No trail," he said. "That means our friend must have come earlier in the day, while there was time for the snow to fill up his tracks."

"Did you look in the shed?"

He nodded. "Nothing there. The horses were fine. The only thing missing was a side of bacon I'd hung in the smoke room." He smiled, trying to put Stella's fears to rest.

"By now the devil's probably off somewhere having himself a nice supper. He— Lord, but you're shivering!"

"I-I'm sorry." Stella gave a little sob. Whether from cold or fear, she was shaking uncontrollably.

Cade knelt, facing her where she sat in the chair, and gathered her in his arms. "It's all right, Stella," he whispered. "You've been a very brave girl. It's all right to let go of it a little. It's all right to be scared. It's all right to need someone...."

He cupped her chin with his hand, lifted her face and warmed her trembling lips with his. His kisses were gentle, soft and lingering. They moved slowly from her mouth to her closed eyelids, to her cheeks and down to her throat. Stella felt herself warming, felt the exquisite stirring of desire deep in her body. She began to feel alive again.

When Cade released her, his voice was husky. "Give me a minute to start the fire. Then we'll warm up the bed and get you into it."

"The kitchen—" Stella protested weakly. "You'll need me to help you clean up the mess."

"The kitchen can wait." He pulled her close again, his mouth rough and searching this time, his fingertips brushing the curve of her breast. "The kitchen can wait all night if it has to."

As he lighted the fire, Stella noticed that Cade's hand quivered slightly. *It's all right to need someone,* he had said. Watching him, Stella knew that the words had been meant as much for him as for her. He was the one who had held back, who had been afraid to show his need for her.

He glanced back over his shoulder. Their eyes met with an intensity that almost made her dizzy. "I forgot to ask you what you wanted to eat. If you're hungry, we can—"

"No." Stella shook her head. She had not eaten since dawn, but suddenly she could not even think about food. "It's all right. It can wait."

He nodded quietly and returned to tending the fire, blowing gently on the small, licking flames, coaxing them to a steady blaze. Then, with its warmth radiating into the cabin, he walked over to the bed. Lifting the mattress back into place, he rearranged the rumpled bedclothes, smoothed them and carefully folded down the top sheet. Then, he turned and walked slowly back to Stella.

Though she was still too weak to stand, her body was ready for him. Every nerve, every cell tingled with the anticipation of his touch.

When he leaned down and lifted her in his arms, she clung to him, her pounding heart echoing his. She closed her eyes as he carried her toward the bed, counting the steps before he laid her gently down on the pillow.

"Cade . . ."

His lips stopped her words. "Hush," he whispered, his mouth skimming hers as he spoke. "Don't try to talk, Stella."

He began with her feet, untying her frozen moccasins, slipping off the heavy wool stockings, then gently massaging the warmth back into her toes, her heels, her high, delicate arches. "No frostbite," he murmured. "That's good."

Next, he slowly unbuttoned her shirt, bending to kiss each part of her body as he uncovered it. His touch was soft and light, his restraint so exquisite that it made her moan.

"Cade—"

"Shh. . . ." His tongue circled the tip of one breast, licking, teasing, puckering the nipple. The sensation sent waves of warmth tingling through Stella's body. She arched upward toward him, wanting more and still more. Her hand caught his and guided it to the buckle of the belt that held her trousers. She felt them loosening, slipping down off her legs.

"Oh, yes, you are cold," he murmured, his lips pausing in their soft, nibbling exploration of her skin. "Come on now, under the covers with you."

He pulled back the quilts a little more and gently eased her under them. She lay there waiting for him while he shed his clothes, knowing better than to speak. They wanted each other, she and Cade. They needed each other. Words would only spoil things.

He stood beside the bed for a moment, the orange firelight turning his lean, muscular body to flame. Stella gasped softly at the sheer power and beauty of that body. She wanted him. She ached and quivered with wanting him.

She held out her arms. He gazed down at her for a long moment, his eyes tender and mysterious. Then he was beside her, slipping beneath the quilts to draw her close.

She felt his arms around her, strong yet gentle, like velvet-wrapped steel. And his warmth... She melted against him, feeling it all around her, the heat, the life of him.

"Stella." He whispered her name as their bodies joined, and that was all. They were lost then, both of them, in the sweet, all-encompassing wonder of each other. When she felt him move, deep inside her, it was like the stirring of her own soul. She whimpered softly as her body responded to him, exquisitely, nerve by nerve, until her entire being vibrated like the singing strings of a violin.

The song rose, building little by little until the pitch of its ecstasy became almost unbearable. Stella gasped, struggled, then let it carry her to a soaring burst of rapture so intense it was almost terrifying. She cried out as they reached the peak of it together. Cade's body shuddered violently as his life flowed into her. Then it was over. They lay in each other's arms, released, exhausted.

For a few moments neither of them moved. Then she began to stir beneath him. He lifted his head and gazed at her, his eyes filled with wonder.

Stella's lips parted as she tried to speak, but the words would not form in her mind. What had happened was beyond her ability to express.

Very tenderly, he bent and kissed her. "Go to sleep, Stella," he murmured. "It's all right now. I'm here."

His gentle tone reassured her. She found her voice. "Don't leave me," she whispered. "Please don't leave me, Cade."

Wind River

"I won't leave you." He kissed her again. "I'm right here. I'll stay close."

"And tomorrow—" she felt herself drifting off "—tomorrow we can go see Moon Bird's baby?"

"Tomorrow we can do anything you like." His lips brushed her eyelids. "Now sleep, love. Get some rest."

His words blurred in Stella's mind. She drifted off to sleep, Cade's arms around her, his warm body close to hers.

She awoke the next morning with sunlight streaming in the window. Outside, she could hear Cade shoveling pathways through the snow. He had already cleaned up the mess that the intruder had made in the kitchen, Stella noticed, and she was glad. The thought that it might have been Gillis still made her shudder. She would never feel completely safe in the cabin again—not unless Cade was there with a gun.

For a moment she let herself lie back in bed, remembering last night. A little of the warmth still lingered. This morning, in fact, she felt...wonderful. Lazily she stretched her arms over her head. She had not slept so well in years.

Cade had come onto the porch. Stella could hear him clearing the snow off his boots. Self-consciously, she untangled her hair with her hands. Last night, she reflected, his defensive barriers had been down. He had been tender, loving and open. Had the morning changed him? She would soon know.

The door swung open, letting in sun and cold air as he stepped inside, closed and bolted the door and flung off his coat. "So you're finally awake," he said. "How about some breakfast?"

Her eyes searched his face—the face she had come to know so well. Were the barriers there? Were his eyes cool and guarded? She had told herself she would know at once. But now, she could not be sure.

There was, at least, warmth in his voice. Stella let herself respond to it. She smiled at him and snuggled down into the bed. "It feels so good not to be cold," she said with a laugh.

"You must be doing better." He came over and sat down on the edge of the mattress, a touch of hesitation in his movements, and suddenly Stella realized that he was as unsure as she was.

"Much better, thanks to you." Summoning her courage, she reached out and laid her hand on his arm. She felt the response, like an electric charge through his body. He leaned forward and gathered her into his arms.

They held each other, both of them trembling. "I need you, Stella," he whispered. "You don't know how much I've needed you, how alone I've been."

His arms tightened around her. She lifted her face and let him kiss her. Again, she felt a surge of desire, a sudden welling of the same sweet, vibrant current that had flowed between them last night. She knew that he felt it, too.

Her fingers fumbled at his shirt buttons. He reached up to help her, his heart drumming so loudly that she could hear it.

"Stella, love—"

He broke off at a sudden sound—footsteps, soft and light on the porch. An instant later, there was a sharp rap on the door.

Cade broke away from her. "Now, who the devil . . . ?"

Stella drew the covers up over her bare shoulders as he strode across the cabin to answer the knock. She saw him pause beside the door long enough to reach for his rifle and cock it. Then he slid back the bolt and swung the door open.

A young Indian stood there. Stella recognized him as one of Washakie's braves. He seemed nervous, agitated, as Cade ushered him inside. His black eyes darted to Stella and then shifted quickly away.

The young man spoke to Cade in Shoshone, the words a rapid verbal staccato that Stella could not hope to understand. But there was no mistaking Cade's response. Whatever the message was, it had disturbed him. He asked a few more questions, then turned back to Stella, his face grim.

"What is it?" she asked, alarmed.

"A party of Shoshone hunters brought in an injured man last night. A white man. He'd been mauled by a grizzly bear."

"Sam?" Stella's hand went to her throat.

Quickly Cade shook his head. "That was my first thought, too. But no, the description of the fellow doesn't match Sam at all. This is a heavy man, a big man...." He paused, as if giving her time to prepare for the news. "A man with a black beard."

Stella felt weak. "Gillis!" she whispered.

"It looks that way." He was flinging on his coat. "I've got to go now. I've got to get over there."

"Wait." Stella reached for her clothes, which were hanging on the back of a chair next to the bed. "I'm going with you!"

"No." He was buttoning his coat.

"Cade, this concerns me more than it does you. I have to see Gillis! I have to talk to him!"

"No." There was something in Cade's face—a black determination she had never seen before. "I'll talk to him myself. I think I can find out what I need to know."

"Cade..." Suddenly she felt cold. "What is it? Why don't you want me to come?"

He hesitated. "You've never seen what a grizzly can do to a man's body. I have. I know what to expect."

She felt the color leave her face. "How badly hurt is he?"

Cade took a deep breath and pulled on his gloves. "They say he's dying, Stella."

Chapter Fifteen

Cade pulled the roan in sharply at the outskirts of the Shoshone camp. He had taken the distance from his cabin at a thundering gallop, outstripping even the young brave, who'd ridden back with him on his swift Indian pony. If the man was Gillis, and if he was dying, seconds could be critical.

He had left Stella behind, half-dressed and still protesting. She had already seen too much blood and death, Cade told himself. She didn't need to see more. Besides, he had questions of his own—questions about Jared. And he wanted to ask them himself.

Near the center of the camp, Cade spotted a crowd of Indians. They were clustered around a crudely rigged shelter of brush and hides. That, Cade calculated, would be where they had put the wounded man. No Shoshone would want his lodge cursed by the death of a stranger.

The small crowd of onlookers parted to let Cade slip past. Someone had laid the injured stranger on an old blanket and bound the worst of his wounds with rags, but no one appeared to be tending him now.

Cade felt his knees weaken as he leaned over to look at the man. He had known what to expect, but seeing the kind of damage a bear could do never failed to wrench his insides. The bearded man's left arm and leg were badly mauled, and the ribs on the left side appeared to have been crushed by the bear's massive jaws. It was a wonder the poor devil had lived at all.

Cade squared his shoulders and made an effort to swallow his pity. If this wretch was really Gillis, he'd done as much and worse to pretty little Amy Corrigan.

"You're Newt Gillis?" he asked, forcing himself to look straight into the man's pain-dulled eyes.

"Johnson . . . Jake Johnson." The answering voice was a pain-soaked rasp. "You—you got any whiskey?"

"No." Cade's hopes of getting some easy answers sank. The man had to be Gillis, but he wasn't ready to talk. "I can get you some brandy," he said, remembering the small supply he kept for visitors. "There's a bottle in my cabin. I can send somebody for it. All you have to do is answer some questions."

The man made a sound that was somewhere between a groan and a gurgle.

"You're Newt Gillis, aren't you?" Cade asked again.

"Johnson—Jake Johnson. Told you. God, get me the brandy!"

Cade struggled with his own frustrations as he bent over the man. With the damage his body had taken, he could die at any time, taking a whole world of unanswered questions with him.

"Gillis, you knew my brother, Jared Garrison. The woman who shot him claims you were there when it happened—"

"Told you—I ain't him. The name's Johnson."

"He's lying." The voice behind Cade made him jump. Stella stood there, pale and trembling, staring into the man's face.

"He's lying," she said again. "He's Gillis. I'd know him anywhere. Even his voice—"

She crouched beside Cade and moved closer to the man. "You know me, Newt Gillis," she said, her voice cold. "You know me from Green River. You broke into my tent and attacked me."

He blinked at her. "All right, I do know ye," he rasped. "You be the gal with the pitcher-takin' machine. But I sure as hell never was in your tent! God, give me a drink!"

"Gillis, you've got nothing to lose," Cade argued. "If you don't die from this, you'll hang for killing Amy Corrigan. Telling the truth could save this woman's life!"

"Don't know no Amy Corrigan...never killed nobody."

Cade sighed with exasperation as he realized what he and Stella were up against. The big miner had the strength of a buffalo bull and a will to match. Even now, he was determined to survive, to escape, to start a new life someplace else. He would die before he told them anything.

Stella touched Cade's sleeve. She appeared shaken by what she had just seen. Yet, as she looked at him, there was a spark of wonder in her eyes. "You believe me, don't you?" she whispered. "You really believe me!"

"Yes. Yes, damn it, I believe you, Stella. But if Gillis dies without talking, that's not going to make much difference."

"Then—" her fingers tightened hard on Cade's arm "—then we've got to save him!"

"Stella, he's lost a lot of blood. Even if he had a doctor—"

"We've got to try. I took care of my father. I know a little..."

Cade shook his head. "I'll help you, of course. But with no disinfectants, no medicine—"

"You said the Shoshone used herbs. How much do you know about them?"

"Not enough. There are so many, it takes a lifetime to learn about them all. We'd need help from a healer, someone who has a good supply of herbs and knows how to use them."

Stella glanced around at the fast-growing crowd gathered outside the shelter. "Would any of them help us?"

Cade sighed. Those among the Shoshone who could really heal with herbs were few, and they guarded their gifts jealously. They would not treat just anyone, especially an evil-looking stranger whom the bear had marked for death. "It won't be easy, but I'll ask," he told Stella. "I'll keep asking till I find someone who'll help us."

The watchers drew back a little as Cade ducked out of the shelter and stood up. Facing them, he spoke in a loud voice. He told them about Jared's death and about Stella and Gillis's part in it. He told them about the trouble Stella was in and why only Gillis could clear her. "If this evil man dies without telling his story, my woman will be judged guilty of murder," he said. "We must try to save his life, but we cannot do it alone. We need help from one who knows healing."

He paused, his eyes sweeping the crowd of, perhaps, eighty or ninety Shoshone. Most of them, especially the younger ones, lacked the full knowledge of healing. Others, Cade knew, possessed the ability, but they were old and bitter. Their feelings toward white people ranged from mistrust to hatred. Not only that, but they guarded their reputations fiercely. None of them would be eager to treat a patient on the brink of death.

"Is there no one who will help us?" Cade looked over the crowd again. His heart sank as he saw some of the old people turn away. Not even Washakie could force them to use their healing knowledge if they did not want to. He glanced back at Stella where she sat beside Gillis. She was close to tears.

After what seemed like an eternity, a stout, gray-haired woman pushed her way forward and stood before him.

"I will help," she said. "I cannot promise to save the man, but I will do my best."

The woman was She-Bear.

Gillis drifted in and out of delirium, muttering and moaning as She-Bear applied fresh poultices to his wounds. All day long, Stella and She-Bear, with Cade helping, had crouched inside the crude shelter, laboring over the big miner's maimed body. Buffalo hides made up three sides of the shelter and kept out the cold. On the open side, a small fire flickered in a pit. This was used for warmth and to heat the teas, ointments and poultices that She-Bear used in her healing.

At first, it had been all that Stella could do to touch Gillis. The feel of his flesh, the rasp of his voice, the smell of his unwashed skin all brought back flashes of that terrible night in her tent. Now, however, with her mind numbed by cold and weariness, she no longer saw him as a man. He was only a body that had to be kept alive, a mass of wounds to wash, dress and change, a head to hold steady while She-Bear spooned her strange-smelling herbal concoctions down his throat.

Gillis's vital organs seemed to be functioning well enough. It was the blood loss that threatened his life. And it was to stopping this blood loss and building up the body fluids that She-Bear directed most of her energy.

Stella marveled at the woman's skill. First She-Bear boiled creosote root to make a tea, which she used to wash Gillis's side, arm and leg. Then she used a stone to grind some dried puffballs into a powder. This, Cade explained as she sprinkled it liberally into the wounds, would help stop the bleeding. The powder was followed by poultices of elder bark.

Stella helped her apply some strong-smelling pine salve to the smaller wounds. The sting of it made Gillis flinch and curse, but he seemed to know they were helping him. When he was conscious, he took the treatment stoically.

Stella found herself wishing she could speak to the older woman, wishing she could learn more about her healing skills. She-Bear, however, worked mostly in silence, pointing when she wanted something from her medicine bag or when the fire needed another stick of wood. Her attitude was plain. She owed Stella a debt—a debt she was repaying with her service. Her friendship and trust were gifts she was not yet ready to offer. They could only be earned, if ever, over a long period of time.

Cade had protested at first when Stella insisted on being the one to help She-Bear. "This is no job for you," he'd argued. "Go on home and let me do it. After all you've been through, you don't have to subject yourself to—to this!"

But Stella had overruled him. "This is my battle, Cade," she had insisted passionately. "I can't leave it to anybody else, not even to you. My own life is hanging in the balance with Gillis's, and I have to be in there fighting. Please understand."

Now, at last, the sun was going down behind the Wind River peaks, setting the snow on fire. Stella's back and legs ached from crouching beneath the low roof of the shelter. Her hands and face were numb with cold. Her senses swam with the deep, rasping sound of Gillis's breathing and the pungent odors of She-Bear's herbs. But she felt a small sense of victory. Gillis, for whatever it was worth, was still alive.

She-Bear turned and said something to Cade, who was tending the fire. Cade nodded, then reached out and touched Stella's arm. "She's finished for the night, love. She says the last tea she gave Gillis should keep him resting till morning."

"He's going to live?" Stella was so tired and cold her mouth could scarcely form the words.

Cade and She-Bear exchanged a meaningful glance. "It's too soon to know," he said gently. "But you can get some rest now. I'll sit up and watch him till morning."

"I'll rest a little while," Stella murmured. "But I'm not leaving. If he says anything, I want to be here."

Cade sighed. "You're a stubborn woman. But all right. Suit yourself. I'll borrow a spare blanket from Washakie."

He was back minutes later with the blanket. By then Stella was reeling with weariness. Without another word, she made a cocoon of the thick, woolen blanket, curled herself next to the fire and drifted off into exhausted slumber.

* * *

She-Bear squatted beside the fire, reorganizing her things—the herbs, the spoons and crushers, the collection of odd little pots and bowls she used for mixing.

Cade watched her through the smoke. Though she had worked over Gillis the entire day, she seemed in no hurry to leave. Her strong, callused hands took their time, sorting the herbs into small doeskin bags, cleaning the utensils with snow and stacking them into piles.

Between the two of them, there was an easy companionship—a mutual respect that was unusual between a Shoshone son and his mother-in-law. His refusal to marry Moon Bird had vexed her sorely, Cade knew. Yet she was still here, lingering as if she wanted to talk. He sat quietly, listening to the deep rasp of Gillis's breathing, while he let her choose the time and the words.

At last She-Bear spoke. Nodding toward Stella's sleeping form, she said, "That one is a good woman, Yellow Wolf."

Cade's breath caught. Coming from She-Bear, the simple comment was a high accolade. He waited, hoping she would say more, but instead she turned her attention back to Gillis.

"I have done my best with him," she said in a tired voice. "The bleeding has stopped and he is getting stronger, but..." She sighed and Cade waited while she stirred the fire with a length of willow. "I may have not done the man a kindness. If he dies now, it will be slower, with more pain. It may be that the bear has already killed him."

Cade nodded, understanding. The claws of a grizzly were tainted with rotting matter from its kills. Gillis's wounds would be teeming with germs. Infection, blood poisoning, gangrene—these were the awful specters that lurked around him now.

"How long do you think he will live?" he asked.

"Nine sleeps...ten. Maybe more. But if the bear has killed him, he will not live to see the new moon."

Cade nodded again and turned up his collar against the nighttime breeze. Adding another log to the fire, he stared into the flames. His mind measured the odds, weighing the alternatives.

Sam Catlin would not be leaving Fort Bridger for several days, he'd said. The best chance, perhaps the only chance, of clearing Stella would be to get Gillis to Bridger and turn him over to Sam—alive, if possible. Otherwise, even if Gillis confessed before he died, a jury might not take Cade and Stella's word that a confession had occurred. That was a chance Cade felt they couldn't afford to take.

He took a stick and began sketching a crude map in the snow. Small bands of Shoshone often traveled between the Wind River and Fort Bridger, even in the dead of winter. The trip was difficult and took several days, but it was not impossible.

The easiest route was the one Sam had taken—winding south out of the mountains and picking up the Oregon Trail. The first part of the trip would be rough and dangerous, especially in the deep snow. But once they were out of the hills, as long as they didn't encounter any blizzards—

"What is this?" She-Bear had moved around the fire and was looking at Cade's map. "Ah. The evil man. You will take him away from here."

"That's right." Cade continued sketching in possible routes.

"To the fort?"

Cade nodded and She-Bear glanced over at Stella. "You will take her with you?" she asked gently.

Cade sighed, thinking of the hardship and danger to Stella. "I must," he said.

She-Bear stared at the map in silence for a time. "My two tall sons know the best way to go," she said. "And because I have taught them a little about healing, they can tend the bad man's wounds on the way. I will ask Washakie, our father, to send them with you."

Stella rode through a world of whiteness—a world of twisting mountain trails, rocks and treacherous, sliding snow.

Two days had passed since they'd left the Wind River Valley. Already it seemed as if there would never be an end to the cold, the wind, the blinding expanse of the snow and the chilling stare of Gillis's eyes.

Washakie had sent an escort of armed warriors with them as far as the first pass to guard against the Sioux. Now, however, they had passed the limits of that danger, and the braves had turned back. Only She-Bear's two sons remained with them. The older of the two, Track-the-Buffalo, was a serious lad of eighteen. His most prized possession was a flintlock rifle, so ancient that Stella could not imagine it ever firing. His younger brother, Falling Arrow, had no gun, but he sported an elegant lance decorated with a long black plume. When the trail became tedious, Falling Arrow would practice his aim by hurling the lance at trees.

Much of the time, the boys were in high spirits. To them, the trip was a lark, a grand adventure away from home. To Stella, however, every day was an ordeal.

Gillis was too badly hurt to ride, so he had been lashed to a travois, a sort of makeshift litter that dragged along the ground between two poles, hitched to a horse. Where the snow was deep and the land smooth, the travois glided easily. On rough ground, however, the jarring of the poles would cause Gillis to scream with agony. At such times, Cade would dose him with brandy to dull the pain or, if the terrain was really rocky, the two Shoshone boys would dismount, pick up the poles of the travois and carry them for a time. Progress was grindingly slow.

The nights were worse. Though She-Bear's two sons took care of Gillis's dressings, Stella had felt she should do her part, as well. She had offered to feed Gillis the gruel that they cooked over the evening fire.

That, for Stella, was the worst part of all. Even Gillis's injuries did not keep him from leering at her and making

suggestive remarks that made her face go hot with rage.
When Cade tried to stop him, he would only grin. "What
will you do to me, eh, squaw man? Beat me?"

The first night, Cade had offered to feed Gillis himself,
but Stella had declined. "I can't break trail, because I don't
know the way," she'd said, trying to make him understand. "I can't carry the travois, and I'm not good at
hunting. We'll reach the fort in another two or three days.
In the meantime, I don't want to feel like useless baggage.
I've got to do my part."

She'd watched him turn his back and go off to tend the
horses. The strain was telling on Cade, she knew. It was
telling on both of them. Fort Bridger seemed an eternity
away.

That night Stella dreamed about Karin Aarnson. She saw
Karin's little hands, chapped and bleeding as she tried to
make a decent home from a hovel in the wilderness. She
saw the tears run down Karin's face as she wept over her
lost baby, heard her screams as the Sioux set fire to the roof
above her head.

Stella had awakened trembling and had lain awake for
the rest of the night, staring up at the stars. She felt lost in
the lonely vastness of this country, trapped by its harshness. There was something about the land out here, she reflected. It did things to people. Either it broke them, as it
had Karin, or it made them hard and unfeeling. It inured
them to cruelty, horror and death.

What was it doing to her? Stella found herself asking.
What would she become if she stayed?

The next night, as she spooned the gruel into Newt Gillis's mouth, Stella felt his right arm encircle her waist.
Startled, she gasped and drew back, dropping the spoon
into the snow.

He laughed, defying the pain it caused. "Liked that,
didn't ye, girlie? I could tell."

Stella picked up the spoon. Cade had told her that they
were within thirty miles of the fort. Tonight would be their
last night on the trail. The knowledge that the ordeal would

end tomorrow when they reached Fort Bridger made Gillis's taunts easier to shrug off. "You're getting stronger," she said, dipping the spoon into more gruel. "Maybe you'll live to hang, after all."

"Ain't nobody got no reason to hang me." Gillis swallowed the spoonful of gruel she had thrust into his mouth. "But you listen t'me, girlie. Just wait till the others is asleep tonight. Then you come over here, an' I'll show ye who's gettin' strong! There be one part of me that grizzly didn't lay a claw on, an' I can tell ye right now, it works jist fine!"

Suddenly Stella had had enough. She had tried not to let his gibes bother her, but the words brought back the full impact of that night in her tent. "You're disgusting," she hissed. "You're an animal! A savage!"

"A savage!" Gillis winced as his own laughter sent waves of pain through his body. "Ye got two Injuns an' one more what might as well be an Injun, too, an' you call me a savage! That's a good one, girlie!"

"I've lived around the Shoshone," Stella said icily. "From what I've seen of them, they're a good deal more civilized than you are!"

"Civilized!" Gillis laughed till he coughed. "Civilized, my ass! Ain't you seed the black thing that young buck's sportin' on the end of his lance? Take a look! It's a damned bloody scalp!"

"Oh, nonsense!" she protested, realizing with sickening certainty that he was right. "Why it's only—"

"Hell, it's a scalp! An' he'd have yours, too, in a minute, girlie, if'n you turned your back on 'im long enough!" He began to chuckle in a low, controlled way that would not hurt him so much.

The sound seemed to echo inside Stella's head as she walked away from him, out of the circle of firelight, farther and farther into the darkness. She wanted to get away from Gillis's pain-racked laughter and obscene taunts, from the snow and the wind, from the icy brutality of this land. But there was no escape for her, no place to run or hide. She was a prisoner here—as surely as if she were locked behind bars.

"Stella...." She felt the touch of Cade's hand on her sleeve. With a little gasp, she turned and stumbled into his arms.

He held her tightly. "I saw you leave. You shouldn't be out here this far. It isn't safe."

She huddled against his chest, saying nothing.

"What is it, love?" His lips brushed her hair. She knew he wanted to kiss her, but she did not raise her head. "Is it Gillis? Is it something he said?"

She only pressed her face into the rough wool of his coat, wishing he could take her away to someplace warm and safe and bright.

"Don't let the bastard bother you," he murmured, his hand stroking her back. "We'll be at the fort by tomorrow night. Then we can turn him over to Sam and be done with it."

"What if Sam isn't there?" she asked in a tight little voice. "What if he's already left...or what if he didn't make it at all?"

"There's no sense worrying about that till the time comes," Cade said. "Lord, but you're in a state tonight, love. I know the trip's been rough on you, but—"

She was trembling. He stopped speaking and lifted her chin with one gloved hand. His eyes narrowed as he studied her face in the moonlight.

"This isn't like you, Stella," he said gently. "Not like you at all. If there's something bothering you, it might help to talk about it."

She pulled loose from his arms. "No, it's nothing. It's silly. Just something I've been too naive to realize."

"What?"

"That black decoration on the end of Falling Arrow's lance—I thought it was horsehair. But it's not, is it?"

Cade sighed. "No, Stella. Falling Arrow took that scalp in a skirmish with the Crow last year. He's...very proud of it."

"He's just a boy!"

"He's a Shoshone. In the eyes of his people, that scalp makes him a man and a warrior."

She turned and walked away from him then, farther into the darkness. The thoughts welling up in her mind were now so awful that she could not bear to look at him.

"Stella." He caught up with her and put his hands on her shoulders. "What is it?"

She kept her back toward him. "*You* are a Shoshone," she said, her throat so tight she could hardly force the words out. "*You* are a man and a warrior."

His silence answered her unspoken question.

She twisted her shoulders loose from his hands. Her chest jerked with unreleased sobs as she heard his voice behind her.

"I won't lie to you, Stella. When the Sioux murdered my wife and sons, I went mad with grief. Something snapped in me—my last ties to civilization, to humanity. For a time, I became an animal—no, a savage. And I took a savage's revenge."

He paused, hoping, perhaps, that she would answer him, but she could not speak.

"When the madness passed and I realized what I had done, I was sick inside," he said. "I—I took the scalps and burned them all. It didn't help. That horrible time haunted me, Stella. It haunts me to this day."

He stopped speaking and waited, his silence pleading for her compassion. But Stella could not even shake her head. She felt as if her whole body had turned to ice.

"I saw things during the war," he said, "things that were ten times worse—" He broke off, knowing he had begun a useless argument. Stella stood stiff and cold, not looking at him.

At last she found her voice—not even a voice, really, only a cold, thin whisper, like the sound a winter breeze through the bare willows.

"I buried Knute and Karin when Red Hawk had finished with them," she said. "They'd been scalped, both of them—only poor Knute didn't have much hair, so they took his ear, too.'' She drew a deep, painful breath. ''Red Hawk...Washakie...Falling Arrow...and you. You're no different from the rest of them, Cade. You condemned me, but you're the savage.''

Chapter Sixteen

Cade knelt in the snow and blew on the fire. The tiny flames that had sprung from the tinder barely caught at the damp kindling.

He had not planned to spend another night on the trail, nor had he wanted to. But one of the horses, the big one that pulled the travois, had gone lame. The resulting slow pace had cost them several hours and left them a good nine miles short of the fort when darkness fell. Rather than risk the night and the uncertain weather, he had decided to make camp.

At least he'd had the presence of mind to send Falling Arrow ahead to the fort on his swift-footed pony. If Sam was still at Bridger, he would know they were coming, and he would wait for them.

Aside from that . . . Cade shook his head as he glanced around at the dismal camp. The entire day had been like a bad dream. Stella had been silent and withdrawn, almost cringing when he came near her. It wasn't her fault, he tried to tell himself. This trip had given her a dose of wilderness life at its worst, and she was exhausted. Still, he could not help feeling hurt by her coldness—especially after what had passed between them back in the valley.

The weather had been gray and cheerless all day, the trail rutted with ice where other travelers had passed. Cade's mood had matched the sky. The slow tedium of their progress with the limping horse had set his teeth on edge.

Wind River

And underneath it all boiled the frustration that Gillis had admitted to nothing. For all the misery of the trip and the pain of his wounds, he was as vile and cocky as ever, still insisting that this whole thing was a mistake. Even the promise of brandy, all he wanted to drink, could not change his story.

Cade sighed wearily as he got up from the sputtering fire and went over to unsaddle the horses. Out of the corner of his eye, he could see Stella rummaging among the cooking utensils. He had long ago ceased to question her innocence in Jared's death. No matter what anybody said, Stella Brannon was not capable of murder. There was too much gentleness in her, too much decency, too much love of life.

But Jared—that was a matter that had chewed at Cade day and night. And every time he looked at Gillis's greasy face, the obsession grew. What had Jared been doing with a man like that, standing by while Gillis forced his way into a woman's tent and tried to rape her at knifepoint? Jared was no angel, true, but he'd always had a gallant heart. What could have explained it? That question ate like lye at Cade's soul.

According to the girl, Martha Jane, Jared and Gillis had played poker together at the bar in South Pass. Did that mean they were friends? Did that mean they were partners in crime? Cade mulled the evidence over in his mind as he hefted the saddle onto a stump and ran his hands over the roan's damp withers. Gillis and Jared. Something didn't fit.

Stella had set up the cooking pot and was mixing the gruel she fed to Gillis. For a few minutes Cade let his eyes drink her in: the glow of the firelight on her russet hair, the graceful movements of her hands. Right then he would have done anything to make things right between them. But he knew the odds were against it. There was no way to change his violent past. As long as Stella couldn't accept what he was, their relationship was at an impasse. Still, he could not stop thinking of her. He had not given up hope, he realized, that somehow she might change her mind about him.

Gillis moaned sharply as Track-the-Buffalo applied a fresh bark dressing to his side. Gillis was a tough buzzard; you had to give him that. No wonder he'd been so hard to break. The wretch was beyond threats, beyond hope; a man who had nothing to lose. Cade had racked his brain for a way to make him talk but had come up empty.

While Stella was feeding Gillis, Cade sliced up the last of the bacon he'd brought and fried it for supper. After the meal, Cade, Stella and the young Shoshone wrapped themselves in their blankets and settled down around the fire. Gillis, still lashed to the travois, lay a few feet away from them. He had already fallen into a fitful, moaning slumber.

Cade stretched out a few feet from Stella, hoping for a chance to talk with her after Track-the-Buffalo went to sleep. It probably wouldn't do much good, he told himself. She'd made things clear enough. But this could well be their last night together. For once in his life, he had to swallow his pride. He had to do whatever he could to keep from losing her.

A soft wind had sprung up, thinning out the clouds that had overhung the day. Here and there, patches of clear sky, bright with stars, could be seen. Cade lay listening to the sound of the stirring trees, gathering his nerve.

When he was sure that Gillis and the Shoshone youth were deep in slumber, he reached out and brushed Stella's shoulder with his hand.

She opened her eyes at once, and he knew she had not been asleep. "I'm sorry," he whispered in a voice too low to wake the others. "I know you're tired. But I couldn't go to sleep without talking to you."

She lay there in silence, her dark eyes catching the red glow of the coals. Cade gulped back his own pride and braced himself for what he was about to say. He knew how she felt about him now. He knew he was opening up painful wounds for them both. But he had to speak up. The thought of losing her, when a few simple, spoken words might make the difference, gave him the courage.

Wind River

"Back there in the valley, we had something, Stella," he began awkwardly. "Something very precious. We both knew it, I think. I—it's something I don't want to lose. And I don't want to lose you, either."

She did not answer, but her eyes glittered in the firelight, as if there might be tears in them. Her body seemed to be trembling.

"It's a lonely life in the Wind River country," he said, trying to keep his voice steady. "But together we could make it a good life. There's a chance for us, Stella, a real chance, if we can just forget the past."

There, he had said it. A handful of words representing a mountain of swallowed pride. Surely she would know what it had cost him to say those words. Surely she would understand how much he wanted her.

She stirred in her blanket and turned over so that she was looking up at the sky. When she finally spoke, it seemed to be as much to the stars as to him.

"I've been thinking a lot about Karin," she whispered. "I've been thinking about how much she loved Knute and about how much he loved her." She shook her head, the firelight catching a gleam of wetness on her cheek. "Love was all they had, Cade, and it wasn't enough. They lived miserably, and when they died—" Her breath caught in her throat. "Nobody should have to live or die the way they did. Love wasn't enough for Knute and Karin, and it's not enough for us. There are just—just too many problems."

Now it was Cade's turn to be silent. He lay on his back, listening to the distant call of a snowy owl. "What will you do?" he asked at last.

"Assuming I don't hang or go to jail—" she gave a bitter little laugh "—I'll most likely go back to Boston. My father's friends will lend me enough money for new camera equipment, I think. After that ... Europe, maybe. I've always wanted to see Italy...."

Her words hung on the air, as flawless as snowflakes in their logic and just as cold. Cade had no answer for them. He had pushed aside his barriers of pride and caution long enough to offer her his future. Now he could feel those barriers moving back into place, this time for good.

He had tried, he reflected. Now there was no more to be said. She would return to her world, and he would remain in his. They would go on, both of them, as if the events of the past few weeks had never happened. But he knew, all the same, that no matter how long he lived, he would never stop remembering....

Cade did not realize he had drifted off till he felt a hand nudge his shoulder. He opened his eyes to find Track-the-Buffalo leaning over him.

The young Shoshone put a finger to his lips to signal silence. "Listen," he hissed. "There's something out there in the trees."

Cade sat up and reached for his rifle. The fire had burned down to a few red coals. He could hear the horses, stamping and snorting. Something, he realized, was spooking them.

Cautiously, he got to his feet and cocked the Spencer. He could see that Stella was awake, too, her eyes big and frightened in the moonlight. Moving silently, he edged over to where the horses were tied. The roan had its ears laid back and was showing the whites of its eyes. The big paint Stella had been riding was tossing its head, jerking hard at its tether.

Whatever was out there wasn't human, Cade guessed. The horses were used to having people around them. It would take a bear or a cougar to get them this upset.

He took a deep breath and moved past the horses into the stand of thin, white aspens. Rifle ready, he scanned the area around him.

Out here, away from the circle of the camp, the night was quiet. The waning moon cast blue shadows on the snow. Cade jumped at a fluttering sound behind him, then relaxed a little as he realized it was only an owl, startled from its perch on a dead stump. He walked a little farther and saw tracks in a line, circling the camp. Bear tracks.

Warily, he bent down and examined them. They were fresh, but not large. The bear was a black, he decided, and most likely a young one—more of a nuisance than a danger. It had probably smelled the bacon and wandered in to investigate.

Cade was about to turn around and head back for camp when a sudden movement caught his eye. There was the bear, silhouetted against the pale trees, not a stone's throw away.

Instinctively he raised his rifle. The bear growled, hesitant to charge or flee. It was no bigger than a good-size sheepdog—a two-year-old cub, most likely, and newly on its own. It would be a shame to have to shoot it.

With a final menacing snarl, the bear turned and ambled away. Relieved, Cade lowered the gun. That was when a sudden notion struck him—an idea so diabolical that it shocked him at first. Then, as he thought about it, he realized it might be the one way to get what he wanted from Newt Gillis.

He walked back into the clearing. Someone had put another log on the fire. Its light cast a flickering yellow glow around the camp. Gillis was stirring on the travois.

"It's a bear, all right," Cade announced, wandering over to warm his hands above the flames. "Couldn't get a shot, but he's out there. I heard him and saw his tracks."

Stella huddled beside him, trying to get warm. "Is it a big one?" she asked in a whisper.

Cade nodded, hating to lie to her, but knowing it was necessary if his plan was to work. "Too big to stop with this rifle, I'm afraid," he said. "We'll have to be on the lookout all night. I've known bears to come right into camp if they get hungry enough." He glanced around at Gillis, who was taking in every word, his eyes bulging.

"They like horseflesh," he continued, setting the bait. "But they're not all that fussy. They'll gladly make a meal of a human if they can catch one. Isn't that so, Mr. Gillis?"

Gillis swore under his breath and twisted against his lashings.

"It's too bad we've gone through most of our grub," Cade said. "If we could throw something out there for him to eat, he'd probably go away and quit bothering us." He let that thought hang on the air while he poked at the fire with a stick. The horses were still spooked. They snorted, squealed and pulled at their tethers as the bear scent filled their nostrils.

"Of course, it wouldn't help to give the bear just a few bites," Cade continued in the same vein. "He'd only want more, and then we'd have him right in our laps. We'd have to offer him something that would satisfy him." He glanced over at Gillis. Yes, it was working. Beads of sweat were breaking out on the big miner's face.

"The horse," Gillis said. "The lame 'un. You could take it off in the trees and tie it up. We—we ain't got far to go. We could make it to the fort with the horses that's left!"

Cade looked straight at Gillis and slowly shook his head. "Horses are worth money," he said. "But you, now, Mr. Gillis. You aren't worth anything to us. Why not put *you* out there for bear bait?"

From behind him, Cade heard Stella gasp. "You wouldn't!" she whispered.

"Why not?" He turned on her, and not all the bitterness in his voice was feigned. "Last night you called me a savage. Maybe I'm about to prove you right!"

He looked back at Gillis and saw that the big miner was shaking like a drunkard. "Ye—ye wouldn't do that to a man!" he croaked.

Cade poked at the fire for a few seconds. "I wouldn't do it if you'd agree to tell us what happened back in Green River. But since you won't, you're no good to us for anything but bear feed. We've brought you all this way for nothing, and we might as well be rid of you!"

Cade paused a moment to let the words sink in. Then he beckoned to Track-the-Buffalo. "You take one pole of the travois," he said, pointing as he spoke in English. "I'll take the other."

Understanding the gesture, the young Shoshone did as he was told. Stella crouched beside the fire, staring at them in horror and confusion. Cade wished he could have let her in on the secret.

As the poles of the travois were lifted off the ground, Gillis's iron control broke. He began to sob and blubber uncontrollably, thrashing around so wildly on the travois that Cade feared he would tear his dressings off. "No...." he moaned. "In the name o' God, man...."

Cade felt a hand on his arm. It was Stella, her dark eyes glittering with tears. "Stop it, Cade," she whispered. "I don't care who he is or what he did, you can't put a human being through this!"

He forced himself to turn away from her. "Come on," he said gruffly, signaling to Track-the-Buffalo. Together, they began to drag the travois away from the camp fire and into the trees. The horses were frantic by now, a sign that the bear was still close by.

"Noooo!" The cry scarcely sounded human. "Damn ye all to hell! I'll tell anything ye want to know! Jist—jist don't put me out there! For the love o' God!"

Cade let his breath out in a long sigh of relief. "All right," he said, nodding to the young Shoshone. "Take him back to the fire."

Gillis's story bore out everything Stella had said about the night Jared was killed. The ironic thing was that none of it came as a surprise to Cade. He had believed her for a long time, he realized, maybe even from the beginning.

There had been some questions, however, that not even Stella had been able to answer. Questions about Jared. Cade wanted the answers to those questions. He would have them now.

"I knowed your brother purty well," Gillis admitted in response to Cade's insistent probing. "Wild young buck if there ever was one. Too damned cocky for his own good!

Never knew when he ought to leave a man alone!" The big miner leaned over and spat in the snow.

"Jared wouldn't leave *you* alone? That's what you're saying?"

"Little bugger claimed I owed 'im money. Kep' after me for it. A hunnert dollars, it was. He'd give it to me t'use in a poker game. I said I'd give 'im double the money back if'n I won. But it weren't my lucky night. I lost it. Figgered it was his loss, too, but he thought different."

"What was he doing with you in Green River?" Cade asked, trying to move the story along.

"Brandy," Gillis muttered. "Got to have it t'talk."

Cade uncorked the flask he'd brought and gave Gillis a long swig. Stella sat a little to one side, just watching, her eyes large and sad.

Gillis licked the last of the brandy off his thick lips. "Met up again with young Jared as I was leaving town, an' right off he started in about the money. Wouldn't let it be. That was when I got the idea." His eyes wandered to the brandy, and Cade gave him another sip.

"Remembered the red-haired gal I'd saw in town that day. Thought if I could git the boy likkered up good an' somehow git him into trouble with her, then he'd wind up in jail an' I'd be rid o' him. Sounded good at the time, an' I had some whiskey on me. Good stuff I'd got off the railroad. We both had a lot, but I saw to it that he got more'n I did. Little bugger was so drunk he couldn't hardly walk! Had to sort of lead 'im 'round like a dog."

Cade was beginning to feel sick inside. He'd blamed himself all along for what had happened to Jared, but Gillis's words drove the point into his conscience like a steel spike. Jared had been too naive and too reckless to survive frontier life on his own. The boy should have been kept at the ranch by force if necessary, or sent back to Saint Louis.

"Didn't mean no more harm'n that," Gillis went on. "Figgered I'd jist shove 'im in that gal's tent an' let her screamin' do the rest. But on the way over there I got t'thinkin' about that gal an' how purty she looked sa-shayin' around with that pitcher-takin' stuff. Figgered 'long as I was there, I might as well have first go at 'er myself.''

Cade could not sit still. He had to get up and walk away to keep from slamming his fist into Gillis's face. Seething with rage, he strode to the edge of the camp and stared out into the darkness. The horses were still nervous, but not the way they'd been earlier. Maybe the bear was moving off.

When he turned around he saw that Stella was giving Gillis another drink of the brandy. "Go on," she was saying. "I have to hear this, too."

Gillis licked his lips again. "'Member I'd had a few drinks," he said. "Weren't thinkin' too straight or I'da saw where things was headed. Once I got the knife on ye, gir-lie, it hit me that you knew who I was now. I'd have had t'kill ye afterwards t'keep ye from talkin'. But I figgered it was all right, 'cause they'd jist blame Jared fer it. An' he was so drunk, he weren't goin' nowhere!''

"Good Lord!" Cade breathed, thinking how fate had twisted Gillis's plan. It could have just as easily been Stella dead and Jared hanging for her murder.

Stella must have been thinking the same thing. She got up without a word and walked away, as far as the edge of the trees. There she stood for a time, her eyes on the stars, her hand resting against one of the bare, white trunks.

After a few minutes, Cade drifted over and stood beside her. At first she did not speak. Then, suddenly, she turned on him, her voice shaking. "I know you had to do it," she said, "but that was inhuman, Cade! It was—"

"Savage?" Cade's throat was tight. "Yes, I had to do it. I had to get Gillis to talk. But it's over now. You're going to be all right, Stella."

She stared into the sky again. "Yes," she murmured, her voice flat. "It's over. It's all over."

Fort Bridger lay on a high, rolling plain dotted with trees and set off by the twin forks of a river. Its original stock-ade walls had burned long ago. Now its clusters of low, whitewashed buildings stood in the open, making it look more like an immaculate little town than a frontier military post. To Stella, after the long, miserable journey, it was a beautiful sight.

When the man who came galloping out of the fort to meet them turned out to be Sam Catlin, she felt weak with relief. She had to pull her horse out of the way as the marshal came thundering up and reined in his big bay, showering the travois with snow.

"I'll be damned!" he boomed, slapping Cade on the back with his Stetson. "Good thing you sent that Injun kid on ahead of you. Otherwise, I'd have been halfway to Green River by now!" He swung his horse around to where he could look down at Gillis. "So this is the murderin' coyote, eh? Lordy, looks like he might not live to hang!"

"He told us everything," Cade said. "His confession ought to be more than enough to clear things up for Stella."

"We'll get it down first thing," Sam said. "Then we'll lock this galoot up somewhere till we can find a doc to look at him." He turned to Stella. "We've got you a place to stay, too, Missus Brannon. Judge Carter, who runs the big army store, said he and his missus would be happy to put you up for a spell. Come on, I'll take you over there." He swung back toward Cade. "Oh, the judge says to tell you you're invited for dinner tonight. You can pick up some fresh clothes at the store and a bath in the officer's quarters!"

Cade nodded. "Tell him I'll be pleased to come."

Stella felt his eyes on her as she rode off with Sam, but she did not turn around. Meeting those eyes was more than she could do today. It would have torn her apart.

The sight of the imposing Carter home was almost a shock to Stella after her time in the wilderness. Even the well-dressed matron on the porch seemed to have been transported from another part of the world—some gentle place where there were no scalpings, murders, lynch mobs or grizzly bears.

"The Carters are from Virginny," Sam whispered to her as they rode up to the house. "When they come here, years ago, they brought a little bit of Virginny with 'em. They've even got a piano in their sittin' room! That's Missus Mary Carter on the porch. Right fine lady.''

Mary Carter clutched her merino shawl around her shoulders and hurried down the steps to meet them. As Stella watched her come, she suddenly realized how Karin Aarnson must have felt when another white woman showed up at her cabin. There was an instant bond between them, a kinship born of loneliness and isolation.

Impulsively, Stella slipped out of the saddle to greet her hostess on foot. The two of them stopped within a pace of each other. Mary Carter was a handsome woman, silver haired, with an erect posture. Stella took swift stock of her expensively made cashmere dress, her smoothly coiffed hair, her onyx brooch and earrings. For the first time in weeks, she became acutely conscious of her own bedraggled appearance. She fought the urge to hide herself.

Mary gazed at Stella's baggy men's clothing, her windburned face, her impossibly tangled hair. ''Oh, my dear child!'' she exclaimed. ''My poor, dear girl!''

She gathered Stella into her arms in much the same way Stella had embraced a weeping Karin Aarnson an eternity ago on the Little Sandy. Stella could have wept, too. But no, she resolved. This was no time to cry, not with her ordeal so nearly over.

''Come on into the house,'' Mary said, keeping an arm around Stella's waist as they walked. ''Sam told us you were coming, so everything's ready. A warm bath, a bed, whatever you need. I even have some dresses that should fit you. My daughters left them behind when they went off to school in the East. Said they were going out of style.... I hope you won't mind that too much.''

''Mind?'' Stella managed to laugh. ''Just look at me! I promise you I won't mind at all!''

The piano in the Carters' parlor was a Steinway grand. It had been hauled all the way across the plains by ox cart, years before the coming of the railroad, and it was still one of the most beautiful objects Cade had ever seen.

As he waited for the other dinner guests to arrive, he leaned over and ran a surreptitious finger across the cool, ivory keyboard. The light movement produced no sound. It was simply a caress, a tribute.

"You play, Mr. Garrison?" Judge Carter, tall and distinguished, with a flowing beard, had come into the room.

"No," Cade said. "But I always wish I'd learned to play something, at least. The Wind River gets awfully quiet at times."

"Yes, I know what you mean," the judge said. "Mary and I came here eleven years ago when I got the chance to open a supply store for the army. I saw it as an opportunity to make some good money, and it's been that." He sighed. "It was hard for Mary, though, leaving Virginia. She's been a good soldier, but sometimes—sometimes I think the one thing that pulled her through the lonely times was having this piano here. It cost me a small fortune to have it carted out, but it's been worth every cent."

Cade glanced around the room, at the shelves filled with books, the oil paintings on the walls, the fine lace curtains at the windows. "You've built a good life here," he said. "I hope I'll be able to say as much for myself in a few years—especially if my ranch pays off the way I expect it to. I've got plans for stables, a barn...and a house as grand as this one someday."

Judge Carter nodded. "Now that the railroad's almost here, the good life's going to be much easier to come by. Just watch—you'll see civilization springing up all over. Towns with fine schools and stores...even libraries and theaters. The frontier will be a thing of the past." He turned and gazed out the window into the twilight. "I guess progress is a good thing. Still, somehow, it seems a damned shame."

"Yes, I know." Cade thought of the Shoshone and how their traditional ways would be threatened. He thought of the dwindling buffalo herds, the shrinking hunting grounds, and felt a sudden, profound sadness. "There's good and bad in everything, I suppose," he said.

"True," the judge agreed with a sigh. "Frontier life can be bleak and lonely. Me—I don't know what I'd have done out here all these years without Mary. Her willingness to make a home here, in spite of the hardships . . . it made the whole experience worthwhile and kept me civilized in the process!" He glanced up at the sound of light footsteps overhead. "I daresay that's the ladies. They should be down shortly. Do you plan on staying around Bridger long, Mr. Garrison?"

Cade shook his head. "I'm leaving at dawn, with the marshal. He's going to need my help in getting Gillis and the other prisoner back as far as the railroad. And that's just as well, since there's a small legal matter he has to help me clear up in Green River."

"Yes." A flicker of a smile crossed the judge's face. "I heard all about your spiriting Mrs. Brannon out of jail with the lynch mob at your heels. Quite an escapade." He gazed out the window for a moment, curling a strand of his long fine beard around one finger. "You think your Mr. Gillis will be sentenced to hang?"

"If he lives. He's as strong as a bull, but he's not out of danger yet."

"I see." The judge sighed. "I've already talked with the marshal about Mrs. Brannon. She's to remain right here, in my custody, till the charges against her are cleared. Once that's taken care of, he'll send me a wire, then she'll be free to go where she likes."

"She talked about going back East," Cade said. "Will you see to it that she gets safely on the train?"

"Certainly."

"I'd like to leave some money with you. Enough for her ticket and a few other things she might need. Could you find a way to give it to her without letting her know where it came from?"

The judge gave Cade a swift, penetrating glance. "Yes, of course," he said. "And don't worry, I won't let her know. I'll think of a good story— Ah! There's the door. It must be some of our other guests. Excuse me. I must go and let them in."

Cade waited in the parlor for a few minutes, his eyes skimming restlessly over the titles of the judge's books. Then, when the judge did not return, he wandered out into the foyer.

The other guests were clustered at the foot of the stairs. Cade had not met them, but it was easy enough to guess who they were. The graying man in the colonel's uniform had to be Morrow, the post commander, with his aide, a well-polished young captain, standing like a chess piece at his side. The other fellow, sporting a fringed buckskin jacket, would be Luther Mann, the government Indian commissioner. They were all looking up, toward the top of the staircase.

Cade followed their gaze, and suddenly his breath caught. Stella glided down the stairs toward him, a vision in pale rose lace. His eyes drank her in. Mary's skillful hands had twisted her coppery hair into a knot at the crown of her head, leaving small, curling tendrils to fall around her face. Amethyst earrings, their color echoing the fabric of the gown, swung as she moved, catching the light of the chandelier in the hallway.

The dress itself was cut low at the bodice, showing her creamy shoulders and just a hint of softly rounded bosom. A full skirt billowed out from her tiny, tapering waist, swirling as she walked.

"By thunder, what a woman!" Cade heard a murmur, and he realized it was the young captain.

Dinner, for Cade, was a blur in which he saw nothing clearly except Stella. As she chatted graciously with the officers and other guests, he realized that this was a side of her he had never seen. And while he was dazzled by her beauty and her sparkle, the sight of her also filled him with dismay.

He had been a fool, he told himself, to even dream that she could be content with the life he had offered her. He could see now that she belonged in a finer setting, with lovely clothes, paintings on the wall, silver, crystal and china on the table. One day, he might be able to give her those things. But not now. Not yet. There was still so much work to do, getting the ranch built up the way he wanted it.

Stella, at least, had had the good sense to turn him down. *Love wasn't enough*—that's what she had said. Seeing her now, as she listened to the exploits of the dashing captain, Cade could only conclude that she was right.

In spite of everything, however, he could not take his eyes off her all evening. And when the other guests were saying their goodbyes and drifting away, he found himself making excuses to stay. He lingered in the parlor, browsing through the judge's books, until even the entranced Captain Vickers had taken his leave.

She came in to him then, closing the parlor door softly behind her.

"Cade—"

"You look lovely," he said.

"You'll be leaving in the morning?"

"I have to help Sam with the prisoners."

"Then..." She turned her face away from him, twisting her hands. "I—I never realized saying goodbye would be so hard." Her voice caught, and he realized she was on the verge of tears.

"Do something for me," he said gently, not touching her. "You said you played the piano..."

"I'm awfully out of practice," she said, "but I'll try. I owe you that much."

"You don't owe me anything. I think there's some sheet music in the bench."

He settled into a leather armchair while she ruffled through the pages of music and found something she knew. "Forgive me," she whispered, seating herself on the piano bench. "It's been so long. I know it won't sound the way I'd like it to."

"That's all right, Stella," he said, his throat tight.

She played for him then, a tinkling little Mozart sonata. Her fingers were shaky, the notes uncertain. Once or twice she nearly stopped, but she made it through to the end, then turned on the bench and sat looking at him, without a word.

Cade rose from the chair and walked over to where she sat. Gently he lifted her right hand from the keyboard, uncurled the long fingers and pressed his lips to her palm.

"Goodbye, Stella," he said.

Chapter Seventeen

Captain Harry Vickers stepped into the parlor, where Stella was waiting for him. She had been at Fort Bridger for a week, and this was the fourth time he had come to call— or was it the fifth? She had already lost track.

He doffed his regulation felt hat. His warm brown eyes took her in greedily from head to toe. "You do look stunning in that riding habit!" he exclaimed.

"Thank you," Stella brushed a speck of lint off the sleeve of the dark blue woolen jacket. "It's amazing how well the clothes that Mary's daughters left fit me. Even the boots. But don't come too close. The mothball smell will knock you flat!"

"Wait till you see what I found in the stable!" he said. "It's a real sidesaddle. Some officer's wife must have left it here. You'll be able to ride like a lady again!"

"That's awfully sweet of you, Harry. I just hope I can remember how." Stella laughed and tossed her curls. After her ordeals in the wilderness, it was pleasant to wear pretty clothes again, to put combs in her hair and dab Mary's eau de cologne behind her ears. It was pleasant, being courted like a proper lady. Even Harry— Oh, she had no illusions about him, but he was handsome, and there was a certain comfort in knowing that she controlled the relationship. With Harry, there was no danger. There was no chance of being swept away by a passion that would tempt her to throw all caution to the winds. She felt safe.

All the same, she mused, there was a strange aura of un-reality to this new world of hers. Sometimes she felt as if she were an actress on a stage with painted scenery, wearing pretty costumes, speaking polite and proper lines she would never have thought of on her own. But maybe that was only because she was still adjusting to the change, Stella told herself. She would come around in time.

She had made up her mind to put the Wind River Valley and its painful memories behind her. Still, there were days when she ached to see the sun on the rocky crags of the mountains, or to go galloping bareback across the pasture astride the unruly little black mustang. And there were times when the raw honesty and sheer physical power of what she had shared with Cade seemed more real than anything she could see or touch here in the safety of the fort. Sometimes—at night, when no one could hear—she cried.

Harry's voice brought her back to the present. "You shouldn't have any trouble riding," he said. "I picked out the gentlest gelding in the stable for you."

"Then I should be able to manage the sidesaddle," she said, thinking of the time she had plunged full tilt down the slope on Cade's big roan, with hostile Sioux screaming all around her. "Look how lovely it is outside. It's a perfect day for a ride. Shall we go now, Harry?"

She turned to leave the parlor and found that he was blocking her way. He stood very close to her, tall and broad shouldered in his well-pressed blue uniform, and smelling lightly of bay rum. His brown eyes, flecked with gold, burned into hers.

Stella's breath caught. Suddenly she was seeing other eyes, pale blue eyes, like winter ice; wolf's eyes. She felt weak.

"Please," she murmured. "Let's just go."

"All right. After you!" He stepped aside and the spell was broken.

Soon they were riding along the side of the parade ground, where the river ran past the fort, their mounts trotting at a leisurely pace. The country was open and rolling, dotted with trees and clumps of brush. At the base of some nearby hills, Stella could make out the clustered lodges and rising smoke of an Indian camp.

"You're lucky to be stationed here," she said, making conversation. "It's so peaceful."

Harry shook his head. "Too peaceful for me. The most exciting thing that happens here is an occasional drunken brawl among the redskins. I'd rather be where the action is!"

"Oh?" Stella's eyes followed the flight of a hawk.

"In fact," Harry said, "I'll let you in on a secret. I've applied for a transfer to a cavalry unit—the papers should come through any day. I'm hoping for the Seventh, since Colonel Custer's been one of my heroes for years. Now, there's a man who knows how to handle Indians!"

"So I've heard," Stella said archly. Her eyes were on the Indian camp and the two slender riders who were galloping out in the direction of the fort. They waved when they saw her, and she recognized She-Bear's two sons. Evidently, they'd been having too much fun at Fort Bridger to go back to the Wind River.

"Look at those two bucks, now," Harry was saying. "What good are they? Either they loll around the fort and take government handouts, or they go on the warpath. America will be a better place when all the Indians are gone, and I mean to do my part in bringing that about!"

Stella sighed. "Harry, the Indians were here first. They have as much right to this country as we do!"

Harry laughed. "Sometimes I don't understand you," he said. "But then again, what's to understand about a beautiful woman?" His eyes flickered over her in a way that Stella found mildly disturbing, but she ignored the warning. She could handle Harry, she told herself.

A cold breeze stirred her hair. Beyond the parade ground, a half mile away, she could see a small rise topped by a stand of bare aspens.

"Come on!" she said, jabbing the horse with her boot heel. "I'll race you to that hilltop and back!"

In an instant they were flying across the parade ground, leaping the creek, spattering snow as they landed on the other side. It was hard hanging on with one knee crooked over the horn of the sidesaddle, but Stella was filled with a sudden surge of recklessness. She took the gelding full-out.

She was leading when they topped the rise. Behind her she could hear Harry's horse, laboring up the slope. Harry looked irritable; it was clear that he didn't enjoy being beaten, especially by a woman.

As she was wheeling the gelding for the return, he suddenly caught up to her, seized the bridle and jerked her mount to a halt. For an instant his eyes frightened her, but they swiftly became gentle again.

She forced herself to laugh. "Why did you do that, Harry? Was it because I was winning?"

"I was worried about you." He eased out of the saddle, still gripping her reins. "A lady's got no business riding like that. She's liable to get hurt."

"You're calling off the race, then?" Stella kept her manner lighthearted.

"There's a nice view from here. Thought we might take a little time to enjoy it, instead of tearing back like a couple of lunatics." He reached up to her. Not wanting to be unreasonable, she let him help her out of the saddle. His hands gripped her waist, lingered, then released her as she turned away from him.

"Oh, you're right, Harry! It is a nice view! A lovely view!" She walked away from him to the brow of the hill, where the snowy, tree-flecked plain stretched toward the horizon. "Look! Isn't that a herd of—"

Her voice broke off abruptly as she felt Harry's hands sliding around her shoulders. She stiffened, as if she had turned to ice.

"There, now, sweetheart." His breath was warm and damp against her ear. "I know what you must be thinking. Back East we'd have time for proper courting, you and

I. There'd be time for balls, parties... walking home from church on Sundays. But this is the West, Stella. We can't count on time out here. We have to make the most of what we've got."

He spun her around. His lips caught hers in a smothering kiss that bent her backward over his arm. Stella neither responded nor resisted. She felt... nothing, really. Only awkwardness, embarrassment and a sense of remoteness, as if she were an actress enduring an overdone stage kiss in a play.

He released her, breathing like a stallion. "There's plenty more where that came from," he said. "If you'll just let me...."

She lowered her eyes, trying not to see Cade's face in her mind. Harry had only kissed her; that was all. And she was a free woman. Yet somehow she felt compromised, cheapened.

"Please, Harry, I think we'd better get back," she said, edging toward the horses. "I promised to help Mary with dinner."

With a swift movement, he blocked her way. "One more kiss," he teased. "That's my price for letting you go, Mrs. Stella Brannon!" He opened his arms, waiting.

His presumptuousness triggered a sudden rise of indignation in Stella. "Thank you, but I don't deal in kisses," she said. "And you've no right to keep me here."

She started for her horse again, but he sprinted around her and stood, again, blocking her path. "You heard my price," he said with a laugh. "If you want to get home in time for supper, then you must pay!"

Stella gave a little huff of exasperation. Harry meant no harm, she told herself. The most graceful way out of her predicament would be to give him a swift peck and be done with it. But he had raised a flag of stubbornness in her.

"I don't give kisses on demand!" she insisted. "Now, let me get on my horse, or I start screaming!"

"Aha!" It had become a game to him, a challenge. "Scream and see how I stop that pretty mouth!" He made a playful lunge for her. Stella spun away, but he caught her by one arm and swung her back against him, holding her fast.

"Now I've got you!" His eyes, inches from hers, gleamed triumphantly. "You can't fly away, little bird!"

Stella's annoyance was rapidly turning to desperation. Maybe Harry wasn't as harmless as she'd thought. Game or no game, if she didn't find a way out of this predicament, she could end up very sorry.

She met his gaze with an icy glare. "Let me go, Harry. I mean it. This isn't funny."

"Funny?" He laughed roughly as his arms tightened around her. "I never meant it to be!"

His mouth came down on hers, forceful, hurting. Frightened now, Stella wrenched her face away and began to struggle.

"That's it, sweetheart." He chuckled, his lips moving lower, to the open neck of her blouse. "Go ahead and fight me a little. Deep down, I know you want this as much as I do!"

"No!" she gasped as his hard fingers began to knead one of her breasts. "No, Harry! I'll report you to the colonel ... the judge—" She was fighting him wildly now, but he was too strong for her. Her movements only seemed to arouse him more.

"Who's going to ... believe you?" His breath was coming deep and hard. "A woman like you ... a fugitive...."

Panic seized Stella as she felt his weight against her, forcing her down on her back in the snow. "Harry— please!" She writhed and kicked beneath him as he jerked her skirt up to her thighs. The whole awful memory of that night in her tent came rushing back over her as she struggled. It was Gillis she was fighting now, Gillis's fingers ripping at her clothes, Gillis's weight holding her down.

A scream tore loose from her throat, only to be stifled by his hand. "Don't be a little goose!" he muttered. "You've had it before and liked it, I can tell! You'll like this, too, if you'll just let me—"

His face froze in sudden surprise. Stella heard a horse snort and saw Track-the-Buffalo looming above them, ready to strike at Harry with a fist-size rock. Behind him, Falling Arrow had just gained the hilltop and was flinging himself out of the saddle to help.

Harry was a seasoned Indian fighter. In a lightning move, he rolled to one side, sprang to his feet and snapped his pistol out of its holster. Seeing the weapon, the two young Shoshones edged back hesitantly.

"Friends of yours, I take it?" Harry muttered, cocking the pistol.

Stella was still on the snowy ground, struggling to get her skirt down. "For heaven's sake, Harry, put your gun away! They're only boys, and they're not even armed!"

"They're Indians. And they were threatening us. I've got every right." He aimed the pistol at Track-the-Buffalo's chest and started to squeeze the trigger.

Somehow Stella made it to her feet. She flew at Harry like a wildcat, hurling herself against his arm. The crack of the pistol shattered the wintery silence, but the shot went wild.

In the next instant, Stella, her fury giving her strength, had knocked the pistol from Harry's hand. The weapon flew into a snowdrift, where it was retrieved by Falling Arrow.

"You fool!" Wild with rage and relief, Stella pummeled Harry with her fists. "You blind, mad fool! They're Shoshone! They're Chief Washakie's grandsons! Do you know what you almost did?"

Harry glared at her in stubborn, cowed silence. Stella's glancing blows hadn't hurt him, but he was not a man who took kindly to being humiliated by a woman.

She spun back to where Harry's horse stood, tossed the reins over its head and whacked the animal resoundingly on its rump. With a snort and a toss of its mane, the horse bolted down the hill.

Still furious, she strode toward her own horse. Her hands, she realized, were shaking like aspen leaves. Her knees quivered as she led the gelding to the side of a fallen log and climbed up to mount. By the time she had pulled herself awkwardly into the sidesaddle, she was shuddering with disgust and delayed fear.

"Stella...." There was a pleading note in Harry's voice. "You—you aren't going to make trouble for me, are you? I was only having a little fun...."

"Here." Stella held out her hand to Falling Arrow, who, very gingerly, gave her the pistol. "I'm taking this for now," she told Harry. "You can reclaim it from Judge Carter after you get back to the fort. Meanwhile, I hope you enjoy walking."

She spurred the gelding to a brisk trot and headed back down the hill, toward the fort. Without being told, the two Shoshone boys mounted and followed her, leaving Harry alone.

No, she resolved as she rode, she would not make trouble for Harry Vickers. She had already experienced enough scandal and notoriety to last her a lifetime. She would make some excuse to explain her disheveled appearance and her having Harry's pistol. Then she would try to put the whole ugly episode behind her.

Outside the fort, she thanked She-Bear's two sons as best she could and sent them back to the encampment. Then she headed for the stable to put her horse away. From there it would be an easy walk to the Carter home.

The stable was quiet, deserted both inside and out, except for the army horses. Stella led the gelding to its stall, feeling the comforting darkness around her, breathing in the fresh, earthy smells of manure and hay. She was all right, she tried to reassure herself. The encounter with Harry was over, like a bad dream.

Still, when she had unsaddled the gelding, she stood in the stall for a long moment, her face pressed against the damp, satiny neck, her cheeks wet with tears. It took an effort of will to dry her eyes at last, to square her shoulders and walk toward the sunlit rectangle of the open stable door.

She had not quite reached it when she heard the clatter of hooves outside, followed by a muttered curse. Her heart sank as she realized it was Harry. Somehow, he had managed to catch his horse and had evidently crossed the open country at full gallop.

Any second he would be coming inside. Unless she wanted another nasty confrontation, she would have to keep out of his sight. Swiftly Stella glanced around for a place to hide. The door at the far end of the stable was closed and bolted—no easy escape. Next to it, however, across from the stalls, she could make out a line of three or four wagons, one of them a covered van.

She ducked behind the van as Harry stepped inside, leading his horse and cursing roundly. Stella shrank back into her hiding place, his pistol still heavy in her coat pocket. What would she do if he found her? Would she have the nerve to draw the weapon and threaten him with it?

He led the horse to a stall, still cursing as he unbuckled the saddle and bridle. "Dirty bitch...." Stella closed her eyes as she caught the words. "Filthy, Indian-loving whore.... Probably sleeps with the bastards!"

She held her breath until he was gone. Then she sank back against the side of the van, the names he had called her still ringing in her ears. It didn't matter, she told herself sternly. What had happened today wasn't her fault. Still, she couldn't help feeling tainted by the whole experience.

The stable was quiet now, except for the placid munching of the horses. Stella knew it was safe for her to leave. But she found that her legs would scarcely hold her. She hesitated a moment, still leaning against the high, painted van while she gathered her courage again.

It was only when she turned to go that some faded hand lettering on the van's side caught her eye. Her heart began to thud as she struggled to make out the words in the dim light.

H. O. Magelby
Photographer
Portraits Made to Order

Stella stood transfixed, as if she had suddenly been struck by lightning. One tentative, quivering hand ventured up to unfasten the unlocked hasp that held the door. Dizzy with hope, she swung it open. For the moment, the unpleasant memory of Harry Vickers ceased to exist.

Riveted, she stared into the van's dusty, dark interior. She gasped as her eyes caught the gleam of glass plates and bottles, the familiar, bulky outline of a camera. "Dear God," she breathed. "Please don't let this be a dream!"

Then she was running out of the stable and into the snowy, sunlit afternoon. She had to see Colonel Morrow. She had to talk to him now, before the day got a minute older!

Washakie gazed intently at Cade and shook his head. "My son, you are not yourself. You have a sickness of the spirit. It shows in your eyes."

"It's nothing. All I need is a good hunt," Cade said.

"Not a good hunt." The old chief grinned slyly. "A good woman in your bed...or maybe even a bad one—that would cure you!"

They were seated, both of them cross-legged, on a blanket beside the entrance to Washakie's lodge. The life of the Shoshone village bustled around them: children gathering sticks for firewood, dogs tagging after them, women scraping hides and fetching water. Moon Bird minced past them, her baby on her back in an ornately beaded cradleboard. In Cade's absence she had been promised to Iron Bow, who was already showering his intended with gifts. Rain Flower's sister appeared self-satisfied and happy.

"Look at me, now!" The chief's eyes followed the colt-like steps of a nubile fifteen-year-old with a water jar. "I have counted more winters than I care to remember. Yet I can hunt and dance with the young braves and not grow tired. And you know why?''

Cade sighed wearily. "Yes, my father, I believe I do."

Washakie threw his head back and laughed. "Ha! I have no secrets from you, my son! But it is true. This old blood can still flow hot when the occasion calls for it.

"You, now..." He turned back to Cade, his black eyes piercing like arrows. "I know what your trouble is. You think the red-haired one has stolen your soul! But another woman can help you get it back again. Red hair or black—in the dark, there is no difference!" He touched Cade's arm, and his voice grew more gentle. "You were happy with my granddaughter, I know. You could be happy again."

Cade stared morosely at the peaks of the Wind River Mountains. Their snowy crags glowed like embers in the setting sun. "Time," he said. "That's all I really need. I'll be all right."

Washakie gazed at him sharply, his eyes narrowed to slits. "No, you need more than time," he said. "If you do not find a cure for your sickness, I think you will go away from here. And then my heart will truly be sad."

Cade pondered the old chief's words as he rode homeward. He had planned to build a life here, in the Wind River Valley. Now, however, without Stella, the idea of a future here filled him with a sense of desolation.

He had begun to realize that the land was too wild, too remote for a man alone. The nights were too cold, too quiet and too lonely. More and more, he found himself longing for warmth, for color, for the sounds of the outside world. He found himself thinking of California or Oregon, maybe even Europe.

Washakie's advice about taking another Shoshone woman was well-meant. At least it might ease the ache of physical desire that had been a torment every night since his return to the valley. But taking an Indian girl would be a selfish act, a counterfeit for what he really wanted. And it would tie him to this valley just when he needed to be free.

Stella's face swam before him in the twilight. She had haunted him since his return. Sometimes he felt as if he could almost catch glimpses of her running with the horses in the snowy pasture or slipping among the trees. At other times he would awaken to the sensation of her bending over him in the night, brushing his face with her hair. The cabin held her fragrance. The pines sang with the sound of her laughter. And the bed contained the memory of their last exquisite lovemaking—a memory so poignant that, rather than endure it, he had taken to sleeping in the loft again.

Cade knew he had to find a way to forget her, but another Shoshone bride wasn't the answer. Somehow, he had to redirect his thoughts and energy. He had to find a new reason for living, and that, as he had told Washakie, would take time.

As he approached the cabin, his senses began to prickle—a sure sign that something was wrong. From this distance, the place looked peaceful enough, with a thin finger of smoke still curling from the chimney. All the same, he pulled the loaded Spencer out of its scabbard and cocked it. Whatever was wrong, it wouldn't hurt to be ready.

As he pulled into the yard, the first thing he noticed was the hoofprints in the snow. Five or six horses, he calculated, and unshod. That would mean Indian ponies.

His eyes followed the lines they made, from the trees to the yard, then back again. Perhaps it was nothing, he told himself. A party of Shoshone braves on a hunt could have stopped by to see if he wanted to join them, then found him gone. That would explain the tracks. But it did not explain the ringing sense of danger going off like a fire bell in his head—a ringing that intensified when he suddenly realized the pasture gate was wide open.

None of the three horses could be seen. Cade swore under his breath. Whoever the thieves were, they had been extremely bold to come this close to Washakie's camp. They must have known exactly what they wanted and where to look for it.

He was turning to go and check the cabin when something caught his eye—something red against the white snow of the pasture. He groaned with dismay as he saw what it was.

Snow-in-Summer, the white filly Stella had loved, lay dead in a pool of blood, her jugular vein deeply slashed. An arrow had been shot into her flank.

Cade's thoughts swam crazily as he moved closer. Though he was still too far away to see the arrow well, he knew, with gut-wrenching certainty, what it would look like. There would be a feather attached to it—the tail feather of a hawk, its tip red with the filly's blood.

His mind went back to the awful weeks when he had stalked Red Hawk's band. He remembered the ghastly games he had played, leaving objects in their camp, coming close only to withdraw again, making sure that each man who died felt the full measure of fear. Now, he realized, Red Hawk was using the same tactic on him.

He reached the filly, wrenched the feathered arrow out of her lifeless body and flung it to the snow. A cry of wounded defiance, savage and primitive, ripped from his anguished throat.

"Red Hawk! It's me you want! Come on out! Come out and take me!"

The cry echoed against the snow, the trees and the frozen hills. It lingered in the air, then slowly died away.

Only mocking silence answered.

Stella slipped out from under the black camera cloth, her focusing completed. "Hold still now," she cautioned the wrinkled Arapaho grandmother she had posed against a rough-textured adobe wall. "You don't want to move and spoil this lovely picture!"

The old woman scowled at the black box, but she did not move as Stella lifted the cap off the lens, then replaced it with expert timing and precision. It was difficult shooting photographs with so much light reflecting off the snow. After the first few overexposed plates, however, Stella had learned to compensate by adjusting the exposure time. Since then, the photographs she'd produced were among the best she had ever taken.

"Bless you, H. O. Magelby. Heaven rest your soul!" she murmured as she slipped the plate out of the camera. It was Colonel Morrow who had told her about the wandering photographer, killed by a party of liquored-up Bannock last year. Why the Indians had not pilfered and burned his wagon, no one would ever know. Perhaps they were too drunk, or they'd been scared off by the pungent chemical odors and odd-looking equipment. In any case, no one had ever claimed the stuff, Morrow said, and he'd be happy to see Stella get some use out of it.

Taking pictures again, Stella realized, had been her salvation. Otherwise, she would have sunk completely into the black despondency that seemed to grow worse with each day.

The blackness was something even she could not understand. Here, in the comfort and safety of Fort Bridger, with her legal problems all but resolved and the genial Carters as her friends, she had every reason to be happy. Instead, she seemed to spend much of her time on the verge of tears.

"It's just the strain, dear," Mary Carter had soothed her. "You've been through a terrible time, and it's just catching up with you. That's all."

The explanation made some sense. But Stella had always been a cheerful person. This erratic melancholy she felt was not like her at all. When she wasn't taking pictures, she could often be found sitting in the parlor window seat, gazing at clouds in the eastern sky, or picking out sad little tunes on the piano. Her nights were filled with wild dreams and longings, in which every voice she heard and every face she saw became Cade Garrison's. She spent hours secretly reliving that last, perfect time they had made love.

Harry Vickers had received the hoped-for transfer to Custer's Seventh Cavalry and had left the previous week. Stella found his absence a relief. She knew he had given his own lurid version of their encounter to his fellow officers. She knew they talked about her. And she no longer cared.

Only when she was taking pictures did some of her old vitality return. Photography lent her a sense of purpose. It helped, in part, to fill the aching, empty void that had opened up in her life since she left the Wind River Valley...and Cade.

Finishing this day's picture taking, she returned to the darkness of the van to complete the developing. When that was done, she straightened the well-equipped interior and closed it up for the night. Tomorrow, she resolved, she would start on a filing system to catalog and organize the photographs she took. At the rate her pictures were accumulating, she would soon need it.

The evening wind was cold. Clutching the long, woolen cape around her, she hurried back to the Carter house. Through the dim twilight, she could see the judge standing on the porch. He seemed to be waiting for her.

As she came up the steps, windblown and a bit out of breath, she could see that he was smiling. There was a piece of paper in his hand.

"I've got some good news for you, Stella," he said.

The first thought that flew into her mind was that it might be a message from Cade. Her lips had already begun to form his name before she realized that it had to be something else. Cade would not have written. Not after the finality of their parting.

The judge beamed as he thrust the paper toward her. "It's the wire from Marshal Catlin. All charges against you have been dismissed by the circuit judge in Green River. You're a free woman, Stella."

"Oh!" The news should not have come as a surprise. But somehow, after all this time, it struck her hard. She felt so weak that she had to clutch the porch railing for support.

"Are you all right?" Judge Carter leaned out and steadied her arm. "You look pale, Stella."

"I-I'm fine," she said, fighting back an inexplicable rush of tears. She had expected to be happy when the news came. Why, then, was the pit of her despair yawning wider than ever? What was the matter with her? She was free!

Free to do what? the echo of her own thoughts mocked her. She could start a new life, any life she wanted, she told herself. Yet the thought of changing again, of abandoning what she had already found, seemed more than she could bear.

"You can go wherever you like," the judge said gently, seeing her distress. "But Mary and I were hoping you'd stay on as our guest for a time, at least till we get a spell of good traveling weather. We've both enjoyed you so much. With our own children all away at school, having you here makes the house less empty."

Stella pressed his hand gratefully. "Thank you," she whispered. "I don't want to impose, but I am very much at loose ends. If I could stay just a little longer, while I get my plans in order..."

"Stay as long as you like," said Judge Carter. "Mary will be relieved to hear you're not leaving right away. She's been as fluttery as a moth on a screen door since that wire arrived." He offered Stella his arm. "Now, don't you fret about things anymore. Let's go on inside and have some supper."

She took his arm and was halfway into the house when she remembered. "Did the marshal say anything about Gillis?"

The judge nodded gravely. "He lived to stand trial in Laramie for killing that young girl. The jury found him guilty, and he was hanged three days ago. You won't have to worry about him anymore."

Stella slept fitfully that night. The next morning, she awakened feeling more tired than when she'd gone to bed. For a few moments she lay there in the feather bed, willing her leaden limbs to move. What was wrong with her?

Mary Carter opened the bedroom door and popped her head in. "William had to go out early," she said. "I've got bacon and eggs and hot biscuits downstairs in the kitchen. Why don't you come down and have some with me? Don't bother getting into your clothes—just throw on a dressing gown."

"Mmm, that does sound nice. I'll be down in a minute." Stella stretched and rolled her legs over the edge of the bed. Maybe with some food in her stomach, she'd feel more energetic.

As she came down the stairs, however, the aroma of fried bacon, which she usually liked, almost sickened her. And when she sat down at the table, the fried egg on her plate seemed to be staring back at her, like a greasy, yellow eye.

Mary gave her a concerned glance as she sat the biscuits on the table. "Are you all right, Stella?" she asked.

"I—I think so." Stella nibbled tentatively on a biscuit. It's just that I— Oh! Oh dear!" She rushed away from the table and headed for the stairs again.

When Mary caught up with her, she was in her room, retching over the basin. The older woman held her head, stroking her hair and making sympathetic little crooning noises.

When the nausea had passed, Mary dampened a cloth and wiped Stella's white face. "Thank you," Stella murmured. "That's never happened to me before. I—I just don't know what's been the matter with me lately. I've been so tired all the time, so…emotional. Not like myself at all!"

Mary pushed the tousled hair back from Stella's face. Her gray eyes were troubled. "My dear, when did you last have your menses?"

Stella's eyes opened wide. She had been so preoccupied with other things, she had almost forgotten. "Why, it was just—" Furiously her mind leafed backward through the days. Not in the Wind River or on the trail—no. Her last menstrual period had taken place while she was at the Aarnson cabin, almost two months ago!

"But I'd been ill," Stella said lamely, her heart beginning to pound. "And under such a strain—"

"Oh, my dear girl," Mary said softly. "I think you're with child."

Chapter Eighteen

Emotions are strange things, Stella was to reflect later. What else could explain the fact that Sam Catlin's wire clearing her of murder charges had thrown her into turmoil, while the revelation that she was carrying Cade's child filled her with a deep sense of peace?

The news, of course, had come as a shock, at first. But once the awareness had settled in, Stella began to feel herself in possession of a miracle. She would never truly lose Cade or the wild, savage beauty of the Wind River Valley. She would see them every time she looked into the face of her child—the child Cade's love and hers had created.

Still there were many questions about the future—questions that would have to be settled soon.

"I really think you should let him know, Stella," the judge insisted over dinner a few nights later. "Cade Garrison impressed me as a man of honor, and I could tell that he cares for you. He'd want to do the right thing by you and the baby."

Stella gazed down at her plate, at a loss to express her hesitancy in words. Cade, she had come to realize, was the only man she had ever truly loved. To have a small part of him growing inside her was a source of wonder and joy. But, as she had told him that night on the trail, love wasn't enough. Much as she might care for Cade, how could she live with what he was, what life in the Wind River Valley had made him? And much as she might be drawn to the valley's rugged beauty, how could she raise their child in a world where violent, savage death was accepted as commonplace?

"But what will you do if you don't go back to him?" the judge argued gently. "A woman alone in the world, with a child. It won't be easy, my dear."

"I know. But I have a profession, and I can make a good living at it. The baby and I won't starve." Stella spoke calmly, trying to hide the growing uncertainty and conflict she felt. Even when she ruled out her love for Cade and tried to think logically, the battles raged. One side of her argued that Cade had as much right to this child as she did, that they owed their child a life together, with two parents. Another side of her argued just as passionately that the Wind River Valley was no fit place to raise a family, and that Cade, with his bloody and turbulent past, would never make a suitable father.

That night she tossed and turned on her pillow, her head filled with eerie dreams. A voice seemed to be calling to her—not a human voice, but the silent voice of mountains, trees and water, the voice of the Wind River Valley. Irresistibly drawn, she followed the call, moving through swirls of mist, through snow that was not cold and fire that was not hot. Something was shining in the far distance, catching glints of sun. She flew toward it, only to find that it was Cade, lashed with rawhide ropes to a great, cold rock. Rushing to his side, she tried to free him, for she could see that he was in pain. But no matter how she tried, she could not part the ropes. It was as if they were made of steel, as if the valley itself were holding him prisoner.

Stella cried out. The sound of her own voice startled her awake. She lay there in the darkness, her eyes wide open, listening to the wind in the trees outside. What a strange sound it made—lonesome, mournful and frightening, like the call of a wolf from a faraway ridge.

"Stella?" It was Mary, slipping into the room, a dim candle lighting her face. "I thought I heard you. Are you all right?"

"I was only dreaming. But listen, Mary. Listen to the wind."

"Yes," Mary sat down on the edge of the bed. "It's what they call a Chinook. When I first came out here, I used to hate the sound of it. It just seemed to add to the desolation of the place. But now I'm always glad to hear it, because it melts the snow."

"Melts the snow?"

"Wait till morning. You'll see. Was your dream a bad one?"

Stella nodded. "You said you used to hate the wind. It must have been hard for you, living out here for so long, raising your family..."

"It was, at first," Mary said. "Just soldiers, mountain men and Indians—not another white woman for miles around. I was lonely, and scared sometimes. But I got used to it. Now it's home to me."

Stella lay back on the pillow. "How brave you must have been. And how strong."

"No stronger than you, dear. And certainly no braver." Mary reached out and squeezed Stella's shoulder. "If there's one thing I've learned out here, it's this. There's good and bad anyplace you go. In the end, what you find is what you're looking for. Life is what you make it, Stella."

Stella lay quietly for a moment, the turbulence in her suddenly still, her resolve suddenly firm. She knew what she had to do. "I'm going to him," she said, sitting up. "To Cade. As soon as I can."

Mary frowned. "Are you sure that's wise, in your condition, dear? Wouldn't it be better to send a message with one of the Indians and let him come to you here at the fort?"

Stella shook her head. "It wouldn't be the same that way. I know it doesn't make sense, but I have to see him there— in the Wind River Valley. That's his home. If it's to be mine, I have to know."

Mary sighed as she stood up to leave. "You're a strong-willed person, Stella, and I know better than to try and talk you out of it. All the same, I wish you'd think it over for a few days."

"I have thought it over. It's the only way to resolve things between Cade and me." Stella reached out and pressed Mary's hand. "You don't know how much your kindness has meant," she whispered. "Thank you so much, for everything."

"Write me when the baby comes, wherever you are," Mary said, brushing away a tear. "I'd like to know—"

"I will. I promise."

After Mary had left the room, Stella closed her eyes. Mary was right; there was good and bad everywhere. She could weigh Red Hawk against Washakie, Gillis and Harry against the Carters. The scale was even—hers to tip the way she chose.

For the first time in many days, she slept peacefully, the tempest inside her at rest. While she slumbered, the Chinook wind blew its warm, dry breath over the land. In the morning, the snow was gone.

The sun was a silvery disk in the dim November sky; the dead leaves thick and spongy beneath the hooves of the Indian ponies. Without its blanket of snow, the land was as pale as thin-washed watercolor, its grays and browns brightened only by the red of bare willows along the streams.

Stella and the two young Shoshone traveled swiftly this time, galloping their mounts over the long, open stretches of the trail. Without the burden of the travois and its awful passenger, the journey was pleasant, almost light-hearted. Much of the time, Falling Arrow and Track-the-Buffalo kept up a good-natured banter, arguing in Shoshone, laughing, breaking loose to race each other to the next bend in the trail.

Though she could understand only a few words of what they were saying, Stella enjoyed their antics. Only now and

then did her eyes wander to the streaming black plume of
hair that decorated Falling Arrow's lance. When that happened, she would force herself to look quickly away before
the dark thoughts could form in her mind.

She was grateful to Luther Mann, the Indian agent at the
fort, for persuading She-Bear's sons to escort her back to
the Wind River. Mann had been more than willing to help.
The young bucks who hung around the agency too long, he
explained, often became dependent on handouts and developed an unhealthy taste for the white man's liquor.
Washakie would be highly displeased if such a thing were
to happen to his own grandsons.

Mann had loaded the two boys down with gifts of cloth,
needles, thread and bullets, and sent them off grinning like
two country lads ending a visit to a big town.

Stella's own departure had been less carefree. She had
entrusted the van, the chemicals, equipment and her photographs to Colonel Morrow, who had promised to keep
them safe till she could return for them. Then she had gone
back to the Carter home for a tearful farewell.

Mary Carter had embraced her. "Don't worry, child,"
she'd murmured against Stella's ear. "Cade Garrison is a
gentleman. He'll do the honorable thing, I'm sure!"

The honorable thing! Even now, as Stella and her two
companions neared the Wind River country, those words
echoed in her mind, filling her with uncertainty. Cade was
a proud man, and she had hurt him deeply. How would he
feel about taking her back? How would he feel about the
baby?

And how would she feel? After all, she had her own
pride. The thought of his merely doing "the honorable
thing" made her writhe inside. It was Cade's *love* she
wanted, not his honor. If she couldn't have that, life in the
Wind River Valley would be unbearable; she would be better off back East, raising her child alone.

Stella battled her emotions as she rode. Part of her ached
with eagerness to see Cade again. Sometimes she caught
herself spurring the horse where the trail was easy, plung-

ing ahead over rocks and fallen tree trunks, making the two Shoshone youths keep pace with her. At other times she dreaded each bend in the trail that brought her closer to the inevitable confrontation with Cade. What would she do if she found he no longer loved her?

Her first sight of the Wind River peaks, wild against the morning sky, brought tears to her eyes. The intensity of her own response stunned her like a blow. Not until now did she realize how much she had missed this country, how much a part of her it had become. Its trees and hills seemed to embrace her, to draw her in with a gentle power that she could not break. Her senses sang with the sound of the streams and the wind in the pines, whispering one word over and over: *home.* The feeling of welcome she experienced only increased the conflict inside her.

The last night on the trail, Stella was unable to sleep. She lay wide-eyed in her blankets, listening to the calls of a faraway wolf pack. Their cries were no longer frightening to her, or even sad. They were simply a part of the night, a part of this fierce and rugged land. And the land was part of Cade Garrison.

How would he feel when he saw her again?

Tomorrow she would know.

By the time the sky had begun to gray in the east, they were on the trail again. They were so eager for the end of their journey that they had not even taken time to eat breakfast. When Track-the-Buffalo tossed Stella a strip of jerky, she caught it deftly and tore into the stringy dried meat with her teeth. Strange how she'd developed a real liking for the stuff, she mused as she chewed it hungrily.

The sun was coming up. Stella slackened the reins a bit while her eyes watched the changing colors of dawn above the peaks. The land was becoming more and more familiar. She could even sense the downward slope of it as they rode. Her pulse quickened as she realized that when they broke out of the pines, they would be riding into the arm of the valley that held Cade's land and the Shoshone camp.

Soon—within the hour, perhaps—she would be seeing Cade again.

Then, it was as if the trees themselves had suddenly come to life. Indians—Sioux, Stella realized from their yellow war paint—surrounded them on all sides. They closed in so fast that Track-the-Buffalo did not even have time to raise his ancient rifle before it was knocked out of his hands and he was dragged off his horse.

Falling Arrow, with a whoop of defiance, reared his mount and flung his lance toward the enemy. The lance bounced harmlessly off a tree as the boy slumped over his horse's withers, stunned by a blow from the flat side of a tomahawk. Stella watched in horror as he slid down the animal's side and fell to the ground, where he lay, dazed and moaning.

The Indians had already seized her, their cruel, brown hands pulling her out of the saddle before she had time to think. Wild with fear, she wrenched and twisted, trying to break loose, to run, or at least to help Falling Arrow. Even now, however, she felt her captors looping rawhide thongs around her wrists. The rough edges bit into her flesh as the Indians pulled the knots tight, lashing her hands behind her back.

In the next minute, they had bound the arms of the two boys, as well. Then the three of them were shoved against the trunks of dead, standing pines and tied fast.

Only now was Stella able to get a real look at the Indians. Most of them were young, their dark faces streaked with yellow paint, their long hair braided. They seemed to have no leader, and, to her surprise, Stella did not recognize any of them.

Then one of the Sioux lifted his head and gave a long, high-pitched cry, like the yelp of a coyote. The cry echoed through the trees and died into silence before it was answered, from a distance, with a long howl that made Stella's hair stand on end. She twisted vainly against her rawhide bonds, sensing what she was about to see.

A few minutes later, three Indians rode into the clearing. Stella gave a little cry of horror and dismay as she saw them—not just because their leader was Red Hawk; that she had expected. But the sight of him suddenly crumpled all her hopes, leaving her sick with despair. The fearsome Sioux war chief was mounted on the Appaloosa mare that had belonged to Cade. And one of his companions was riding her little black mustang.

Cade was chopping wood when the horse broke out of the distant trees. He lowered the ax, shaded his eyes against the still-bright sunset and watched it come. It moved toward him across the yellow-gray flat in an erratic trotting pattern, as if its rider were drunk.

As it got closer, he realized the horse was carrying double and that something was very wrong. The two riders were slumped forward over the big paint's neck, almost as if they had been tied that way. Except for a slight jouncing from the motion of the horse, they were not moving.

Snatching up his rifle from where he'd propped it against the fence, Cade slipped the bridle onto the roan and galloped out to meet them. He knew with grim certainty that what he was about to see would not be pretty. And he knew with the same certainty that he'd been meant to see it.

A hundred yards out from the cabin, he came abreast of the horse, caught the slack reins with one hand and pulled it to a halt. She-Bear's two young sons, their bodies covered with welts and bruises, were lashed to its back. Cade's heart lurched as he saw Falling Arrow's eyelids flutter open. They were alive, thank heaven! Both of them!

He got them to the house and cut them loose. They slid to the wet ground, too weak to stand or walk. A cursory inspection showed that their injuries were not serious. But they'd been clubbed and whipped unmercifully. Hardly an inch of their young flesh had been spared.

As he laid the two boys across the bed and began to sponge their wounds with a clean, damp cloth, Cade gave silent thanks that Stella had not returned to the valley. By now, she would be free, her pardon official. With luck, she would already be on the train, safely away from the nightmare that his life had become since his return to the valley.

Falling Arrow lay quietly, his eyes fluttering open from time to time. Track-the-Buffalo, however, seemed highly agitated. He kept rolling his head back and forth, trying to speak, but his swollen mouth would not form the words. Cade managed to get a trickle of water down his throat, but it helped only a little. The boy continued to moan, pausing to tug furiously at Cade's sleeve with his left hand.

That persistent hand—was that part of the message? Yes, something was twisted around Track-the-Buffalo's wrist. It was muddy from the ride and caked with the boy's own blood.

Cade drew his knife to cut it loose. The color drained from his face as he recognized it.

It was a lock of Stella's hair.

As Cade gazed at it in horror, Falling Arrow suddenly opened his bruised mouth and, with great effort, began to speak. "Red Hawk..." he gasped, each syllable an agony. "He says...come. When the sun is...down. Come alone...or she dies...."

Cade clasped the boy's hand. "Come? Come where?"

"He...he said you would know...."

Cade closed his eyes for a moment as a shaft of pain passed through his memory. "Yes," he said, his voice a hoarse whisper. "Yes, I do know. I will be there."

Stella had been tied to the back of a horse and half led, half dragged for what seemed like miles. Now she sat at the foot of the tree where she'd been tethered like an animal, too exhausted to move. Her clothes were torn, her arms and legs bleeding from bramble scratches. But she was alive, she reminded herself. And so far, at least, the Indians had done nothing to hurt her.

Watching them beat the two boys had been the worst part. When the Sioux had finally tied them to the big paint horse and led it away, she had not even been sure whether they were still alive. But at least they were gone from this place. And maybe the horse would carry them home.

But what would happen to her now? she wondered. The fact that the Indians had not really harmed her yet was no reason to feel safe. They were probably just saving her for something spectacular, something truly diabolical. She shuddered as she remembered that Knute Aarnson had shot his wife to keep her from falling into the hands of these same Indians. Knute, she was sure, had known exactly what he was doing.

As her strength slowly returned, Stella began to glance around the camp. There were about twenty Sioux in all, she calculated, all of them ignoring her for the time being. One of them had shot a deer, and great hunks of meat were roasting on spits, set up over a central campfire. The flames leaped and danced in the twilight as Red Hawk himself bent over and cut off a slice of half-cooked meat, spearing it with his knife and jamming it into his mouth. He chewed it savagely, meat juice running down the sides of his chin. As he ate, he kept scanning the darkening woods with his eyes, listening, as if he were waiting for something. He seemed as nervous as a cat, jumping at every sound, every movement around him.

The camp had been pitched in a small open area, its boundaries so straight and even that it looked as if the land had once been cleared. The ground was covered with grass and dead leaves, with an occasional young pine poking knee-high out of the earth. There was something strange about this place, Stella thought. Something important.

Forcing her tired mind to concentrate, she made a visual sweep of the clearing. At first she saw nothing unusual. Then, suddenly, she noticed it, on the far side of the open area, almost hidden by tall brambles. It was a rock chimney, half tumbled over, its stones blackened by fire. There had once been a cabin here.

Stella gasped out loud as the realization struck her. She'd always assumed that Cade had built his new cabin on the site of the old one. Now she realized he had not. This was the spot where Cade's first cabin had stood, the place where Rain Flower and his sons had died.

And then she knew Red Hawk had not brought her here by chance. She was part of a master plan—a plan of revenge against Cade. And killing her here, where Cade had suffered so much pain, would make that revenge complete.

She stole another glance at Red Hawk. He was watching her now, squatting before the fire as he ate. Yellow light gleamed on his scar and on the ugly white streak in his hair.

What was he planning for her? Stella wondered. Whatever it was, it had to involve Cade. Perhaps Cade was already a prisoner and Red Hawk was simply waiting for him to be brought here. That, at least, would account for Red Hawk's having Cade's two horses. Or maybe Cade was still free somewhere, and Red Hawk was using her as bait, to lure him close.

The last glow of red had faded from the western sky, and darkness was moving like a blanket over the land. Stella stretched her cramped legs and tried to get comfortable. Cade would come—she knew that now. One way or another, he would come.

Red Hawk had gotten up from his place by the fire. Wiping the grease from his mouth with one hand, he walked slowly over to where Stella sat. The eyes that looked down at her glittered with cruel anticipation. Moving slowly, he drew his broad-bladed knife from its sheath and tested the blade with his thumb. Then he bent lower and moved the blade toward her throat. Stella felt her heart jump as it came closer, then closer still....

All at once Red Hawk stiffened as a call rang out from beyond the edge of the clearing. Stella could sense the sudden agitation in the big Sioux war chief. She could almost smell the blood lust, the terror in him, as he peered into the trees.

Stella gave a little sob that blended relief and fear. There was no mistaking that voice. Cade had come.

Chapter Nineteen

Cade pressed himself into the shadowed crevice of a big, gnarled stump as he waited for Red Hawk's reply. In a way, it was a stroke of luck that Red Hawk had chosen his old homesite for their final encounter. Cade knew every tree, every rock and hollow of this ground. He was using that knowledge now, to hide himself while he negotiated with his old enemy.

He had already circled the small camp and seen where they had Stella, tied to a tree near its center. The first sight of her had left him almost dizzy with relief. She was alive, at least, and didn't appear to have been hurt.

Still, he had cursed under his breath as he assessed the situation. Surrounded as she was by twenty armed Sioux, there was no way he'd be able to cut her loose and get her safely out of there. His mind devised plan after plan, only to reject them all as too risky. If any kind of skirmish broke out, the first thing Red Hawk would do would be to kill Stella.

Why had she returned? The question tortured him. Why would she have made the long, dangerous journey back to the Wind River unless she had changed her mind—unless she wanted to stay with him, after all? Whatever the reason, her return had brought her to this. He had to free her, and there was only one way.

He slipped out of his hiding place, shifting his position so the direction of his voice could not easily be followed.

"Red Hawk!" he shouted again. "You bloody bastard! You killer of women and children! Here I am! Take me if you dare!"

Cade moved back into the shadows and waited. Though he had spoken in Shoshone, he knew that the Sioux war chief would understand him. In his boyhood, Red Hawk had spent nearly a year as a Shoshone captive. He had picked up a fair amount of the language—especially taunts and insults—before escaping to rejoin his people. Cade was banking on the hope that some of his braves would understand a little of it, as well.

There was a long silence, broken only by the fragile breath of the wind. Then Red Hawk's voice screamed out from the middle of the camp. "Show yourself, slinking coward, or your woman dies!"

Cade's nerves were quivering bowstrings. This was the game, the delicate balance of bluff against bluff, with Stella's life as the stakes. Jab and retreat. Push the devil just far enough, but not too far.

"That would suit you!" he taunted. "Everyone knows Red Hawk would rather kill a helpless woman than fight a man!"

"Stay where you are, then!" Red Hawk shrilled his reply. "Stay there and listen to her scream!"

Cade felt something claw at his insides. He knew the kind of things Red Hawk could do to a woman. "Touch her and you'll never see me again!" he called in a firm voice. "You'll never have the satisfaction of facing me and taking my blood! I will be again what I once was to you—a ghost, a shadow across your path. And one day, when you least expect it, you will feel my knife at your throat!"

There was no reply this time, but Cade could feel the tension, the hatred in Red Hawk's silence. He let it build until the pressure of that silence became unbearable.

"Red Hawk!" he shouted again. "The woman is nothing to you! I'm the one you want!" He waited a few seconds, and when Red Hawk did not reply, he continued. "A trade! That's what I'm willing to give you! Let her go free, and I come in to you unarmed. You have my word!"

Again, only silence. Sickening, maddening silence.

"Think of it!" Cade cajoled. "Your old enemy in your hands! Yours to deal with in whichever way would give you the most pleasure! You can have that, or you can murder a helpless woman who has never harmed you! The choice is yours!"

"Your word?" Red Hawk's question rang through the cold, November darkness. Cade felt himself break out in a sudden sweat.

"My word for yours!" he answered. "We may be enemies, you and I, but we are not without honor!"

The Sioux leader laughed harshly. "I could send my braves into the forest to take you, Yellow Wolf! Then I would have you *and* the woman. I could kill you together!"

"You would never take me alive!" Cade retorted swiftly. "If you want the pleasure of killing me with your own hands, there is only one sure way to have it. Choose, Red Hawk!"

"Your word!" Red Hawk's voice rang out again in the gathering darkness. "You come in alone, unarmed!"

"When you let the woman go!" Cade felt fear and relief churning together inside him. Relief because Stella would have a chance to live. Fear because there were no tricks to his plan. He was simply offering his life for hers. Soon he would die, and Red Hawk would make his death an unforgettable spectacle of slow agony. That much he knew.

"Come to the edge of the clearing." Red Hawk's voice still carried a note of distrust. "When you see the woman, throw out your weapons. We will release her as you come in."

"Your word on it!"

"My word as the son of my father! But one false step, Yellow Wolf, and she dies!"

"I'm coming, then. Bring her out where I'll be able to see her." Cade moved cautiously, zigzagging from shadow to shadow. His eyes scanned the woods, alert for any sign of treachery. But he saw nothing—nothing except the flickering yellow haze of firelight through the pines.

Even now, every step he took seemed familiar. How many times in years past had he walked this very ground, checking the boundaries of his world while his loved ones slept? How far had he come since those nights? Cade sighed raggedly. This was no time to be philosophical, but if he had to choose a place to die, right here, where he had known happiness, would be as good as any.

Then, suddenly, he could see Stella. She was on her feet now, silhouetted against the light of the fire. Two braves, one on either side, grasped her outstretched arms. They seemed to be restraining her, waiting for him to appear.

Taking a deep breath, Cade stepped into the clearing and threw down his rifle. The Colt pistol and his hunting knife followed. Stella gave a little moan as she saw him and realized what he was doing. She struggled, trying to pull loose from the two Indians who held her arms.

"Let her go," Cade said. "On your word, Red Hawk."

The tall war chief was standing beside the fire, arms folded across his chest. Cade could almost feel the hatred emanating from his powerful body. This, he realized, was the most perilous moment of all. How much trust, how much honor would Red Hawk feel he owed such a bitter enemy?

Cade tensed, ready to make a rush for Stella at the first sign of betrayal. An eternity seemed to crawl past before Red Hawk gave an imperious nod, and the two braves let go of Stella's arms. Still straining against them, she fell forward. Then, with an awkward little stumble, she caught herself and plunged across the clearing to where Cade stood.

He caught her in his arms. They had seconds, perhaps, certainly no more. "When I let you go, run!" he whispered, holding her desperately close. "Don't stop and don't look back! Keep going in a straight line, and you'll come to a little creek. My horse is tied on the other side. Take him and get to someplace safe!"

"No! How can I leave you?" She was crying softly.

"You must. I'll be all right. I'll come to you as soon as I can."

Stella was silent for a moment. Then Cade felt something go through her. She stood straighter in his arms, and when she looked up at him, her great, dark eyes were full of quiet courage. He had not fooled her, Cade reflected. She knew he was lying.

"I love you, Stella," he whispered. "Whatever happens, always remember that."

"I love you, too," she said, her eyes brimming with unshed tears. "And if our child is a son, I will give him your name!"

For an instant Cade stood transfixed with joy. But there was no more time. He forced his arms to thrust her away from him. "Run, Stella!" he rasped, masking his emotion with harshness. "For God's sake, *run!*"

With a little sob, she spun away from him. Then she was running hard, bounding like a doe in a wild sprint through the trees.

Cade followed her with his eyes till she disappeared into the darkness. He could only pray that she would have no trouble finding the roan. Alone and on foot she would be vulnerable—easy prey if Red Hawk was to send his braves out after her. But mounted, Stella at least had a chance of reaching safety. The big red stallion could outrun any Indian pony alive.

The Sioux were circling him now, closing in warily, like wolves intent on bringing down a great bull elk. Cade used his last few seconds of freedom to fill his mind with thoughts of Stella, their love and the child that love had conceived. Then, bracing himself for the ordeal to come, he turned back to face Red Hawk.

Blinded by tears, Stella stumbled through the dark underbrush. Emotions tore at her like thorns as she pictured

Cade in Red Hawk's hands, facing torture and death. It took all her strength of will to keep running, to fight the powerful instincts that called her back to die at his side. Only the awareness of the life she carried kept her moving. For the sake of Cade's child, she had to live.

Cade had told her that if she traveled in a straight line she would come to the creek where the roan was tied. But with so many fallen trees and boulders in the way, keeping to a single course was impossible. She had no idea how far she had veered from her original direction, but she had found no sign of either the stream or the horse.

For perhaps the tenth time, she paused, her ears straining for the watery hiss and tumble that would tell her the creek was nearby. But the only sounds in the icy night were the faint, savage war whoops from Red Hawk's camp, somewhere off behind her. Stella knew what those war whoops meant, and it took all her self-control to keep from screaming out her anguish. Don't listen, she told herself firmly. Just keep moving. You've got the baby to think of.

But why was it taking her so long to find the horse? she wondered desperately. Why, when every second that passed was so crucial?

She moved ahead a few steps, then paused to listen again. That was when she heard it—the faint snap of a twig from a footstep whose rhythm did not quite match her own.

She froze in sudden panic as she realized what was happening. Now that Red Hawk had Cade, there was no more need for him to keep his bargain. He had sent some of his braves out to find her and bring her back.

Stella shrank into the inky shadow of a pine tree, trying to keep calm. Her pursuers appeared to be on foot. If she could find the roan before they got to her, she would be all right.

She held her breath. Behind her, she could hear them coming through the underbrush, no more than a good, long, stone's throw away. How many there were and how fast they were moving, she could not tell, but she had to keep out of their sight. It was her only hope.

She glanced at the eastern sky. The pale glow above the horizon told her that the full moon was rising. In a few minutes, it would be flooding the land with light. She would have an easier time finding her way then, but so would the Sioux. If she did not reach Cade's horse by the time the moon rose, she would be easy prey for them.

Think! she urged herself, pushing her weary, tortured mind to its limits. Where would a creek be found? Where would it flow? Downhill! Always downhill, seeking the lowest level of the land! Look for a slope, even a slight one!

From shadow to shadow, she began to move, trying always to be sensitive to the contours of the ground. Behind her, she could hear the Indians tramping through the brush, making no effort to be quiet. They were so close now that she could hear them muttering.

Above the trees, the moon was showing its thin, silver edge. Stella quickened her steps. Her eyes and ears strained till they ached.

Then at last she heard it, the rush and fall of the creek ahead of her, beyond the trees. Guided by the sound, she fought her way through the thick tangle of willows to the water's edge.

By now, the moon was all but fully risen, spreading its luminous glow through the forest. A whoop from behind told Stella she had been seen. She plunged into the water. It swirled around her knees as she struggled to reach the opposite bank. She had gained the shallows when she almost collided with an immense, looming, dark shape. She gave a little shriek of alarm before she realized it was the roan.

By now, the four Sioux were almost upon her. Stella flung herself into the saddle with two of them clasping at her legs. Ripping the reins loose from the bush where Cade had tied them, she swung the big red horse around hard. She heard shrieks and splashes as two of the braves were knocked into the creek. Then, in another moment, the roan's powerful legs had carried her out of their reach.

They flew like the wind, through pools of moonlight and darkness. Stella lay low against the great stallion's neck, her ears straining for the sound of the creek. Its downhill course, she calculated, would lead her out of the wooded foothills and into the open meadows of the valley. From there, if she rode hard enough and fast enough, there might be a slim chance of reaching the one person who could help Cade—before it was too late.

Cade counted it as a triumph when Red Hawk's four braves returned to the camp without Stella. Their failure so enraged Red Hawk that he shrieked like his namesake and flailed at them with the handle of his tomahawk. Humiliated, they slunk off to the fringes of the camp to lick their wounds and glower while Red Hawk turned his full fury on Cade.

Cade had been lashed to a tree for general tormenting while Red Hawk waited for Stella's return. The jabs from hot lance tips and burning branches had been nothing compared to his concern for her. When the four braves had stepped into the circle of firelight, wet, bruised and empty-handed, Cade had almost laughed with joy. He knew that his love—and their child—were on their way to safety.

Unafraid now, he looked into Red Hawk's seething eyes. "Such is the honor of Red Hawk," he said, his voice dripping contempt. "Now that you have no woman to torture before my eyes, what will you do with me?"

Red Hawk's hand shot out and struck him across the face so hard that the impact wrenched Cade's neck muscles. Hiding the explosive pain, Cade managed to smile at his enemy. "Tie me up and beat me to death with your bare hands? Is that enough to satisfy you?" He shook his head. "I'm disappointed in you, Red Hawk. From a mind like yours, I would have expected something more…inventive."

Red Hawk glared at him, his black eyes exuding pure, venomous hatred. "This is what I will do next," he growled, drawing his knife. "I will cut out your tongue before it can make any more trouble!"

Cade felt a shiver of fear pass through his body. Red Hawk, he knew, would not hesitate to carry out such a threat. "Your young braves are watching you," he said, as if he had not heard. "They will remember this night all their lives! They will sing of it around their campfires—how Red Hawk, their brave leader, fought his battle against an enemy who was tied to a tree!"

"If you speak again..." The Sioux's knife gleamed red in the firelight.

"How will you kill me?" Cade pressed his point relentlessly. "Is there enough blood in this body to slake your thirst, Red Hawk? Is there enough life, enough capacity for pain to satisfy your vengeance?"

Red Hawk's mouth was tight. The scar that marred his face lay dead white against his dark skin.

"You can only kill me once, then it's done," Cade said, speaking very slowly. "If I were you, I'd try to make it worth remembering."

His eyes shifted to the circle that Red Hawk's men had made around them. All the braves were watching intently. At least some of them, Cade hoped, would know enough Shoshone to understand what was being said. "These young braves," he continued, "they look to you to show them how a real warrior deals with his enemy. Is that what you will show them, Red Hawk? Or will you show them how a coward kills a man he is afraid of?"

A murmur rippled its way around the circle of watchers. Yes, Cade decided. A few of them did understand. They were translating his words for those who did not. The murmur grew; a shout went up from a young Sioux in the back of the ranks, its tone contemptuous.

An animal's growl came from Red Hawk's rage-tight throat as he turned on them. But even then, the muttering continued. "Listen to them!" Cade taunted the powerful chief. "They are tired of watching you scalp dead women and slaughter horses! They want to see you fight me—like a warrior! Like a *man*!"

Red Hawk spun back toward Cade, his tomahawk quivering above his head. Cade felt a flash of fear as he braced himself for the blow. But it did not come. Instead, with a grunt of exploding anger, Red Hawk flung the weapon to the earth. The watchers howled their approval. They would have their fight, after all.

While the circle widened, two of the young braves untied Cade's bonds. The rules were ancient and known to everyone there: two men and one weapon, in a struggle to the death. The fighting took place within a given area, where no one else could interfere. If the victor was a prisoner, he would be allowed to go free. Outside of these rules, anything was permissible.

Red Hawk's angry gesture had designated his tomahawk as the weapon. It remained where he had flung it, handle up, head half-buried in the earth. It seemed to be waiting, while the circle was measured and drawn around it.

Cade took the time to rub the circulation back into his cramped arms and roughen his hands with dirt. His eyes took in the details of the circle: the ground with its cover of wet, decaying leaves; the small pines, pushing up to knee height here and there; the scattered stones from the foundation of his old cabin.

Red Hawk was stripping off his buckskin shirt, his skin gleaming like bronze in the firelight. The Sioux war chief was bigger than Cade, with a massively powerful chest. In age, agility and fighting experience, Cade judged the two of them to be near equals. Emotionally, however... Cade stopped to weigh his own state against Red Hawk's. Strange how calm he felt, as if, now that he had saved Stella, he was fully prepared for whatever came next. Red Hawk, however, had not anticipated this kind of encounter. He was angry enough to be reckless, but he was fearful, as well. If these conflicting emotions could be played upon, Cade calculated, they might give him the edge he needed.

The ring was ready, the watchers massed around its edge. At an unspoken signal, Cade and Red Hawk moved to op-